ONE Summer AT THE LAKE

KIM LAWRENCE   MICHELLE MAJOR   SUSAN CARLISLE

ONE Summer COLLECTION

June 2016

July 2016

July 2016

August 2016

August 2016

September 2016

ONE Summer AT THE LAKE

KIM
LAWRENCE

MICHELLE
MAJOR

SUSAN
CARLISLE

MILLS & BOON

First Published in Great Britain 2016
By Mills & Boon, an imprint of HarperCollins*Publishers*
1 London Bridge Street, London, SE1 9GF

ONE SUMMER AT THE LAKE © 2016 Harlequin Books S.A.

Maid for Montero © 2013 Kim Lawrence
Still the One © 2013 Michelle Major
Hot-Shot Doc Comes to Town © 2013 Susan Carlisle

ISBN: 978-0-263-92232-5

09-0716

MAID FOR MONTERO

KIM LAWRENCE

Kim Lawrence lives on a farm in Anglesey with her university lecturer husband, assorted pets who arrived as strays and never left, and sometimes one or both of her boomerang sons. When she's not writing she loves to be outdoors gardening, or walking on one of the beaches for which the island is famous—along with being the place where Prince William and Catherine made their first home!

CHAPTER ONE

SOME MEN IN Isandro's position would have whined about press intrusion. He didn't. He considered he had little to complain about in life, and he knew it was perfectly possible, even for someone whose financial empire drew the sort of global media attention that his did, to have a private life.

Of course, if his taste had run to falling out of nightclubs in the small hours or the routine attendance of film premieres with scantily clad models, it might have been more difficult, but neither pastime held any appeal for him.

He viewed security as a necessary evil, a side effect of success—like midges in the Highlands—but he was hardly a recluse who lived his life behind ten-feet-high walls.

If he had had a family to consider, possibly he might have seen potential danger lurking around every corner, but he didn't. He only had an ex-wife, with whom he exchanged Christmas cards these days rather than insults, and a father he had very little contact with. Given that he was confident in his ability to look after himself, Isandro was not alarmed when the electronic gates that guarded the entrance to his English estate—which did

actually have ten-feet-high walls—did not swing open
as he approached, for they were already open.

Slowing his car, he swept the area with narrow-eyed,
irritated speculation. While he didn't automatically assume this suggested anything dark and sinister, it did
suggest a carelessness that he did not expect from those
who worked for him.

The groove between his dark, strongly defined brows
and his level of irritation deepened as his glance lighted
on a brightly coloured bunch of balloons attached to an
overhanging branch that looked incongruous beside the
discreetly tasteful sign that simply read 'Ravenwood
House: Private'.

He had owned Ravenwood for three years, and in
that time on the admittedly rare occasions he had visited he had never found cause for complaint, which was
nothing less than expected. He employed the best, be
they corporate executives or gardening staff, paid them
extremely well and expected them to earn their salary.

It was not a complicated formula but one that he
found worked, and if it didn't… He was not a man re-
nowned for patience or sentimentality in his professional or personal life. If those in his employ didn't
perform to the high standards he expected and deliver
the goods they did not remain in his employ.

He opened the window, reached out and caught hold
of the string dangling from the balloons. As he tugged
two popped on the branches and the rest rose into the
air, embracing their freedom. Following their merry
progress with his eyes, he frowned before he pulled his
head back in. He was not ready to read anything significant into the open gates or the balloons, but there
had been a recent staff change, and the housekeeper did
play a pivotal role at Ravenwood.

The previous postholder had not only been efficient, but had combined excellent man-management skills with the ability to blend into the background. She had never been obtrusive.

Under her watch he could not imagine open gates, invisible security or balloons. It was always possible none was connected with the new housekeeper, and he kept an open mind on the subject, innocent until proved guilty. No one could say that he wasn't scrupulously fair, and he made allowances for human error.

What he couldn't live with was incompetence.

He was prepared at this point to believe that the new housekeeper was as perfect as his personal assistant, who had interviewed the candidates, had indicated. He trusted Tom's judgement, as the younger man had always shown it to be excellent and it had been his efforts and diplomacy that had gone a long way to soothing local ill will when Isandro had bought the hall.

Three years ago the local community had greeted the change of ownership of the local estate with deep suspicion bordering on hostility. The family that had given the house and the village their name had contributed nothing tangible to the local economy in decades, and the previous owner spent more time falling out of nightclubs and entering rehab clinics than repairing the roof or earning money to do so—so the locals' blind loyalty to them seemed perverse to Isandro.

With Tom's help he had addressed the situation with his usual pragmatism. He did not wish to be best friends with his neighbours, but neither did he want the inconvenience of being at war with them. The initial stream of complaints had faded to a trickle and visits from officials with clipboards from conservation and heritage groups that had halted work on the house and grounds had lessened and eventually vanished. He made a point of employing only local artisans and firms on the restoration work and made a donation that had put a new roof on the leaking church.

He considered the situation resolved.

Of all the houses he owned, this was the one where Isandro felt as close to relaxed as he ever did. It was beautiful and he enjoyed beauty. He invited none but his closest friends, and even then rarely. He never drove through the gates without feeling he was shedding the pressures of work.

He anticipated the next few days of rare relaxation, his wide sensual mouth twitching into a half-smile as he drove slowly through the pillared entrance. A moment later he was reversing.

The balloons snagged in the branch could have been accidental; this was not. Bizarrely tucked in beside one classical pillar was an upturned packing case.

With a mixture of growing incredulity and irritation, Isandro read the handwritten sign propped on it that informed him the eggs were free range and cost one pound per half dozen. There was no sign of the eggs mentioned, just a jar that was stuffed with coins and several notes suggesting trade had been brisk—the area had an unusual level of honesty.

Long brown fingers beat out an aggravated tattoo on the steering wheel. He had driven halfway down the long horsechestnut-lined driveway and was trying to rediscover his mellow mood when the noise hit him—a mixture of music, laughter, dogs barking and loud voices.

'What now...?'

Angular jaw set, he swore and floored the accelerator. A moment later he hit the brake, bringing the vehicle to a screaming halt on the top of the rise that gave him the first view of the delightful Palladian mansion considered by those in the know to be an architectural gem set in a parkland setting complete with lake, folly and beautifully tended formal gardens.

The manicured west lawn, where on occasion he watched invited guests play a game of croquet—and where he had spent the journey from the airport picturing himself enjoying the silence and solitude, sipping some brandy and perhaps catching up on some reading after the month of intense negotiations—was barely visible beneath the massive marquee, several smaller satellite tents, makeshift stage, cluster of stalls and what appeared to be a small…yes, it was a funfair of sorts, he realised as he identified the giant teacups slowly spinning to the strains of an early Tom Jones number, the volume so loud even at this distance to vibrate in his chest.

Staring in unwilling fascination at the surreal spectacle, he started like someone waking from a nightmare as a voice over the loudhailer system announced the winner of the best behaved pet competition to be Herb—a result that, judging from the volume of the cheers and clapping, was popular.

Isandro swore loudly and at length in several languages.

The person responsible for this outrage would not be around to regret this invasion and misuse of his trust for long. For that matter he might sack the bunch of them because while this might have been the brain child of one person—presumably the new housekeeper—the rest of his staff must have sat back and let it happen, including his highly paid so-called professional security team.

Great! So much for leaving stress behind. His resentment levels rose as he mentally said goodbye to his much-needed, greatly anticipated break… So what if after a couple of days he'd get bored with the inactivity and grow restless? The point was he wouldn't have the option of being bored now.

The feeling he had wandered into some sort of alternative universe intensified as a balloon that had presumably followed him up the drive floated past his head. It snagged on a branch and popped—the sound breaking Isandro free of his teeth-clenched scrutiny of the disaster scene.

His dark eyes as warm as ice chips, he reversed with a screech of rubber back to the intersection in the drive and took the secondary road that led directly to the stable block at the rear of the house, which seemed blessedly free of the insanity taking place elsewhere on his property.

Entering the house via the orangery, he snapped grapes from the vine that grew in coils across the roof as he went. He made his way to his study, not encountering a soul to demand an explanation of or vent his simmering anger on. When he reached the inner sanctum, however, he did discover someone: a small child he had never seen before, who was almost hidden by his desk as she spun around in his swivel chair.

The child saw him and grabbed the desk to slow herself, leaving a neat imprint of sticky finger marks on the antique wood. His lips twisted in a grimace of distaste. He had few friends with children and his exposure to them had been limited to brief appearances at baptisms bearing appropriate gifts. None had reached this child's age yet… Five? Six? he speculated, studying the grubby freckled face.

'Hello. Are you looking for the toilets?'

The question was so unexpected that for a moment Isandro did not respond.

'No, I am not.' Was it normal for a child to be this self-possessed? She definitely didn't seem even slightly fazed to see him.

'Oh.' Hands on his antique desk, she began to twist in the seat from side to side. 'The lady was but the other man was looking for Zoe. Are you looking for Zoe, too? I can do fifty spins and not be sick. I could probably do more if I wanted to.'

Glancing at the Aubusson carpet underfoot, he cautiously caught the back of the chair before she could put her boast to the test. 'I'm sure you could.'

'You picked grapes.' The kid stared at the grapes he had carelessly plucked from the vine as he had walked through the orangery. 'You're not meant to do that,' she said, shaking her head. 'You'll be in big trouble, and maybe even go to jail.' The thought seemed to please her.

'Thanks for the warning. Want some?' She seemed so at home he almost began to wonder if the place had been invaded by squatters and nobody had seen fit to mention it to him!

'Can't. You're a stranger. And they're sour.'

'Georgie!'

Isandro's head lifted at the sound of the musical voice with just a hint of attractive huskiness.

'I'm in here!' The kid bellowed back into his right ear, making him wince.

A moment later a figure appeared in the doorway. The body that matched the voice was not a let-down—anything but! Tall, slim, dark-haired with the sort of figure that filled out the faded denim jeans she wore to perfection. His immediate impression was of sinuous supple grace and an earthy sexuality that hit him with the force of a hammer between the eyes. Though the main physical response to her appearance was somewhat lower than eye level.

Isandro's aggravation levels reduced by several notches as he studied this new arrival, who didn't just have a great body but a vivid, expressive face he found himself wanting to look at. Stare at.

She possessed the most extraordinary eyes—electric blue that tilted slightly at the corners—and a mouth that made any man looking at it think of how it would feel to taste those plush pink lips… Isandro exhaled and reined in his galloping imagination. He had a healthy libido but he prided himself on his ability to control it.

'Georgie, you shouldn't be in here. I've told you. Oh…!' Zoe stopped halfway through the open doorway of the study. Her blue eyes flew wide as she sucked in a tiny shocked breath, registering the presence of the tall figure who was towering over her niece.

The strange reluctance she felt to enter the room was strong, but not as strong as her protective instincts, so, with a cautious smile pasted in place, Zoe stepped forward.

There had been many occasions in her adult life when she had been accused of being too trusting, too inclined to assume the best of others, but since Zoe had acquired responsibility for her seven-year-old twin niece and nephew she had developed a new caution that bordered, she suspected, on paranoia, at least when it came to the safety of her youthful charges.

Under the pleasant smile, her newly awoken protective instincts were on full alert. She moved towards the man whom she had not seen outside. And she would have noticed him, because despite the casual clothes—expensive casual—he definitely wouldn't have blended in with the carefree and relaxed people milling around outside.

She doubted that face did relaxed or carefree.

Without taking her eyes off the incredibly handsome stranger any more than you'd take your eyes off a stray wolf—and the analogy was not inappropriate, as he had the entire lean, hungry look going on—she held out her hand to her niece.

'Come here, Georgina,' she said in a tone meant to convey a sense of urgency without overly alarming her niece. Not that the latter would be likely—Georgie was friendly to a fault and she had no sense of danger whatsoever. Real parents probably knew how to make their kids sensibly cautious without scaring them witless and giving them umpteen issues later in life…but Zoe wasn't a real parent and most of the time she felt like a pretty sorry substitute for not one but two brilliant parents.

She took a deep breath and fought her way clear of the oppressive weight of emotions that continued to hit her when she wasn't expecting it. There wasn't time to feel angry at fate or the drunk driver whose carelessness had taken away the twins' parents. There was barely time to comb her hair some days!

'I'm sorry. I hope Georgina wasn't bothering you.' It was more polite than 'what the hell are you doing in here?' but in her experience it was always better to try a smile before you brought out the big stick.

Though it would take a very big stick indeed or even a small army to make this intruder leave if he didn't take the hint, she thought, sliding a peek at him under her lashes and looking away quickly. The heat climbed into her smooth cheeks as she realised her scrutiny was being returned, though there was nothing remotely surreptitious or apologetic about the way his dark eyes were wandering over her.

She flicked her plait back in a businesslike manner over her shoulder and, raising a brief cool hand to her cheeks, she wished that her protective instincts were the only reason she could feel the heavy, frantic beat of her heart in every inch of her body.

She'd never come across a man who exuded such a raw, sheer maleness before and it was deeply weird, not in a pleasant way, to find her indiscriminate hormones reacting independently to the aura he projected. She pressed her hand protectively to her stomach, which was quivering the way it did when she found herself in any situation that involved high places and the possibility of falling.

Logic suggested he was no danger to Georgie, just another visitor to the Fun Day who'd got lost or was just plain nosy but…the fact that she was the person whose job it was to protect the twins from everything bad in the world meant that Zoe was taking no chances.

'Now, Georgie, please.'

With a show of reluctance and a big sigh the copperheaded little girl responded finally to the note of command and slid out of the chair. But Isandro wasn't watching. His eyes were trained on the sliver of pale, toned midriff that was on show. The tantalising flash of flesh vanished as the woman's hand closed over the child's. Drawing her in, she bent to speak, saying something to the kid that made her nod before running out of the door.

Isandro watched as the young woman straightened up, throwing the fat plait of glossy dark hair over her shoulder again, exposing the firm curve of her jaw and the long elegant line of her pale throat.

The recognition that his response to her had been primal, out of his control, produced a frown that faded as he put the situation in perspective. Just because he had experienced an unexpectedly strong physical response did not mean he couldn't control it... Since his failed marriage he had never been in any form of relationship that he couldn't walk away from, and he never would.

She straightened up. 'Sorry about that.'

Now the child was gone some of the tension seemed to have left her slender shoulders, though a degree of caution remained in the blue eyes that studied him now with an undisguised curiosity mingled with a critical quality he was not accustomed to seeing when a woman looked at him.

Isandro's smile held a hint of self mockery... If she had not been beautiful would he have chosen to be amused...?

His appreciation of beauty was not restricted to architecture. He put this woman somewhere in her early twenties, young enough at least to wear no make-up and look good. Her clear skin was flawless, pale tinged with the lightest of roses in her smooth, rounded cheeks. She was not just sexy, she was beautiful.

Not in the classical sense perhaps, and absolutely nothing like the sort of woman he normally found attractive. For starters he dated women who worked hard at and took pride in their appearance. This woman's grooming left a lot to be desired, but her oval face with wide-set, slanting blue eyes, delicate carved cheekbones and wide, full lips had an arresting quality that combined sexiness with a sense of vulnerability.

Vulnerability was another thing he avoided in women.

Needy was just too time-consuming, and time was a precious commodity.

His response simply proved that sexual attraction was not an exact science. Her look was not even smart casual, more scruffy casual. Despite his unflattering assessment of her style he was conscious of a heaviness in his groin by the time his eyes had made the journey up the length of her lusciously long, denim-clad legs. Tall and slender but with feminine curves that the oversized white shirt she wore did not hide, she really did have a delicious body—and she would scrub up well, he decided, picturing her in something silky and insubstantial, and then in nothing at all.

He found his mood mellowing some more. The day might not be a total washout after all. He found himself more attracted to her than he had to a woman in months… It was possible that part of the appeal was she was not his type, not a samey clone. That and the clear-eyed stare, plus the extraordinarily sexy mouth, and the fact he felt confident that he could slide his fingers into her hair and not come away with a handful of hair extensions. Now that had been a real mood killer!

What had the kid called her…?

Not Mum, and she wasn't wearing a ring, but that didn't mean anything, so he remained cautious.

There were enough complications in life without inviting them, so Isandro kept his love life simple. He didn't do long-term relationships and was upfront about it, and even so he had never had to work hard to get a woman into his bed.

Married women, single parents, women who wanted commitment were not conducive to simplicity, so he ruled them out. He had learnt from his mistakes, and an expensive divorce that had lost him both a wife and a best friend provided a steep learning curve. Quite frankly there was no point in inviting problems when there were any number of attractive unattached women who did not come with baggage.

He could fight for a prize when it was required, but it was not his style to fantasise over the unattainable. He had no problem walking away from temptation, however attractively packaged, so he was surprised to recognise that in this instance it was a struggle to adopt his normal take-it-or-leave-it attitude.

Now that her niece was safely away from strangers she should have been able to relax slightly, but Zoe discovered she wasn't.

Obviously she had registered the fact he was not ugly the moment she entered the room, but she hadn't noticed the ludicrously long eyelashes, the jet-black, deep set heavy-lidded eyes they framed, or the incredible sculpted structure of his patrician features. Each strong angle and plane of his face was perfect.

He was her idea of a fallen angel—fatally beautiful and seductively dangerous—supposing angels were six-five and wore designer black from head to toe.

He smiled. It was usually possible to tell when a woman felt a reciprocal tug of attraction, and in this case it definitely was… She either wasn't attempting to hide her reaction or she didn't know how, not that she was trying to flirt with him, which was actually refreshing. Even a perfect vintage could become pedestrian if a man drank it for breakfast, lunch and dinner; he enjoyed flirtation to a point, but once you knew the moves of the modern mating ritual it could on occasion become painfully predictable.

A sense of expectation buzzing through his veins,

he bit into the grapes. They were sour, as predicted, but he smiled.

The flash of white teeth and the intensity of the stranger's hard dark eyes sent a shiver through Zoe's body unravelling like a silken ribbon of desire. It was a relief when she finally discovered a flaw, which should have made him less attractive but had quite the reverse effect. The imperfection was relatively minor—a scar, a thin white line that began to the right of one eye and traced the curve of one chiselled cheekbone.

Zoe swallowed and plucked at the neckline of her shirt as the palpable silence in the room stretched. Her tingling awareness of him was so strong that there was a delay for several seconds before her body responded to the desperate commands of her brain. She was close to applauding with sheer relief when she managed to gather up the shreds of her self-control and lower her gaze.

'I'm afraid you shouldn't be here, either.' She pitched her tone at friendly but firm, it came out as breathy. Nonetheless, she was happy—breathy was a big step up from open-mouthed drooling!

Isandro's gaze lifted from the logo plastered across the T-shirt she was wearing—not that he had read a word of the inscription, but mingled in with the mental image of him peeling the shirt over her head an astonishing idea had occurred to him, making the pleasurable picture fuzz and fade.

Surely not... She couldn't be...could she?

Had Tom lost his mind?

If she was, he definitely had!

Or had his normally super-reliable assistant been thinking with a different part of his anatomy when he appointed this woman to the post of housekeeper?

No, she couldn't be, he decided, clinging to his mental image of the perfect housekeeper—a woman of a certain age with an immovable iron-grey helmet of hair and a brisk manner. He didn't expect the new housekeeper to possess all the attributes of her predecessor but this woman—girl!—couldn't be…?

'This part of the house isn't open to the public, actually,' she admitted, softening the gentle remonstrance with a smile.

Madre di Dios, she was! Tom actually had lost his mind.

'None of it is but people keep wandering…' She heard the sharp note of anxiety that had crept into her own voice and closed her mouth, shaking her head as she smiled brightly and concluded in her best 'fasten your seat belt' tone, 'So if you'd like to follow me…?'

The irony of being asked to leave his own study was not lost on Isandro, but instead of putting this person in her place he found himself considering the question.

Would he like to follow her…? Yes, up the sweeping staircase and into his bedroom, which was not possible as he didn't date employees. It was a no-exception rule. But he was about to sack her, which would make her not his employee…?

Maybe Tom had been having similar thoughts when he had decided this woman fulfilled the brief of experienced and efficient. Maybe she possessed both these qualities in the bedroom? Maybe his assistant already knew…?

The possibility that his assistant had given his girlfriend a job she was patently unsuited to because of her skills in the bedroom sent a rush of rage through Isandro.

Was he mad because Tom had broken the rules, or

mad that Tom had broken them before Isandro had got the chance?

Responding to the voice in his head with a heavy frown that drew his dark brows into a single disapproving line over the bridge of his nose, Isandro gave a frustrated grunt of tension.

When the tall, unsmiling stranger with his film-star looks and smoky eyes didn't react to her invitation to leave, Zoe felt the panic she had been struggling to keep at bay all day surface before she ruthlessly subdued it.

She could panic when this day was over, even though right now it felt as if it never would be.

How could anything that had started so innocently become this monster? she asked herself despairingly.

The answer was quite simple: she'd lost the ability to say no… She'd agreed to so many things she'd forgotten or more likely blocked half of them; by this point if the Red Arrows did a fly past she wouldn't have been surprised.

CHAPTER TWO

IT WAS A total nightmare. In the past five days, she had lied more—by omission, which amounted to the same thing—than she had done in her entire life!

It was that first lie that had kicked it off and started the snowball effect, but the snowball was now the size of an apartment block.

It had seemed so innocent and she had been so desperate to help when poor Chloe, her dead sister's best friend—Chloe who always put on a brave face—had broken down in tears after inviting Zoe to a coffee morning.

'Who am I kidding? A coffee morning!' She shook her head in teary disgust. 'Do you know how much Hannah's operation costs?'

Zoe shook her head, guessing that such ground-breaking medical care in the States did not come cheap.

'And that's without the cost of travel to America. And time's running out, Zoe, while I'm organising coffee mornings and treasure. Baking isn't going to get Hannah to that hospital—it'll take a miracle!' she sobbed. 'In three months' time the disease might have progressed too far and the treatment might not work… They might not even agree to try and she'll be stuck in a wheelchair for life!'

Her heart bleeding for the other woman, Zoe hugged her, feeling utterly helpless.

'This isn't you, Chloe. You're a fighter. You're tired, that's all.' And small wonder. God knew when she had had a break; she commuted almost daily for Hannah's hospital appointments. 'Everyone's behind you, so involve us! We all want to help.'

She shook her head, wishing she had more than platitudes to offer the other woman. Then it came—the inspired idea—and she didn't pause to think it through, just blurted it out.

'Have your coffee morning at the hall. You know what people are like—they'll come just to have a nosy. We could put up some trestle tables in the garden and I'm sure Mrs Whittaker would bake some of her scones.' She knew that the entire community were gagging to see the changes made by the enigmatic new owner of the hall almost as much as they were gagging to see the man himself!

'Really?' Chloe had taken the tissue Zoe offered and dried her eyes. 'Won't Mr Montero mind? I wouldn't want to get you in trouble. I know when we asked if we could use the cricket pavilion for the charity match we got the thumbs down, though he did provide a nice shiny new cup for the winners,' she conceded with a sniff.

Wasn't hindsight grand? Of course it was easy now to recognise that this had been the moment to admit she'd have to run it past him, but she hadn't and neither had she run it past him afterwards because she knew what the reply would be. Chloe had been right: her new employer did not want to continue any old traditions or start any new ones of his own. He wanted, as Tom had explained, to keep the village the other side of the ten-foot wall.

'Not that he's not a great guy,' the loyal assistant had assured Zoe when he saw her expression. 'He's just private and he doesn't like getting personally involved. He's very generous, does heaps of stuff you don't hear about, but any charitable donations he makes are through the Montero Trust.'

The Montero Trust was apparently involved itself in such diverse projects as adult literacy programmes and providing clean water to remote Third World villages. It seemed worthy, but a solution loaded with red tape, and Chloe needed help *now*; she didn't have time to be at the bottom of a pile of worthy causes.

'Let me worry about that.'

And she'd been worrying ever since, but her reward had been Chloe's smile. She thought about that smile every time she got a fresh attack of guilt, which was often.

What had Tom said at her interview? 'He'll expect you to work without supervision, show initiative.' She suspected that today might be classed as too much initiative, but it wasn't as if the man would ever know. And his standing in the local community had been massively raised without any effort on his part. It was a win/win… or lose/lose for her if he found out!

No matter how hard she tried to rationalise what she'd done, Zoe knew that she had overstepped her authority big time and, as she was still working her trial period, if her actions were discovered the 'inspiration' could well lose her her job!

Her job…which meant her home and a roof over the twins' heads.

Small wonder she'd not had a decent night's sleep for the past week. And that was even before it had all got horribly out of hand. For some reason, once she had started saying yes she couldn't stop! Everyone had been so enthusiastic and generous, contributing their time and talents, that it had seemed churlish to be the one dissenting voice. The tipping point was probably the bouncy castle. After that Zoe had stopped even trying!

The only thing she could do today was stay on top of things and make damned sure that the grounds were returned to pristine condition once the day was over. She had an army of volunteers lined up for the task.

But right now what she had to do was get rid of this man—not as easy as it sounded because he made no effort to move as she stood back to let him pass—then check nobody else had wandered into the house.

'If you were looking for the toilets, go past the tombola and the refreshment tent and follow your nose.' In his case the nose, narrow and aquiline, was just as impressive as the rest of him. As she made a conscious effort not to stare their glances connected, only briefly but long enough to make all her deep stomach muscles contract viciously.

Seriously shaken by the extent of her physical response to this man, she huffed out a tiny breath from between her clenched teeth to steady her nerves and focused on a point over his left shoulder.

'You can't miss it.'

He still didn't take the hint. Instead he set his broad shoulders against the panelled wall and looked around the room.

'You have a beautiful home.'

Zoe folded her arms, hugging tight to hide her involuntary shiver. He had the sexiest voice she had ever heard and the faint accent only added another fascinating layer to it.

'No, yes…I mean it isn't mine.' It crossed her mind

that he was being sarcastic. 'As I'm sure you can tell,' she murmured, flashing him an ironic grimace before extending a trainer-clad foot and laughing.

His hooded stare made a slow sweeping survey from her extended foot to her face. 'I try not to judge by appearances,' he drawled.

Her eyes narrowed. 'That's not always easy.'

Like now it was hard not to judge this man by the faint sneer and the innate air of superiority he exuded. She supposed arrogance was natural for someone who looked in the mirror each morning and saw that face looking back…and his body, from what she could see, was not exactly going to give the owner any major insecurities! Her gaze moved down the lean, hard length of his long body. Not only did he look fit in every sense of the word, he was supremely elegant in an unstudied, casual sort of way.

Her smooth cheeks highlighted by a rose tinge, she brought her lashes down in a protective sweep. If there was a time to be caught mentally undressing a stranger, this was not it.

'Actually I just work here…' The sweep of her hand encompassed the elegant room with its warm panelled walls and antiques. 'It is beautiful, though, isn't it?' A cross between a museum and a very expensive interior designer's heaven, the place, in her view, lacked a lived-in-look. There were no discarded newspapers, open books or sweaters draped over the backs of chairs, no sign at all that anyone lived there—it was just too perfect.

But then essentially no one did live here. It amazed her that anyone could own such a beautiful place and barely spend any time here at all.

The staff had been more than happy to fill her in

on the many houses owned by their elusive boss, and
the many cars and private jets… Isandro Montero obviously liked to buy things whether he needed them or
not. Zoe had always suspected that people who needed
status symbols were secretly insecure. Mind you, having a bank account that hovered constantly just above
the red made a person feel insecure too. Zoe knew all
about that sort of insecurity!

His mobile ebony brows lifted in response to the information. 'So the owner has allowed his home to be
used for this…event?'

Zoe felt her cheeks heat.

'How generous and trusting.'

If he had been trying he couldn't have said anything
that made her feel more terribly guilty. Her eyes fell.
'He's very community minded.'

If he could hear me now, she thought, swallowing a
bubble of hysteria as she imagined the expression on
the face of the billionaire who didn't want to rub shoulders with the locals.

Her blue eyes slid to the wall lined with valuable
books. Did he spend his time here reading the first edi-
tions on the shelves or were they, like the cricket pavilion, just for show…part of the entire perfect English
Country Home?

What was the point in restoring a cricket pavilion
if you never intended to use it? What was the point in
buying books you were never going to read?

'The house is out of bounds today.'

He did not comment on the information. He was staring with what seemed to her far too much interest at a
painting on the wall.

She went pale as for the first time she realised how
vulnerable the house was. If he could just walk in here,

how easy it would have been for someone to wander in—still was, and…not just someone! Her blue eyes suspicious, she turned to look at the tall stranger who continued to stare at the painting. God, she had been so sidetracked by physical awareness of him that it hadn't even crossed her mind that his presence here might not be accidental!

'There is an excellent security system in place, and security guards.'

He heard the nervousness in her voice, saw the sudden alarmed dilation of her pupils and smiled slowly, without feeling any sympathy. Well might she be worried, he thought grimly. The odds were that some of his valuables were even now in the pockets of light-fingered visitors. His security team would be lucky to come out of this with jobs.

'So I couldn't just pick up…' He made a show of looking around the room, then reached out and picked up a gilt-framed miniature from its stand. It was one of a pair he had outbid a Russian oligarch for six months earlier. He did not begrudge the inflated price, as he liked the sense of continuity—the miniatures were coming back to where they had been painted. 'This?'

The casual action made her tummy muscles flip. When she had first arrived she had literally tiptoed around the place, seriously intimidated by the value of the treasures it housed and scared witless of damaging anything. Though she had relaxed a bit now, seeing this valuable item treated so casually was alarming.

She gave a nervous laugh and thought, Calm down—no genuine thief would be this obvious…would they?

'No, you couldn't…' She sucked in an alarmed breath and fought the impractical urge to rush forward and snatch it from him. She didn't have a hope in hell of taking anything away from six feet five inches of solid muscle. She looked at his chest and swallowed, her tummy giving a nervous quiver as she pressed a hand to her middle where butterflies continued to flutter wildly.

'Is it genuine?' he asked, holding the delicate gilt frame between his thumb and forefinger.

'A clever copy,' she lied, nervousness making her voice high pitched. 'All the valuable stuff is locked away in the bank.' I wish!

'So that's why you're not concerned about stray visitors putting a souvenir in their pocket and walking out.'

Zoe swallowed as she watched the miniature vanish into the pocket of his well-cut jeans, but was able to maintain an air of amused calm as she returned his wolfish grin with a shaky smile of bravado and shook her head. What did it say about her that even at a moment like this she had noticed how rather incredible his muscular thighs were?

'We're not actively encouraging it, but if anyone's tempted we have a very strong security presence.' She saw no need to explain that this presence was at the moment helping out with directing people in and out of the parking areas. She felt extra bad about that because she had pretty shamelessly taken advantage of the absence of the head of the security team to persuade his deputy to relax the rules. She had used every weapon, including moral blackmail and some mild but effective eyelash fluttering.

'So I would be stopped before I left the building…?'

Even though she positioned herself strategically in the doorway, Zoe was well aware that he would find her no obstacle to escape if he wanted. Though she was not sure he wanted to—he seemed just as happy taunting her as making good his escape.

Zoe placed her hands on her hips, lifted her chin to a don't-mess-with-me angle and resisted the temptation to return an 'over my dead body' response. He might decide to take it too literally. Instead she said calmly, 'Definitely not. I'll have to ask you to return the miniature. It's very valuable.'

'Yes, it was quite a find.' The blue eyes he held blinked and a small furrow appeared between her dark feathery brows. He experienced a stab of guilt. She was obviously scared stiff and he did not enjoy scaring women even if on this occasion she deserved it.

'Find?'

He tilted his head in acknowledgement of her bewildered echo. 'The lady here was considered a great beauty of the day, but she was trade—the daughter of a wealthy mill owner. The marriage caused quite a scandal when Percy there brought her home.' He glanced at the twin of the portrait he held still sitting in its stand. 'It turns out that old Percy started a trend in the family, though I'm afraid the other heiresses that subsequent male heirs married were not always so easy on the eye as Henrietta here.' He studied the painting, taking a moment's pleasure from the masterful brush strokes and eye for detail shown by the artist. 'He really caught her... Such a sensual mouth, don't you think? Personally I think this is better than the Reynolds on the staircase.'

His eyes were trained, not on the portrait in his hand as he spoke, but her own mouth. The effect of the dark-eyed stare was mesmerising. Zoe didn't respond, mainly because she could barely breathe past the hammering of her heart against her ribcage, let alone speculate on how he knew so much about the history of the house and family.

'Maybe they were in love?' Her voice sounded as though it were coming from a long way away.

He laughed. The throaty sound shivered across the surface of her skin, raising a rash of goosebumps. 'A romantic.'

The amused mockery in his voice made Zoe prickle with antagonism. What was she doing discussing love with a possible art thief? Was he? He certainly seemed to know more than she did about the artwork in the house.

'Actually, no, I'm not.' Her chin lifted. 'But if I was I wouldn't be ashamed of it. Now, Mr... I have things I need to attend to. If I could ask you to—'

'Shame is a very personal thing,' he mused, cutting across her. 'I wonder if Percy was ashamed of his heiress? You call it love, but I call it symbiosis.'

She compressed her lips. 'I wasn't calling it anything. I was simply not discounting the possibility.'

He tilted his dark head in acknowledgement of her interruption. 'Well, there is no doubt that she had money and he had social position, the ability to guarantee her acceptance into society, though maybe looking at that mouth there might have been other factors involved?'

He levelled his obsidian gaze on Zoe.

'Do you not think she has a sensual mouth?'

Now there was a case of pot calling kettle, she thought, dragging her gaze from the firm sculpted outline of his own mouth.

'I'm no expert on sensuality.'

'I'm sure you are being modest.' He arched a satiric brow and the speculation in his smoky stare sent a rush of embarrassed heat over her body. 'Well, I shall continue to think that our Henrietta was a woman of passions...and that perhaps Percy was a lucky man? We will, I suppose, never know. What we do know is that when there were no more rich social-climbing heiresses, the family sold off treasures and land until finally there was nothing left. There is a certain sense of continuity in seeing this pair back where they started.'

'That's very interesting but...' She stopped, the colour fading from her face. His manner, his accent, the fact he displayed no sign of discomfort being caught in the house... Of course he had acted as though he owned the place, because he did!

How could she have been so stupid? Because he wasn't what she had been expecting, of course—if she'd walked into a room and found a short, balding man using expensive tailoring to hide an affluent middle-aged spread she would immediately have considered the possibility that she was looking at her employer.

She squeezed her eyes shut. Small wonder the stable girl who had shown the double-page spread to her in the society magazine had looked at her oddly when she'd responded to the Welsh girl's enthusiastic, 'Isn't he utterly unbelievably lush?' with a polite but surprised response that he wasn't really her type. He hadn't been the man in the photo handing out the cup at the polo tournament—he'd been the one receiving it!

She had left the stables that morning reflecting sadly on the number of people who saw a man's bank balance before anything else. If the stout, balding man handing over the cup to the Latin-looking polo captain had not had the odd billion in the bank pretty Nia wouldn't have looked twice, and there she was acting as if he were some sort of centrefold pin-up.

My God, he was the centrefold!

Struggling to accept the evidence of her own eyes

and lose the invented image in her head, she watched the polo-playing captain put the portrait back in its place.

I just knew this job was too good to be true.

CHAPTER THREE

'My name is Zoe Grace.' She lifted her chin and clung to a shaky façade of calm. 'I'm your new housekeeper, Mr Montero. I'm sorry, we weren't expecting you,' she apologised stiffly.

'So I was looking for Zoe after all.' He met her confused blue stare before his glance fell to the hand extended to him and, ignoring it, he continued in the same conversational tone. 'I think you'll find you're my ex-housekeeper. You may have managed to con Tom...'

Zoe's shock at the calculated insult was followed swiftly by anger that she couldn't check. 'I didn't con anyone!'

'Then I can only assume you're sleeping with him because I can't think of any other reason why Tom would employ someone so stupendously unsuited to this or, as far as I can see, any other position of trust. And before you waste your time fluttering your eyelashes at me I have to tell you I'm not Tom. I enjoy a good body and—' he paused, his eyes making a cynical sweep of her face before he delivered a crushing assessment '—passably pretty face, but when it comes to staff I prefer to keep the lines firmly drawn. It cuts down on confusion and time-consuming, messy litigation.'

Zoe hated him before he was halfway through the scathing tirade.

Dismay widened her blue eyes. He was already turning away. In the grip of panic she surged after him, catching hold of his arm. 'You can't sack me!'

He arched a brow and looked down at her hand.

Zoe let it go, biting down on her full under lip as she backed away, shaking her head.

'I mean, you can, obviously you can, but don't…' She swallowed and bit her lip. Unable to meet his eyes, she lifted her chin, a note of sheer desperation creeping into her voice as she added huskily, 'Please.'

There were times when a person had to swallow her pride and this was one of those occasions.

Of course, if it had been just her she would have told him where to stuff his awful job. In fact if there had been just herself to consider she wouldn't be doing the job to begin with.

But there was more than herself to consider now.

Even if she could get some sort of job locally that would enable the twins to continue going to their school—they'd had enough disruption in their lives without being snatched away from everything that was familiar—Zoe couldn't have afforded the rent on a property within the catchment area. As for buying—she would have been laughed out of any bank.

The property prices were inflated in the village because of the number of affluent parents eager to move into the area due to the success of the local state school. Laura and Dan had frequently joked that they were sitting on a fortune, but their lovely little thatched cottage had been taken by her brother-in-law's creditors along with everything else they had.

Though his expression did not soften, Isandro did after a short pause turn and face her.

'I need this job, Mr Montero,' she said, wringing her white hands in anxiety at the prospect of being jobless and homeless.

His expression held no hint of sympathy as he read the earnest appeal in her blue eyes.

'Perhaps you should have thought of that before you turned my home into a circus. Unless this is all someone else's fault…?'

Zoe didn't even consider passing the buck. She lifted her chin and thought, You got yourself into this, Zoe, now get yourself out—crawl, grovel, whatever it takes. 'No, this was all me.'

'And you're not even sharing the profits of this little enterprise…?'

Anger made Zoe momentarily forget her determination to grovel. 'Are you calling me a…?' She lowered her gaze and added quietly, 'I'm not making money from this. Nobody is!'

He arched a sceptical brow. 'No…?'

'All the money goes to a good cause a—'

He lifted an imperative hand. 'Please spare me the sob stories. I have heard them all before. And as for appealing to my community spirit, don't waste your breath. I don't have any.'

Or a heart, either, Zoe thought, trying to keep her growing sense of desperation and panic under control.

She bit her lip. 'I know I overstepped my authority but I didn't see how a coffee morning could do much harm.'

His ebony brows hit his hairline. 'A coffee morning?'

She flushed and lowered her gaze. 'I know, I know… things got out of hand. It's just they were so enthusiastic and—' she lifted her eyes in appeal to his '—it was such a good cause that it was hard to say no.'

A flash of irritation crossed his lean features. If this woman expected he would react to a combination of emotional blackmail and big blue eyes she was in for a disappointment. 'It is always a good cause,' he drawled carelessly.

Zoe had to bite her lip to stop herself reacting to his contempt.

She bowed her head. If he wanted humble, fine, she could do that... She had to do that. 'We weren't expecting you.'

'How inconsiderate of me to arrive unannounced.' The sarcasm brought a flush to her cheeks. 'I admit I'm curious—what part of your designated role as someone responsible for the smooth running of this establishment did you think you were providing when you decided to turn my home into a cheap sideshow?'

'I thought...well, actually...I've already said it did get a bit out of hand, but it's not as if you are ever here.'

'So this is a case of while the cat's away. You have a novel way of pleading your cause, Miss Grace.'

'I need this job.' It went against every instinct to beg but what choice did she have? Speaking her mind was a luxury she could no longer afford. 'I really need this job. If you give me a chance to prove myself you won't regret it.'

His lifted his magnificent shoulders in a shrug. 'Like I said, you should have thought about that.' He studied her white face and felt an unexpected flicker of something he refused to recognise as sympathy as he could almost taste her desperation. 'Have you actually got any experience of being a housekeeper?'

She was too stressed to give anything but an honest answer. 'No.'

'I think it might be better if I do not enquire too far into the reason my assistant saw fit to offer you this job.'

'He knew I needed it.'

Her reply drew a hard, incredulous laugh from him. Actually, he had some sympathy for his assistant. If her performance at interview had been half as good as the one she was delivering now, he would not have been surprised if the man had offered her more than a job.

He would be having words with Tom.

'If when I take an inventory there are any valuables missing you will be hearing from me. Other than that I shall expect you to have vacated your flat by the morning.'

Zoe gave a wild little laugh. Short of falling to her knees, which might give him a kick but would obviously not change his mind, what was she meant to do? She had no skills, nothing to sell... The sheer hopelessness of her situation rushed in on her like a black choking cloud.

Falling back on the charity of friends was her only option, and that was only temporary.

She made one final attempt.

'Please, Mr Montero.'

His mouth thinned in distaste. 'Your tears are very touching, but wasted on me.'

She looked at him with tear-filled eyes. There was no longer anything to lose by telling him what she really thought. 'You're a monster!'

He shrugged. Being considered a monster was to his way of thinking infinitely preferable to being a sucker.

Zoe lifted her chin and, head high, walked towards the door, feeling the honeysuckle-scented breeze blowing through the open window stroke her cheek as she walked past him.

She was so blinded by the tears she fought to hold back that she almost collided with the vicar who was entering the room.

'Oops!' he said, placing both his hands on her shoulders to steady her. 'Zoe, dear, we were looking for you.' In the act of turning to include in this comment the woman who stood beside him with the child in a wheelchair he saw Isandro and paused, his good-natured face breaking into a beaming smile as he recognised him before surging forward.

'Mr Montero, I can't tell you how grateful we are… all of us.'

Isandro, who had met the man on one previous occasion, acknowledged the gushing gratitude with a tilt of his head. 'The work is finished on the new roof?'

'New roof? Oh, yes, that's marvellous but I am talking about today. This totally splendid turnout. It warms the heart to see the entire community pulling together.'

He didn't have a heart to warm, Zoe thought as she saw the hateful billionaire tip his dark head and hide his confusion behind an impassive mask of hauteur. Actually it wasn't a mask; it was probably just him. Cold, cruel, vindictive, positively hateful!

'Mr Montero, oh, thank you… Hannah, this is Mr Montero, darling. Come and say thank you.'

Startled to find himself being hugged by a tearful woman, Isandro stood rigid in the embrace, his arms stiff at his side. Oblivious to the recipient's discomfort, Chloe sobbed into his broad chest and told him he was marvellous.

Zoe took a small degree of comfort from the discomfort etched on the Spaniard's handsome face. She'd have preferred a job and a roof over her head but it was something.

When Hannah propelled her wheelchair over, her little face wreathed in smiles, and informed the startled billionaire that he could have a puppy from the next litter, his expression almost made her smile…though that might have been hysteria.

'Bella is the smartest dog, even though she was the runt, and everyone wanted her last puppies, though this time we think the father might be… Well, that's all right, you've plenty of room here and you look like a dog person.'

At a loss for once in his life, the dog person swallowed and wondered if the entire community here were off their heads.

Chloe still bubbling, her face alight, stopped her daughter's chair before it hit the desk. 'You two made this happen…' She took Zoe's hand and then that of the man she considered benefactor and pressed them palm to palm before sealing them between her own.

Standing there with a frozen smile on her face, Zoe had to fight the urge to tear her hand free. The only comfort she found in the situation was that he had to be hating this as much as she was.

'We made the target, so you won't have to shave your head!'

Zoe, forgetting for a moment her own situation, smiled happily, without noticing the expression on the tall Spaniard's face as he watched her light up with pleasure.

'Oh, Chloe, that's marvellous! Is there enough for John to come with you?'

'Not quite,' the older woman conceded. 'But he wouldn't be able to take that much time off work anyway. And we'll have so much to tell Daddy when we come home, won't we, Hannah?' She released the two hands she held and ducked down to her daughter, leaving Zoe standing there with her fingers curled around the long brown fingers of Isandro Montero.

While Chloe was kissing her daughter, and the vicar was taking off his glasses to study one of the paintings on the wall, Zoe took the opportunity to wrench her hand free and sling a poisonous look up at his face.

'Oh, Zoe, you've worked so hard. How will we ever be able to thank you? And don't you worry—we'll be here bright and early to clear away.' She stretched up to kiss Zoe's cheek. 'I wanted you to know first. Now I think we should go and tell everyone else...Vicar?'

'Yes, indeed. Mr Montero, you have a very impressive art collection here...amazing...' He wrung the younger man's hand with enthusiasm before following Chloe from the room. Zoe, who had tacked on behind them, was stopped by the sound of her name.

'Miss Grace, if I could have a moment...?'

Half inclined to carry on walking but knowing if she did the likelihood would be that the story would come out, Zoe paused and turned back, promising Chloe she would catch up. She knew it was inevitable that her friend would feel in part responsible for her sacking, but she saw no need to cast a cloud over this happy moment for the family who had not had a lot to be happy about recently.

She held herself rigid as he walked past her and closed the door.

'So?'

She shrugged and matched his tone. 'What?'

'Would you like to tell me what that was all about?'

Now he wants to know. 'I was trying to explain.'

Isandro's jaw tightened. He was furious to have been put in the position of being treated like some sort of hero and not having a clue why, and his anger was aimed at the person he held responsible for it.

'Well, explain now.'

'The fund-raiser was for Hannah.'

'The child in the wheelchair?'

Zoe nodded. 'Hannah had surgery for a spinal tumour. It was successful, they got all the tumour, but the pressure on the spinal cord caused damage and she can't walk. The doctors can't do anything, but Chloe, her mum, found a hospital in Boston that might be able to help. The treatment is experimental but so far the results have been really good.'

'And all this today was for that cause?'

She nodded.

His dark brows drew together in a straight line above his hawkish nose. 'Why on earth did you not tell me this straight away?'

She stared at him, staggered he could ask the question with a straight face... Priceless—the man was incredible. 'Possibly because you didn't give me a chance?'

Before he could respond there was a tap on the door and Chloe poked her head into the room.

'I almost forgot—we're having a party tomorrow at our house. Please come, Mr Montero.'

'Isandro.'

'Isandro,' she said, smiling. 'I'm sure Zoe will drive you if you want a drink,' Zoe was mortified to hear her friend suggest warmly. 'Her being the teetotaller she is.'

Zoe tensed, dreading the man would respond with a crushing refusal to the invitation, but to her surprise he simply nodded and said, 'Most kind of you.'

'Great—we'll see you both at seven.'

The door closed. 'Don't worry, I'll make your excuses. I'm assuming that as you know I'm not some sort of con artist you'll allow me to work my notice. I'm not asking for myself, but the children—'

Frowning, he cut across her. 'They all seem to be under the impression that I gave the go-ahead for this… this…'

'Fund-raising Fun Day.'

'Fun?'

'It started out as a coffee morning and then it just…'

He produced the sarcastic smile that made her want to stick a pin in him.

She clenched her teeth. 'Got out of hand.'

'It would seem you have a problem saying no.' He looked at her mouth and imagined her saying yes to a lot of things…yes and please. 'Did it not occur to you to tell me what this was about?'

She lifted her chin in response to his daunting disapproval and countered, 'Did it not occur to you to tell me who you were?'

The retort drew a frown. 'You have placed me in an impossible situation,' he brooded darkly.

Logic told him his hands were tied.

Sack her now and he would go from being the hero of the hour to the villain in a breath, and while he did not care overly for his standing in the local community, what bothered him was the press getting a sniff and running with it.

With the Fitzgerald deal in the balance the timing was as bad as it could be and this was the sort of story that the tabloids loved. The wheelchair-bound child, the rich landowner… He could see the headlines now, closely followed by the deal he had spent the last six months pulling together going down the drain along with all the jobs it would bring.

As tempting as it was to let the dismissal stand— every instinct he had was telling him she was nothing but trouble—Isandro knew the more sensible alternative was letting her stay. He had no doubt whatever that he would not have long to wait before she provided him with ample legitimate reasons to dismiss her.

An image of the pale freckled face flashed into his head. 'The child could not be treated in this country?'

Zoe smiled—the day had done some good. 'No, the surgery is ground-breaking.'

'And shaving your head?' He directed a curious glance at her glossy head, the light shining from the window highlighting natural-looking glossy chestnut streaks in the rich brown. 'A joke?'

Zoe lifted a self-conscious hand and flicked her plait over shoulder. 'Not really. Chloe has bad days sometimes and to make her laugh I said if the day didn't raise the money she needed I'd shave off my hair to raise more.'

'No!' The strength of his spontaneous rebuttal startled Isandro as much as it appeared to the owner of the hair.

She blinked, startled. 'Pardon?'

'It would not be appropriate for my housekeeper to go around with a shaved head.'

For a moment Zoe stared at him, her hope soaring despite the voice in her head that counselled caution. 'Housekeeper. Does that mean…?'

'I will be back tomorrow and I expect—' He broke off as a great roar went up from outside. 'I will expect things to be back to normal.'

'So you're not sacking me?' Zoe lowered her gaze, appalled to find her eyes filling with weak tears of relief.

'I will give you a trial period.' He gave her a month.

'You won't regret it.'

He probably would. 'The child…?' He touched the back of the chair she had been spinning around in. 'The one with the ginger hair.'

'Auburn. That was Georgie…Georgina.'

'She is…?' he prompted impatiently. It was like getting blood out of a stone.

'My niece.' She beamed happily. He could look down his aristocratic nose at her as much as he liked—she was no longer homeless, jobless and virtually destitute.

'She is staying long?'

'She lives with me and her twin brother, Harry.' In her head she could hear Laura on the phone when the scan had revealed she was carrying twins… One of each, Zoe, how lucky are we?

In the act of opening a diary on his desk, he stopped, his hands flat on the desk as he lifted his head. 'You have two children living here? No, that is not acceptable. You will have to make other arrangements.'

Zoe stared at him, breathing deeply to distract herself from the rush of anger. 'Arrangements? What,' she asked, 'did you have in mind?'

His eyes narrowed at the edge of sarcasm in her voice. 'I know nothing about children.'

'Except that you have no room in your twenty-bedroom house for two small ones.'

'So you're suggesting you move into my home.' He arched a sardonic brow and watched her flush. 'Or perhaps you already have?' It struck him that this might not be so far from the truth—the child had looked very comfortable in his chair.

Zoe flushed and bit her lip. 'Of course not.'

'So you would agree that the accommodation that comes with the job is not suitable.'

'It's fine.' It was free and in the catchment area of the twins' school, which made it not just fine but incredible!

His dark eyes sealed to hers as in interrogation mode he ran a hand across his jaw, shadowed with a day's growth of stubble. 'Correct me if I'm wrong…'

Oh, sure, I bet that happens a lot, she thought, struggling to keep her placid, perfect housekeeper smile pasted in place. She could see him now surrounded by little yes men falling over themselves to tell him how wonderful he was.

'But I was under the impression that the house-keeper's apartment had one bedroom?'

'A very big bedroom, and it has a perfectly comfortable sofa bed in the living room.'

'You sleep on a sofa bed?'

He could not have looked more appalled had she just announced she dossed down on a park bench or in a shop doorway.

'The arrangement works very well.' She smiled brightly in the face of his undisguised scepticism. If he was looking for an excuse to give her the push, she wasn't going to give him any. 'I'm always up before the twins, and they are in bed before me.' It wasn't a room of her own that kept Zoe awake at night, it was balancing her budget.

'In other words it is a perfect arrangement.'

Zoe pretended not to recognise the dry sarcasm. 'Not perfect,' she conceded calmly. 'But a workable compromise.' Like he knew a lot about compromise, she thought, but, smothering the prickle of antagonism, she continued serenely, 'And if you're thinking that the twins have a negative impact on my work, actually the reverse is true.'

'Indeed?'

'Having a family and responsibilities makes me ultra-reliable.' And totally lacking in pride, suggested the scornful voice in her head.

'You mean you need this job so you'll bite back the insult hovering even now on the tip of your tongue.' His hooded dark eyes slid to the soft full outline of her quite spectacularly sexy lips.

The words hovering on the tip of Zoe's tongue involved telling him to stop staring at her mouth.

She found herself thinking with nostalgia of the days when her temporary cash shortages had been dealt with by not buying the pair of shoes she'd been drooling over, or cutting back on the number of coffees she bought in a week. Things were no longer so simple. She was still reeling over the cost of new school uniforms for the twins, who had both shot up the previous term.

'You are speaking as if this arrangement is permanent. I assumed the children were spending their holiday with you.'

And I could have let him continue assuming that—the man is here so rarely he wouldn't have known the difference—but no, I had to go open my big mouth.

'No. They are my sister's children.' She swallowed. She didn't discuss the details of the accident that had killed her sister and her husband or mention the under-age drunk driver going the wrong way on the motorway who had been responsible for the simple fact that she was afraid if she did she would start shouting. 'She and her husband died. I'm the children's guardian.'

'I am sorry.'

She nodded, not trusting herself to speak.

According to the grief counsellor anger was normal... It would pass, she said. There might be a time when she would stop being angry, but six months after that terrible day Zoe could not imagine a time when she would come to terms with it, stop wanting to beat her bare fists against a brick wall at the sheer terrible waste.

'You are very young to have such responsibilities.'

'That's relative, isn't it?' Only last week Zoe had watched a programme that followed a week in the life of children who were the main carers for their disabled parents. It had made her feel ashamed—compared to them she had it easy.

'Surely there is someone more suitable who could take care of these children?' He scanned her up and down and shook his head.

'My sister was my only family and Dan didn't have any family. It's me or social services.' She'd do what it took to stop that happening. The children would enjoy the sort of childhood she'd had... It was far too short as it was.

Zoe closed her eyes, remembering Laura's face the day she met Dan, and swallowed, concentrating on the anger, not the pain, as the same old question followed—why? Why Laura of all people in the world? Why did it have to be her?

He eyed her beautiful face cynically. 'I am assuming that housekeeping was not a career choice for you.'

Zoe moistened her lips, trying to decide what the right answer to this question was. In the end she kept it simple and honest.

'I never really knew what I wanted to do with my life.'

There had never seemed any hurry to make up her

mind. She liked to travel; she liked new experiences and meeting new people.

Well, now it was her turn to step up to the mark and, yes, she would beg and be tearfully grateful to this awful man. She would grovel if necessary, even if it killed her. She would do whatever it took to keep her family together.

She gave a quietly confident smile. 'But I never give any less than a hundred per cent, and I'll do whatever it takes to keep this job… Anything,' she added fiercely.

'Anything…?'

Something in the way he said it made her feel less secure, but she wouldn't back down—she couldn't. She nodded.

'Absolutely.'

Expression impassive, he brushed an invisible speck off his dark top with long brown fingers.

'"Anything" covers a lot of territory so if you're offering sexual favours I should tell you I normally get it for free.'

Zoe's hands curled into tight fists at her sides as she breathed through the energising rush of anger. He was taunting her, but he knew full well she couldn't respond and in her book that made the man a bully. She rubbed the hand that tingled to slap the expression of amused disdain off his smug, impossibly handsome face, and tilted her chin to an enquiring angle.

But would she…?

She pushed away the question and willed herself not to blush, unwilling to give him the satisfaction of seeing her squirm. At least she was safe from any unwanted attentions—the man was obviously too much of a snob to consider sleeping with the help.

But if he did?

Her body reacted to the unspoken question and Zoe had no more chance of halting the visceral chain reaction than she did stopping her fingers jerking back from a hot object.

Taking a deep breath, she brought her lashes down in a protective sweep and wrapped her arms across her middle in a hugging gesture, glad that she was wearing a loose-fitting top. She was saved the added embarrassment of having her shamefully engorged nipples on view, but it didn't stop her being painfully conscious of the chafing discomfort of her bra or the heavy liquid ache low in her pelvis.

Closing down this internal dialogue as her temperature rose, Zoe managed to break contact with his disturbing steely stare and lifted her shoulders in a tiny shrug.

'Jokes aside, I can promise you I shall be totally professional.'

He arched a brow and didn't look convinced by her claim. She felt panic trickle down her spine and thought, God, please don't let him change his mind.

'You won't be sorry.' Her fingernails gouged crescents into the soft flesh of her palms as she held her breath awaiting his response, feeling like a prisoner in the dock waiting to hear his sentence read out.

His tall figure framed in the doorway, Isandro turned. He already was regretting it.

'I am sorry for your loss, but I have to tell you I do not allow sentiment to sway my judgement, so do not expect any special favours here.'

Just how well would his judgement withstand the pressure of great legs and a stupendous mouth?

Her smile was cold and proud. 'I won't expect any.'

'We'll see. I judge by results, not promises.' Or lips,

he thought as his gaze made an unscheduled traverse of the lush pink curve of her wide mouth before he could think better of it.

'I never had any complaints.' The unintentional innuendo after his previous comment brought a flush to her cheeks. 'In any of the jobs I've had,' she added hastily.

'That cannot be many. How old are you?'

'Twenty-two, and actually—' She lifted a hand, about to list the jobs she had done, and dropped it again, not wanting to give the impression that she didn't have staying power. As it happened, it was too late, as his next disturbingly perceptive remark revealed.

'What is the longest time you have remained in one job?'

Outwardly cool, inwardly thinking, Why, oh, why can I never keep my big mouth shut? she furrowed her smooth brow. 'Is that relevant?'

'It is if you walk after a week.'

'I have done a number of jobs, it's true, but who hasn't in this job market?' As if he knows such a lot about this job market. He may employ a lot of people in his various empires, but to him they are statistics on a chart. 'I've never left anyone in the lurch. I'm totally reliable.'

'But you don't like to stay in one place long? You have no staying power?'

'I have…' She forced her lips into a smile and bit back a retort even though it choked her to do so. 'Please don't judge me on first impressions. I have responsibilities now that I did not have previously.'

'We'll see.' He flicked his wrist and glanced at his watch. 'My chef will be here later. You will make the arrangements.'

She nodded and produced a smile that oozed professional confidence. 'Of course.' She wrinkled her nose. 'What arrangements would they be?'

Unable to decide if she was joking, he regarded her with an expression of stern disapproval. 'This is not a work experience position, Miss Grace.'

'Of course not, Mr Monster...Montero.' Thrown into confusion by the horrifying Freudian slip, she almost fell over in her haste to get to the door before him to open it.

'I do not require grovelling. I require efficiency.'

She tipped her head meekly. 'Of course.' What he required, in her opinion, was taking down a peg or several hundred. She just hoped she was around to watch when it happened.

Passing through the door, Isandro revised his month estimate. She wouldn't last a week. If she had mouths to feed that was not his problem—he was not a charity.

CHAPTER FOUR

IF HE FOUND so much as a curtain fold out of place she'd eat her rather grubby trainers, Zoe decided, doing a final survey of the room.

The army of volunteers had cleared away any sign of yesterday's festivities in the grounds. The word had got around that the boss had put in an unexpected appearance the previous day and the staff had really gone the extra mile on the house. The rest of the rooms were equally pristine, about as lived-in as your average museum, but presumably cosy was not what he wanted.

Thinking the word 'cosy' in the same thought as Isandro Montero made her lips quirk, but not for long. She had spent a really awful night reliving yesterday's encounter, by turns breaking out in cold sweats when she thought of how close she'd come to losing the roof over their heads and seething with resentment that she'd had to crawl to keep it.

The couple of times she had managed to drift off she hadn't been able to escape the awful man who held their fate in his elegant, over-privileged hands. Shivering, she pushed her fingers into her hair and shook her head. Typical. She normally forgot the contents of her dreams the moment she woke up. But the dark erotic images from last night remained disturbingly fresh, as did the lingering shivery feeling in the pit of her stomach that did not diminish with each subsequent flashback.

Get a grip, Zoe, she told herself. The man only comes here once in a blue moon, so grit your teeth and give him no opportunity to criticise.

'You don't have to like him.' And you definitely don't have to dream about him, she added silently as she rubbed a suggestion of a smudge off the surface of a mirrored bureau door with the sleeve of her sweater.

Catching sight of herself, she gave a horrified gasp. The house and grounds looked terrific but she didn't!

Rushing out into the square marble-floored hallway, dominated by the graceful curving staircase that rose to the second floor and the glass dome above that flooded the space with light, Zoe couldn't help glancing nervously at the big front door, her heart beating fast in reaction to the image in her head of it opening to reveal the master of the house. A shiver travelled the length of her spine before she shook her head, laughing.

Master?

'Really, Zoe!' She shook her head again, ignoring the fact her laugh this time had a breathless sound to it. Living with all this history was making her thoughts turn positively feudal, she decided, exiting through the door that led into a long winding inner hallway and in turn to the sturdy door that led outside into the quadrangle of outbuildings at the rear of the building.

She headed across the cobbled yard, past the rows of stone troughs filled with artistically arranged tumbling summer flowers, and up the stone steps that led to the flat above what had once been a coach house but now housed what was by all accounts an impressive collection of vintage sports cars.

Inside the flat she closed the door and leaned against

it, relieved that he hadn't put in an appearance while she was looking like a scarecrow. Walking across to the fitted cupboard that housed her clothes, she grimaced at her reflection in the full-length mirror inside the door. Not exactly the image of cool efficiency she was determined to exemplify.

Stripping down to her bra and pants, she folded her jeans. When the space was limited neatness was essential but fortunately she didn't have many clothes, which made her choice of a suitable outfit pretty easy. Padding through the living room and through the twins' bedroom into the en-suite, she popped her dusty top in the linen basket, then pinned her hair up before she stepped into the shower. Though she would have liked to wash her hair, it took an age to dry and she was short of time.

Fifteen minutes later, wearing a crisp white blouse, a pair of narrow-legged tailored black trousers and with her hair in a fat plait down her back, she slid her feet into a pair of sensible black leather loafers. She gave herself a critical once-over, bending at the knee to see the top of her head in the angled mirror. Resisting the temptation to jazz up the sombre outfit with a pink scarf dotted with orange roses, she slid a pair of gold hoops into her ears. The sound of them jingling brought a smile to her lips as she lifted her head, more confidence in her stride as she headed across the courtyard. She was determined to make up for the disastrous first impression she had made; she could do it.

She had to do it.

Her smile faded slightly as she approached the building, tensing as she heard a car in the distance, but the vehicle that drove through the arch was a delivery van from the local butcher's. She started breathing again, delivering the silent advice, Cool it, Zoe, before she paused to thank one of the gardeners for donating a box full of the vegetables from the kitchen garden to the raffle the previous day, and admiring the magnificent lavender tumbling from a group of barrels.

'The smell always makes me think of summer and at night it fills the flat,' she told him, adding warmly, 'The flowers you cut for the house were marvellous.' She had spent a pleasant half-hour filling bowls in several of the rooms with the fragrant summer blooms.

He tilted his head in acknowledgement and looked pleased with the compliment. 'The other one here before you sent up to London for fancy arrangements every week. I told her it was a criminal waste.'

'I'm sure they were very beautiful.' The gardener might approve, but Zoe suddenly felt less secure about her amateur attempts to add a touch of colour to the house; they were hardly professional.

Resisting the impulse to run back to the house and remove all the flowers, which in her mind were fast becoming tasteless and ugly displays of amateurism, she chatted a little longer to the man before she finally excused herself.

In the end she couldn't bring herself to dump the freshly cut flowers, deciding as a compromise not to volunteer the information she was responsible—unless directly asked, which seemed unlikely. She walked around the place a final time to double-check everything, leaving it until the last possible moment before she jumped in her car and set off to pick up the twins from school.

For all she knew Isandro Montero might not arrive until midnight; he might be a total no-show—if she was very lucky.

The narrow country lane that led to the village was

in theory a short cut, but Zoe got stuck behind a tractor, and the children were already waiting at the gate when she arrived, chatting to Chloe and Hannah.

'I'm sorry I'm late!' she exclaimed.

'You're not late,' Chloe soothed. 'They only just got out.' She took in Zoe's outfit and her brows lifted. 'Wow, you look very…'

'Weird,' supplied Georgie bluntly.

'Very sexy librarian,' Chloe corrected.

'Are librarians sexy?' Harry asked.

Chloe exchanged a look with Zoe, who suppressed a smile and said, 'In the car, you two.' Adding, 'Do you want a lift, Chloe?'

The older woman shook her head. 'No, I'm picking up some glasses for tonight from Sara on my way back.'

'I hope you all have a great night, I wish I could come but…' She lifted her slender shoulders in a regretful shrug; her babysitting arrangements had fallen through that morning.

'You can… I know, just call me fairy godmother. You know how John's mum is having Hannah? Well, she's offered to have your two as well. John will pick up the twins on his way home and he'll fetch them back in the morning.'

'Oh, Chloe, that's really kind but I couldn't impose…'

'It's not imposing. Maud offered and they'll have a great time, you know they will.'

'Yes, but—'

'Yes but nothing, Cinders, you're going to the ball and don't forget the invite includes your utterly gorgeous boss… I tell you, if I was a few years younger I'd give you a bit of competition there.'

Zoe struggled to smile at the joke. 'He's not here, I'm afraid.' She felt a guilty tug as her friend's face fell.

'I thought he was due back today. John's going to be so disappointed—he wanted to thank him personally and return his hospitality. Half the people there only came because they wanted to take a look at the hall.'

Zoe's unease increased. Short of admitting that the hospitality they wanted to return had not been given freely, she had no way of preventing the decision to treat the new lord of the manor as a community-minded philanthropist.

'He was…is…due today,' she admitted. 'But when I left he hadn't arrived.'

'But he might do.'

'Anything's possible,' Zoe admitted, but the thought of Isandro coming to a party where the glasses were borrowed and the food was provided by guests! Possible but not very likely, thank goodness!

'Well, promise you'll remind him if he does turn up? Tell him that we'd love to see him and he seemed very keen to come. He's obviously making an effort to be part of the community.'

Zoe didn't have the heart to shatter this illusion and explain that the man had only said yes to cut the scene short and get rid of them as quickly as possible.

'If he does I will,' Zoe promised, imagining with horror the admittedly unlikely scenario of Isandro putting in an appearance at the party. Him spending the entire evening with his lips curled contemptuously would suck the joy out of any occasion and Zoe wanted to save her friends that. On a less unselfish note she wanted to save herself from spending her precious off-duty time with a man who made her skin prickle with antagonism even before he opened his mouth and said something vile and unpleasant. The fact that half the vile things he said were actually the truth was neither here nor… Losing track of her train of thought, she shook her head slightly to banish the image of the lips that combined overt sensuality with an underlying hint of cruelty.

She was getting fixated on the man's mouth when it was the things that came out if it that she ought to worry about.

'John will be by around six to pick up the twins.'

Isandro did not get involved in other people's lives. His charitable donations to selected good causes were made anonymously, and he never responded to any form of moral blackmail or sentimental sob stories, but the story of the little girl and her 'last chance to walk' trip to America continued to play in his mind.

Admit it, Isandro, the kid got to you.

This perceived weakness was responsible for putting the indent between his sable brows. His father had been a sentimental man, a kind, trusting man who was moved by the suffering of others. A man who taught his son the importance of charity, and led by example.

And where had that got him?

Universally liked and admired certainly—but at the end he had been a broken and disillusioned man.

Isandro had been forced to stand by helplessly and watch while the woman his father had married and her daughter had systematically robbed the family business, stealing not just from his father but from major clients. He had no intention of emulating his parent, had no room for sentimentality in his life, expected the worst from others and was rarely disappointed.

Experience had taught him that everyone had an angle and the most innocent of faces could hide a devious heart, like his stepmother and her daughter. Forced to brake hard to avoid a cat that shot across the road out of nowhere, he shook his head, banishing the thoughts of the pair of con artists who had with clinical efficiency isolated his father, alienating him not just from trusted friends and colleagues but his family, ensuring that when Isandro had passed on the concerns expressed by senior staff it had been treated as jealous spite.

Isandro would never be the man his father had been; he'd make sure of that. The possibility that his name was synonymous with cold and heartless was to his way of thinking infinitely preferable to being considered a mug.

A faint smile flickered across his face. According to the lovely Zara he was both cold and heartless among other things. She had lost it big time and reverted to her native Russian, a language Isandro had only a smattering of, so some of the choicer insults had been lost on him, before she swept majestically out of the restaurant on her designer heels.

He exhaled, feeling a fleeting spasm of regret. The woman looked magnificent even when she was spitting fury, and the sex had been excellent.

Great sex had been about the only thing they had going for them, and it had been pretty much the perfect relationship while Zara's demands had stayed in the bedroom, but recently… He shook his head. He was not into post-mortems but if he'd lived last night again he might not have replied so honestly when Zara had pouted and asked, 'Have you listened to a word I've been saying all night?'

If he'd contented himself with an honest, no frills 'no' he might have cajoled her out of her sulks and things might not have escalated so noisily, but he hadn't.

He'd irritably gone into more detail, rather unwisely revealing that he had minimal interest in shoes, the latest way to remove a skin blemish, or minor royals.

To Zara's frigid, 'I'm so sorry if I'm keeping you awake,' he had responded with an inflammatory:

'Barely.'

Zara's wrathful intake of breath had caused heads to turn and half the room had heard her hissing, 'Do you want to split up?'

The ensuing scene could have been avoided. His error of judgement had been assuming she expected to hear him say yes.

He still wasn't sure why he'd said it. It wasn't as if Zara had ever been anything but shallow, but that had never been a problem. In fact it had always suited him. It wasn't her fault that her beauty budget for a month could have paid for a disabled child's medical treatment.

Dios, but the child had really got to him, he thought, seeing not the child's face but the disapproval and contempt etched on the beautiful face of his new housekeeper.

There were no balloons along the driveway, just a peacock who sauntered across the road at a leisurely pace, forcing him to wait, then one of the team of gardeners at the wheel of a lawnmower on the now empty lawn as he drove past. Superficially at least everything was back to normal.

It wasn't until he drove into the courtyard that he realised how hard he had been searching for a legitimate cause for complaint. Frowning as much at the flash of insight as at the beat-up Transit van parked beside one of the estate Land Rovers, he opened the door and peeled out of the low-slung sports car he was driving.

He had taken a couple of steps across the cobbles

when he saw a denim-clad bearded figure he assumed was the driver of the eyesore vehicle, who up to that point had been concealed from Isandro by his van.

He wasn't alone. He held in his arms a tall slender figure. Isandro stopped dead at the sight. The woman wrapped in the circle of another man's arms had her face hidden from him but the slim body was that of his housekeeper.

Anger flooded into his body, the speed and strength of the flood of emotion leaching the colour from the sculpted bones of his strong features. For the space of several heartbeats his ability to think was obliterated by pure fury as he stood with his hands clenched into fists at his sides.

As the woman emerged from the embrace, pulling away from the man's chest, he kept hold of her upper arms, saying something that made her laugh before jumping into the van and closing the door behind him with a bang.

It was the musical sound of her laughter and not the reverberating sound of the door being slammed that shook him from his fugue.

Isandro inhaled and loosened his clenched fingers. His temper had been a problem when he was a boy but he was no longer a boy—he was a man who was known for his control and objectivity.

And he had objectively wanted to drag that guy off her. It wasn't an overreaction, but a perfectly legitimate response to having his trust abused. This wasn't about a public kiss—though you had to wonder at the woman's taste. The point was this was not only his home, it was her workplace. This little scene represented a total lack of professionalism. He had given her a second chance, hoping that she would blow it, and she had not disappointed.

Feeling more comfortable having a satisfactory explanation for his moment of visceral rage, he began to walk towards her, the sound of his footsteps drowned out by the van's engine as it vanished through the arch. He knew for a fact that he did not do jealousy, especially when the woman concerned was his employee. A jealous man would not have been amused rather than angry when his lover of the moment had been caught on camera by the paparazzi being as friendly as a person could be in public without being arrested.

Waving as John's van drove away, Zoe held up her hand even after the van had vanished. Then taking a deep sustaining breath, she dropped it and turned around to face the figure she had been aware of in the periphery of her vision as John had given her a goodbye hug.

Before reaching him, her gaze swept over the low-slung powerful car parked the opposite side of the courtyard. It was a monster, low, silver and sleek. She hadn't heard it arrive but then the noise of the running engine of John's van had presumably drowned out the sound of the Spanish billionaire's arrival. It had been the prickling of the hairs on the nape of her neck that had alerted her to the presence of the tall dynamic figure as she stood there saying goodbye to John.

If she'd acknowledged him then she'd have had no choice but to introduce him to John, which was something she wanted to avoid if possible.

She had promised Chloe she'd ask him about tonight and she would. This way she could sugar-coat his response—that it would be no was a given, that he wouldn't go out of his way to frame his refusal nicely was an equally safe bet.

'Good evening. I hope you had a good journey—'

He cut across her, launching without preamble into blighting speech. 'I do not find the sight of my house-keeper with her tongue down the throat of a tradesman a particularly edifying sight. In the future I would be grateful if you kept your love life or what passes for it behind closed doors and on your own time the next time you fancy a bit of rough.'

For a second she was too startled, as much by the icy delivery as his interpretation of a simple goodbye hug, to respond to this ludicrous accusation. But when she did her voice shook with the effort to control her response. She took a deep breath and closed off her furious train of thought, tipping her head in an attitude she hoped suggested humility while she badly wanted to slap the look of smug contempt off his face.

'I'll keep that in mind when I feel the urge to force myself on some passing tradesman.' Focusing her thoughts on the price of school sports kits helped her stay calm as she levelled a clear blue gaze at his dark lean face and finished her thought. 'Though actually, for the record, on this occasion I was simply hugging a friend goodbye.' Like it's any of your business, you sanctimonious creep. 'You're right, he is a tradesman, but not rough at all,' she added, unable to keep the note of shaky indignation out of her voice. 'John is sweet.' She lifted her chin. 'And not the sort of man who judges people by appearances or what they do for a living.'

Politely framed or not, it was impossible to miss the fact he was being called a snob. For a moment Isandro was too astonished to be angry. For a long time in his life now there had been no one who would presume to tell him if he was out of line.

The moment passed and astonishment gave way to anger that caused the muscles along his angular jaw to tighten and quiver. 'I do not care what the man does for a living!'

She arched a feathery brow and said politely, 'Of course not.'

Isandro clenched his teeth, seriously tempted to give her her marching orders and to hell with the consequences, then he recalled the delicacy of the deal on the negotiating table and the outcome was by no means a given. Any hint of scandal now would make the old family firm walk away from the table.

'What I care about is the man conducting his sex life on my doorstep!'

She stared, her blue eyes widening to their widest before narrowing into angry sparkling slits. He made it sound as if he'd discovered her having an orgy! What she couldn't understand was how could anyone have seen anything sordid in a perfectly innocent hug?

He was madder than he had been when she had given him cause. His reaction to her using his house to raise funds without his permission had been clinical, but there was nothing at all clinical about his reaction to her imagined sin now.

'The next time get a room.' The snarled suggestion triggered a free-fall avalanche of images that made him lose his thread.

'Get a room? John is married!'

His nostrils flared. 'All the more reason, I would have thought, to show a little more circumspection,' he declared austerely.

'I would not have an affair with a married man!' She

took a deep breath. It really hurt to have to explain herself to this man but what choice did she have? 'What you witnessed, Mr Montero, was simply a goodbye hug between friends,' she told him stiffly. 'That was John, Chloe's husband. You remember Chloe?'

Taking his silence to be a yes, she explained further. 'He was picking up the twins. They're staying with his mother tonight. She's babysitting, because John and Chloe are having a party…you remember?'

He remembered.

'I saw—'

'You saw nothing, because there was nothing to see.'

His mind replayed the image that had caused him to jump to conclusions and he realised he had not seen anything beyond two people close. His expression froze, his discomfiture revealing itself in the faintest deepening of colour along the slashing angles of his sybaritic cheekbones. Isandro cleared his throat. Embarrassment was a foreign sensation and one he did not enjoy.

He stopped his jaw tightening. 'I apologise. I made a mistake.'

Zoe fought a smile. Clearly every syllable of his apology had hurt. 'Apology accepted. I left your mail on your desk. I wasn't sure if you wanted it forwarded. If you let me know what time is convenient I'll let the maid know when she can clean your study. Oh, and shall I let your chef know what time you'll want dinner, sir?' She took a breath and thought, Wow, I'm good.

His brows lifted. 'I assumed that we would be dining out.'

Zoe shook her head, losing control of her 'perfect housekeeper' smile. 'Dining?'

'What time did your friend say—seven?'

She gave a little laugh, her face clearing. 'The party! Oh, goodness, you don't have to come.'

'Then the invitation is not genuine?'

'Yes, it's genuine—Chloe and John are very genuine people. I just thought that under the circumstances...'

He arched a questioning brow. 'Circumstances?'

This deliberate display of obtuseness brought her full lips together in a pursing line of annoyance. 'They are going to want to thank you, and I'd assumed that you'd find that embarrassing.'

Of course her analysis was dead on, but it turned out his reluctance to attend this party was not as strong as his enthusiasm to not follow the script she clearly wanted him to.

Where women were concerned Isandro did not consider himself complacent, but neither did he anticipate rejection. It was his male pride responding, rather than common sense, as he bared his white teeth in a smile that did not reach his dark eyes and framed his silky response.

'It is always pleasant when people are grateful.' Some women would be grateful to be offered the chance of sharing an evening with him. 'You will find I'm not easily embarrassed.'

Zoe struggled to hide her dismay. 'Does that mean you want to come?'

While he knew it was illogical to put himself through what would be an uncomfortable and almost certainly boring evening, the dismay in her voice that she didn't have either the skill or the good manners to disguise hardened his stubborn resolve to attend the damned party with her at his side—and she'd damned well enjoy it! he thought.

'It's not a matter of want. I gave my word.'

She struggled to read the expression on his lean sardonic face and faltered. 'They'd understand if you...'

'What time will you pick me up?'

Zoe's heart sank to her boots and she shook her head, feigning incomprehension.

Isandro smiled. She was a very bad actress—an actress with the most incredible mouth he had ever seen.

'Was that not the arrangement—you take me...?' he asked, utilising his much more polished acting skills. 'Of course, I can arrange a driver if you have other plans.'

Her only plan at that moment was to retreat to her little flat and bang her head on a brick wall! Inevitably he would be a back-seat driver. The sinking sensation in the pit of her stomach as she thought of being forced to share such a small space with him raised goosebumps over her body, but she cheered herself with the mental image of his elegant length folded into the not at all elegant confines of her Beetle that had seen better days. She squared her slender shoulders and ran her tongue across the surface of her dry lips.

Time to accept the inevitable and make the best of the situation. She was still mystified why he would want to come. Perhaps he just enjoyed having people tell him what a great guy he was, she thought scornfully, but the reality was it was going to happen so she'd better stop fighting it and make the best of the situation. It was one evening of her life, and she was probably worrying unnecessarily—his social skills were probably not nearly as bad as she feared.

'No, that's fine. I thought I'd leave around seven, if that suits you?'

He lifted his shoulders in a fluid shrug. 'I will be waiting.'

Her brave smile tipped his emotions over into amusement tinged with determination. He had always found it hard to resist a challenge. By the time this evening was over he would have Miss Zoe Grace eating out of his hand.

CHAPTER FIVE

GIVEN THE LIMITED storage space in the flat it was lucky Zoe didn't have a lot of clothes. Those that didn't fit into the cupboard in the hallway she kept in a case under the twins' bed.

On her knees she dragged it into the middle of the room, then sat back on her heels and went through the contents. The choice did not take long as she only possessed two half-decent summer dresses. After a few moments of narrow-eyed contemplation, she chose the maxi, mainly because it had fewer creases. Putting it on a hanger she hung it over the bathroom door and turned on the shower, hoping the steam from it would smooth out the few there were in the light chiffon fabric that she was a bit nervous about pressing because she still hadn't got around to replacing her iron with its dodgy thermostat.

Fifteen minutes later, some light make-up applied, her hair loosened from the plait and brushed into silky submission in waves that almost reached her waist, she switched off the water in the bathroom and was pleased to see that it had worked—the creases had virtually all fallen out of the misty blue fabric.

Slipping it over her head, she adjusted the shoe spaghetti straps and stooped down to get a glimpse of herself in the mirror. She hardly recognised the grave young woman who looked back at her, and allowed herself a complacent smile. When was the last time she'd dressed up? So long ago she couldn't remember. It was a shame that on this occasion she had that terrible man along for the ride.

With any luck he would get bored and leave early.

Hugging this comforting thought to herself, she walked across the courtyard back to the big house and found him waiting outside the porticoed entrance.

The sound of the fountain drowned out the noise her heels made on the cobbles, so she was able to study him unobserved for a few moments. He was wearing an open-necked shirt and dark tailored trousers. She was admiring the way he looked, hard not to, and reflecting that it was a shame that someone who had everything physically should be so lacking in the personality department when he turned suddenly, startling her enough to make her fall off the strappy wedge she was wearing.

He was at her side supplying a steadying hand to her elbow with startling speed. Flustered, she lifted her face to his, the pupils of her dramatic cornflower-blue eyes dilating as they connected with his dark ebony burnished stare.

She caught her breath sharply as a shimmy of sensation that slid down her spine made her shiver. The man had a sexual charisma that really was off the scale!

'I'm not used to the heels.' She pulled and his hand fell away from her elbow. 'I'm afraid my car's not very...' Her voice faded as she picked her way with more care now across the cobbles.

Isandro had been pierced by an arrow of sheer lust the moment he had seen her walking towards him. Walking behind her gave him the opportunity to admire her delicious bottom and the long elegant line of her seemingly endless legs, revealed rather than hidden by the long skirt that clung and flowed as she walked.

'The seat belt's a bit…' She took the football he held and with a grimace slung it into the back seat on top of the motley collection of toys and turned the ignition. 'It takes a few times before it… Sometimes…'

'Will you stop apologising?' He nodded towards the back seat. 'Your nephew plays football?' He spoke not out of any genuine interest but a desire to stop himself asking her if she had a boyfriend. It wouldn't make a difference—she worked for him and some rules he did not break. Still, there was no rule against looking.

'Harry?' Zoe laughed and shook her head. 'No, Harry hates sport. The ball is Georgie's. Harry is… quieter.' A man like Isandro Montero would never understand a sensitive boy like Harry. Her brow furrowed. Harry was a worry; he was such an easy child that he tended to be overlooked.

She glanced towards her passenger, and her lips twitched at the thought of anyone overlooking the scorchingly handsome Spaniard. It should have been laughable to see him squashed into her Beetle, but Zoe was unable to raise even a smile. The fact they were virtually rubbing shoulders made her feel a lot less comfortable than he appeared to be.

Being in this sort of enclosed space with him made Zoe want to crawl out of her own skin.

'It's not far.' Thank God for small mercies.

'I will sit back and admire the scenery,' he said, studying her profile. He had thought she would scrub up well and he had been proved right—she was stunning.

A few minutes later she crunched the gears and

winced as she drew up outside the local convenience store.

'Your friends live here?'

'No, they live the other side of the village. I need to stop to get a bottle of wine.'

'I thought you didn't drink.'

'I don't, but other people do,' she said shortly without looking at him.

'You should have said. There's plenty of wine in the cellar.' Good wine was always a sound inflation-proof investment.

A small choking sound left her lips as she thought of the vintage stuff stacked in the hall's cellar being served from borrowed glasses and drunk by people who in her hostess's case preferred her wine mixed with lemonade.

'Don't worry about it. I'll get this.'

Inside the store she snatched two of the second-cheapest bottles off the shelves and took them to the checkout.

'Nice stuff this, so they say,' the man at the till approved, putting the bottles into a bag for her while she dug into her purse. It became embarrassingly clear pretty quickly that she was short of cash to pay and her plastic was at home in the drawer, which had seemed the safest way to avoid temptation while she adjusted to her new straitened circumstances.

'Sorry, it'll have to be the Spanish one—do you mind if I change them? Fifty pence short, I'm afraid.' She nodded towards the stacked coins.

'No problem, it's very nice too, love.'

Her hand had closed around the bottles on the counter when a big hand covered it. 'Let me get those.'

Looking from the warm hand covering her own to the face of the tall, sleek, exclusive-looking man who had moved to stand beside her, Zoe shook her head, struggling to recover her composure and painfully aware of the tingling pain in her peaked and aching nipples. She was shamed and embarrassed by her weakness.

'No, really, I'm fine. I'm going to have the Spanish one…wine, that is…' she corrected and promptly felt like a total idiot.

'I hate to be disloyal, but take it from a Spaniard—that is not wine,' he told her with a shudder.

'It's not a wine snob sort of party.'

He was prepared to swallow the insult, but not the wine on the shelf. 'No, I insist, the least I can do since you are being my taxi,' he said, taking his wallet from his pocket and handing over the money.

Short of having a fight right there in the shop, Zoe had no choice but to accept the offer with as much grace as possible.

With his hand on the small of her back he guided her out of the shop and back towards the car. She didn't enjoy the light physical contact—actually any contact at all with this man made her feel uncomfortable—but she could tell that the natural courtesy came as second nature to him.

He held the door open for her, then went around to the other side of the car. The entire vehicle shook as she slammed the door closed. 'Do you not drink out of choice or because you have a drink problem?'

Her lips tightened. Was the man worried that his new housekeeper was an alcoholic? 'Neither, sir.' She emphasised the title before adding factually, 'I simply can't metabolise alcohol. I get drunk on the smell.'

'I rather think it might be more appropriate if you do not call me sir tonight.'

She shrugged and steered her car past the others parked along one side of the narrow lane. 'Is that an order, Mr Montero?'

'If you like, and try Isandro. It is my name. Relax,' he recommended. 'This is a party. I will not cramp your style…'

'It's not that sort of party and be careful there's a…' She stopped and hid a smile, adding as he surveyed his muddy shoe, 'A bit of a ditch that side.'

Zoe had been concerned for her friends' feelings, but slowly let down her guard as she realised that, far from looking down his nose at her friends, he was charming them. She could relax and enjoy herself; why not? Against all her expectations he was not being aloof or even icily polite. From the moment they had arrived and he had been swept away by Chloe, who had wanted to show him off, he had given the appearance of enjoying himself.

Watching Isandro talk easily with John and the local vet—who, according to Chloe, had not worn low-cut blouses before her divorce—it was Zoe who found herself feeling like an outsider. She felt her resentment rise as the red-headed divorcee threw back her head and laughed throatily at something Isandro had said, giving him an excellent view of her cleavage. Zoe's teeth clenched—and he looked, of course; he was a man!

How predictable. Shaking her head in a combination of contempt and cynical amusement, she felt embarrassed for the woman who was being so obvious. And he wasn't doing anything to discourage her, she thought. Her eyes narrowed as the woman's hand came to rest on his arm and stayed there, her long nails showing as flashes of scarlet as they curved over his biceps.

Zoe couldn't decide if the woman was pathetic or predatory...and whether she herself was embarrassed or envious.

Ignoring the laughable possibility that she wanted to touch Isandro, she directed her stubbornly critical glance over his strong, arrogant profile, pushing away the image of moving her hands over the hard muscular contours of his body, waiting for the hot hormone rush that tinged her cheek with pink to recede.

This was insane, she told herself. How could the man be all the way over the other side of the room and still manage to jangle every nerve ending in her body? His masculinity really was totally overwhelming. She sipped her drink, wishing that there were something stronger than fruit juice in it—though maybe not; the last thing she needed was her social restraints vanishing. Zoe had not exaggerated when she explained her reaction to alcohol; she had learnt after a couple of deeply embarrassing experiences that she and booze were not a good combination.

Common sense told her this was about hormones. She'd just have to accept it as an uncomfortable fact, like a pollen allergy, and deal with it. No point whatsoever in overanalysing the primitive physical response he had awoken in her, and it didn't really matter if this was all about timing or that he had been the catalyst for kicking her dormant hormones into life. She would treat it as an inconvenience rather than a disaster. There were always coping mechanisms and for the rare occasions there weren't, you avoided the problem. Like her body's inability to cope with alcohol—she didn't touch it; she wasn't going to touch Isandro. Simple.

What would be a disaster or at least an unwanted distraction would be to think too much about the primitive hunger she sensed was somewhere inside her. She should acknowledge it and forget about it. She was human; she had rotten taste in men. But she must not go there.

The vet, on the other hand, had clearly no such qualms about going where God knew how many women had been before, Zoe thought, her lips moving in a grimace of distaste as the older woman and her curves moved in closer. She had all but trapped him in the corner now...not that he showed any inclination to escape.

Her lips were still tightened in a cynical sneer of superiority when, without warning, Isandro turned his head slowly as though sensing her scrutiny. His dark eyes sought and connected with hers across the room. It was as if he possessed some radar that told him exactly where she was standing...where she was staring.

Their eyes locked, and for a long, heart-thudding moment Zoe could feel her own pulse over every inch of her skin, the vibrations reaching her tingling fingertips. She stopped breathing. Her stomach muscles quivered; her legs felt weak and oddly heavy; her knees literally shook.

The contact might have lasted moments or an hour, she didn't have a clue, but by the time she managed to bring her lashes down in a protective fan her insides had dissolved. Her throat was dry as she raised her empty glass to her lips and struggled to regain some semblance of self-control.

She closed her eyes, her lashes brushing her cheeks. As she willed her body to relax they shot open at the sound of her name.

'Sorry, I was miles away. How are you?' she asked Chloe's elderly aunt who was lowering her bulk into a chair.

'I can't complain, but of course I do. Thank you, dear,' she added as Zoe retrieved her stick that had fallen to the floor. 'Unless you want your man going home with someone else I'd get over there, Zoe.'

Blushing, Zoe followed the direction of the old lady's sharp-eyed stare to where Isandro stood, looking like the personification of a predatory male. And the hunter was still being hunted, she saw, her mouth twisting as she watched the redhead lean into him and stroke his sleeve. 'I'm his taxi, not his date. He's my boss.'

'In my day it was most girls' dream to marry their boss. I did—not, of course, that George ever looked like that.' She saw Zoe's expression and gave a chuckle, adding, 'I'm old, child, not blind.'

'And I'm not thinking of getting married.'

If she ever did it would not be to a man like Isandro Montero, she thought, summoning a mental picture of a man who would treat her as an equal, a man who would love the twins as much as she did. Her brow furrowed as her employer's face superimposed itself over her mental image, causing her eyes to drift across the room to where…he was no longer standing, and neither was the voluptuous vet.

Maybe she wouldn't have to put up with his aggravating company on the return journey…?

'Very wise. Of course, in my day it was different. You couldn't have sex outside marriage…if you were a nice girl, that is. We didn't have your freedom.'

'Actually, I don't believe in casual sex. Not for me anyway.'

Zoe was wondering why she felt the totally uncharacteristic need to discuss her feelings on the subject, when she realised that the old lady was not looking at her, but past her.

Her stomach quivered; she knew without turning who was standing there. Had he heard what she'd said?

His expression told her nothing.

'I was wondering if you are ready to go home?'

'I thought you'd already left.'

'What gave you that idea?'

'You make friends very easily.' The moment the remark left her lips she regretted it. She glanced guiltily over her shoulder to where a distinctive throaty laugh placed the vet. The woman had by all accounts been dumped by her husband of fifteen years for a younger model. Who only knew what insecurities her flirtatious behaviour masked?

Zoe felt a stab of shame. The woman was vulnerable and needed sympathy, not catty remarks behind her back. She actually deserved admiration—she had come out fighting after being kicked in the teeth.

'Actually, I don't.'

The comment brought her attention back to the tall Spaniard. It was clear he had not been canvassing the sympathy vote, simply stating a fact.

'I think you've made a few today.' Not a single person she had spoken to had had a bad word to say about him, and several had told her how lucky she was to be working for him.

Frankly, all the rave reviews were beginning to grate. People were so superficial they didn't look past the handsome face, perfect body and incredible smile. How many people but her had noticed him empty his glass of wine into the pot plant? Possibly the ones who hadn't taken their eyes off him all night? No, they acted as if he'd done them a favour by deigning to show up.

Zoe had been forced to bite her tongue on several occasions. She'd hoped he'd behave well and not upset anyone but she hadn't bargained on him turning the entire community into his devoted fans, who wouldn't believe that the man had sacked her within two minutes of setting eyes on her, that he was still looking for an excuse. Oh, yeah, he really was a great guy!

Friendship required trust. Isandro did not consider his inability to trust easily a character flaw; rather he valued his true friends all the more because he knew how rare they were.

His eyes brushed her face and he was struck again by the directness of her blue stare. 'I have many acquaintances, but few friends.'

And you're not even an acquaintance, Zoe. You're an employee. The taxi driver, not the date. 'I suppose it's difficult to tell if someone loves you or your bank balance.'

'I do not require love.' His brows lifted. 'Or are you talking about sex?'

'Sex?'

By some horrid twist of fate her yelped echo coincided with a lull in the conversation.

Oh, let me die now, Zoe thought as everyone turned to look at her.

'Strange how that always happens.'

'Not to me, it doesn't.' She struggled to see him as gaffe prone. 'If you'll excuse me, I see...' She made a vague gesture and headed across the room, accepting a few good-natured teasing comments as she went.

'What I need,' she muttered, 'is to cool down.'

'God, yes, it's warm in here, isn't it? Try one of these.' Once again her comment had reached more than its target audience—herself.

She looked at the tall glass that clinked with ice in

her hand, and opened her mouth to ask the person with the tray what it was, but he was gone.

Walking out through the open French windows, she sniffed it warily before picking out a floating strawberry to taste. The overwhelming flavour over and above the fruit was pineapple. It seemed innocuous enough, and a tentative sip reinforced this analysis. Satisfied it was one of the delicious mocktails that Chloe had made, she took a swallow.

She passed a group of men chatting, then wandered out onto the steep sloped lawn shaded by a row of tall oak trees in the field beyond. She sat down on the stump of a recently felled tree and swallowed some more of the fruit concoction. It was actually so delicious it made you wonder why people bothered with alcohol.

Tipping her head back to look at the starry sky, she thought that a person really should stop occasionally and just enjoy being alive. Lie on the grass and feel the earth…and why not?

Lying flat on her back, staring up at the stars, she began to hum a little tune softly to herself before she closed her eyes. Did she drift off?

'I can't, I really can't take this…' She half lifted her head at the sound of John's voice. Why was he ignoring her? She let out a small giggle and thought, Because he can't see me! I'm lying down.

'Yes, you can. Just think how much better it will be for Chloe and Hannah if they have you there to support them.'

This deeper voice with the sexy accent—she recognised that, too!

John and Isandro.

'I don't know what to say.' There was the sound of

crinkling paper and a gasp. 'Hell, that's too much…
no…I couldn't.'

'All tax-deductible. The only thing is that I'd prefer
this was private between you and Chloe and me. I'm
not comfortable with…'

'Understood. We won't forget this.'

Zoe lay there turning the conversation over in her
head. It took her foggy brain a little while to process
what she had overheard, but when she did tears of emotion sprang to her eyes. Isandro had just given John the
money he needed to join his family in Boston—and
more than enough, by the sound of it.

'That is so, so incredibly lovely!'

Isandro turned in time to see a figure rise from the
mist, hovering over the grass at ground level like some
sort of spectral vision.

'Zoe, what were you—?' The glorious goddess-like
figure flew towards him like a heat-seeking missile.
Madre di Dios, she was plastered!

'I heard everything, and I think you're w…won…
marvellous,' she declared earnestly.

'I think you should sit down.'

'I will, but first…' Standing on her tiptoes, she
reached up and took his face between her hands. 'You're
a very beautiful man and I've been mean to you, very
very very mean. I'm so ashamed! But that's all over.
You're a hero.' She leaned in closer, her soft breasts
crushing against the barrier of his chest as she fitted
her mouth to his.

The warm, soft mouth that pressed against his tasted
of booze. Standing rigid, his hands wide, he knew if he
touched that body, drunk or not, he would not be able
to stop himself having her right there on the grass. He

somehow managed to resist the blandishments of those luscious lips.

The effort brought a sheen of sweat to his skin and a great deal of pain to his groin, but he held out. Though the throaty little mewling sound of complaint she made in her throat when he didn't respond almost broke him.

'I think…I think I might sit down.' Clutching her head, and without warning, she sank gracefully to the grass and sat there cross-legged.

Isandro sighed and picked up the almost empty glass he saw there. He dipped his finger in the contents and licked it. A lot of fruit juices and vodka. Not a lot, but it was there.

Behind him he heard Chloe and John approach.

'Is that Zoe?'

'Hi, guys…yes, it's Zoe,' Zoe said, waving her hand. 'Chloe, you musht give me the recipe for that mocktail.'

'Oh, God!' Chloe gasped.

'He's not a monster, Chloe, he's a hero—did you know that? A real-life hero. He doesn't like me, though…sad.'

Isandro handed John the glass. 'It's pretty innocuous.'

'It doesn't matter. It's a metabolic thing with Zoe— she couldn't have known. What are we going to do with her? We've got a full house tonight, not even a spare sofa.'

Isandro saw them both looking at him.

Isandro, who never did anything he did not want to, heard himself say, 'I'll take her home. Don't worry, I've not been drinking.'

Once they got her in the car she immediately went to sleep curled up like a kitten, her mouth slightly open.

'Will she remember when she sobers up?'

'Oh, yes,' said Chloe, a wave of sadness crossing her face. 'Or that's what Laura always said.'

Isandro nodded. He was pleased with the reply. It only seemed fair that she would remember, because he surely would. It was hard to forget the extremely painful cost of being a hero; he was pretty sure that the resulting frustration would cost him a night's sleep.

Zoe continued to sleep like a baby all the way back to the hall, which was good because he wasn't sure his response would be quite so noble if she made another attempt to jump him.

When he opened the passenger door the cool night air woke her. He was amazed and relieved that she had recovered enough to make it up the stone steps to the flat without any assistance from him, but he followed behind just in case.

'You'll be all right?'

She looked at him blearily. 'I think there was something in my drink.'

'Vodka.'

'Oh, God! I thought it… Sorry…' She had no idea what she was apologising for, but it seemed safe to assume that there was something. 'Goodnight, Mr Montero.'

Isandro watched the door close. He was quite pleased with his demotion back to monster. Monsters were not obliged to behave with honour—they could take what they wanted.

CHAPTER SIX

ROBBED OF HIS early morning ride after discovering his horse had pulled a shoe, Isandro returned to the house, leaving the stallion in the capable hands of his groom. An hour on a cross-trainer in the gym did not really touch his frustration levels.

Heading downstairs after his shower, he reached the galleried landing when he almost fell over her.

'What the hell are you doing?' If she appeared at all this morning he had imagined she would be nursing a hangover, not on her knees singing to herself.

Seemingly oblivious to his presence, she continued to bang the hand-held vacuum into a crevice under a console table, still humming along to the music playing in her ears. Her singing voice was totally flat but her behind was not. Isandro, who had opened his mouth to deliver his demand again, closed it as she reached further forward, the action causing her delightful bottom to tighten against the pair of jeans she was wearing.

Lust hit him like a hammer blow to the chest. Beside his sensual mouth a nerve quivered, beating out an erratic tattoo as in his head he saw himself dropping down beside her, tipping her onto her back... His chest lifted as he sucked in a deep breath and swore through gritted teeth. He had never experienced this degree of blind, relentless lust before. Not even in his teens had he felt so obsessed.

He swore under his breath and bellowed, 'What the hell are you doing?'

One hand on the floor to steady herself, Zoe turned her head, a questioning furrow in her smooth brow. She saw Isandro and her half-smile faded with a speed that under other circumstances he might have found amusing.

'It is always nice when people are glad to see me,' he muttered under his breath.

'Pardon...' Zoe lowered her voice, murmuring a self-conscious, 'Sorry.' She pulled the earphones out of her ears and looked up at the figure who towered over her. 'I didn't see you there.' She stopped herself from asking whether there was anything she could do for him, afraid that he might tell her—and even more afraid that she might deliver his request.

She was probably worrying over nothing. Last night he hadn't even kissed her back.

It was the ultimate humiliation. She had offered herself up on a platter and he had said no, thank you, and she remembered every mortifying, cringeworthy detail. It had been about three a.m. when she'd sat bolt upright in bed and it had all come rushing back to her.

Unable to resist the masochistic compulsion to relive the scene over and over, by this morning she didn't see how she could face him. And now it felt just as awful as she had imagined.

Should she mention last night? Wait for him to? Or should she pretend it never happened?

'I said what the hell are you doing?'

'I'm vacuuming the carpet.' She held out the hand-held vacuum she was using to reach the crevices, flicking the switch into the on position to demonstrate as she got up from her knees.

'I can see what you're doing.' He reached over and flicked the switch off. 'What I want to know is why?'

'Susie couldn't come in this morning.'

'That does not answer my question, and who the hell is Susie?'

'Susie is one of the cleaning staff. She lives in the village.'

He folded his arms across his chest and looked unimpressed by her explanation. 'Will you stop waving that thing at me?'

Zoe lowered the vacuum, but lifted her free hand to shade her eyes from the shaft of strong morning sun that shone in from the tall floor-length window behind Isandro, framing his tall figure in a golden haze of light. As if he needed any help to look as though he'd just stepped down from Mount Olympus! It was like a massive conspiracy to turn her into some sex-starved bimbo.

'You're really not a morning person, are you?'

A gleam flashed in his dark eyes. 'I've never had any complaints.'

It took a few seconds, but when the penny dropped her face flamed. She brought down her lashes in a protective sweep to shield her eyes. Head down, she swept off the scarf she had tied over her hair. Ruffling it with her hand as it slipped down her back, she struggled to maintain a professional attitude given the reel of lurid images now playing in her head.

Isandro felt the hunger flare, his body hardening as he watched the river of glossy silk settle down her narrow back. The sexy little black outfit was gone and she was back in jeans, complete with a tear in one knee and belt loops he could have hooked his fingers into and jerked her… The effort to suppress his lustful imagination drew a short harsh rasp from his throat.

'This still doesn't tell me why I find you down on your hands and knees like some…'

Her head lifted; her blue eyes shone with anger. 'Servant?' she bit back. 'Maybe because I am.'

'You are the housekeeper.'

She shrugged, not sure why he was making such a big thing of this. It wasn't as if the workings of a vacuum cleaner were alien to her. 'Call it multitasking…'

'I call it inappropriate. What sort of first impression would it give if I had walked in with a group of important guests and the first thing they see is the housekeeper down on her knees?' He shook his head.

'You didn't walk in with…'

Isandro's expression made her wish she had held her tongue.

'It is totally inappropriate to your position here.'

'What was I meant to do? Drag poor Susie in with her abscessed tooth? Her mother says the poor girl is in agony.'

'You were meant to delegate.' It amazed him that she had not grasped this basic precept.

'I don't like telling people what to do.' Zoe found it was easier and less stressful to do things herself.

'Delegation is part of your job. Scrubbing floors is not.'

His coldness hit her like a slap in the face. 'I wasn't…' She bit her tongue and bowed her head.

The show of humility did not fool Isandro for one second. He knew full well it was an act. She was about as humble as a battle cruiser.

'Part of your job is also learning the difference between showing sympathy and being a soft touch.'

Zoe's head lifted at the suggestion. 'I'm not a soft touch!' she protested indignantly.

'People take advantage of you.' His annoyance that she was either unable or unwilling to see this was etched on his hard features.

'You didn't!' She closed her eyes and lifted a hand to her head, let her chin fall to her chest and thought, Please let me die now. 'Sorry. I didn't mean to say that. It just sort of slipped out.'

'Not because I did not want to, if that is what is bothering you. Did you get any sleep?' The violet smudges under her eyes showed up clear against her translucent skin, as did the handful of freckles across the bridge of her nose.

She nodded. 'And I woke with a bit of a headache.'

His mobile lips twitched. 'Called a hangover.'

Zoe shuddered as she got to her feet. 'I can't imagine why people drink.'

'Not everyone has your zero tolerance. For some people it's their drug of choice, and it's legal.'

'What's yours, or don't you need one? Sorry…I keep forgetting… Can I take your order for dinner, sir?'

'You can't go from trying to kiss my face off to calling me sir. Neither are what I expect of my housekeeper. I will settle for a happy medium.'

The mortified colour rushed to her cheeks as she pressed her teeth into her full lower lip. 'I am sorry for last night. I really am. But what you did for Chloe and John, that was…very kind.'

His features froze. 'That stays within these walls. Is that understood?'

Before she could reply to this terse warning, the front door swung open and the twins rushed in. At least Georgie rushed. Harry walked with his nose in a book.

'No, not here. I've told you, the flat—'

'We know. You forgot to put the key under the mat.' Georgie looked at Isandro and grinned. 'We have to keep out of your way.' She wrinkled her nose. 'Don't you like kids?'

'It depends on the kid.' He strolled across to the boy, a skinny child with strawberry-blond hair. 'You're Harry.'

Harry nodded.

'Run along, children.' She pulled the key fob out of her pocket and tossed it to Georgie. 'I've left you some sandwiches for eleven. I'll be over at lunchtime.'

'What's that you're reading?' Isandro looked at the title on the spine. 'You like the stars?'

Of course he did. Skinny, undersized boys with books and no friends always did. Isandro knew because he had been one himself. In his case he had grown twelve inches at sixteen and gone from being the despised wimp to the jock that everybody wanted to know.

Harry nodded, his face suffused with pink.

'On the wall on my desk I have a photo of the Horsehead nebula. Have you seen it?'

'We're not allowed in the house. Especially your office.' So Harry was not a rule-breaker. 'I like looking at the night sky, but I want to be an astrophysicist when I grow up.'

Zoe blinked. This was news to her.

'Cool,' Isandro said.

'Run along, children.' She was both pleased and relieved when they both did as she asked—with Georgie, you never knew.

'You, too,' Isandro said when they had left. 'Ring the agency first and get a replacement for…whatever her name is.'

'Susie.'

'Then take the rest of the day off. I'm off to London.'

She assumed when he left that they would not see him for some time. She had understood that this was the norm. But over the next few weeks he kept arriving unexpectedly, sometimes spending a night, sometimes not even that long.

At first mystified by his behaviour, she realised that he was hoping to catch her out, though it did seem a lot of trouble to go to. Never knowing when he would turn up made it difficult to relax…and though trying to catch her out made sense, it didn't explain the occasion he brought Harry a book full of photos of galaxies and nebulae.

The little boy looked forward to his visits…but was he the only one? Why would anyone look forward to a visit from someone who blew hot and cold? Who was cold and remote one moment and relaxed and friendly the next?

As they approached the crossroad Alex slowed for a red light. Isandro shut down the tablet and looked through the window, dragging a hand through his dark hair. He had planned to spend the weekend in London, but at the last moment had decided to drive down to Raven-wood, reasoning he could spend the weekend reading the report without distractions. Sure, no distractions at all, mocked the voice in his head.

'Is that…?'

Pushing away the thought, Isandro followed the direction of his driver's nod. 'Yes, it is, Alex,' he confirmed.

'Are they alone?'

Isandro, who had been looking for that glossy dark head attached to a body he had spent some time thinking about, nodded. All right, not just some time—a lot of time. He was finding it pretty much impossible to think about anything but his housekeeper, who did not know the meaning of 'unobtrusive'.

'It looks like it.'

Which in itself was strange. While Zoe Grace might not be about to win any prizes for her housekeeping skills, when it came to her youthful charges she took the role extremely seriously. He could not imagine her allowing the twins to wander around town unaccompanied.

'Shall I pull over?'

Isandro nodded and unclipped his seat belt as the car drew to a halt on a double yellow. When he reached the twins they were still on the pavement. They appeared to be arguing—and more significantly there was still no sign of their aunt.

It was Harry who saw him first. Seeing the relief on his freckled face, Isandro experienced an emotional tightening in his chest.

Isandro controlled his strong inclination to hug him, aware that the boy had already measured him up as an unlikely male role model. It would be nothing short of cruel to allow the boy to become reliant and then fade out of his life.

Instead he gave the boy a manly pat on his painfully skinny shoulder. The kid could do a lot better than him for a father substitute. Did his aunt's determination to sacrifice her own needs for her charges extend to her choice of partner? Would she choose the 'good father' material over a good lover? The woman was probably determined to be a martyr. She'd probably end up alone or with some boring loser whom she deemed solid and responsible.

'We've lost Aunty Zoe. Actually, we ran away and now we're lost, too.'

For which Isandro correctly read his sister had run and he had followed. There was no doubting who the dominant and reckless twin in this equation was.

'We're not lost,' his sister interrupted. 'And if you hadn't made me come back…'

'It was stealing!'

'It was not stealing. We were bringing it back, and that's borrowing, isn't it?' she appealed to Isandro for support.

'Borrowing without permission is stealing. And running away from your aunt is… Have you any idea how worried she will be?' An image of a terrified Zoe flashed into his head and he hardened his heart against their stricken expressions. 'She will be frantic!'

The twins exchanged worried glances.

'We didn't think,' Georgie admitted.

Isandro steeled himself against the quiver in her voice and struggled to maintain his stern expression as he ushered them towards the car. The sniff was too much for the ruthless captain of industry to withstand.

'Don't worry,' he soothed. 'I'll ring your aunt and let her know—'

'You can't,' they said in unison.

He shook his head. 'Why can't I?'

'Her phone wasn't charged. It died on her when Aunt Chloe was talking.'

He exhaled. If he had been in Zoe's position—which was unlikely, because not only would he not have let his phone battery run down, he certainly wouldn't have taken on responsibility for this pair of demons—he would now be retracing his footsteps.

The demons regarded him with the expressions that said they had total faith that he would come up with a solution.

'Right, then, where were you when you ran away, and where were you before that?'

The terrible clawing panic in her stomach when she had turned to tell the twins to get a wriggle or the car would be clamped would stay with Zoe for ever. When she found them she would never let them out of her sight again…always supposing she didn't throttle them.

She jogged along the pavements, retracing her footsteps, stopping occasionally to ask people if they had seen two children, oblivious to the stares that followed her progress. She kept telling herself over and over like a mantra, Tomorrow this will just be a memory. I'll laugh about it with Chloe.

Tomorrow seemed a hell of a long way away, though, and Chloe was still in Boston!

By the time Zoe had worked her way to the boat-hire booth her heart was thudding so hard she felt as if it would crack her ribs. She was only kept going by the strong conviction that had gradually taken hold that the twins were out there on the river.

It was so obvious. Why hadn't she smelt a rat when the wilful youngster who would never take no for an answer had not argued or even tried to cajole when she'd refused to take them out in a kayak. Now of course it made sense. Georgie hadn't suddenly become malleable, she'd simply cut out the arguing, and she'd dragged Harry with her.

The ticket booth was closed, but before a frantic Zoe

could think of what to do next a boy came around the corner carrying a padlock and a large bunch of keys. He removed the earphones from his ears when he saw her.

'Sorry, we're closed.'

'I'm looking for my niece and nephew,' she said before he could put the earphones back in. 'They're seven years old. I think they might have gone out in one of your kayaks.' The effort to stay calm and not sound like an unbalanced lunatic made her voice shake, but she was pretty proud of her effort.

'Sorry, we're closed.'

She watched, her pent-up fear tipping over into rage, as he began to insert the earphones.

Her eyes narrowed, she stepped forward and snatched them out, drawing a yelp from the boy. 'My niece and nephew—they wanted to go out in a kayak. Have you seen them?' she yelled, fighting the impulse to shake the information from the stupid boy who was backing away from her.

'I don't know what your problem is, miss, but the public are not allowed here. There's a sign. It's health and safety.' He pointed to a no-entry sign on the wall of the booth.

Give me strength! 'I've been trying to tell you what the problem is. I'm looking for two children, a boy and girl. So high...' She held her palm at the appropriate height. 'They wanted to go out...' She closed her eyes, seeing Georgie's expression when she had refused their request. God, but she really should have seen this coming. 'I think they might be out there.' She swallowed as her eyes moved to the horizon where the grey water of the river met the darker grey sky. 'In one of your canoes.'

'No children allowed in the kayaks without a responsible adult. Besides, we're closing early—there's a storm coming.' His phone rang and he wandered away with it pressed to his ear.

When Zoe took the situation into her own hands the youth was close enough for her to hear him say, 'No way…outside the pub at five.' But not close enough, thanks to a tree, for him to see her wade into the shallow water and push out a stray canoe that had not yet been dragged onto the artificial beach.

She'd been kayaking before, she reminded herself as she managed on the third try to clamber into the swaying boat. Of course on that occasion Laura had been paddling, and she'd been only five years old, but this was a detail. How hard could it be?

Five minutes later Zoe had gone several hundred yards. But she had no idea whether she was heading in the right direction. She didn't have the faintest idea where they were! She was acting on intuition, but wasn't that another name for blind panic?

She squared her shoulders and dipped her oar into the water. She had to stay positive.

The obvious sensible thing to do would have been to go to the police…so why was she just realising that now when she was literally up the creek? Then the rain started.

The downpour was of biblical flood proportions. Within two minutes she was drenched. Her hair plastered against her skull; the water streamed down her face, making it hard to see. More worrying than her wet clothes was the water sloshing around in the bottom of the canoe.

Trying to see past the rain that was now being driven horizontally by a gale-force wind into her face, she recalled the weather man's prediction of light showers and laughed.

The hysterical sound was whipped away by the wind, which was again blowing her in the wrong direction. Head bent, she paddled hard but, despite the fact her arms felt as though they were falling off, she made no headway. She put oar down for a moment to ease the burning pain in the muscles of her upper arms and shoulders, flexing her stiff fingers as she balanced it across the canoe.

She saw it happening as if in slow motion. She lunged forward, one arm outstretched and the other holding onto the edge of the wildly rocking kayak. Just as her fingers touched the oar a current carried it away out of reach. Her centre of gravity lost, Zoe struggled to pull back, but just when it seemed inevitable she would be pitched into the grey swirling water she managed to recover, collapsing back with a sob of laughing relief into the canoe.

It hardly seemed possible that a couple of weeks ago she had decided that this stretch of the river, with its series of shallow waterfalls and half-submerged stone slabs where people sunbathed and children paddled in shallow pools, made for a really lovely afternoon stroll. Pretty, but not dramatic.

Today it did not lack drama. The river was wild white water, full of dark swirls and hidden obstacles. The boulders she strove to avoid were only just visible above the foaming white water. Zoe paddled with her hands but soon recognised it was hopeless. The kayak would never survive.

Feeling surprisingly calm in the face of impending disaster, Zoe was in the middle of telling herself she was overreacting when the kayak hit a submerged rock.

The jarring motion as it glanced off sent the flimsy craft rocking sideways. Thrown off balance, Zoe lurched sideways, throwing her body weight sharply to one side to right the canoe. For a moment it seemed to work, but it was hit by an extra-strong squall of wind and simply carried on going.

This time there was no reprieve and the immersion in the shockingly cold grey water took her breath. For a moment she panicked, flailing around blindly as she tried to free herself from the upturned canoe, hampered by clothes that dragged her downwards. When she did she surfaced almost immediately, choking as she gasped for air. Behind her the canoe was making its way upside down through the churning white water, before it vanished over the top of a weir.

That could have been me.

But it won't be. The twins would be all alone, they need me. Focusing on that one thought and not the cold seeping into her bones, she struck out strongly, aiming for the opposite bank, where she would be likely to see someone who could raise the emergency services. Zoe was a strong swimmer with no fear of the water, but even so the going was tough and her progress, hampered by her clothes, was torturously slow.

As she swam she was distantly aware of a sound above the echoing roar of the water and her own heartbeat but she didn't allow it to distract her. She couldn't stop. She had to keep going. Every second she wasted the twins could be… *No, she wouldn't think like that. She needed to focus.*

'Focus, Zoe,' she said to herself—but the water filled her open mouth and, choking, her head went under.

As she was lifted unceremoniously out of the water she continued to kick feebly, right up to the moment she was hauled over and left utterly disorientated in an inelegant heap in the bottom of what seemed to be a small motorboat.

She grunted as the boat swerved, sharply throwing her against a wooden seat. The locker underneath was open and a child's inflatable vest spilled out. Oh, God, the children were out there somewhere!

She began to cry great silent, gulping sobs that racked her entire body.

Once the boat was away from the immediate danger of hitting the rocks and in the relative safety of open water, Isandro cut back on the throttle and turned his attention to the sodden bundle of misery sitting in the bottom of the boat.

He experienced a gripping sensation in his chest almost as strong as the one he had felt when he had seen her head vanish under the grey water—though without the soul-destroying terror.

'What the hell did you think you were doing?' he blasted.

She recognised the voice but was convinced she was dreaming. Except in her dreams he hadn't sounded angry... Zoe dragged her hair back from her face. My God, it was him!

It was Isandro! Looking furious, very wet and not dressed for sailing!

'Isandro...how...?' She stopped. It didn't matter how he came to be here. 'No,' she croaked, grabbing at his leg and tugging. 'I've got to go back.'

'You want me to throw you back in the water? Do not tempt me,' he growled, seeing her vanish beneath the grey water again and feeling the visceral kick of fear in his gut again. He never wanted to relive the moment when he saw her go under.

'No, Isandro, you don't understand! I think the twins...'

Some of the anger died from his face as he placed his hands on her shoulders and dragged her up onto the wooden bench seat beside him. Shaking so hard that her teeth chattered, she transferred her desperate grip to his jacket. Frantic to communicate the urgency of the situation, she grabbed his lapels and pulled.

'The twins—'

'No, Zoe—'

'Listen, will you?'

He caught hold of her hands. 'The twins are with Alex, who is not, I admit, the most likely child-minder. In fact it is highly likely that he is even now teaching them to play poker. But they are safe.'

Zoe blinked as she shook her head, trying to clear the fog in her brain. Why couldn't she think straight?

'The twins are all right?' Without waiting for a reply, she pushed her head into his chest and began to cry in earnest.

His arms went out wide as he looked down at the head of tangled hair. His anger had vanished and he refused to recognise the feelings that had rushed in to fill the vacuum as tenderness. Her cries tore at him; finally the mewling sounds as she burrowed in deeper snapped his resistance and his arms closed around her. He lifted her body into the warmth of his.

'*Madre di Dios*, you're an imbecile, a raving... You make me want, you make me feel—' He stopped and thought, you make me feel...too much. Digging his fingers into her wet hair, he stroked her scalp and let her cry herself out.

He had stopped resisting the sexual desire he felt for her. Physical desire was normal, not complicated. It was something that he understood and accepted, not a weakness. It did not require that he surrender any control; it was not about trusting. He wanted her on his terms—he would have her on his terms. He would not fall into the trap of allowing emotions to cloud his judgement.

He was not his father.

Finally peeling herself away, Zoe straightened up, blinking like someone waking up.

'I'm…' She gulped and shook her head again as he removed his jacket and draped it around her shoulders.

'It's wet but better than nothing.'

The lining was still warm. 'Sorry,' she said, not meeting his eyes. She was too embarrassed by her total meltdown. Why did she always make a total fool of herself around him?

He kept one hand on her shoulder, the other on the tiller, guiding the boat towards the mooring.

'Sorry…I…I thought…' Her lips quivered as she struggled for composure. 'I thought they'd gone on the river…' She gave a frown, trying to remember the sequence of events as much for her own benefit as for his. 'We'd been to the craft fair in the park. When we started back it was late and I thought they were with me. I was running—they were going to clamp the car…' Wrong tense, she realised, they probably already had clamped the car. But having faced what she had thought was a real disaster, car clamping faded into insignificance.

She pushed the wet strands of hair from her eyes and pressed the heels of both hands to her temples before slowly turning her head to stare at him.

'What the hell made you go out on the water? Are you suicidal?'

'The twins—'

'And what would have happened to the twins if you

had drowned?' Her horrified little gasp felt like a knife sliding between his ribs, but Isandro didn't allow his expression to soften as Zoe went several shades whiter. The only colour in her face was her dramatic sapphire eyes and the blue discoloration around her lips.

'I was not going to drown,' she protested through chattering teeth.

Faced with this refusal to acknowledge, let alone show any remorse for, the total bloody selfishness of her reckless actions, Isandro was tempted to throw her back in the water.

'My mistake,' he gritted through clenched teeth. 'I can see now that you had the situation totally under control.'

Unable to tear her eyes off the nerve that was throbbing in his lean cheek, she shook her head. 'No, really, I'm a strong swimmer...obviously I'm grateful but...'

'But really you didn't need my help at all.' He gave a shrug and, cutting the engine, steered the gliding boat expertly between the moored vessels.

Before Zoe could respond he leapt out of the boat, landing lithely on the wooden pier where he proceeded to tie off the boat.

'I really am grateful, Isandro. It was really lucky you had a boat.'

'I don't have a boat.' A faint smile flickered across his face. 'Not here anyway.'

'But this?' The boat wobbled as she got to her feet. With a grimace Zoe sat down again abruptly. Her knees were still shaking and she had no desire to repeat her earlier immersion.

Considering the question, Isandro thought of Georgie's defence and smiled to himself. 'I borrowed it.'

'You stole it!' she cried, but then, not wanting to

come across as ungrateful again, she added, 'But I suppose it was an emergency.'

'What made you think they were heading for the river?'

'Georgie wanted to go out in a canoe and I said no. We really didn't have time…'

'You do not have to justify your decisions to me, Zoe.'

'Georgie is…'

'Determined?'

Zoe acknowledged the dry suggestion with a shrug. 'She didn't fight it, which isn't like her. Saying no is like a red rag to her. I should have known.' After a fractional pause that was not lost on Isandro, she accepted the hand he held out to her and rose unsteadily to her feet. The boat swayed again and she lurched, making an awkward leap as he tugged.

As she landed clumsily on the boarded walkway Zoe heard a splash. Letting go of Isandro's hand, she twisted around and saw the jacket that had been draped over her shoulders floating on the water.

'Oh, God!' On an adrenaline high still, she moved quickly without thinking and almost reached it.

An arm like a steel band around her waist hauled her back from the edge.

'What the hell are you doing, woman? Do you have some sort of death wish? I have to tell you once is my limit when it comes to fishing suicidal maniacs out of the drink.'

Zoe didn't struggle against the arms banding her. She leaned back into his big, solid, hard body, allowing herself the luxury of feeling safe. She wasn't going to drown and the twins were all right.

She was still shaking with the chill of the ice in her

veins but in the shelter of his arms she was protected from the wind. The feeling of security was an illusion but as illusions went this one felt good.

'Your lovely jacket.'

Isandro rested his chin on the top of her head, closed his eyes and shook his head... Jacket!

'I have others.' The woman was in need of professional help. He shifted his stance to ease the pressure on his groin and thought, *Dios*, she is not the only one!

CHAPTER SEVEN

HER LIPS TWITCHED faintly. 'The man who has everything.'

'You read the article.'

Two weeks earlier a Sunday paper had decided to dedicate half their glossy supplement to him. *The Man with the Midas Touch* was to his mind shockingly unoriginal and a perfect example of the dumbing-down of the press…ten pages that said nothing new.

He had everything? He supposed he did. But to Isandro his wealth represented not luxury or self-indulgence but the freedom to live his life just as he wanted. Did that make him selfish? Did it make him happy…? Was anyone happy?

He shook his head. *Dios*, this was not the time for a philosophical debate. This was definitely a time for action, decisive action, and the priority was warming up Zoe before she became hypothermic.

It did not take him long to weigh the options. Decision-making was, as the article author had suggested, Isandro's area of expertise.

'Chloe gave me her copy,' she admitted between chattering teeth. 'The entire village bought the paper. They were sold out. You're a local hero…for real now…'

'Even if you didn't need my help.'

Her lips twisted into a grimace. 'I really am grate-ful... Stop! You can't—!'

Isandro took no notice of her protests as he began to stride up the path from the river.

'I can walk! Put me down...please put me down.'

He flashed her a look. 'You won't jump back in the river?'

'Don't be stupid.'

'Seriously, though, you're chilled through. You need to dry off and warm up.'

'I need to see the twins.'

'You think that's a good idea, looking this way? You'll scare the life out of them,' he predicted. 'Which in Georgie's case might not be such a bad thing. But seeing you like that is likely to give Harry nightmares for a month.' He arched a brow. 'What, no "you know nothing about children, so butt out"?'

Zoe shook her head, biting her lower lip to stop it quivering. He had summed up the twins pretty accurately.

'You're right. It's me who knows nothing about bringing up children,' she wailed.

A hissing sound of exasperation left his lips as he hefted her a little higher with apparent ease. On another occasion when she wasn't busy contemplating her fail-ure at parenting, Zoe might have been impressed. She was not exactly petite. 'I find it infinitely preferable when you are defensive and rude. This self-flagellation is boring.'

Finding herself unexpectedly placed on her feet, Zoe waited a moment for her head to stop spinning before she raised her swimming eyes to him, her quivering lips tightening. 'Oh, I'm so sorry I bored you.'

He smiled. 'Better,' he approved. 'Now, come on.

What you need is a hot bath, a brandy—or maybe not brandy, you might kiss the concierge—and a change of clothes before you return to your niece and nephew.' Placing a hand on her elbow, he guided her past the selection of gleaming top-of-the-range cars parked in front of the hotel whose gardens went down to the river.

'Nice thought, but unless you have them in your pocket…' She tried a smile but her teeth were chattering too hard. Every squelchy footstep was uncomfortable. 'Where are you parked?'

'I'm not. Alex took the twins back to Ravenwood. I'll ring him, and he'll tell the twins we'll be back later.'

Belatedly Zoe realised his intention.

'You're kidding—no way!' She shook her head and shrugged off the guiding hand on her shoulder as she stared up at the recently restored art deco façade of the five-star hotel with a reputation that drew a lot of people to the area.

She'd often thought it would be nice to sample the food there—but not looking like this!

'Why would I be kidding?'

'You can't just walk in there looking like this.' She glanced at him and made the mental adjustment that while he could, she couldn't. Isandro's clothes might be sodden, but he had not been swimming, and even if he had, she acknowledged reluctantly, he would still have the presence to make any door open for him.

'Why not?'

'Well, I don't know what the dress code is but I'm pretty sure this isn't it.' She held her hands wide to reveal her sodden muddy clothes. 'They'll throw me out. They won't even let me walk across the hallowed threshold.' She took a step backwards, shaking her head in response to the gleam in his eyes. 'And before you suggest it, being carried won't change anything.'

Except possibly her pulse rate. She knew that later that night she was going to remember every little detail of being carried in his arms, which would have made her a disgrace to modern liberated womanhood had she not suspected that inside most modern independent women lurked a secret desire to be swept off her feet. And if a man like Isandro was doing the sweeping, she suspected that few would find the experience objectionable.

She couldn't help but wonder what it would have felt like if his motivation had not been totally practical—a scenario that would have required her not looking like a drowned rat and for him to not be her boss...

But this is the real world. And once more, as far as he's concerned, you've shown yourself to be a pain in the backside.

'I was not about to offer. The fact is you're not as light as you look, especially wet.' His grin widened in response to her indignant squeak. 'Who exactly do you think is going to stop us?'

Zoe, who felt oddly light-headed, didn't react to the question. 'Just take me home, Isandro.' She clutched her spinning head, suddenly feeling nauseous as frames of the past hour flashed before her eyes. 'I turned around and they weren't there, and I...'

Observing the blue discoloration of her beautiful lips, Isandro released a hissed imprecation from between clenched teeth before taking her chin firmly between his thumb and forefinger. He turned her face up to his. The problem was not so much her imminent collapse or her stubborn refusal to enter the hotel as his struggle to maintain the necessary level of objectivity.

'Look, adrenaline was the only thing that kept you on your feet, and it's crashed.' So had she.

'I do feel a bit…'

'You look a bit, too.' His glance drifted over the curve of her cheek, delineated by classic high cheekbones. Her perfect skin was marble pale, the only colour in her face was supplied by her eyes, which stood out as a flash of startling colour in a monochrome film.

'You didn't succeed in drowning yourself, so now you are inviting hypothermia.' The effort to conceal the concern her fragility evoked in him made Isandro's voice cold and flat. 'We need to warm you up, get you out of those wet clothes.'

The words had barely left his lips before a stream of images that Isandro could have done without flashed through his head. He was regaining his shattered control when a sly voice reminded him that skin-to-skin contact was a well-known treatment for hypothermia His control went out of the window!

Even a sub-zero body temperature was not going to save him from the spike of lust that hardened his already half-aroused body. *Madre di Dios*, he was turning into a sad adult version of some sex-starved teenager! For a man who prided himself on his self-control it was…not tolerable. The only thing that was going to restore him to sanity was spending a week in bed with Zoe Grace.

He exhaled. The first step to solving a problem was admitting it existed. This he had already done. The next step was to work out a strategy. He needed to treat this problem like any other and apply logic and cool objectivity. The problem was that where his housekeeper was concerned he struggled to think objectively, and as for logic—he'd just stolen a boat, for God's sake!

'I know what you're thinking,' Zoe said, looking at

him over the soggy tissue she had produced and was now sniffing loudly into.

The prosaic action was rather touching, but not touching enough to hold his attention when the competition was the heaving contours of her breasts under the thin layer of drenched cotton through which her peaked nipples were clearly outlined.

'I rather doubt that, *querida*.' His thoughts were pretty rampant.

'You think I'm not fit to look after a cat, let alone two children,' she wailed, in full self-pity mode.

He did not respond with any comforting denials, but glanced rather pointedly at his watch.

This callous behaviour drew a hiss of annoyance from between her chattering teeth. 'So sorry—am I keeping you?' she said, wondering why she had thought for a second that her problems would do anything but bore the pants off him.

Her eyes dropped, running the length of his long legs, then making the journey back once she had reached his now muddy boots. She could see that, for some women, getting his pants off by whatever method would be considered a good result but she... Who was she kidding? Even on the brink of what felt like imminent hypothermia she could not stop lusting after him.

'Not at all. Feel free to go ahead and beat yourself up,' he encouraged. Zoe tried to bear her teeth in a snarl but she was shaking too hard and she bit her lip instead, drawing a pinprick of blood and his disturbing dark stare. 'But do you mind if we continue this conversation indoors?'

Zoe glanced at the hotel entrance. The golden light shining through the doors looked warm and inviting... and she was very cold. She lifted a hand to the hair that was plastered to her skull. His was, too, but in his case the effect was not drowned rat.

'I can't.' It was an invitation for him to contradict her, and he accepted it.

'Can and will,' he said, catching hold of her hand. 'We need a room.' On so many levels they needed a room!

'You can't walk in and book a room for a few hours,' she said, pointing out the obvious. At least it seemed obvious to her.

'Why not? People do. Oh, I see.' He laughed. 'You're afraid your reputation will be ruined if you're seen going into a hotel room with a man.'

'Of course not. And nobody is going to think that you…me…we…unless you normally have to half drown a woman before she'll have sex with you.'

'Not so far.'

Before she could interpret the odd inflection in his voice he had tightened his grip and virtually dragged her up the shallow flight of steps.

The warmth inside the hotel foyer hit her like a wall. So did the stares. It seemed to Zoe that a thousand eyes followed their progress.

But, as he predicted, nobody attempted to stop them, though it would have taken a very brave person to approach Isandro, who had adopted what she privately called his 'to hell with the lot of you' expression. His antagonism was probably aimed at her. This couldn't have been the way he had intended to spend his day, but the people who cleared a path for him weren't to know that.

It was amazing, she reflected enviously, as at her side Isandro gave every appearance of being genuinely oblivious to the stares and hushed comments that followed their progress across the lobby. But then he was probably used to people staring. And who could blame them? she thought as she directed a covert sideways look through her lashes at his stern profile, dishevelled but beautiful.

Even as someone who had previously not been totally sold on the dark brooding aura, she was willing to admit he was a fantastically good-looking man, who didn't just have the perfect face and body but also the indefinable extra factor. Confidence, sheer arrogance—whatever it was, he had it, and being extremely damp with his clothes spattered with mud and badly in need of a shave did not lessen it. The liberal sprinkling of stubble on his jaw lent an extra layer of air of danger, and did not exactly diminish his appeal.

So who could blame people for staring? she thought, making a conscious effort to emulate some of his attitude. And promptly tripping over the sodden hem of her jeans. It would happen when one stared at a man and not where one was going!

The ripple of laughter at her near pratfall brought her chin up. Trotting now to keep up with Isandro, Zoe suddenly thought, To hell with this! and gave the person who had laughed an enquiring look, even managing to inject a little hauteur into it. The culprit looked away before she did.

Zoe smiled and looked ahead. No amount of shoulder hunching or wishful thinking was going to make her vanish so she might as well borrow some of Isandro's attitude, even if she couldn't carry it off with his style.

'May I help you, sir?' A man whose lapel badge identified him as the manager intercepted them when they were halfway across the lobby. He guided them towards the reception desk where the eager-to-please attentiveness continued.

The people behind the reception desk almost fell over themselves being helpful to the point of obsequiousness, but Isandro, who was firing off his list of requirements, didn't appear to notice. This was probably his life, she mused, giving impossible orders and having people fall over themselves to deliver.

After a few moments he turned to a shivering Zoe. He hadn't forgotten her after all. 'I'll be up presently. You go along.'

The manager reappeared holding a large blanket, which, on an approving nod from Isandro, he draped almost reverentially over Zoe's shoulders. 'Jeremy will show you the way, miss.'

Jeremy, neat in his uniform, nodded and motioned for her to precede him into the glass lift that he explained was for the exclusive use of the penthouse. Penthouse… Zoe almost laughed. She was well aware that if she hadn't been Isandro's satellite she wouldn't have got through the front door, let alone been given this VIP treatment.

In the second before the doors closed Isandro turned, zeroing in on her like radar. His smile flickered as he caught her eye and tipped his dark head.

As the door swished closed her heart was still beating fast. The moment, a mere nothing in reality, felt strangely intimate to Zoe, as if they were exchanging some private secret.

'I had a slight boating accident.' A half-smile flickered across her face as she realised that if Isandro had been there he would have been mystified and probably irritated by her need to explain herself to a hotel employee. Jeremy made a sympathetic noise but did not volunteer an opinion.

As soon as the door to the suite was closed, Zoe explored her palatial surroundings only as far as the bathroom that adjoined one of the bedrooms, conscious that she was leaving a trail of wet, muddy footprints.

The place was…well, wow! She had only seen hotel rooms like this in films. It felt like the set of an old movie, and she ought to be wearing a long slinky gown.

Instead she was wearing…ugh! She glanced down at her ruined clothes, her lip curling in distaste. As she peeled off the soggy garments she made an active choice not to look at herself in the mirror. It wasn't easy, as the room was full of them. Definitely a room for someone with no body issues, she thought, shedding her clothes with relief.

Free of her clothes, she did glance in passing at her reflection in a mirror. She saw long legs, a slightly rounded stomach… While she would have liked more inches up top and a bit more flesh to cover her prominent hipbones, Zoe was happy enough with her figure.

Would a man be so happy?

Her eyes half closed, her stomach muscles quivered faintly as she stroked a hand slowly down her flank. Would her first lover think her hips too narrow, or find her bottom too—she moved her hand over the curve and stopped. Her hand fell away. She was shocked—the man she saw in her mind as she imagined standing naked in front of her lover was Isandro!

Now that would be a tough audience!

The hollow-sounding laugh was not convincing and did not stop a wave of scalding shame heating her cold skin.

Refusing to dwell on the man who had now invaded,

not just her life, but her subconscious, too, she walked
briskly away from the sodden pile of clothes—leaving a
widening pool of water on the mosaic-tiled floor—and
past the massive bath set on a raised pedestal, copper
and big enough to swim in. She would normally have
loved to try out this opulent fantasy tub but at that moment she did not feel much like swimming, so instead
she decided on the more practical option: the massive
shower behind a glass wall.

As she stood under the warm spray, liberally applying the luxury bath products supplied by the hotel, she
focused her thoughts on safer subjects. Just how much
did it cost to spend a night here? Perhaps Isandro would
take the cost from her pay?

'No!' Fear and anger bubbling inside her, she picked
up a sponge and began to apply it roughly to her skin.
Why was it that the wretched man managed to infil-
trate her every thought? When she finally stopped rubbing and dropped the sponge, her skin was glowing
and tingling pink, and her mind was a blissful, exfoli-
ated blank.

Picking up the shampoo, she lathered her hair for
a long time after it was squeaky clean. She stood still
like an alabaster statue, her eyes closed, her face lifted
to the warm spray, thinking nothing.

The nothing vanished the moment she emerged from
the shower and heard sounds of activity in the sitting
room. Immediately tension slid down her spine.

'For goodness' sake, Zoe, get over yourself!' she told
herself impatiently. 'You fancy him. Big deal! Half the
planet fancies him so what makes you so special, other
than the fact he thinks you're an incompetent idiot?'
She sniffed and reached for one of the gowns hanging

from a hook. 'And staff. He doesn't kiss staff even when they kiss him.' That mortifying memory was going to stay with her for a long time.

She wasn't even a colleague. She was the help.

She took a deep breath as she tightened the belt on her robe and flicked her wet hair back from her face.

As she entered the sitting room cautiously it was immediately clear there had been considerable activity in her absence. The table beside the open doors that led to the Juliet balcony had been laid with silver cutlery and fancily folded Irish linen napkins, and the antique candelabra in the middle was lit. It looked like a classic stage set for seduction... She could only assume that the staff had got the wrong idea.

She didn't immediately see Isandro, who had been sitting on a leather chesterfield in an alcove. She was alerted by the creak of leather before his throaty drawl.

'Feeling better?'

She flinched and spun around just as he got to his feet. Her skin had tingled when she'd ruthlessly scrubbed it, but now the tingle went deeper... I was better, but I'm not any more, she thought as she pasted on a polite smile.

'Yes, thank you. That smells good.' She nodded towards the domed covered serving dish set on the console table before looking at him—or, rather, past him.

'Clothes maketh the man' was not a phrase that applied to Isandro. He looked good in clothes, but he looked equally good, actually much better, without them...well, almost without them. He was wearing a robe similar to her own but on him the superior hotel-issue garment reached his thigh and revealed more of his dark hair-roughened skin than she was comfortable with.

'I almost came to look for you.'

It had taken all his willpower and the seemingly constant flow of waiters through the place not to follow the sound of the running water and his own instincts.

His own shower had been ice cold, which had given him a temporary partial relief from his agony, but the moment she'd walked into the room with a freshly scrubbed face and nothing more than an ankle on show he had been painfully aroused and unable to think about anything but throwing her on the bed. His desire had no subtlety; it was sheer primal hunger.

He wanted her so badly he could taste it.

'I only need rescuing once a day.' Her lips formed a smile but her eyes conspicuously avoided making contact with his. Isandro could feel her tension from where he stood. 'Did you contact Alex?' she asked, as businesslike as someone could be when bare-faced and barefoot. She ran her tongue across her dry lips. She didn't even have any lipstick to hide behind, though it was doubtful if a slash of cherry red would have made her feel more confident.

'Yes, he's got Rowena to come over and babysit.'

'Rowena.' Zoe gave a sigh of relief, losing some of her stiff formality as she smiled. 'Thank you.'

Isandro's eyes travelled up from her bare feet to the top of her wet head. The section in between was covered in a thick layer of fluffy white bathrobe, but the suggestion of curves, the thought of the soft skin it hid, sent his imagination into overdrive.

'What can I get you?' He walked over to the table and lifted a lid on one of the dishes.

You on a sandwich, she thought, but bit her lip. 'Thanks, but I can't eat. I should get back.' Before I make a total fool of myself.

'Why?' He looked irritated by her response. 'The twins are being well cared for. Or don't you think Rowena can cope?'

'It's not a matter of her coping.' Rowena was totally capable. The young woman's parents had been good friends of Dan and Laura, and the twins loved their daughter, who ran the local stables. 'I don't want to take advantage.'

Her sister and brother-in-law had had a lot of friends and it was good to know that in an emergency they were there. But it was important to her to stand on her own feet and not become reliant. Or infatuated, she thought, looking directly at him for the first time.

He arched a strongly delineated ebony brow. Everything about his face was strong. 'Have you ever said no when someone asks a favour? No, you haven't. But when they want to return the favour it becomes "taking advantage"?'

The mockery in his voice as he adopted a very shaky falsetto to mimic her brought a lump to Zoe's throat.

'I'm glad I give you something to laugh about.'

'I'm not laughing. I admire independence but not when it becomes bloody-minded stubbornness.' Sometimes he wondered when she slept, or if. His critical glance moved to the violet smudges beneath her spectacular eyes. She was struggling to fit into a job she was unsuited for, and struggling to be the perfect parent. It was admirable but impossible. Why couldn't the woman embrace her imperfections? He had!

The insight sent a stab of shock through Isandro. She roused feelings that he flatly refused to recognise as protective tenderness. He refused because he associated the emotions with weakness. It made him angry. *She* made him angry!

'What are you trying to prove, Zoe?' he asked, his voice hard.

'I'm not trying to prove anything!'

Glaring, her eyes slid down his body as he sat down and leaned back on the leather sofa. Stretching his long legs out, he folded one ankle across the other. The hair-roughened skin of his muscular calves looked very dark against the white of the hotel robes. She was wearing nothing underneath. Was he…?

Shivering, she stopped the speculation from progressing into dangerous territory and dragged her gaze back to his face.

'In that case take five minutes off from being a martyr and give us all a break.'

She sucked in a gulping breath, embracing the rush of anger as she clenched her fists. 'There's nobody here but you and me.'

'Exactly, and I won't tell if you fall off your perfect parent pedestal. Just you and me…what could be cosier?'

The question drew a gurgle from her throat. 'Oh, I don't know—how about hang gliding over an active volcano?'

And there was something combustible about him, even when he was still and silent like now, his long, lean body relaxed. She had the impression that he could explode into action at any moment.

He let out a low chuckle, his expression sobering as he added, 'Are you planning to put your life on hold for the next ten or fifteen years?'

'Fifteen years!' She snorted. 'I'm not thinking any farther ahead than next month's bills.' She found his anger inexplicable. 'I'm a single parent. My priority has to be the twins.'

'Single parents have been known to have sex.'

CHAPTER EIGHT

ZOE BLINKED, THE COLOUR flying to her cheeks as she lost any fragile illusion of composure. 'Since when were we talking about sex?'

'It's part of a healthy, well-balanced life. We're always talking about sex, even when we're talking about the weather. It's the subtext.'

She flushed and snapped in protest, 'I was drunk when that happened before.'

'You're not drunk now.' So there was zero reason for gentlemanly behaviour. 'And I'm not a teenager. I'm tired of the game.' And the frustration was killing him.

He had come up with a workable solution. Now all he had to do was sell it. Isandro did not doubt his ability to do so. That was what he was good at: selling ideas; producing packages that made everyone think they had a good deal.

Zoe had anticipated his anger. After all, from his point of view she was a grade A nuisance. But she had not imagined this level of simmering fury. Even while he had been yelling at her over capsizing the boat, there had been an underlying gentleness, almost a tenderness, in his manner.

Searching his lean, handsome face now Zoe could

see no trace of the tenderness. The gleam in his deep-set dark eyes was hard and calculating… She shivered.

'I don't play games,' she protested. 'And I happen to think that someone who changes his girlfriends like socks and never sees them during daylight hours is not qualified to preach to me on what constitutes a healthy, well-balanced life!'

Having said her piece, she sat down with a bump on the sofa opposite him, her cheeks burning. She drew the folds of the robe around her like a tent and pulled her knees up to her chest.

'Obviously, how you live your life is none of my business, but that goes both ways. I work for you, but that doesn't give you a right to criticise my lifestyle unless it impinges on my ability to do my work.'

'Pardon me for stepping over the line,' he drawled, tipping his head in mock apology. 'But I think that line has been blurred from day one with us.'

Eyes trained on the gaping neckline of her robe and the exposed curve of one smooth shoulder, he exhaled through flared nostrils, combating the stab of lust by focusing on the disruption this woman had caused in his life, and not the fact he wanted to touch her skin.

This situation was of his own making. He had broken a fundamental rule. He had allowed the lines to become blurred, and he needed a strict demarcation between his personal and professional lives.

Her eyes lowered. 'I know I made a bad first impression, but I hoped that by now you'd see that I really am capable of—'

'Drowning yourself?' An image of her vanishing under the water began to play on a loop in his head, the images accompanied by the dull bass soundtrack of his blood pumping in his ears.

She flashed him a reproachful look. 'No. Being a good housekeeper.'

He laughed, and it sounded cruel to Zoe, who sat hunched watching him. 'You're a terrible housekeeper.'

A part of her despised wanting to cry. She held the tears back by sniffing and concentrating on the part of her that wanted to throw something at him.

'I've made a few mistakes,' she conceded.

His brows hit his hairline. 'A few! You can't give the most basic instruction, you fall for any sob story and you invite people to take advantage of you.'

'I think more of people than you do. I trust them.'

'I know—that's why you're sacked.'

He hadn't intended to deliver the news quite so brutally, but a combination of need and frustration bypassed his subtlety circuits. And diplomacy did not come easy when you had a slow-motion nightmare playing on a loop in your head. He prided himself on his ability to apply cool logic to all situations, but for a moment back there on the water, even though he'd known the boat would get him to her quicker, he had been within a whisper of following his instincts and diving in.

If he had, who knew what the outcome might have been? She called herself a strong swimmer but he knew what he had seen. Though he actually was a strong swimmer, there remained a question mark—could he have reached her in time?

It was possible they might both have perished.

She stiffened as she shot to her feet, every muscle in her body clenched and defensive, refusing to acknowledge the cold fear in her belly. Clasping her hands together, she blew out her breath slowly and flicked back her wet hair.

'What did you say?' Her tone was conversational. She had obviously misheard him—nobody would be that brutal, that totally...totally vile.

'You're sacked.'

Desperation overcame her anger and she crumbled. 'I'm really trying—'

'Do not beg, Zoe. This is not open for discussion.'

She bit her lip.

'It doesn't matter how much you try. You're uniquely unsuited to the role of housekeeper. I think it'll be easier all around if we cut our losses rather than drag this out. You are not the sort of housekeeper I need.' You're the sort of sex I need.

Panic made her voice shrill as she came back, 'I could be. It's just I can't relax around you...' She caught his look and added quickly, 'Because you're my employer.'

Quite suddenly he was tired of this pretence. Sensual mouth compressed, his chiselled cheekbones jutting hard against his golden skin, he silenced her with a sharp jerk of his head as he rose to his feet. 'That situation has got nothing to do with the fact I pay your wages. A strong sexual connection makes all our encounters less than relaxing, especially when you work so hard trying to pretend it doesn't exist.'

Zoe turned her head, her mouth open to produce a strong rebuttal, her eyes connected with his glowing dark gaze. Her biggest fear had been him guessing the way she felt, and now he had. So what, she thought despairingly, was the point denying it?

'Don't you find it exhausting, Zoe?' he asked softly.

She stood there mutely staring at him. Inside she was dying of sheer mortification. This was her boss saying he knew she secretly lusted after him. What was she meant to say to that?

For a split second his resolve wavered. She looked so pale, so vulnerable. But it only wavered briefly. Another month like this one and he'd be a basket case.

'I can only assume you've had some problems in the past with female staff and…crushes, but I promise you're safe from me.'

He didn't want to be safe from her.

'Good to know, but you're still sacked.'

She flinched. The bastard had said it the way someone remarked on the weather. Somewhere deep inside her, rage stirred. 'Because I don't fancy you.'

'If that were true, there would be no problem.'

Her chest swelled as she flung him a look of withering contempt. 'Even if you were right I have my own rules, too. And the first one is that I never have sex with a man I don't respect. Believe you me, that rules you out, you contemptuous little snake!'

He gave a low throaty chuckle.

'Why didn't you just sack me on that first day?' That would have been bad but this was worse. Thinking her job was secure, she'd allowed herself to relax, she'd allowed herself to sit here thinking stupid ridiculous thoughts about him, imagining that they might even… Stupid…stupid…stupid! She was so angry with herself she wanted to scream. She took a deep breath and slung a look of loathing his way.

'I didn't sack you at that point because my company is in the middle of some sensitive negotiations which could mean a lot of…' He made a dismissive gesture with his hand. 'You are not interested in the whys, but the success of this deal will mean something in the region of a thousand jobs over a five-year period.'

'What's that got to do with me?'

'It's about protecting my company's brand. Any negative publicity would send the clients running for the hills, and the story of me sacking a woman because she used my property to host a charity fund-raiser would be the worst-possible PR.'

Trying to think beyond the static buzz in her head, a combination of anger and panic, she only really processed one word in two of what he was saying. 'I don't know what you're talking about.'

'Because you are an innocent.'

How long would her savings last…a month, two…? After that what was she going to do?

'I really hate you.' Her snarl was shaky but filled with venom and her eyes gleamed with loathing as she glared up at him. She grabbed at a side table, afraid that her shaking knees were about to give way. This body blow on top of the events of that afternoon had taken a physical as well as mental toll.

'Calm down. There's no need to react this way. It's not as though you enjoy the job.'

Calm down? What planet did this man live on?

'We can't all do jobs we enjoy. Some of us do jobs because we need to survive.' This job had been her plan A, and she didn't have a plan B. She wiped her brow as she felt the panic crowding in on her again.

'Will you stop acting as though you're a heroine in a Victorian melodrama and I'm the villain?'

She flashed him a look of sheer incredulity and shook her head. He made it sound as though she was overreacting. 'If the black hat fits…?'

With an exaggerated roll of his eyes he placed his hands on her shoulders, exerting enough pressure to force her back down onto the sofa. 'If you'd stop for a minute and let me explain. I'm not throwing you out anywhere. I'm suggesting that you move to the end of the drive, that's all.'

'What are you talking about?'

'The gatehouse.' The solution had been staring him in the face all along! Now that he had had his eureka moment, he couldn't understand why he hadn't thought about it earlier.

'The one you've just decorated?'

The building in question had not been included in the initial refurbishment of the estate because there had apparently been some planning dispute over a proposed extension, but this had recently been resolved. Zoe had not been involved with the renovation but the builders had packed up and left a couple of weeks ago and the team of decorators had literally finished the previous day.

'If I'm not working for you how can—?'

'I'm suggesting you and the children move into the gatehouse, pay a nominal rent...'

'With what?' No job meant no money, which meant... Oh, God, she couldn't think what it meant. She was no longer in a position to sleep on a friend's couch until she sorted things. The twins needed a home and stability—they needed a guardian who didn't go around losing her job!

I am such a loser.

Well, if she was a loser, he was a total bastard!

'I have a friend who has bought an art gallery. She is looking for someone to front it. I have spoken to her about you...'

Polly's astonished response when he had explained that his unsuitable housekeeper's domestic situation

meant he couldn't simply let her go without providing some sort of safety net was still fresh in his mind.

'Since when did you worry about dismissing someone who wasn't up to the job, Isandro? And why are you
going to so much trouble to help find the girl a job?'

She had accepted his explanation without question.

'So this is about avoiding bad PR. What a relief. For
a moment there—' she laughed '—I thought you'd become a bleeding heart!'

'She is happy to offer you a trial,' Isandro told Zoe.

'What makes you think I'd be any less terrible at
running an art gallery than I am running a house?'
Zoe asked bitterly.

'You are artistic.'

'How would you know?'

'Had you not been accepted on a fine arts degree
course before your sister and her husband died?'

In the middle of a miserable sniff, Zoe lifted her incredulous glance to his face. 'How did you know that?'

He shrugged and dropped his gaze. 'Tom might have
mentioned it.'

'But why would your friend give me this job?'

'I asked her.'

'A permanent job?'

'Very few things in life are permanent, but there
would be a very good severance package,' he told her
smoothly. 'Enough for you to pay your way through
art college as you planned and employ childcare in the
meantime. I understand they run an excellent foundation fine arts course on an evening basis at the local
college.'

'I don't understand. Why would this woman pay
me a—' her nose wrinkled; what had he called it?
'—severance package?'

'She wouldn't.'

Zoe shook her head as the confusion deepened.

'I would.'

'But I wouldn't be working for you.'

'Not as such,' he conceded. 'The point is, Zoe, the attraction is not one-sided. I want you in my bed and I am a man in a position to make my fantasies come true. You are my fantasy, Zoe.'

Things fell into place in her head with an almost audible clunk. She shot to her feet—no longer shaking, no longer terrified, just furious.

'Let me get this straight. This job you're talking about, it's as…your mistress?'

He shrugged. 'That's an old-fashioned term.'

She stuck out her chin, her blue eyes sparkling with wrathful contempt. 'I'm an old-fashioned girl.' He had no idea how old-fashioned. 'Though I suppose you think I should be flattered. Isn't it a bit of a risk, though? We've never even slept together. How would you know that I'd be…any good in the bedroom?'

'It takes two, and I think when a woman literally shakes with lust when I look at her I'm willing to take the risk on a sight-unseen basis—'

'My God!' she gasped. 'You really think I'm shallow enough to want to sleep with a man who is obviously deeply in love with himself. A man whose only redeeming feature as far as I can tell is a pretty face and a moderately all right body.'

Fingers crossed, because that was a lie. He had the body of an Adonis. She gave a derisive sniff and arched a brow before laughing.

'Yes, I do.' His sloe-dark eyes drifted over her lush sinuous curves shrouded beneath the robe, and his mouth grew dry at the thought of slipping the loose knot of the belt looped around her narrow waist.

It was an uphill struggle to act as though his slow, sexy smile was doing nothing to her. She knew that sex appeal wasn't just about looks, but the idea that she was any man's erotic fantasy—let alone a man like Isandro—was shocking. She swallowed and pressed both hands to her stomach, shamefully aware that the deep quivers that rippled low in her pelvis were not caused by shock. What he was suggesting was wrong on more levels than she could count, it went against every principle she held dear, yet she was excited... What does that say about me?

'Besides, we don't have to wait. This is the perfect opportunity to find out if it's as good as I think it will be.' The sweep of his hand took in the big bed piled with cushions, the open French door against which the light curtains fluttered in the breeze.

In the distance Zoe could hear a flock of geese landing on the water. She went hot, cold, then hot again.

'I'm not selling my body.'

'That's good, because I've never paid for sex.'

'What do you call what you're suggesting?'

'I'm suggesting we remove the barrier that is preventing us both doing what we want to. If you are no longer on my payroll we can be equal.'

'I'll never be equal to you. I'll always be superior!'

'Bravo!' he drawled.

Her lips tightened. 'Don't you dare patronise me! And why make up that stupid story about your friend?'

'That is not invented. It is real. I do have a friend who owns a gallery.'

Zoe felt a stab of something she didn't immediately recognise as jealousy. 'A female friend?'

Could you sound more jealous if you tried?

'Her name is Polly Warrender. She inherited a theatre from her husband.' Zoe had heard of the Warrender theatre, but then pretty much everyone had. 'When she diversified and bought into an art gallery she came to me for advice.'

She stifled a theatrical yawn, but the gesture unwittingly drew his eyes to the soft full curve of her rosy lips. 'So, let me guess, she listened to you and made a fortune,' she inserted with a roll of her eyes.

'Actually she ignored my advice and bought it and, yes, made a fortune.' He gave a faint smile. 'A smallish one.'

'So you were wrong?'

He reached out and tangled a wet curl around one long brown finger and drawled, 'You've discovered the chink in my infallible armour. Please do me a favour and keep it to yourself.'

As he released the curl his finger brushed her cheek. It barely made contact, but Zoe, who had been holding her breath, felt an electric tingle pass through her body all the way to her curling toes.

His voice was a soft attractive buzz. She could hear what he was saying, but over and above the words was a louder buzz—a combination of her own heartbeat and the thrum of the deep hunger that was coursing through her veins with each beat of her heart as she stared at the deep V of golden chest dark against the white towelling.

It took every ounce of her self-control to stop herself reaching out and touching him… She curled her hands into fists and tucked them behind her back.

'I put her onto the decommissioned church that was up for sale in town as a possible site for a new gallery. She has wanted to expand into this area for some time, so she owes me a favour. She is genuinely looking for someone to run it, and you have an art background... So it is perfectly feasible for you to live here and commute to do the foundation course.'

'And amuse you in bed.' He acknowledged her bitter addition with a tilt of his head. 'You have it all worked out.'

He gave a smile. 'The secret of success is taking control of events and not allowing them to control you.'

Yeah, you carry on telling yourself that, Isandro, if it makes you feel any better. The fact was he had felt out of control since the moment he had met this woman. From day one she had managed to turn his well-ordered life into chaos.

She shook her head. 'Don't you dare smile. I'm not listening to a word you're saying.'

He took the hands she had pressed to her ears and pressed them against his chest. Then holding her eyes with his, he brushed his lips across her cheek.

'You're not shouting, though,' he murmured against her mouth.

She wasn't. Zoe was barely breathing. Her body felt strange and tingly, as though it didn't belong to her. Her arms and legs felt heavy as though a great weight were dragging her down. Dizzy, she clutched at the towelling of his robe. Somehow it parted and her hands were flat on his skin, the warmth seeping into her cold fingers, the heavy thud of his heartbeat mingling with the frantic clamour of her riotous pulse.

Common sense told her to push him away.

'This isn't going to happen.' Why was she whispering? She should be shouting.

'If you say so, *querida*.' His big hand sank into her wet hair, cupping the back of her skull. His long fingers tangled in her hair while his thumb trailed tingling paths down her cheek. His breath was coming fast and hot against her neck.

Her knees gave out, but before she could slide to the floor his arms snaked around her waist. He was so close that his face was a dark blur. She could see the predatory glow of his beautiful eyes. Her own eyes burned but she couldn't blink, she couldn't look away, not until he tugged at the soft pink flesh of her lower lip, holding it between his teeth. Then her eyes squeezed tight closed as she released a soft sibilant sigh and opened her palms flat on his chest, pushing them under the thick fabric of the robe, up over his warm skin to his shoulders.

Still she didn't push. Like someone in a dream she clung, and still he didn't kiss her. The scent of his warm male body in her nostrils, she was desperate for the taste of him. The need consumed her utterly, so strong that it blotted every other thought from her mind. He radiated raw power, and it excited her unbearably, sent a primitive heat sweeping through her in waves crashing over her. She felt herself going under.

Need, primitive need, raw and all-consuming, blinding lust controlled his actions as he tilted her face up. *Dios*, but he had wanted to kiss her for… It felt like a lifetime.

His tongue slid between her parted lips and Zoe's brain closed down as instinct took over. Her moan was lost in the warm recesses of his mouth as her lips parted to deepen the sensual invasion.

She kissed him back, greedily drinking in the taste of him, wanting more…wanting everything. He hauled her body into him. His hands slipped down to her bottom as, cupping it, he lifted her off the ground. Without thinking, she wrapped her long legs tight around his

waist as she framed his face between her hands, gave a
throaty sigh and whispered, 'God, but you are so beautiful…the most beautiful man.'

With a deep groan that rose up in his throat he plun-
dered Zoe's mouth, kissing her with barely controlled
desperation, stealing the breath from her lungs, lighting a passion that flared into violent life. As she kissed
him back with a wild and unrestrained hunger, satis-
fying the mutual need between them, everything else
ceased to exist.

Her fingers dug into the muscles of his shoulders,
her legs tightening around his waist as she fought to get
closer to him, her strength fuelled by the primal desire
to be joined with him…be one.

Joined with her that way still, he walked blindly towards the bed.

Zoe felt as if she were falling—and then she was
really falling and he was falling on top of her. A pillow
beneath her head, she barely noticed the weight of his
body on top of her until he levered himself off.

Panting, her eyes as dark as midnight, she gave a
small cry of protest, then she saw what he was doing.
Kneeling over her, Isandro was shrugging off his robe.

'Oh, my God!'

He was long and lean, his skin gleaming like burnished gold. Not an ounce of excess flesh blurred the
perfect lines of his powerful body. Every bone and
sinew of him was perfect, like a bronzed statue. A ram-
pantly, fully aroused bronzed statue.

She bit down hard on her full lower lip as heat
washed her skin with a warm rosy flush. Her initial
shock at the earthy image was replaced by a stomach-
clenching, incapacitating, lustful longing that closed
down every logic circuit in her brain.

His grin was fierce and his laughter strained as he husked, 'If you look at me like that, *querida*, this thing is going to be over before it has begun.'

'I want you,' she whispered, pulling herself up onto her knees. 'So badly…' She reached out and touched him, unable to believe her daring as she curled her fingers around the shaft of his erection. Silky smooth and rock hard, he pulsed hotly against her small hand. 'You feel—' her breasts quivered as she gave a fractured sigh and continued to stare, fascinated, at him '—incredible.'

A hiss left his lips as he caught her wrist.

'Too much,' he muttered, pressing her body back onto the bed before he joined her. Arranging his long lean length beside her, he kissed her, a kiss full of passion and promise that made words redundant. Lifting his head, he stroked her face and held her eyes as he reached for the tie on her robe.

The embarrassment she had anticipated did not materialise but the voluptuous pleasure did as he whispered fiercely, 'You are exquisite, flawless.'

His searing gaze swept upwards slowly, greedily drinking her in as it took in every detail from her narrow feet and ankles, the long elegant length of her legs, and over her belly. Then finally to her lovely, pertly pointed breasts.

His hand came to cover one perfect soft mound. Her skin was flawless. He could smell the perfume of the soap on her skin, and the faint but distinctive delicate, musky scent of her arousal made his vision mist red.

As he massaged the smooth skin, his touch firm but sensitive, running his thumb with slow deliberate strokes across the sensitised peaks, Zoe gasped and muttered his name. Her head thrashed wildly back and forth on the pillow. The pleasure was so intense—

beyond words, she clenched her hands into fists at her sides as she felt herself losing her struggle to stay in control.

Then his mouth was on her breasts, his hands on her body, touching her awakening senses. With a soft sigh of surrender, she stopped trying and gave herself up to the desire flowing like warm wine through her veins. She almost felt like laughing with the sense of release. Who knew that losing control, feeling enough trust to give it over to someone else, could feel like this?

She reached for him, her fingers tangling in his dark hair, holding him against her as she stroked the skin of his muscled shoulders. The raw power in him, the dramatic contrasts of his hard angularity and her own softness, her roundness, was more exciting than she could have dreamed possible.

Isandro lifted his head and smiled at her with his glorious eyes, a dark fierce smile filled with promise, then he kissed her belly, drawing a hoarse gasp from Zoe, and ran his tongue over the quivering skin, drawing a line that terminated just above the apex of her thighs.

At the first touch of his hands between her legs need exploded through her. She loosed a keening cry as her hips lifted off the bed. Her entire body ached and trembled with desire; her mouth opened but she had no words, just his name, which she said over and over. And when she stopped he lifted his head and said, 'Again, say it again.'

She did, and at the same time opened her legs in mute invitation, inviting skilful touch of his fingers over the slick, moist, swollen folds of her femininity, and the tight, sensitive nub they protected.

The first skin-to-skin contact was electric. Then, as her arched spine made contact with the bed and he pressed down on top of her, it was totally, utterly bliss-ful, a cocktail of intoxicating physical sensations that made her senses spiral and spin. Bright lights exploded behind her eyelids as she closed her eyes.

Her hips moved in a grinding motion as she rubbed herself against his erection as it dug into her thigh, then her soft belly. The pressure building inside her made her thrash around, bite his neck as she dragged her fin-gers down his back, clutching at the firm contours of his tight, muscular buttocks.

Unable to bear the erotic friction of his erection against her any longer, she grabbed his hair, drawing his face to hers, and kissing him hard, whispered, 'Please!'

With a savage smile he held her eyes as he drove deep into her body. The breath left her in a shocked gasp that was drowned out by his deep growl of pleasure. Her heart racing, her eyes closed tight, she concentrated on the intense pleasure of each slow, measured move-ment of his hips as he moved inside her body. There was layer after layer of sensations that she had never imagined she could feel.

Each thrust built the erotic pleasure that she encour-aged with each sinuous, sensuous grind of her hips responding to age-old instincts she was delighted to discover.

When the climax hit her, she was unprepared for the strength of the expanding wave of pleasure and her eyes flew wide with shock.

'Perfect, just go with it, my clever, beautiful…' His eyes held her while she rode the wave. He waited until she reached the vortex of the storm before he allowed himself to find his own release and thrust one final time into her.

When Zoe floated back to earth, she was curled up

in his arms, her head resting against his thudding heart, her sweat-slick limbs tangled with his.

'Well, I never saw that one coming. I remember hearing you say you did not approve of casual sex but I never equated that with… Was there a bad experience that put you off sex I should have known about?'

It seemed the only explanation for how a woman as sexy and passionate as Zoe Grace could be a virgin. And her surrender had been total; she had held nothing back. He had sensed the passion beneath the surface, but what he had released had startled and delighted him almost as much as the discovery she was a virgin.

'No bad experience, I just… I've moved around a lot and never got time to make any sort of lasting relationship. Not that this is lasting…obviously.' There was a short awkward pause. Dear God, it was a strange world when she was embarrassed to admit that, a secret romantic, she had always felt uneasy about casual sex.

'You must have had boyfriends.'

'Of course I have—I'm not a freak. I had boyfriends but they all seemed to suggest I was not very…good at that sort of stuff.' Her last date had culminated in a nasty little scene when the man who invited her to dinner had accused her of being a tease when she could not agree that the correct payment for a dinner was a make-out session in the back seat of a car.

He gave a throaty laugh of incredulity. 'I think you have been keeping the wrong company.'

She twisted in his arms and flipped onto her stomach, resting her chin on her elbows and affording him an excellent view of her breasts. 'And you're the right company?' she challenged.

He was definitely the right lover.

'It felt pretty right to me.'

'So what happens now?'

His wicked grin flashed. 'Give me five minutes.'

'I mean after this?' Had he really been serious about moving her and the twins into the gatehouse?

CHAPTER NINE

'I THOUGHT I had already made that clear.'

'But after?' Isandro was hot for her now, but Zoe did not anticipate the situation would last and when he lost interest, what then? 'When I am no longer flavour of the day?'

'That moment,' he purred, stroking the silky smooth skin of her forearm, 'feels like a long way off.'

'But it might not be.'

'Well, that is catered for. You will continue to live in the gatehouse for as long as it pleases you. It seems to me a win, win situation.'

He could say that but he wasn't on the brink of falling in love. Who was she kidding? Zoe thought bleakly. She was already in love and had been for the past weeks. She was going to be devastated when this was over, but she was going to be devastated anyway so why not have some weeks of delicious mind-blowing sex with this gorgeous man to remember and some financial security for the twins?

'All right, but no.' She twisted away from the hand that reached for her, knowing that once he touched her she wouldn't be able to think straight, let alone consider consequences. 'There have to be some rules.'

Isandro stared at her, taken aback—he made the rules.

'I don't want this to affect the twins. I don't want them to know about us. We have to be discreet. We know this is just sex but they are just...' Whichever way she looked, there were aspects to this arrangement that didn't feel right.

He tipped his head. 'That seems fair.' He tangled his fingers in her hair and kissed her mouth. 'Do not look so worried. We have weeks of pleasure ahead of us. You are not some little girl seeking the attention of men and mistaking it for love. This is an equal relationship of two people who know what they want.'

'What do you want?'

'You, *querida*, you in so many ways.'

She shivered. 'Many ways?'

His smile made her heart flip. 'Come here and let me show you.'

Zoe and the twins had been established in the gate-house for six weeks. Her passion with Isandro had not flagged, and six weeks was new ground for him. Abiding by rules set by someone else was also new and on occasion frustrating.

There came a tapping on the window of his study—which had recently been knocked through to make room for the extra office equipment he needed since he had made the decision to do more work from home.

Isandro looked up from the computer screen.

When the red-headed figure at the window saw him she began to gesticulate wildly. A second later she vanished, and there was a clattering sound.

With a sigh Isandro levered himself up from his chair, stretching the kinks from his spine as he walked towards the window. Pulling up the sash, he leaned out. Georgina was lying beside an overturned crate she had presumably dragged over to the window and fallen off. She was picking herself up.

'What are you doing?'

'Looking for you, obviously.' Ever irrepressible, she dusted off the seat of her jeans.

'Did you hurt yourself?'

The kid treated the question with the scorn she appeared to think it deserved, shaking her head and looking offended by the question.

Like aunt, like niece, he thought.

'I would have gone to Chloe but they're not back until tomorrow. I can't wait to see Hannah again and she's walking with crutches, and there isn't really anyone else.'

So not first choice, or even second. 'I feel honoured.'

'If Zoe died, would we get put in a home?'

His half-sardonic smile snuffed like a candle caught in a chill draft and Isandro did suddenly feel as though a cold fist had plunged deep into his belly.

'Zoe is not going to die.'

'No...?' Her niece sounded scarily uncertain.

'What has happened to your aunt Zoe?' he asked, ruthlessly reining in his imagination and struggling to keep his tone light.

'She says she's fine but she doesn't look fine and she—'

He held up a hand. 'Wait there. I will be with you momentarily.'

Snatching up his jacket on the way out, he paused only to close his laptop before leaving the house. Outside Georgie was trotting around the side of the house to meet him when he emerged.

'Zoe sent you?'

She shook her head. 'She'll be mad with me,' she predicted gloomily.

'She doesn't need to know that you came to get me.'

Her eyes flew wide with shock. 'That would be lying!' Children were a minefield.

'Of course it would, and of course you should never lie…especially to your aunt.'

The child looked unconvinced as she climbed into the passenger seat of his car.

'Now tell me what is wrong.'

When they arrived at the lodge they entered through her open back door where Harry, his face scrunched in concentration, was standing on a kitchen chair trying to open a tin with an opener that looked like an antique. His small fingers looked perilously near the razor-sharp edges.

Conscious it might not be a good idea to startle him, Isandro walked across and, after a friendly pat on the shoulder, extricated the tin from his grip.

'Let me—there's a knack to this. There you go.' He glanced at the label. 'Chicken soup.'

'Mum always gave us chicken soup when we were sick. I thought I'd make Zoe some.'

'Good idea, but let's wait until we see if she wants to eat just now.'

'Until she stops throwing up, stupid,' his sister inserted critically.

'I'm not stupid.'

Isandro cleared his throat. 'How about if you two go?' Two expectant faces turned to him. 'Go to the shop and get me some…' He paused. 'Are you allowed to walk to the shop?'

They both shook their heads.

'Right, well...' *Madre di Dios*, give me a room of CEOs any day of the week.

'We could clean out your car. It was very messy. For money,' Georgie offered.

Her brother cast her a sideways warning look. 'For free.'

His sister sighed heavily.

'That would be very helpful.' His car had been valet cleaned the previous week. 'I will go and see how your aunt is feeling, but don't worry. It sounds like she has the flu bug that is doing the rounds.' He moved towards the hallway.

'Are you Zoe's boyfriend?'

Isandro might not be good with children but he did not fall into that trap. He paused and turned. His amused expression was not a direct denial but he hoped they took it as such. 'Is that why you came to get me? Because you think I am her boyfriend?'

'No, we came to get you because she was saying your name in the night. She woke us up and when we went in she was awake but really hot.'

'I told you it was just a nightmare,' Harry said.

A woman's nightmare...children certainly had a way of keeping a man's ego in check.

Isandro made his way to the bedroom at the front of the cottage. The door was ajar, and he pushed it open and found the curtains in the airy room pulled shut. The light filtering through the striped fabric illuminated the figure in the bed lying with one arm curled around her head.

He was used to feeling the tug of sexual attraction when he looked at her, used to feeling the electrical tingle when she was close. As he stared at her now, looking both vulnerable and utterly desirable—they were both there but there was something else in the mix, something he struggled to define as he stood nailed to the spot while something imploded in his skull.

Then she moved and shifted, groaning softly before she licked her lips as her eyelashes fluttered against her cheek. 'Harry.'

'Not Harry.'

The eyelashes parted to reveal blue blurry eyes. 'Oh, God,' she groaned. 'What are you doing here?'

He had had more enthusiastic welcomes. 'How are you feeling?'

She raised herself groggily up on one elbow, causing the nightdress she wore to slip over one shoulder. He felt a stab of inappropriate lust.

'Fine,' she croaked.

'I admire the stiff upper lip, naturally, but an honest answer would be more helpful.'

Zoe turned her head on the pillow and aimed a look of simmering dislike on him. He wanted to know what she felt like? Fine, she'd tell him.

'I feel like death warmed up. Happy?' She lowered herself with a groan onto the pillow. 'And I suppose I look that way, too.'

'Pretty bad,' he agreed, his mocking smile vanishing as her lips began to tremble. 'Are you crying?'

'Oh, well, so sorry I couldn't manage to put on my make-up for your benefit, but nobody asked you here.' Her brow furrowed. 'What are you doing here anyway?'

'Georgie came to get me.'

'Oh, God, she shouldn't have.'

'They are worried.'

Zoe clapped a hand to her aching head and groaned. 'I told them I'm fine. It's just a bug or something.'

'Symptom-wise, could you be a little more precise?'

'If I tell you will you go away? I have cymbals playing in my head, I ache all over and I feel sick…' She gave a him a narrow-eyed glare of 'Is that precise enough for you?'

'Very succinct. I am assuming our date tonight is off.'

Zoe didn't have the energy to prise her eyelids apart but she found the strength to correct him.

'We don't have a date. It's just sex. Do I know it's just sex? he asks me, like I'm a total idiot,' she mumbled. The comment he had made in the aftermath of the frantic love-making session they had fitted in while the children were having their riding lesson had been playing in her head all through the long interminable night.

'So how is our patient?'

This time Zoe's eyes didn't open as she resisted the temptation to declare she was nobody's patient.

'Doctor, who sent for you?' He had to have heard what she'd said. She comforted herself with the thought that doctors, like priests, couldn't blab about their patients. Presumably the Montero name, or possibly the cheque book, had made the man forget that GPs no longer made house calls at the weekend, she brooded, with a cynical sniff that became a cough.

Neither man answered her question.

'Beyond the general crankiness, she has a headache, joint pain and obviously a high temperature.' Isandro's glance slid once more to the figure lying on the bed. Her nightdress clung damply to her and the pinpoints of bright red colour stood out livid against the pallor of her skin. 'Nausea…have you been sick?'

Now they decided to acknowledge she was there. 'Mind your own damned business!'

The middle-aged medic laughed and suggested that Mr Montero might like to leave while he had a chat with the patient.

The doctor confirmed that Zoe had a dose of the bug doing the rounds and suggested she take an analgesic for her temperature, get plenty of rest and take lots of fluids.

'Which is what I was doing,' Zoe told Isandro.

'What can I get you?'

'Just go away and leave me alone.'

When the cranky invalid refused point-blank to be nursed or cosseted he did the next best thing—he offered to take the twins off her hands for the rest of the day.

An offer that did not strike him as odd until with the twins in tow he bumped into a school friend of Dana's in a hands-on science exhibition. Emma, who had her youngest in tow, was one of the few mutual friends that he had stayed in contact with after the divorce. Her parting shot of 'I'd really like to meet the woman who has domesticated you!' had stayed with him.

Ridiculous, of course—he hadn't changed in any fundamental way. He could walk away from this relationship at any time. He enjoyed the twins, they amused him…though they were exhausting.

Denial, Isandro, mocked the voice in his head.

The next day Zoe felt tired. Her head ached and things still hurt, but she was well enough to get up, which was just as well as she had promised to go the airport this morning to pick up Chloe, John and Hannah. She also needed to drop the kids off for their science field trip before—oh, God, just thinking about the day ahead made her headache worse.

'Get a wriggle on, you two!' she yelled, pulling open

the front door as Harry vanished to find his rucksack he had left 'somewhere.'

'What the hell do you think you are doing?'

Zoe reacted to the angry voice like a bullet zinging past her ear and spun around to face the tall figure who was striding up the path to the front door. He looked dauntingly angry, but Zoe, refusing to be daunted, pressed a hand to her throbbing head and returned belligerently, 'I might ask you the same thing. I thought you had a meeting in Paris today.'

'It was cancelled.' The lie came smoothly. Intercepting the direction of her gaze, he lifted the hand that held a large bouquet of flowers. 'The gardener heard you were unwell.'

It seemed unnecessary to Isandro to explain that he had told him. 'He says you prefer the flowers that have a scent to the hothouse roses…?'

'I do! How lovely of him,' she exclaimed, taking the fragrant ribbon-tied posy and lifting it to her nose. 'I must thank him.'

'I will pass on your message and you will go back to bed.'

Her chin went up at his dictatorial attitude. 'You can't just waltz in here and order me around. I'm fine and I have to pick up Chloe and co from the airport after I've taken the twins to—'

'Bed!' Isandro thundered just as the postman opened the garden gate.

'Nice morning,' the man said as he handed a pink-faced Zoe her letters.

'Well, thank you for that.' Zoe glared up at Isandro.

Georgie's voice cut across her. 'Isandro's here, Harry, he's taking us to school.'

Mortified, Zoe shook her head. The boundaries of

their relationship did blur on occasion but she was sure they would not stretch to the school run! 'No, no, he's not… Georgie, go—'

'Yes, I am. Go get in the car,' he said, directing this order to the twins, who ran out before Zoe could say a word.

'You're not!'

'I am.' Ignoring her squeal of furious protest, he snatched the car keys that were dangling from her fingers and put them in the pocket of his well-cut trousers. 'Now be a good girl and go back to bed.'

'Do not treat me like a child.' Even if I sound like one.

He looked impatient. 'You are clearly still unwell. You look terrible.' It was not his job to make her better, so why the hell had he taken it on himself to do so?

She gave a twisted smile. 'Thanks.' He must be right otherwise the comment would not have made her feel like crying.

'If you drag yourself out of bed unnecessarily you will only delay your recovery.'

In a perfect world another twenty-four hours would have been nice. 'So now you're a doctor.'

'You are a very bad patient.'

'I need to—'

'Has it not occurred to you that Chloe and her family will not thank you for infecting them with your flu bug?'

Zoe's face fell. 'I hadn't thought of that.'

Hands on her shoulders, he turned her around. 'So go back to bed, and for once in your life, woman, let someone else be in charge.' He broke off at the sound of a car horn. 'That is my car.'

He was being summoned by a pair of kids, and he was responding!

Zoe tried to remember the last time she had felt in charge and gave a small bitter laugh. 'This from the world's biggest control freak!' she muttered as the door closed.

By the time she reached her bed Zoe was too tired to undress. She fell on top of it fully dressed and fell into a deep sleep.

When she woke, the afternoon sun was shining through the window and she wasn't alone. She raised herself up on one elbow and gazed down at the man lying beside her. He too was fully dressed and sound asleep.

Or maybe not.

Isandro opened his heavy-lidded eyes and stretched a hand above his head; he had not slept the previous night but fortunately he survived well on catnaps.

He looked so gorgeous that it hurt; the pain was physical.

She was trailing her fingers lovingly down his cheek when it hit her. 'Chloe!' she yelped, glancing with horror at the time on the digital display of her alarm. 'I thought you were—'

She bit her lip—an assumption she should not have made. He had taken the twins to school because that had been pretty much a fait accompli, but the last thing Isandro wanted was involvement in her domestic life. He just wanted her in bed...for how long?

She pushed away this depressing thought.

'Relax, I have sent a car for them.' He gave a yawn. He was sure that nursing did not involve falling asleep beside your patient, but the last twenty-four hours had taught Isandro that he was not a natural nurse and when

Zoe had thrashed around restlessly and muttered his name in her sleep he had found himself unable not to respond. His physical closeness had seemed to soothe her.

'Their flight arrived on time and they are on their way home.'

'Thank you…I'm really sorry about being a nuisance…'

He reached and placed a hand behind her neck, his fingertips sending little flickers of electricity through her body as they pushed into her hairline.

'You are always a nuisance.' She turned his ordered life into total chaos and yet still he kept coming back for more…?

Zoe struggled to read his expression. 'The twins can be very—'

'I never do anything I do not want to do, *querida*.'

'You can't want to run the twins around and—'

He dragged her face down to his until their noses were touching. 'Right now I want—'

'Do you always get what you want?' she whispered against his warm lips… God, but he smelt incredible.

'I have that reputation.'

'What was that for?' she asked huskily when the long, languid kiss ended.

'Chloe sent her love.'

'Not like that, she didn't.'

His throaty laugh made her grin.

'You shouldn't be kissing me. I'm probably infectious.'

He stroked her cheek. 'I have an excellent immune system. I never get ill.'

You never get in love. She pushed the thought away. Why spoil what she had by wishing for something she never could have? It was hard sometimes.

'Thanks for this morning.'

He shrugged and levered himself into a sitting position before dragging both hands through his sexily ruffled dark hair.

'You should go. The twins will be home soon.' She swung her legs over the side of the bed, not seeing the flicker of annoyance that moved across his taut lean features. 'I really am feeling better now. I needed that sleep.'

After scanning her face, he nodded and got up from the bed. 'I have arranged for Rowena to pick up the twins after their field trip,' he said, rising with fluid grace to his feet. 'And there is something that Mrs Whittaker called a casserole in the fridge. Apparently all you have to do is heat it up.'

'That's so kind of her.'

'I'm flying to Paris in the morning.'

By the time he turned back at the door Zoe had wiped her face clean of the ludicrous disappointment she had felt at his casual disclosure. 'Oh, and Polly is not expecting you in work until Monday.'

As the door closed she picked up the phone. 'Polly—no, that's why I'm ringing. I'm fine—I'll be in work tomorrow.'

Even if it killed her it was too late not to fall in love with Isandro, but she was damned if she was going to let him micro-manage every aspect of her life. She had to make her own decisions, stay independent. He wasn't going to be around for ever.

CHAPTER TEN

INITIALLY IT HAD BEEN scary working in the gallery, but Zoe had soon gained more confidence and now she loved it. Especially since Polly had begun to give her responsibility, which she thrived on.

Today had been a good one. A buyer for an insurance firm had left having purchased several very expensive pastels by a new up-and-coming artist, and there was a spring in her step when Zoe finally locked up the gallery and fastened her jacket against the cold breeze blowing down the street. She was wondering if she'd make the early train when the loud honk of a car horn made her look up.

Pulled up beside the pavement, showing a selfish disregard for the parking restrictions, was a car she recognised. Her heart picked up tempo as she walked towards it, and as she reached it the window on the driver's side rolled down.

'What are you doing here?'

Isandro smiled. He hadn't actually known where he was heading until he had arrived just as she was emerging from the gallery. The sight of her slim, trim figure had, if not lifted his spirits, definitely alleviated the gloom.

'I'm heading home. Do you want a lift?'

The terse delivery made her look more closely at him, her brow furrowing as she studied his face. There was nothing specific, but she could tell that something was wrong.

'That would be good—my feet are killing me,' she admitted.

They had been driving along in total silence for ten minutes before she spoke. 'So what's wrong?'

He flashed her an impatient sideways glance. 'Nothing is wrong... What makes you think anything is wrong?'

'You haven't said a word.'

'Can't a man enjoy a little silence? Do we have to indulge in an endless stream of boring, meaningless drivel?'

She let out a long silent whistle. 'If you're going to speak to me in that tone you can drop me off.'

By way of reply he pressed his foot on the accelerator. 'Don't be so bloody touchy.'

'Me! So are you going to tell me what's wrong?' She gripped the door and closed her eyes as they approached a hairpin bend. 'Or are you going to drive us off the road?'

'I am perfectly in control of this car.'

Despite his reply she was relieved that he did perceptively slow his speed as the powerful car came out of the bend.

'I heard from my father today.' He compressed his sensual lips hard enough to rim them with white in a physical effort to stem the flow of information.

'That's nice.' Clearly it wasn't, and prodding gently was a dangerous strategy but she couldn't think of any other way to get him to open up. It was obvious to her he needed to even if he was too pig-headed to admit it.

Was there some problem between him and his father…? He had mentioned his mother once in past tense,
and as he'd never said anything about his father she had
always assumed that both his parents were dead.

'Nice!' he snarled.

Zoe's confusion and concern grew as her gaze travelled from his white-knuckled hands on the wheel to
his taut profile.

'Sorry, is it bad news?' He couldn't accuse her of
prying when he had introduced the subject…not that he
wouldn't if it suited him, she thought with a wry smile.

'He's invited me to his wedding.' He elaborated, but
as the additional information was in his native Spanish
she was none the wiser.

'I suppose it's hard to see your father moving on.
Has your mother been dead long?' Her blue eyes shone
with sympathy as she looked at him through her lashes.

'Moving on!' His teeth came together with an audible grating sound. 'You think this is my problem?'

'It's only natural, especially if you were close to your
mother—'

'My father moved on so fast the headstone was still
being carved. My father—' He broke off, a nerve in his
taut jaw clenching as he stared with white-faced intensity at the road ahead.

'There's a layby up ahead. Pull over, Isandro,' she
said quietly.

'Why?'

She had wondered why he had chosen the minor
road, a slightly longer route, in preference to the shorter
journey on the motorway. Now she was glad; at least
this road was almost empty.

'Because I don't particularly want to end up a road-
traffic-accident statistic.' For a moment she thought he

was going to ignore her, but to her intense relief at the last moment he swerved into the layby, sending up a shower of gravel.

He turned off the engine, and without a word got out of the car. Leaving the door wide open, he began to pace up and down on the grassy verge of the road.

Zoe didn't follow him. Isandro was a man who needed space, so she let him walk while he fought the devils that drove him. He couldn't not be elegant—the animal grace was an integral part of him, and even vibrating with anger he was riveting to watch.

This was a part of his personality he concealed behind a carefully contrived mask. This was the part of his personality that he liked to deny—the passion and fire—allowing it out only behind closed doors. She knew from experience that driving something underground didn't make it go away; it just consumed you.

Ignoring the fact she had fallen in love with him had not lessened her feelings. It had just meant that when it surfaced... She shivered and wrapped her arms protectively around herself, hugging tight. She wouldn't let it surface.

She stayed silent when he finally slid back into the car.

'What do you think?'

'About what, Isandro?'

'I was twenty-one when my mother died, and already married.'

Zoe had lost her own father when she was a baby and she had no memory of him. Her mother's death remained a strong and sad memory, even though at the end it had been a release.

'My father was a wreck. Then two months after she died, out of the blue he rang and told me he'd met a

wonderful woman who reminded him of my mother.'
His lips curled into a contemptuous smile. 'Turned out
the wonderful woman had a sweet daughter who he
planned to adopt. And yes, the likeness to my mother
was startling. It became obvious pretty quickly to everyone but him that she was a con artist. Friends, colleagues told him...'

'You told him?'

Isandro nodded. 'He told me I was jealous. When
they finally did a flit, he was one step away from bank-
ruptcy. He'd mortgaged my mother's home, sold off her
jewellery, and...' His chest heaved as he struggled to
contain his feelings.

'And now he's met someone else?'

'Apparently.'

'And he's invited you to the wedding?'

She got another nod.

'Do you really want to know what I think?'

'I asked, didn't I?' The belated realisation sent a
wave of shock through his body. One of the reasons
Dana had cited for the breakdown of their marriage
was the fact that, according to her, he never listened to
her, or asked her opinion.

*I need to be needed, Isandro, and you don't need
me—you don't need anyone.*

He had not disputed it, because it had been true...
It still was.

Zoe arched a delicate brow and wondered about the
odd expression on his face. 'That doesn't mean you
won't yell if I say something you don't want to hear.'

He pushed his dark head back into the leather head-
rest and gave a half-smile as he looked at her from under
the dark mesh of his preposterously long eyelashes.

'Since when has that stopped you?'

Zoe was the only woman who ever challenged him. She didn't go out of her way to say what he wanted to hear, and sometimes it seemed to him she took a perverse pleasure from winding him up.

'I think you should go to the wedding and wish your father well.'

He clenched his jaw and swore under his breath.

Zoe didn't let his response throw her. It was pretty much what she had anticipated. 'Well, not going isn't going to stop him. I know he screwed up once, but who doesn't?'

'He didn't just screw up, he—'

'He thought he was in love. That's not a crime.' Though Isandro's expression suggested he thought it should be. 'I'm sure he feels pretty stupid about what happened. Ashamed and embarrassed.'

'I suppose so.' Isandro rubbed his jaw. Had he ever really thought about how his father felt? Would a stronger man have shown more compassion?

He turned his brooding gaze on Zoe. Such uncomfortable thoughts had never come to him before.

'And I expect he knows you're still angry with him.'

'I'm not…' He caught her eyes once more and sighed, dragging a hand through his sable hair until it stood up in tufts around his bronzed face.

'All right, I am angry… How could he take the word of that woman and not his friends, people who he had known for years?'

'You, you mean?'

He shrugged and issued his response through clenched teeth. 'It is not important.'

Zoe felt her heart squeeze in her chest in sympathy. 'It must have been hurtful.'

Isandro looked from the blue eyes brimming with

sympathy to the hand that lay on his arm and thought, What the hell am I doing?

Regretting the outburst that had made him reveal so much of his feelings, and equating it with weakness, he slid his arm from under her hand. He was not a man who shared his problems. His cure for extreme frustration was mind-numbing laps of the pool, or a run that battered body and mind into numbness.

This time he had not sought the pool or donned his running shoes. He had... Why had instinct made him seek out Zoe?

'What was hurtful, as you put it,' he countered in a harsh voice, 'was being forced to put my own life on hold and pull in every favour I had owing in order to stop the firm going under and my father ending up in jail. It wasn't just his money the bitch got. He'd "borrowed" from clients' accounts.'

Zoe watched the shutters go back up, hearing the lack of emotion in his hard voice. She could have screamed in sheer frustration, but instead she put her hand back in her lap, her feelings see-sawing violently between empathy and a strong desire to shake him.

Did he imagine allowing her even a glimpse of the man beneath the mask gave her some sort of special power?

'Don't worry, Isandro, I'd already guessed you're actually human.' Their glances connected and Zoe saw the shock he was not quick enough to hide flicker in the second before his hooded eyelids lowered, leaving her looking at the gleam of his eyes through the mesh of his eyelashes. 'But I won't tell anyone. Your secret is safe with me,' she promised.

His lips tightened, but the faint flush along the angle

of his cheekbones suggested she had made her point. 'I am not in the mood for word games, Zoe.'

'Fine, is this straightforward enough? Your dad made a mistake once…all right, a big mistake,' she conceded in response to his snort. 'That doesn't mean there isn't an outside possibility he actually loves this woman.'

His lip curled contemptuously. 'My father believes in fairy tales.' While he despised the childlike credulity, there had been moments when Isandro almost envied his father.

'Isn't that a good thing? That the awful woman didn't win?' she said softly.

The suggestion caused Isandro to turn his head sharply to look at her, the compassion glowing in her eyes as much as the statement causing him to frown. A nerve jumped spasmodically in his lean cheek. A man was allowed some privacy, yet she continually ignored the 'keep off' signs and crossed the boundaries.

Didn't you invite her in when you offloaded your emotional garbage?

His frown deepened as he pushed away the question and barked, 'How do you figure that one out?'

Watching as she stuck out her chin to a belligerent angle, he felt his anger slipping away to be replaced with an emotion he was less comfortable putting a name to. The woman had more guts than anyone he had ever met.

'If your father had come out of the experience a cynic she would have won, but he hasn't. He hasn't become bitter, cynical and twisted.'

She saw the flicker of an emotion she could not name in his dark eyes before he turned his head away from her. The rain had begun to drum against the window.

'Are you saying I have?'

Instead of responding to the question, she voiced one

that had popped into her head during the conversation. 'Is that why your marriage failed?'

He turned to face her and instead, as she half expected, of telling her to mind her own business, shook his head and repeated the question.

'Is what why my marriage failed?'

Did he lay the blame for his failed marriage at his father's door? It would certainly go a long way to explain why, all these years later, he could not forgive and forget. Common sense told her this was a subject she shouldn't broach but a need to understand this man who had captured her heart was stronger. 'You were forced to concentrate your energy on saving your father and the firm and you didn't have time for your...' Her voice faltered as she stopped and gave a self-conscious shrug. 'It's none of my business. I just...'

'Want to pry and prod.'

Encouraged that he sounded amused, but not antagonistic, she lifted her gaze, studying his face as he replied.

'No, my marriage did not fail because I was busy rebuilding the company. Though I imagine it might have speeded up the process. Simply put, my marriage was never my priority. We married too young—we both wanted different things from life. Marriage requires compromise.' His dark eyes brushed her face. 'I do not do compromise.' He gave a sardonic smile, to which she had no response. 'The end was inevitable.'

Did this clinical analysis hide a broken heart Isandro could not admit to even to himself?

'I was not surprised when Dana left.' One side of his mobile mouth lifted in an ironic half-smile. 'Though I was not expecting her to leave with my best friend,' he conceded.

Unable to control her reaction, Zoe gasped.

Isandro placed a finger under her chin and lifted it. 'The open-mouth look is not so bad on you.' Head tilted a little to one side, he drew back slightly to look at her face, realising as he did so that nothing was a bad look on her.

His eyes darkened as he ran the pad of his thumb down her smooth, downy soft cheek. Inhaling the scent of her warm skin through flared nostrils, he felt the desire that was always close to the surface. Unable to resist the lush softness of her mouth, he bent his head, feeling her sigh as she opened her mouth to deepen the penetration of his tongue, winding her fingers into his hair, pulling him in close.

When he lifted his mouth they stayed that way, her nose pressed to the side of his, her fingers in his hair, their warm breaths mingling.

Reluctant to break physical contact, she slid her hands slowly down over his broad muscular shoulders before crossing them across her stomach in a protective hug. She was still shaking in response to the soul-stripping kiss, the barely leashed violence in his embrace; the simmering hunger still in his eyes made it hard for her to speak, let alone focus.

She felt his hand go to her breasts, cupping them through her clothes, as his other hand skimmed down the side of her face.

She was breathing hard now; her fingers went to his belt.

'If anyone comes…' she said thickly.

He pulled down his jeans and reached across to slide her skirt up her thighs, his fingers sliding up her silky warm skin under the hem of her panties.

'They won't.'

His hard, predatory expression made her shiver inside. Excited and aroused beyond reason or caution, she climbed onto his lap, facing him. His hands moved in a sweeping motion up and down her back and down her buttocks before coming to rest on her hips.

He wanted her so badly that he couldn't breathe; all he could think about was sinking into her. It was crazy and intense.

Zoe reached down to caress his shaft, waiting until he was groaning before she raised herself up and impaled herself on the hard, silky, hot length. Perfectly in tune, they moved together fast and hard in perfect harmony until they both came in a hot, violent flood.

Adjusting her clothes, aware that beside her Isandro was doing the same, she could hardly believe what she had just done. Anyone could have driven by and seen them, and she hadn't cared.

Her body still warm with the flush of desire, she turned to look at him.

'I'm sorry. I didn't know about… It must have been terrible for you.' Dana was a beautiful name. Had she been beautiful? Of course she'd been beautiful.

And he'd loved her… Zoe was shocked by the animosity she felt towards a woman she had never met. Had he been thinking about her while he made love just now?

It took him a few seconds to realise what she was talking about—his ex-wife! They had just made devastating love and she was talking about his ex. He didn't want to talk about Dana; he wanted to talk about where this was going. He wanted to talk about having Zoe in his bed nights.

'I was a hell of a husband. Basically I lived my own life and expected her to take it or leave it. In the end, she left it. I do not blame her. She was lonely and Carl was able to give her the things she wanted.' He held her blue eyes as he said, 'Some men are not meant for marriage.'

The warning was implicit. Wondering uneasily what she'd done to make him feel the need to spell out the obvious, she pulled her hands out from the warmth of his and laughed.

'I suppose there's still time to cancel the engagement notice I sent to the paper. Relax, Isandro, I'm not about to propose.'

And not even in her wildest dreams had she ever imagined Isandro doing so. She had accepted that what they had would never be deep and meaningful for him. What choice did she have? She was taking it one day at a time, enjoying the moments when they were together. Perhaps the knowledge that they would not last gave them a sweet bitterness, but she was determined not to waste a second.

Isandro leaned back in his own seat and turned his head to look at her. 'So you think I should go to my father's wedding?'

'Does it matter what I think?'

'Sometimes an objective view is good.'

Zoe laughed, the sound dredged from somewhere deep inside her bubbling from her lips. She couldn't help herself—objective where Isandro was concerned was something she could never be.

Biting her lip to stem the flow, she responded to his quizzical look with a shrug. 'I thought I was emotional and illogical?'

'You have the occasional lucid moment,' he threw back with a lazy grin.

'So will you go?'

'There is no point in burning my bridges.'

Zoe nodded and lowered her gaze. She had burnt her bridges some time ago. Would she regret it…? She shook her head; she didn't want to think about that now.

She glanced at her watch and was shocked to see how long they had been here. 'I need to pick up the twins. I promised Chloe's mum-in-law I'd pick them up at half past.' It was almost that time now. While she was being utterly selfish she would never let her own selfish desires come ahead of her duty to her sister's children.

'Calm down—it won't take long.'

It didn't. He delivered her to the cottage door only five minutes late. Zoe got out of the car. About to join her, Isandro paused and responded to the bleep of his mobile.

He scanned the screen and with a curse slid it back into his pocket. 'Are you all right getting home alone?'

'Of course.'

'I will see you…' He paused, as if unable to commit himself even to a minor thing like a time, and, nodding curtly, slammed the door and drove off.

CHAPTER ELEVEN

STRUGGLING TO PUSH all thoughts of Isandro from her head, Zoe tapped on the cottage door and walked inside the warm, homely, farmhouse-style kitchen. A second later the impossible was achieved: she wasn't thinking of Isandro.

'Oh, my God!' She dropped to her knees in front of the child seated at the table, her face creased in lines of anxiety as she touched the uninjured side of her nephew's face. 'Harry!'

'It's fine.'

Maud was on her feet, laying a hand on Zoe's shoulder.

'Seriously, it's a lot worse than it looks, dear.'

'How on earth...? Who did this? Has a doctor seen...?'

'The nurse at school cleaned the cut.' Georgie, who had come to stand beside her brother, provided the information to a stunned Zoe.

'But who did this to you, Harry? Why didn't the headmaster inform me?'

'Sit down, dear, you've had a shock.' Maud pushed Zoe down into a chair beside Harry and produced a cup of tea from somewhere. 'The head tried to ring you but you'd already left and your mobile was switched off.'

'He wants to see you tomorrow,' Harry muttered, licking his bruised and swollen lip.

'And I want to see him! I want to know the little thug who—your poor face...'

'It wasn't Adam, it was Harry. He just went for him.'

Zoe turned her head to look at Georgie. 'Harry fighting...?' She shook her head. The image of gentle, sweet Harry brawling was one she simply couldn't accept. Now, if it had been Georgie...

'He was. I saw it.'

'But, Harry, why?'

The little boy shook his head and looked away. It was Georgie who responded.

'It was the things Adam was saying about you and Isandro. I was telling him he was stupid but Harry came in just when Adam called you a bad name and Harry went for him... He was brilliant,' she enthused, turning an admiring look at her twin.

Digesting the information in shock, Zoe recovered enough to knock this on the head. 'It is never brilliant to fight,' she said numbly.

Oh, God, this was her fault!

Of this Zoe had no doubt. The child in question was the son of the attractive vet who had made a play for Isandro at Chloe's party. The woman had gone out of her way ever since to be unpleasant to Zoe, and she had no doubt the kid was only repeating what he had heard at home. Probably everyone was saying the same with various degrees of contempt.

How could she not have considered the possible fallout for the twins when she had embarked on this affair? She had thought that by keeping the affair from them she was protecting them... Some protection, she thought, self-disgust bubbling like acid in her stomach.

She patted Harry's curly head. 'Don't worry, I'll make things right with the headmaster.'

'I told you not to tell, Georgie. Look, she's crying now.'

Zoe gave a watery smile and sniffed. 'No, I'm not crying. And I'm very, very cross with you.'

The kiss she then planted on Harry's head might have given mixed messages, but what mattered was putting this right. And she would. The sooner, the better. No gingerly easing off the plaster—it was a straight in there, hold your breath, grit your teeth and rip it off. The brutal approach might sting a bit at the time but why prolong the agony?

So the analogy was not perfect. No matter what spin she put on it, Zoe knew that this was going to hurt more than losing a few superficial layers of epidermis, but the important thing was not giving herself time for her resolve to weaken and waver.

That had been the theory anyway. But it was after eleven when the doorbell finally rang and by this time Zoe had gone through nail-biting apprehension and nervous pacing and come out the other side.

She let the doorbell ring a second time before she took a deep breath and headed for the hall. I'm totally calm, she told herself, serene even.

Her serenity lasted all the way up to the door and it swung inwards to reveal a tall, lean figure looking sleek and exclusive in a designer suit and, frankly, well out of her league. It hadn't been intended to last… They were a total mismatch outside the bedroom. She took a deep breath and pushed away thoughts of the bedroom and reminded herself all she was doing was hastening the inevitable.

So suck it up, Zoe, you're a grown-up, a parent…

running away or, even worse, running into his arms is not an option.

'Sorry I'm so late...' Drawn irresistibly to her body heat and softness, he began to lean forward, but was forced to draw back when she whisked away and began to walk towards the sitting room. His expression thoughtful, he watched her retreating back. It grew less thoughtful as his heavy-lidded eyes lingered on her rounded bottom. He shook his head to clear it. 'I hope the food isn't spoilt.'

'I didn't make any food.' Her spine stiff with tension, she walked ahead of him into the sitting room, trying desperately to remember her carefully prepared speech. It had vanished into the ether, or at least into some dark dead end of her stressed brain.

He had caught the negative vibes even before she avoided his embrace. Isandro's expression grew contemptuous as he asked himself what point exactly he had been making when he hadn't rung to say he'd be late.

It was simply another example of his increasingly pathetic attempts to pretend that this was all casual. Who was he kidding anyway?

Well, there, he'd admitted it, but this wasn't the time to rush on and make any dramatic declarations. Clearly if he wanted to keep Zoe in his bed and in his life he would have to bend some of his normal rules.

The painful acknowledgement had an aftertaste of relief to it... He felt a little of the tension in his shoulders release. Why on earth had that been so difficult? It wasn't as if he hadn't been bending the bloody rules to breaking point from the moment her blue eyes, sinuous curves and smart mouth appeared in his world.

Life was about to change, and he wasn't infatuated; he was…past infatuation.

Still unwilling to follow this insight through to its conclusion, he closed the door of the sitting room behind him. He should be opening doors. The contemplative furrow in his brow smoothed.

It was not a weakness to accept he wanted more from this relationship than sex, it was a weakness not to accept it.

He clapped a hand to his head. Will you listen to yourself, Isandro? the analytical portion of his brain mocked. This was exactly the reason he didn't go in for all that self-analysis crap. It could drive a man crazy and get him nowhere, especially when he'd not had a full night's sleep for how long…?

Before, he had never spent a full night with a woman out of his own choice. But now the roles were reversed and, back in his own bed, for some reason he just lay awake unable to sleep without her warmth in his arms.

Boyfriend… He tried the description on for size in his head. He'd never actually been anyone's boyfriend. The whole idea seemed…not him.

Her initial impression of intense weariness was more pronounced when he walked into the small living room. It was palpable. It took every ounce of her self-control to fight the compelling urge to rush to him.

He paused, appearing to sense her mood before he tilted his head towards the ceiling and said in a hushed voice, 'The children?'

'Are asleep.'

He expelled a sigh, silenced the narrative in his head and extended his arms. It did not cross his mind for one moment that she would not run into them. Zoe was more responsive to him than any other woman he had

ever met. If his passion for her was unquenchable, so
was hers for him.

She was infatuated.

She's in love.

Zoe stood, her feet glued to the spot, and shook her
head. The effort caused beads of sweat to form on her
upper lip, but she dabbed them with her tongue and
shook her head.

He did not approach her, but instead closed the door
behind him and leaned his broad shoulders against the
wall. He looked very pale. His dark eyes were weirdly
blank, they reminded her of someone in shock.

He cleared his throat. 'Problem?'

She laughed even though she felt like crying. That
was so like Isandro, who never used two words when
one would suffice. Then, gathering her determination
in both hands, she nodded.

'This isn't working.'

He would appreciate brevity, she decided, stifling
an irrational stab of guilt. It wasn't as if Isandro had
invested any emotions in this relationship. It would be
a mistake to imagine that he would feel as though he'd
lost a limb if she vanished from his life.

The highly charged silence stretched and pulsed,
then he laughed and broke the spell.

She cleared her throat. Either he was more all right
with this than she had imagined or he was not taking
her seriously. 'I'm not joking. I think we should agree
to call it a day.'

He stopped laughing. 'You do?'

She nodded, then cleared her throat. She had seen
granite walls more revealing than his expression. The
only things moving were the muscles in his brown

throat as they rippled under the surface of his bronzed skin. 'Yes.'

Isandro closed his eyes, fighting the urge to yell. The children were upstairs sleeping and he could not yell; he had to appear invisible.

Her insistence on maintaining the unrealistic illusion they were nothing but passing acquaintances had not seemed a big ask at the time. It had even seemed like a good idea. However, it had ceased to feel like a good idea some time ago.

There was a certain dark irony to the situation. He had always avoided having his name linked with a woman, and now he was with a woman who seemed ashamed to acknowledge they were sleeping together.

It should have been the ideal situation, but it wasn't.

The previous week he had driven past the school when she was picking up the twins. They had waved and Zoe had pretended not to see him. He had been contemplating leaping out of the car and hauling her into his arms and kissing her in front of the entire damned gossipy village whose opinion seemed to matter so much to her. It wasn't as if they didn't all know they were sleeping together anyway.

But he hadn't, because he wasn't a Neanderthal. Though lately he had seen there were certain advantages in following your baser instincts.

Obviously he did not want to set up house, but neither did he want to be treated like a dirty secret... It was demeaning for any man.

'You need a drink.'

Zoe felt panic as she watched him shrug off his jacket before walking across to the cupboard where she had put the half-drunk bottle of wine he had opened the previous evening.

'I don't drink, remember?' She took a deep breath, lowered her voice from the shrill, unattractive level it had risen to and reminded him, 'We agreed that when this didn't work we would simply call it a day. Look, I know it must be strange because you assumed—actually so did I—that it would be you who ended things.' She gave a sad smile. 'It's nothing personal,' she added earnestly.

He studied her face for any sign of irony but there was none. 'Well, I do want a drink,' he said, pouring the remnants of the bottle into a glass and swallowing the contents without tasting.

'So nothing personal, which of course makes all the difference,' he drawled, setting aside the glass with elaborate care while in his head he saw it smashing to a million pieces as he threw it into the fireplace.

'Please don't be like that,' she begged. 'This is hard.' She bit her trembling lip. She could not afford to lose her focus now, she could not afford to allow him to touch her...

'This is bloody ridiculous,' he contended, thrusting his balled fists into the pockets of his well-cut trousers and glaring at her.

Zoe recognised the cause of his belligerence but she was not in the mood to show much understanding for injured male pride. So maybe he had just been dumped for the first time in his life. There were any number of nubile women who would be gagging to massage his ego.

She, on the other hand, might never fall in love again. This man was her soulmate, and all he could do was sulk while her heart was damned well breaking.

Well, at least he should remember her, though for all the wrong reasons—as the woman who dared to dump him!

'I know you said we could stay on here,' she said formally, 'but that wouldn't be right. I have made alternative arrangements.'

'You have what?' he roared as his smouldering temper sparked into full-blown conflagration. 'Since when is this not working?'

She kept her chin up, not easy when a man who appeared to be ten feet tall was towering over her like some sort of damned volcano. 'Since Harry came home with a black eye and a split lip after brawling with a boy who called me a cheap tart, among other things.'

Isandro took a step back, the air leaving his lungs in one audible, sizzling hiss.

CHAPTER TWELVE

'IS HE ALL RIGHT?'

Mingled with the protective outrage Isandro felt was a surge of pride that the boy had stood up for his aunt; he had protected her honour.

Which was more than he had done. The guilty knowledge that this situation was one of his making scratched away at Isandro's conscience like a nail on a blackboard.

No complications? He had known that was a total impossibility from day one. He had tried extremely hard to tell himself otherwise but he had known that this thing could get very complicated. He had taken refuge in technicalities—Zoe no longer worked for him; he never spent the entire night. He should have seen this coming. But he had wanted her...needed her with a hunger that was totally outside his experience. And in order to satisfy that hunger he had been prepared to break any and all rules.

She nodded, the concern now in his dark eyes making her tear up. 'He will be.'

She rubbed a stray tear with the back of her hand, and the gesture made Isandro's throat tighten.

'This is a small village and people gossip. It was

unrealistic of me not to expect this, and selfish of me not to consider the effect this sort of affair would have on the twins.'

'So you think that nobody in this village has sex outside marriage?'

The sarcasm in his voice brought a flush to her pale cheeks. 'That's not the point.'

'What are you going to do—take a vow of chastity until the twins leave home? No boyfriends? That is your idea of preparing them for the real world?'

'You're not my boyfriend. We don't have a relation-ship—we have sex.'

'Or do you need a ring on your finger? Is that what this is about?'

'Of course not. It's not sex outside marriage, it's sex with you!' she yelled before she remembered the sleep-ing children.

He did not respond to her announcement at all, though his feet-apart stance and stony, tight-lipped si-lence did not exactly convey happiness.

'I don't want to argue.' She gave a weary sigh and looked at him through her lashes, head tilted a little to one side. Seeing the familiar attitude, he felt his anger levels decrease.

'But it's true—you're not my boyfriend. And I didn't mean it to sound the way it did about sex with you, but it is true as well... How can I tell the children that sex within a loving, caring relationship can be a beautiful thing, when I'm having sex with you?' While it might be beautiful for her, she knew that for Isandro it was simply an act of physical release.

If ever she had come close to reading more into his exquisite tenderness and mind-blowing passion, she reminded herself of this: it was just sex for Isandro, for all that he did 'just sex' very well indeed.

He arched a sardonic brow. 'So you are only sleeping with me to pay for the rent.'

The suggestion brought a rosy tinge of anger to her pale cheeks. How dared he act like the injured party?

'Of course I'm not! I'd sleep with you if I had to crawl across a desert to get into your bed.' Her blue eyes held his, shining with passionate fervour, before she dropped her gaze, remembering a few crucial seconds late that she was ending a relationship, not declaring he was her drug of choice…legal but, oh, so addictive.

'But this isn't about what I want.' She inhaled and struggled to clear the haze of desire in her brain. The memory of Harry's bruised little face did the trick better than a bucket of cold water. She squared her slender shoulders and lifted her chin. 'It's what I need to do for the twins. I have to send out the right message and I know full well that even—'

His eyes held a complacent gleam as he added helpfully, 'You would crawl across a desert to sleep with me?'

As if he didn't already know that! Zoe slung him a cross look and sniffed. He wasn't making this any easier.

'A figure of speech,' she muttered, knowing it had been much more than that and hoping he didn't. 'We're really not discussing how great you are in bed.'

'Sex with you is worth the odd desert crossing, too.'

Even above the presence of his painful arousal, Isandro was conscious of a strange heaviness in his chest as he made a conscious effort to capture Zoe's eyes. She seemed determined to look anywhere but at him. The moment of success when he welded his sloe-black eyes on her bright burning blue… The heaviness in his chest bordered unbearable… Yet he felt strangely exhilarated. Was he having a heart attack?

Zoe licked her dry lips and struggled to think past the static buzz of electricity in the room.

'Thanks…' she said, not knowing what else to say, and not hearing the huskiness in her voice above the deafening clamour of her pounding pulses. 'Children can be very cruel.' She gave a loud sniff. 'So you see that I can't continue to live here to be your…mistress.'

'You are not my mistress.'

His offended hauteur in his attitude struck her as weird. 'I live here, and you own the place.'

'You pay rent.'

'A token amount. And the fact is you wouldn't have offered me this place if we hadn't been having sex.'

'I have never paid for sex.'

'We can play table tennis semantics all night, but it won't stop other people seeing me as a kept woman.'

'I don't give a damn what people think.'

'That's not a luxury I can afford, Isandro,' she said sadly. 'It stopped being the day I took on the twins. It's my job to be a good role model for them. Even if they didn't have to contend with the sort of teasing that happened today, what sort message am I sending?'

'Parents do have sex. That is the reality, and you cannot protect them from every hurt along the way. I will have a word with the headmaster.'

She stared at him. 'I can't believe you just said that!' she yelped, dropping into a chair.

'Neither can I,' he admitted honestly.

'You will not have any words with the headmaster.

You will not go near the school… I want the children to know about adult relationships, know that sex should happen within the confines of a loving relationship. Not like…I may have…' Her eyes filled as she trawled her vocabulary for a word that would cover what she had.

'You're overreacting,' he accused.

She thought of Harry's face and shook her head. 'No,' she said. 'I'm not.'

'You want the children to go to school here. Where will you live? I know Polly well enough to know she's probably paying you a pittance.' Polly would have squeezed a stone dry if it put up her profit margins, and Zoe was too self-deprecating to know her own value.

'I'm learning. She's paying me a fair wage and I've already been looking for suitable accom—'

'Looking!' He pounced on the word like a circling tiger looking for a weakness. 'So this thing with the twins is just an excuse? It's not spontaneous. You were already planning—'

She bit her lip. 'I wasn't planning—preparing.'

Sally at the shop had some holiday lets by the canal— a row of terraced cottages that were empty now the season was over. She was willing to let Zoe have one until she sorted herself something more permanent.

'You can't. I won't let you.'

'You can't stop me. It's my choice.'

'And you think it will be so easy, do you, to spend your nights alone in your solitary single bed?'

She reacted to this deliberate cruelty with a display of stubborn defiance. 'The cottage runs to a double. And who says I'll be alone?'

He was out of his chair and beside her, hauling her to her feet, before she had even finished speaking. His warm breath brushed her cheek as he bent in close. 'Have you been preparing for that, too? Have you met someone?'

She closed her eyes, feeling faint, smelling the citrusy scent of the soap he used. Every instinct she possessed was telling her to sink into all his male hardness, but Zoe fought and from somewhere dredged up the strength to put her hands against his chest and push away.

'I thought your speciality was painless break-ups,' she panted as she drew her hair back from her face with a shaky hand. 'Or is that only when you're dictating the timing?'

He didn't respond to the accusation. He was watching her rub her arm where he caught hold of her. He swore and touched her hand lightly; her fingers immediately curled around his. 'Let me see…?'

Zoe shook her head and didn't let go of his finger. The thought of letting go permanently left a great aching hole in her chest.

Would it ever go away?

'It's nothing.'

'The thought of you with another man makes me…' Their eyes connected.

'How could you think there's another man, Isandro?'

'I didn't…I don't. I'm just…' He stopped, let go of her hand and raked his fingers through his hair. 'You can't go, Zoe.'

'Why can't I go?'

'I need you…I love you.' He blinked and looked like a man waking up from a dream. '*Dios*, of course I do. I love you!' he yelled.

She hitched a startled breath and stared up at him. 'Is this your idea of a joke?' she asked him shakily.

'Anything but, *querida*,' he retorted throatily.

'Are you saying this to get me into bed?'

His head reared back as though she had struck him. 'I suppose I deserve that for being so bloody stupid,' he admitted quietly. 'I have been a fool. I was so busy not being a loser like my father that I almost became a loser like me…the biggest loser in the world if I let you walk away from me.'

'You love me?' It still didn't seem real.

'Is that so hard to believe? I can barely stand to have you out of my sight for two seconds. The thought of losing you sent me into a blind panic. I just couldn't admit it, couldn't admit that my fate was no longer in my hands, but that I had put it in yours.' It had taken the prospect of losing her to make him wake up to himself and see what he strongly suspected everyone else already had.

Everyone but Zoe.

He captured her small hands and lifted them to his lips, looking deep into her eyes with an expression that brought tears of joy to them.

'I love you, Isandro.'

'I sort of guessed that.'

She gave a laugh. 'And I thought I was being so subtle.' He pulled her to him and kissed her, a hard, passionate kiss full of promise and love.

'Say it again, Isandro?' she begged huskily.

'I love you, *querida*.' The words that he had been afraid of now came easily; the problem now might be not saying them every second of the day.

'Shall we get married at the hall? Or would you prefer—?'

She drew back her eyes wide. 'Married?'

'Well, how else can I face this headmaster and sort things out for Harry? A boyfriend is not going to have the same pull as a fiancé.'

She blinked, unable to believe this was commitment-phobic Isandro talking. 'You'd do that? Take on the twins?'

'I think the question is more whether they will take me on.'

'Oh, I think they might be OK with it.'

'And you, my love—are you OK with it?'

She smiled and flew into his arms. 'So OK with it, Isandro, so very OK.'

Two months later they attended the wedding of Isandro's father, Raul, in Seville.

It was a lovely wedding, though not, to Zoe's way of thinking, a patch on her own the previous month.

It really pleased her to see Isandro and his father on such good terms. Their little family was growing and soon it would be even bigger.

She had kept the secret to herself two whole days and as the organist struck up the 'Wedding March' she could hold it in no longer. She leaned across and whispered in Isandro's ear.

He frowned at her and mouthed, 'What?'

She whispered again with the same result. Rolling her eyes, she leaned in and yelled, 'I'm pregnant!'

Of course, it coincided with the music stopping and her announcement echoed off the rafters of the church.

'Why do these things keep happening to me? What is wrong with my timing?'

Isandro, his eyes gleaming, bent towards her. 'Your timing is perfect and as far as I'm concerned you can shout it from the rafters every day… I want the world to know I'm the luckiest man alive.'

Zoe, who had never cried at a wedding before, cried at the second one in two months…tears of pure joy.

* * * * *

STILL THE ONE

MICHELLE MAJOR

To Matt, for believing in my dream.

And to Lana and Annie,
for helping me make it come true.

Michelle Major grew up in Ohio but dreamed of living in the mountains. Soon after graduating with a degree in journalism, she pointed her car west and settled in Colorado. Her life and house are filled with one great husband, two beautiful kids, a few furry pets and several well-behaved reptiles. She's grateful to have found her passion writing stories with happy endings. Michelle loves to hear from her readers at www.michellemajor.com.

Chapter One

Lainey Morgan clutched the paper bag, avoiding the corner already stained with grease. "Please," she whispered. "I need this food."

Yanking the sack across the Formica counter, the waitress wagged a finger in Lainey's face. Small sunbursts glinted on the tips of her acrylic nails. "I don't know how it's done where you're from, sweetheart, but around these parts people pay for what they eat."

"I don't have the cash. If you'd let me pay with a credit card—"

When bells above the diner's door jingled, Lainey glanced over her shoulder. At the sight of the man gesturing wildly to a teenage busboy, she inched toward the far wall feeling like she'd been sucker punched. The last thing she needed was to see a familiar face, let alone her ex-fiancé. She knew it had been a mistake to return to her hometown, and just five minutes here proved it.

If possible, ten years had heightened Ethan Daniels's raw appeal. The boy was gone, replaced with a man more suited to the stark desert plains of New Mexico she now called home than this sleepy North Carolina town.

He pointed to the front window and her gaze followed. "No animal should be left in this heat—"

The rush of blood in Lainey's head drowned out his voice.

She needed to get out of the diner. Now.

"You okay, hon?" The waitress had followed her to the end of the counter. "We don't accept plastic for such a small amount. But I guess I can make an exception this once. You look like you could use a decent meal."

She darted a glance at the woman's name tag. "Thank you, Shelly." Adjusting the baseball cap lower, she pushed away the camera around her neck and slid her credit card toward the waitress.

Shelly's voice rang out over the din of the restaurant. "Hey, Doc, what's got you so bothered on a Sunday morning?"

Lainey swallowed hard against the awareness that pricked at her body. Today's agenda did not include puking in front of the weekend rush at Carl's.

"Some fool left their dog roasting in the sun." Heat and frustration rolled off him. "Can I get a cup of water, Shelly? I swear people think two legs and half a brain gives them the right to treat an animal any way they want."

Even angry, Ethan's voice flowed through Lainey like music. The fact he could still affect her after all this time irritated the hell out of her.

"Whose is it?" Shelly asked.

Out of the corner of her eye, Lainey saw a tanned hand settle on the counter. She swallowed hard, praying the floor would swallow her whole.

That prayer, like countless others, went unanswered.

"Can't say." He blew out a breath. "Every canine within

fifty miles has been through the clinic, but I've never seen that mutt."

Lainey scribbled the total plus a hefty tip on the receipt and reached for the bag. The waitress held it tight.

"You know anything about an abandoned dog?"

"She's not abandoned," Lainey muttered. Not yet, she added silently. She gave the bag a hard yank and stumbled when Shelly let go. As an arm reached out to steady her, Lainey looked up into Ethan's dark eyes. Recognition dawned, and with it his gaze filled with anger. Maybe she deserved it, she thought. The way she'd left town ten years ago, why would he show her any kindness now?

"Good lord," he said.

"Nope." Lainey hitched her chin a notch, with the tiny bit of pride she had left. "Just me."

"What are you doing here?"

"My mom—"

"I know about Vera." He ran a hand through thick hair that curled against the collar of his faded Duke T-shirt. "I didn't think you'd come."

"She had a stroke. Of course I came."

"Hold the phone, people." Shelly's heavily lined eyes blinked several times. "Are you…" Glancing at the card before handing it back to Lainey, she said aloud, "Melanie Morgan."

A hush fell over the diner.

Shelly's gaze shifted to Ethan. "She's *the* Lainey Morgan. *Your* Lainey."

A muscle ticked in his jaw. "Not mine," he said. "Just Vera's daughter." A subtle patchwork of lines etched the bronzed skin around his eyes, highlighting their deep chocolate color.

A blush rose to Lainey's cheeks. This was *so* not the way she'd pictured her morning. "I have to get out of here," she said to no one in particular.

"Not so fast, girlie." Shelly leaned across the counter, her twang thicker with every syllable. "Your mama is in a delicate state. She don't need anyone upsetting her."

"I'm here to help," Lainey said through clenched teeth, hating how defensive she sounded.

"Vera Morgan is a saint, I tell you." This from an elderly woman two stools down.

Lainey glanced around the crowded diner. If looks could kill, she'd be a goner a hundred times over. Those angry stares were what had kept her away for so long. And the reason she already regretted returning. Cradling the bag of food against her belly, she raced for the door. To know why people loathed the sight of her didn't make it any easier to stomach.

When the door to Carl's slammed, Ethan blew out a breath. "I need the water to go." He forced an even tone and raised his eyebrows, willing Shelly to remain silent.

She didn't speak. The entire diner was eerily quiet, but the pity in her smile made him grit his teeth. He'd tolerated enough pity for two lifetimes. He'd gone from the town's golden boy to a humiliated laughingstock because of Lainey Morgan and had no intention of repeating that mistake.

He stalked outside where the dog lay under the iron bench. Water sloshed over the side of the cup and dripped down his fingers as she lapped up greedy gulps.

"What are you doing?" Lainey asked behind him. She held a small bowl of water in one hand, balancing the take-out bag in the other arm.

In an instant, her scent surrounded him, different than before—still sweet but with a hint of something he couldn't name. "Shouldn't you be halfway to the county line by now?"

"Not that it matters, but my mother called *me*. Or had Julia call me. I'm not running away."

"We'll see how long that lasts."

"She needs help—"

"I've worked with Vera a long time. I know what she needs." He paused then said, "It's been tough, between the stroke and rehabilitation. She's not used to doing what other people tell her."

"That may be the understatement of the century." She sighed, a small, sad sound.

He pushed his fingers into the thick fur around the dog's neck then looked at Lainey. "No collar," he muttered. "What idiot…"

She crossed and uncrossed her arms over her chest, avoiding his gaze. Finally she reached out and smoothed the hair on top of the animal's head. "I'm the idiot."

Her voice was so quiet he wasn't sure he'd heard right.

"This is my dog. Sort of. Not really." A wave of pink stained her cheeks.

"Your dog?" He looked back and forth between the two. The dog pushed against Lainey's hand as she halfheartedly scratched behind its ears.

"Her name's Pita. For now."

"And you left her in the sun?" He grabbed the blue rope tied to the bench's armrest and worked his fingers against the knot. "Didn't you learn anything from your dad?"

She took a step back as if he'd struck her. Regret flashed through her eyes before they turned steely cold. "I was getting a hamburger for the dog at the diner and her water dish from my car. I'd have been here ten minutes ago if the waitress hadn't insisted I pay cash."

Ethan glanced at the paper bag Lainey still held. "Plus you're feeding her greasy table food. Nice."

Her finger stabbed into his chest. "Excuse me, Dr. Doolittle, but I ran out of dog food and there was nothing off the backwoods highway on my way in this morning." She rolled her eyes. "In case you weren't aware, Piggly Wiggly doesn't open for another hour, and I need to get to the hospital."

She whirled away. Tugging hard on the dog's leash, she stomped toward an ancient Land Cruiser parked near the curb.

He touched her arm but she shrugged him off.

"Lainey, wait..."

She spun back around and shook her finger in his face.

"One more thing before you send the Humane Society after me. I said this dog was *sort of* mine. She's been hanging around my house for a couple weeks. I posted reward signs all over the neighborhood but strays are pretty much the official dog of New Mexico."

She continued wagging the finger and moving toward him until he was flattened against the diner's brick exterior. "She stowed away in the back of my truck—not a peep until the Oklahoma state line. Too late to turn around."

Pausing for a breath, she bit down on her lower lip. Ethan's heart skipped a beat.

Her voice softened and she looked at the dog. "Believe me, Ethan, I am *well* aware I can't even be a decent dog mom."

He didn't understand the sorrow that clouded her gaze. He'd bet the farm it had nothing to do with Pita, who gazed at her with the sort of unabashed adoration only dogs and teenage boys could manage. "I didn't say—"

She flicked her hand. "I've been driving two solid days. I'm going to the hospital and taking the dog with me. If you think I'm that bad, find a good home for her. For now, I'm all she's got."

She stared at him with a mix of defiance and wariness, as if she expected him to challenge her right to the dog.

A breeze kicked up, and she pushed away a curl that escaped her ball cap. Even her face had changed. The soft roundness of youth had given way to high, defined cheekbones and an angled jaw that made her beautiful but not at all the girl he once knew. Her eyes were the same. A color green that turned stormy gray when she was riled up. The same impossibly long lashes.

Memories flooded his mind, almost drowning him with their intensity.

Maybe he'd overreacted about the dog. So what? She wasn't going to make him feel like a jerk. He wasn't the jerk here.

Despite his mistakes, he'd tried to do the right thing. He'd stepped up to marry her, to give her the family he knew she'd wanted. She was the one who'd left him standing at the altar in front of God and most of the damned county. He'd learned his lesson about putting himself out there. About caring too much. Whatever homecoming Lainey got in Brevia, she deserved.

"Good luck, then." He tipped his head and walked past, not trusting himself to speak again. He had to get a hold of himself fast, or this was going to be one long summer.

Lainey didn't watch him go. She didn't need another view of the way the faded jeans he wore hugged his perfect butt. Seeing him bend over the dog had seared that particular image into her mind.

Not that she'd ever truly forgotten.

She bent forward and fiddled with Pita's rope for several beats before glancing over her shoulder. An older couple walked toward her along the sidewalk; otherwise, the street was empty.

Balancing the bag of food on one hip, she opened the back hatch of her SUV. Pita jumped up and plopped onto the navy canvas dog bed Lainey had bought at a pet store outside Memphis.

The dog whined as Lainey opened the paper sack and pulled out two hamburgers, breaking them into pieces over a plastic food dish.

"Look at the mess you've gotten me into." Lainey's fingers trembled as she unscrewed a bottle cap and poured water into another bowl.

When Pita finished the food and water, Lainey piled the two dishes into a corner of the cargo space and closed the hatch. By the time she climbed behind the steering wheel, the dog waited for her, perched on the passenger seat.

"I hope that was worth the trouble." Lainey turned the key and hot air blew from the dash. She sank back against the leather and drew in a ragged breath.

Pita nudged the crook of Lainey's arm.

"Slobber isn't helping." But she reached for the dog, letting the rhythmic petting soothe them both. "Give me a minute to pull it together. I didn't expect…"

What? For the man who broke her heart to be the first person she ran into in Brevia? For the "could have been" chorus to drown out the "for the best" refrain she'd told herself for ten years the very moment she saw him? She shook her head. Enough already. Geez. The dog was not her therapist.

She wasn't strong enough for too many hometown walks down memory lane. From the moment her sister Julia had called three days ago, Lainey hadn't let herself think about anything beyond getting here. Otherwise, she never could have forced her foot onto the gas pedal.

She flipped down the visor and grimaced into the tiny mirror. She'd showered at the dumpy roadside motel, but that was it. She hadn't applied a stitch of makeup or bothered to tame her crazy hair.

Ethan looked better than ever, his body strong and muscular underneath the T-shirt. She'd never been in his league. Why would a decade away change anything?

Pita's tongue flicked her bare arm like a salt lick. "I know. I'm a sweaty mess." Lainey didn't have the energy to push her away. "You act as disgusting as I feel."

Pita barked in response.

Chapter Two

Fifteen minutes later, Lainey pulled into the parking lot of the hospital. As a rule, Lainey avoided hospitals. She brought Pita in with her, needing the distraction and companionship the dog offered. After a quick lecture about the importance of therapy dogs in rehabbing patients and a crisp twenty slipped to the young girl at the desk, she and Pita walked down the narrow hall, the clip of the dog's nails on the linoleum floor the only sound.

The entire building smelled of ammonia and something sweet—like those hard butterscotch candies she'd find buried in her Nana's purse. Lainey climbed the steps to the third floor and stopped at Vera's door. As if sensing something unusual, Pita tugged at her leash. "We're both stuck here," Lainey whispered.

Lainey heard her mother before she saw her. Vera's breath came out in raspy puffs, not quite a snore but in a rhythm that announced sleep. Sunlight filtered through venetian blinds on the other side of the bed.

Lainey approached, her grip tightening on Pita's leash until her nails dug half-moons along the inside of her palm. Vera lay on her back, the left side of her face drooped noticeably and one arm curled at an unnatural angle as it rested on the covers.

Her mother was a force of nature, a whirling dervish who accomplished more before noon than most people did in a week. She looked tiny and frail in the big bed, her skin as pale as the white hospital sheets.

"Oh, Mama." She'd whispered the words but Vera's eyes flew open.

"You came," she began, her voice garbled. Only one side of her mouth moved, and it was an obvious struggle to form the words.

Lainey inched forward, wrapping her fingers around Vera's tightly clenched hand. "I got here as soon as I could." She kissed Vera's sunken cheek, the skin paper-thin against her lips. "Don't talk if it's too hard."

With her good hand, Vera tapped the leash looped across Lainey's palm.

It took her a moment to realize what her mother meant. "I've got a dog. For the moment."

As if on cue, Pita jumped onto the foot of the bed and carefully made her way to Vera's side.

"Pita, off," Lainey said in a harsh whisper.

The dog wasn't huge—blue heeler mixed with more random breeds—but she was no lapdog. Instead of climbing down, she sniffed the covers then curled into a ball, resting her head against Vera's hip.

"Pita, no." But when Lainey pushed at the animal, her mother's good hand swatted at Lainey then settled on Pita's back. She closed her eyes and breathed deeply. The dog sighed and snuggled closer.

Lainey shook her head. Vera's way with animals was legendary. It's what propelled her how-to book on training shelter dogs into a national bestseller. Even Oprah had called for help with a spaniel adopted from a puppy mill raid.

Rescuing and rehabilitating unwanted animals had become her mother's great passion after Lainey's father died. Lainey knew that would be the hardest part of the stroke, putting her work on hold until Vera regained her strength—if she ever did.

They sat in silence as Vera petted Pita. Her voice seemed stronger when she finally spoke, although her speech was still halted. "Good you're here. Need you."

Lainey squeezed her mother's hand. "I'll work on arrangements for your therapy, call the insurance—"

"Adoption fair…"

A trickle of dread rolled down Lainey's spine at the mention of the marquee event the animal shelter hosted each year. "What?"

"So much to do." Vera's eyes fluttered shut and her breath came out in shallow gasps. "I can't…"

Pita whined and Lainey sat up straight. "Mom, calm down. The adoption weekend will be fine. Julia can take over—"

"No." Vera smacked her good hand on the mattress. "Can't do it…baby…need you…"

Lainey reached for the nurse's call button the same moment the door flew open and her sister ran to the far side of the bed. "What did you do?"

"Nothing." Lainey backed up several steps. "She started talking about the adoption fair and went crazy."

Vera prided herself on her "steel magnolia" persona. Her display of fierce emotion complicated things—made her mother seem human. Made Lainey feel responsible.

Julia ran a hand along Vera's arm. "It's okay, Mama. Relax now. I'll explain to her."

Vera's gaze traveled between her two daughters, but Lainey couldn't stop staring at Julia.

Her mouth went dry.

Julia shot her a tentative smile. "You made good time."

"You're pregnant." Lainey's voice came out a frog's croak.

Julia pressed a hand to the mound under her floral sundress. "About seven months now."

"Baby," Vera repeated. "Need you, Lainey."

It was too much. The last time Lainey had been in this hospital, she'd been the pregnant one. Only one floor up was the room where she'd lost her baby. Ethan's baby. Where complications from the miscarriage had changed her life forever. Lainey forced her gaze back to her mother. "What is it you want, Mom?"

Vera looked at Julia, who nodded and turned to Lainey. "Most of the plans for 'Paws for the Cause' are in place. Loose ends need to be tied up, sponsor and press stuff, getting the site ready. I can help, but I'm having issues with preterm labor. If I don't take it easy I'll be on bed rest."

Lainey's mind raced as she tried to absorb Julia's exact meaning. "Why didn't you tell me you were pregnant? Did you think I wouldn't come?"

Julia shook her head. "It wasn't like that. When I called about Mom it had been ages since we'd spoken."

"Ten years." *Not long enough to make this reunion any easier.*

"Right. So it didn't seem like the best time to fill you in on my life, you know?"

Lainey did know, but that didn't lessen her shock. "The shelter event is when?" she asked, trying to focus on the topic at hand.

"September 15."

"That's over a month from now." She paced the room. "I can't stay for six weeks. I have an assignment at the end of the month." The thought of being in one place—in this place—for the entire summer had her stomach clenching.

"I need you," Vera repeated. "We all need you."

Lainey focused her attention on Pita, still resting next to her mother. The dog met her gaze and cocked its head as if to say, "If you bolt, I'm coming, too."

Julia leaned forward across the bed. "Are you okay?"

Lainey was many things, but "okay" didn't top the list. "You were trying for a baby? Mom never said…"

"I wasn't." A tiny crease marred Julia's smooth brow. "Not exactly. I'm kind of putting the cart before the horse, but Jeff and I will get married as soon as his work settles down."

She'd never met Julia's anthropology professor boyfriend, but the reports Vera had insisted on giving her over the past three years hadn't been positive. She knew it wasn't right to pick a fight just so she could channel her mixed-up emotions, but it didn't stop her. "Too busy for a wedding," she answered slowly. "Sure, I get it."

Julia's shoulders stiffened, but to Lainey's shock she didn't come out swinging. "The baby is a surprise, but a welcome one. It just sort of…happened."

Right. Just happened. Since childhood, everything in life had come easy for her sister—friends, grades, their parents' approval. Ethan Daniels falling in love with Julia as Lainey, nursing a wicked crush on him, watched from the shadows. Why should a baby be different?

"I can't blow off my assignment…" she began.

Vera shook her head, the movement jerky. "You stay here. This is for Dad, his memory. Need you, Melanie."

Lainey stared at her mother, wondering how she knew the exact thing to say to cut into Lainey's well-guarded heart. A million excuses ran through her mind. A thousand rationales why she should walk out and not look back.

She knew what it meant to take this on but understood the shame of leaving even better. The last time she'd left Brevia had been her wedding day. When she couldn't bear the thought of marrying a man she knew didn't love her. Of never being able to have the family she'd craved since childhood. Yes, Lainey had run away once. Made a career of circling the globe in search of the perfect photo, the constant travel required of her job helping her to pretend her life had purpose.

Her mother met her gaze. The silence stretched so long Julia finally broke it. "If you can't get the time off, I'm sure I'll be able to—"

"I'll stay."

Lainey wondered what this decision would cost her emotionally. How long it would take her to get her life back on track. But she couldn't say no to Vera. Lainey's relationship with Ethan had torn her family apart, and this might be her only chance to mend fences. She had no choice but to try.

A lopsided smile stretched across her mother's face. She reached out and placed her hand on top of Lainey's. *Here comes the emotion, the gratitude.* She would stay, but she wouldn't let herself get emotionally involved. This was a final payment for past mistakes, she told herself. Nothing more. Lainey ratcheted up her mental defenses at the same time the little girl inside her waited anxiously.

"Get coffee," her mother said. "You look tired. Lots of work now."

Lainey shook her head. So much for the tender reunion.

Wasn't that typical and one heck of a welcome home.

Lainey climbed the back porch steps of her mother's house later that night. Pita sniffed the rosebushes that ran the length of the house.

"You can't imagine how much I don't want to be here."

The dog nudged her nose into Lainey's knee.

"Please don't pee in Vera's garden. She'll kill us both."

She paused at the top, running one hand over the white-washed post. How many times had she come tearing out of the house for the woods around back, hand sliding along the railing so she didn't lose her balance?

Too many to count. She'd felt at peace exploring the thick underbrush of the forest—as much of a loner then as she was now. Things were easier that way, not so much mess.

The sky took on a pinkish cast at twilight. A brief summer storm had blown in a few hours earlier, tempering the blazing heat but sending the humidity so high she could practically see the cloud of thick air that surrounded her.

As a photojournalist, she'd traveled all over the world, from Antarctica to some of the thickest jungles of the Amazon. Nothing overwhelmed her senses like a summer night in North Carolina.

Shaking off nostalgia, she reached for the door. Through the four-pane window she saw a man seated at the old trestle table, his large hands cradling the rounded belly of the woman in front of him: Julia.

Her heart thundered in her chest as memories and long-buried pain rushed in.

Ethan had no way of knowing Lainey had been in love with him since she was barely more than a girl. He'd started dating Julia in high school and they'd been Brevia's perfect couple. Everyone had been shocked when Julia left for New York during Ethan's first year of med school, taking her big dreams and his heart with her.

Devastated, he'd turned to Lainey, who was at the same university campus, as a friend. Very quickly it led to more, and Lainey couldn't resist—being in Ethan's arms made her feel like all her dreams were coming true.

She'd thought it was safe because her sister had ended things and moved on with her life. Only when Lainey had become pregnant a few months later and Julia returned to re-kindle her relationship with Ethan did Lainey see how stupid and selfish she'd been. It didn't matter that Julia and Ethan had been broken up or that Lainey had secretly loved him for years. She should never have given in to her heart.

All hell had broken loose in their family as Ethan chose his duty to Lainey over his history with her sister. Ultimately, Lainey's love story was still doomed.

Julia had left town again after finding out Lainey was pregnant with Ethan's baby. She had no idea what Lainey had lost or the emotional and physical pain she'd suffered.

Lainey thought she'd gotten over the sorrow, but the image in front of her was exactly what she'd imagined for herself. To watch the moment unfold between Julia and Ethan was simply too much. She threw open the door.

Pita scampered over to Ethan, resting her head against his thigh. Lainey narrowed her eyes at the unfaithful mutt.

"Sorry to interrupt…"

"You didn't." Julia moved to the far end of the kitchen. "The baby's active. I wanted Ethan—someone—to feel how hard he kicks." She stepped closer. "You want to try?"

Lainey backed against the doorframe like Julia had pulled a knife on her. "No!" Her hands shook and she crossed her arms over her chest. "Not now. It's been a long day."

"Sure, I understand." Julia looked confused but busied herself with arranging a bowl of apples on the center island. "How was Mom when you left?"

"Sleeping."

"She's happy you're here." Julia laughed without humor. "She hated the idea that I'd try to run the adoption fair and screw it up."

Before Lainey could answer, Ethan's chair scraped on the wood floor. "Do you have bags in the car? I'll bring them in."

"It's unlocked."

As he stepped past her out the back door, she came farther into the kitchen, walking back in time. The walls were painted the same warm yellow she remembered, and a short valance with bright red cherries hung from the bank of windows framing the breakfast nook.

She faced Julia across the large island. "What are you two doing here?" she whispered, glancing over her shoulder.

"I picked up groceries." Julia held up an apple. "Vera's command. Keep you well fed and you'll have more energy to do her bidding." She arched one brow. "Ethan was in the driveway when I got here. Maybe he was waiting for you."

"Doubtful. He ripped my head off this morning at Carl's."

Julia's big eyes widened farther. "You'd seen him before you got to the hospital? That was quick, even for you."

Ouch. The comment stung although she understood the insinuation behind it. Julia had only been gone a couple of months before Lainey and Ethan had begun their brief relationship. But when you'd loved someone forever the way Lainey had loved Ethan, timing didn't matter the same way.

At least it hadn't to her. Now she knew better.

"I never wanted to come back."

Julia put away a gallon of milk and moved a box of Cheerios to the back of the counter. "We're adults now. We can make it work."

Unconvinced, Lainey nodded, willing the words to be true. "Did Mom command you to say that?"

Julia sighed. "Maybe."

Ethan's heavy footfalls sounded on the porch. "Where do you want these?" he asked as he came through the back door carrying two large suitcases.

"In my old room. First one on the left."

"I know which room is yours," he mumbled under his breath.

Right.

She watched him maneuver the luggage through the doorway and down the narrow hall that led to the stairs. Muscles bunched under his T-shirt as he hefted the larger bag over the table in the entry.

Julia studied her with an unreadable expression.

"What?"

Julia raised her hands, palms facing forward. "Nothing at all, Lain-Brain," she said.

"Don't call me that. It was awful when I was ten. Now it's downright rude."

Julia walked around the side of the island. "I'll see you at the hospital in the morning. Visiting hours start at eight."

"You can't leave," Lainey whispered. "Shouldn't you and Ethan walk out together?"

Julia shook her head. "I don't think so. He wasn't lurking around the garage for me."

"Do not go…"

Julia's pace didn't slow. "The question is does the nickname still fit?" she called over her shoulder.

"Julia!"

"Is there anything else I can bring in?"

She whirled at the sound of Ethan's voice. He filled the doorway between the hall and the kitchen, a lock of hair falling across his dark eyes.

Once upon a time, she'd spent hours gazing at him, memorizing every bit of his face. Now she only wanted to forget. She tried to muster the anger she'd felt that morning but couldn't find the energy for it.

"I don't think so." She wrapped her arms tighter around herself. "Just so you know, I got dog food."

"I left a couple bags in the garage, too."

"Excuse me?"

He stepped toward her then stopped and ran one hand through his hair, the same unconscious gesture he'd had since high school. "It's important to Vera that you came. Buying a bag of kibble is easier than giving you grief about what you feed your dog."

She could deal with anger from him, but not kindness. Kindness might melt her frozen heart, and Lainey couldn't risk the heartbreak again. "Like I told you, she's not exactly *my* dog."

When he didn't respond, she walked to the counter to continue unloading groceries. "So if you know of anyone who needs a new pet…"

"How long are you staying?"

Her hands stilled on a bag of mini-carrots. "Mom wants me to run the entire adoption fair."

He nodded. "I figured as much. That weekend means the world to her."

Lainey laughed. "Then it's hard to believe she'd trust it with me. We'll see. I've got a couple assignments I need to reschedule. A summer in Brevia wasn't part of the plan."

He rocked back on his heels. "I saw your feature in *Outside Magazine* on the volcanoes. And the pictures of Everest from *National Geographic*. Amazing."

Never in a million years could Lainey have imagined this conversation. The life of a nomadic photographer was so different than the future she'd planned it was almost comical. But she knew Vera paraded the magazines with her pictorials by anyone who crossed her path.

Even though she shot for a number of national publications, every picture was personal. She put a piece of her soul into each photo and it made her uncomfortable knowing Ethan had seen them. Even stranger that he actually remembered her spreads.

She couldn't put into words the way traveling had saved her, allowed her to escape from her mind and the constant pain of losing her baby and the man she'd loved. She hadn't been able to talk about the tragedy ten years ago, and she certainly wouldn't now. Instead she told him, "I'm lucky to have the job I do."

He watched her for several seconds like he'd forgotten what she'd just said. "That's cool," he answered finally.

What were they talking about? Her work. Right.

"Cool," she repeated. "That's me."

Not quite.

At this moment, she was unbelievably not cool. She felt off balance, not sure how to navigate this new water when she'd vowed to keep an ocean between her and the man standing across the room.

"You've taken Dad's practice to the next level," she said, groping for a topic that wasn't so personal to her. As soon as the words were out, she realized her father's legacy made it worse.

"I'm still grateful for the opportunity your father gave me," Ethan answered, his voice so solemn it made her throat ache. "His reputation is the backbone of the clinic."

This wasn't right either. His words were too serious in the quiet intimacy of the kitchen. Lainey didn't do intimacy anymore. If the past had taught her one thing, it was not to let emotional connections influence her life. That only ended in pain for everyone involved.

She cocked her head to one side, hoping to lighten the mood. "When did you become such a Boy Scout? What happened to badass Ethan Daniels?"

His back stiffened, his molten eyes going icy. "In case you've forgotten, me being a badass tore your family apart. I changed a lot after you left. I changed fast."

"I haven't forgotten anything," she whispered. "What happened wasn't your fault." She didn't realize how much she needed to say those words until they were out.

She'd come to see her miscarriage and the complications that resulted in her infertility as a sign that she was never meant to be a mother. A punishment for reaching for something she couldn't have. The blame sat squarely on her shoulders. She suddenly needed Ethan to understand that. "I was the one—"

"Don't go there." His hand chopped through the air. "I didn't come here to rehash ancient history."

"So why *are* you here?"

The ten-million-dollar question, Ethan thought. He'd been surprised to run into her, but what shocked him more was how quickly his initial anger had disappeared. Because Lainey looked as miserable as he'd felt for so long, and despite how she'd hurt him, he didn't think she deserved that.

He forced himself to remember how she'd run off when he'd put himself on the line for her. He'd had way too much experience with being deserted by the women he loved and had learned the hard way that he couldn't rely on anyone else. He needed to keep his distance from her.

"I'm here for Vera." Best to leave the past where it belonged. For everyone involved.

"Okay." She gave him a tentative smile. The hair on the back of his neck stood on end.

He forced himself to look away, glancing out the window where night had fallen in earnest. The kitchen glowed in comparison, creating a strange yet familiar sense of closeness between them.

Ethan cleared his throat. "I care…" he began but lost his train of thought for a moment as he watched her chest rise when she sucked in a deep breath.

"About?" she prompted, her green eyes turning dark.

"I care…about your mom," he finished, keeping emotion

out of his voice. "We've worked together for a long time. She and your dad were more a family to me than my own crazy father. Vera has always supported me. We're friends, and I hate to see her in the hospital. It's not right."

Lainey jerked her head in agreement but didn't speak so he continued. "I'll do whatever I can to help her. The clinic has a big stake in the adoption fair."

He paused, wondering if his convoluted thoughts made more sense spoken out loud. "This will be easier if things aren't messed up between us. The way I see it, stuff happened. We were kids. It doesn't matter now."

"It doesn't matter," she repeated, as if absorbing each word.

He nodded. "Water under the bridge."

"Yesterday's news," she countered.

He thought about that one for a moment. The glint in her eye told him he was on shaky ground. "Or maybe not."

She pushed herself away from the counter. "You should go now, Ethan."

He took a step closer. "If you need me to..."

"I don't," she said, almost yelling as she backed into the kitchen sink. She closed her eyes for a moment. When she spoke again, her voice was calm, her gaze emotionless. "I don't need anything from you."

Her words poured over his head like a bucket of cold water. He turned away. "I guess some things never change," he called over his shoulder, "because the way I remember it, you never did."

He slammed the door behind him and stalked down the stairs, pausing at the bottom when he heard something clatter against the kitchen wall.

He wanted to charge back up the steps but knew whatever had smashed into the wall had clearly been meant for his head.

She didn't need him, he repeated. How long would it take before he'd finally be clear on that? Ten years ago, he'd offered her everything he had: his heart, his name, the rest of his life. She'd thrown it all back in his face, walked away without even a goodbye.

He headed across the driveway to his truck. Vera told him the universe makes you repeat your mistakes until you get them right. If that was the case, this summer was bound to be the biggest lesson of his life.

Chapter Three

Lainey rapped her fist against the door a second time. "Come on. I know you're in there." She glanced at the Land Cruiser, running her fingers through her tangled mess of hair. Her mother had told her Ethan was staying at the clinic, and she didn't know where else to go.

She turned back when the door opened. Ethan stood in the doorway, the house dark behind him. He wore a pair of faded cargo shorts and nothing else. She blinked, momentarily distracted by his bare chest and the muscles corded along his stomach, disappearing beneath the waistband of his shorts.

If there'd been any doubt, she now knew for certain the boy she remembered was long gone. From the shadow of stubble that covered his jaw to the powerful arms, Ethan's body was one hundred percent man.

He squinted against the morning light peeking through the surrounding trees. "Lainey?" His voice was rough with sleep.

"I need you," she began then realized how stupid she sounded after last night.

A look of disbelief flashed in his eyes before his gaze darkened. "That was quick." He leaned against the doorjamb. "I get it because you're only human and all. But there is no way—"

"Not like that. It's Pita."

He straightened. "What happened?" he asked, all business.

"She didn't eat last night or this morning—" Lainey worked to keep the panic out of her voice. "She threw up then had an accident in the middle of the night. There was blood in it…more this morning." Tears clogged her throat. "She's bleeding, Ethan."

He wrapped his big hands around hers, using his thumbs to pry apart her clenched fists and rub her palms. "It's okay," he said, his gaze never leaving her face. "I'll take a look at her."

"I don't know anything about her, her history or age. I don't even know if she's been fixed." Her voice trembled and he squeezed her hands harder. "She isn't really mine…"

She knew she was overreacting but couldn't stop it. She'd compartmentalized her own pain, avoided any connections that might lead to more hurt all the while telling herself she was okay. The past was in the past. But she wasn't healed emotionally and her irrational fear over the dog made her wonder if she ever would be. "What if she's pregnant and…" Her voice trailed off. "There's a lot of blood."

He drew her into a tight hug. "We'll take care of her."

Lainey wanted to pull away but pressed her cheek into the crook of his neck. His skin was warm, and the hair on his chest tickled her face. He smelled like sleep, soap and the spicy male scent that was intrinsically him—a scent that hadn't changed in ten years.

He kept his hands on her, running his palms along her bare arms, looking deep into her eyes. "Are you okay?"

Lainey wiped the back of her hand across her nose and nodded. "I'm fine," she said around a hiccup.

"Uh-huh." He cocked his head to one side and studied her.

"Really, I am." She didn't want this. Hated feeling so exposed, like he could see into the depths of her soul.

He looked unconvinced. "Let's get to it then."

It wasn't even 7:00 a.m., but Lainey guessed the temperature had already climbed past eighty degrees. Still her skin felt impossibly cold when he let her go. He disappeared into the house for a moment then stepped back onto the porch in a wrinkled polo shirt.

She led him around the SUV. The hatch was already open. The dog lay on a makeshift bed of blankets Lainey had piled into the cargo area.

"Hey there," Ethan cooed. Pita lifted her head in response. Her tail thumped once, but she didn't jump up. After a moment she pressed her face into the towel and whined.

"Hold her still."

Lainey positioned her hands on the side of the dog's head. Pita yelped when Ethan pushed his fingers into her belly. Her large brown eyes found Lainey's.

"It's all right," Lainey whispered. "You are going to be just fine, my sweet pain in the ass."

Ethan's hands paused.

"Pita." She huffed out a breath. "Pain in the ass."

One side of his mouth kicked up as he moved his fingers along the dog's abdomen. "Cute."

Lainey couldn't pin her hopes on this man. His rejection ten years ago had burned so badly she'd sworn never to give herself like that again to anyone. She'd spent a long time getting Ethan out of her system, remaking herself from the lovestruck girl who'd literally fallen at his feet to an independent woman who didn't need anyone—any man—to rescue her.

"What's going on with her? Will she…"

"I need to take X-rays. It feels like there's a blockage. Probably something she ate."

Lainey's fingers flew to her mouth. "Oh, no. The hamburger." She bent forward to kiss the dog's head. "I'm so sorry."

"It wasn't the hamburger." He leveled a serious look at her. "This isn't your fault. Animals eat things they shouldn't. Keeps me in business most weeks. With any luck she'll be back to normal in a day or so."

"So she's not…"

"She's not pregnant, Lainey."

Relief mixed with a fleeting sense of disappointment welled inside her. She tried to keep her expression neutral, but Ethan must have read something because his eyes narrowed and he turned away.

"I'm going to move her to the clinic. Steph comes in at seven. She can help."

"Stephanie Rand?"

"She's my tech," he answered with a nod. "You two hung out in high school, right?"

Lainey swallowed. "Best friends since second grade."

He scooped Pita into his arms. "Let's go then." He strode across the dirt path that led to the main clinic building, carrying Pita like he was cradling a baby.

Lainey stood alone next to the Land Cruiser. Stephanie Rand was another person Lainey hadn't spoken to since she'd hightailed it out of Brevia—one of the few people who knew the full extent of what had happened to Lainey ten years ago. She'd wanted Lainey to tell Ethan everything right away— her parents, too. But Lainey couldn't admit how badly she'd failed them all.

Maybe that was why Lainey had cut ties with Steph when she'd left, hadn't returned her friend's calls or answered emails. Any reminder of the past hurt too much.

Ethan's voice brought her back to the present. "Are you coming?" He waited at the back door of the clinic.

She reached up and slammed shut the SUV's rear hatch. "Yes," she called, and he disappeared inside the building.

Lainey's footsteps crunched on the gravel driveway. She looked around the property that had once belonged to her father's family. The clinic stood where it always had, tucked into a far corner of the lot in a converted farmhouse where her dad had grown up.

To the left stood the original barn that housed any large breed animals under the clinic's care and the All Creatures Great & Small Animal Shelter her mother had founded after her father died.

Guilt stabbed at her chest, the same guilt she always felt when she thought of her dad. She'd been on assignment in a remote section of India when he'd died. She'd missed her chance to say goodbye, lost the opportunity to reconcile with him.

When she'd phoned her mother two days later from Bangladesh, Vera had told her she wasn't needed. "Ethan and Julia are taking care of things" had been her mother's exact words. Lainey had drowned her grief in a bottle of cheap wine, blamed the dull ache in her head on a hangover and flown to Nairobi for a shoot covering that country's dwindling elephant population.

She'd done what she did best: run away from her pain and try to convince herself she was living her perfect life.

Right now her feet itched to scurry to the Land Cruiser. But not even a soul-crushing fear was strong enough to make her desert the dog. She would not inflict the pain of abandonment on another living being, even one of the four-legged variety.

She followed Ethan through the back door of the animal hospital and found him bent over Pita in one of the exam rooms. Lainey crouched near Pita's face. "I'm right here, girl."

Ethan straightened. "Steph's getting the X-ray equipment warmed up. We need to figure out what's causing the blockage. Surgery's an option but a lot riskier. It would be easier if she could get it out on her own."

"She poops like a goose," Lainey murmured to herself.

"Hopefully," Ethan said with a short laugh, "that will work in her favor."

Lainey was too worried to be embarrassed by discussing her dog's potty habits with her ex-fiancé.

Ethan lifted Pita again. "I'll have her back to you in a few minutes."

Lainey sank into the mud-colored vinyl chair that sat against one wall. She closed her eyes but refused to pray. There was a time when she'd spent days on end praying, holed up in her bedroom, her knees hugged in a fetal position. She'd offered prayers, promises, threats—anything so she wouldn't lose the life growing inside her.

In the end, nothing had worked. Lainey had given up on prayer just like everything else.

The door creaked open. She stood, expecting Ethan and Pita. Stephanie Rand stepped into the room. "He'll be a few minutes more," she said. "I wanted to say hi."

"Hey, Steph." Lainey wondered for a moment if she would have recognized her old friend if she passed her on the street. "You look great."

The other woman gave a bark of laughter and finger combed her high bangs. "You always were a bad liar, Lainey." Steph smoothed a hand across the front of her purple scrubs. "I still have twenty pounds to go on my baby weight."

"You have a baby?"

"Three boys. Although Joe Jr.'s eight and the twins turned six last month."

Lainey's eyes widened. "You married Joe Wilkens?" she

asked, picturing Steph's high school boyfriend. "Your last name…"

"He's my ex."

"Sorry."

Stephanie smiled. "There you go again. You told me Joe was a no-good loser thirteen years ago. He split when the twins were eight months."

"That's awful."

"He was a terrible daddy and a worse husband." She flashed a rueful smile. "Too bad I never lost the hots for him. He looked at me and I got pregnant." She slapped her hand against her mouth. "I'm sorry. I didn't mean…"

"It's okay," Lainey said, surprised to find she meant it. She took a deep breath and said, "I've missed you, Steph." She meant that, too, although she hadn't realized it.

Tension seemed to ease from Steph's shoulders. Her smile turned watery. "Me, too."

"Maybe I could meet your boys sometime."

"They'll have you wrapped around their grubby fingers in five seconds flat," Ethan commented as he walked through the open door. He'd changed into a pair of khaki pants and a navy polo shirt with the clinic's name sewn above the pocket.

Stephanie gave him a playful slap on the shoulder. "Not everyone's as big a sucker as Uncle Ethan."

Uncle Ethan. He'd always loved kids, wanted enough for a football team he'd joked with her.

Wanted to try again.

Another layer of the pain she'd buried uncurled in her stomach.

"Lainey?"

She looked up. Ethan and Steph stared at her. "Where's Pita?" she asked.

Ethan's brows furrowed. "I just said she's asleep in one of the kennels. She was a trooper for the X-rays."

"Right." She tucked a loose strand of hair behind her ear. "What did you find?"

He flipped a switch on the metal box hanging on the wall and it lit with an iridescent glow. "There's definitely something in there." He slid the X-ray into place. "I'm not sure… uh…what exactly…"

The two women stepped closer to the bright light.

"Oh, no…" Lainey gasped. She recognized the scalloped edges that were white within the dark area that must have been Pita's stomach.

Steph whistled under her breath. "Wowee, Lain, I wouldn't have pegged you for a thong girl."

Within seconds Lainey's cheeks were as hot as asphalt in the middle of August. "There's no way…" She leaned in inches from the machine. "You can't tell that's a thong."

"Lots of dogs are partial to skivvies." Steph traced the tip of one short nail along the X-ray. "But even twisted like that, there's not enough fabric for regular undies. The question is who are you shopping at Victoria's Secret to impress?"

"Steph!" Lainey and Ethan shouted at once.

Embarrassed beyond belief, Lainey made herself focus on Pita. She hitched her chin and turned to Ethan. "The question is can you get them out? I'm not sure I could take it if this killed her."

"Kinky," Steph muttered.

"Stephanie!" Lainey and Ethan yelled again.

"I'm going to check on the patient," Steph said.

"Good idea." Ethan ran his hands through his hair. "You've got about fifteen minutes until your first appointment."

Ethan nodded and closed the door. He turned to Lainey, trying hard not to think about the unmistakable lace shining in the light of the X-ray machine. "I'm going to give her something that will soften her digestive track, move the object through."

He prided himself on his emotional detachment from his patients, convinced the distance made him a more effective doctor. Maybe it was the fact that he'd gone without his morning caffeine fix. Or his body's haywire reaction to Lainey. He felt punch-drunk with relief that her dog had a good chance at recovering.

"Can I take her home?"

"She needs to stay where we can monitor her. If there's no progress by tonight, I'll schedule her for surgery in the morning."

Her eyes widened. "Surgery?"

"She can't keep your panties…the obstruction needs to come out. It's too dangerous otherwise."

She nodded but looked down.

His insides coiled with frustration. He'd seen too much pain in her eyes—been the cause of most of it—to take any more. As much as he wanted to hate her, he couldn't turn her away.

Steph opened the door. "Edith McIntire and Bubbles are waiting in Exam Two."

Damn. "I'm coming."

"Can I see her?" Lainey's voice was barely a whisper.

"Of course. Leave your number with the front desk. I'll call if anything changes." He forced himself to turn away. "Steph, would you take her to the back?"

"You bet."

As she moved past him, he grabbed Lainey's arm. "I'll take care of her."

Her chin bobbed.

"She's going to be okay," he assured her. "I promise."

She sucked in a breath and recoiled as if he'd slapped her. He realized his mistake, but it was too late to take back the words. The same words he'd whispered to her in a hospital ten summers ago.

Her eyes searched his. "You should have learned by now." Her tone held no reproach, only sadness. "You shouldn't make promises you don't have the power to keep."

She walked out, but her voice pounded like a sledgehammer inside his head. He'd promised her the baby—his child— would be fine. But nothing had gone right that summer. She'd lost the baby, he'd lost her and neither of them had ever been the same.

It took several minutes for his mind to clear enough to officially begin his morning. Even a full load of patients couldn't stop thoughts of Lainey from consuming him. Her stiff shoulders and guarded expression, the sadness in her eyes.

Lainey had left him high and dry, and part of him wanted her punished for it, but he'd also shared in the blame. He'd known about her crush on him and should have never gotten involved with her in the first place. He could have spared them both a world of heartache by just leaving her alone.

The breakup with Julia had been a blow, more to his ego than his heart. They'd outgrown each other long before she'd dumped him. Still, his emotions had become numb, and being with Lainey made him feel so alive. Maybe he should have given her more, told her that he was falling in love with her, but every time he needed someone he ended up hurt.

His own mother had abandoned him and his dad when Ethan was just a kid. He remembered sitting on the bed as she packed her overstuffed suitcase. She'd told him it was better for all of them, but Ethan's father had made it very clear that the blame lay completely on Ethan's narrow shoulders.

He'd been shy, always staying close to his mom, who was the one person who made him feel safe. His boyish need had become too much for his free-spirited mother, his dad told him. She couldn't handle being shackled in that way.

He figured that was why his relationship with Lainey had been so mind-blowing—he'd needed her with an intensity he hadn't felt for years. And despite his trying to hide it, she'd felt it, and the weight of his love proved too much yet again.

He couldn't rewrite the past, but if he could put aside his own pain and resentment and keep his need for her out of the equation—even for a few short weeks—he might have the chance to make amends for shattering both their lives.

Once and for all.

Downtown Brevia looked much the same as Lainey remembered. Redbrick buildings and Victorian-type storefronts with colorful awnings lined the main street. Instead of the pharmacy and family-owned furniture stores she knew growing up, signs for boutique-type clothing and craft retailers welcomed the overflow of tourists from the Smoky Mountains and nearby Asheville.

She wondered absently how many of these new merchants were locals or whether some of them were recent transplants to the small southern town. Hoping for the latter, she reached for the door of the local newspaper, *The Brevia Times*. Vera had wanted her to meet the reporter who'd been the media contact for previous adoption fairs, and as nervous as Lainey was about facing anyone in Brevia, she needed to keep herself occupied and her mind off Pita.

To her surprise, the man who leaned against the desk in the lobby was a familiar face. "Tim?" she asked with pleasure. "I didn't know you worked here."

"Hey there." Tim Reynolds, one of her closest high school friends, stepped forward to hug her. He looked a lot like he had back then, shaggy blond hair and small wire-rimmed glasses. Smart and serious, that was Tim. "I'm the editor of this little paper now. I heard you were coming in today and wanted to make sure you got a warm welcome."

Lainey released a nervous breath. "I thought you were in Atlanta."

He shrugged. "Brevia may not be much of a news hotbed, but it's hard to stay away."

"Tell me about it," Lainey agreed with a sharp laugh.

He didn't let go of her arms. "How are you?"

She tried to shrug out of his grasp, pulling back sharply when he didn't release her right away. "Okay, I guess."

He adjusted his belt over the stomach that was a little large for his slight frame. "It's so good you're back."

"I'm still shocked to be here, but it's only for the summer." She thought about Pita but decided against mentioning her worry over the dog. Tim knew Ethan well—they'd gone to the same university, and although Tim was Lainey's age, his older brother had been Ethan's best friend growing up.

Tim had been at the church on her wedding day. He'd been the one to find Lainey shaking uncontrollably at the back of the sanctuary as she went to leave Ethan the note explaining her decision to leave. Tim hadn't seemed shocked and hadn't tried to argue with her. He'd simply taken the letter with a promise to deliver it and assurance that everything would be all right.

He'd been wrong, but Lainey was still grateful for his unconditional support. Now she appreciated that although he'd been a friend of Ethan's, she saw no judgment in his gaze.

"If you need anything while you're in town, just let me know." He stared at her so intently, Lainey had to look away. "In fact, I'm going to take over coverage of the adoption fair this year."

"Are you sure?" Lainey figured that should make her happy, but instead her stomach flipped uneasily. "Don't you have more important things to do?"

"Nothing is more important than you," he answered.

"Oh." Lainey gave herself a mental shake. She'd been worried about the anger she'd encounter but now was uncomfortable at Tim's friendliness. "I mean, thank you." She took a small step back and patted her large tote. "I brought this year's press kit. Should we take a look?"

He studied her another long moment then nodded. "We'll make a great team, Lainey," he said, gesturing down a long hall. "This way to my office."

Chapter Four

"You wear a thong? Really?"

Lainey leveled a look at her sister. "One—why is that so hard to believe? And two—it's not really the point of the story."

"I know, I know." Julia held up her hands. "I just figured you more the granny panty type."

Lainey didn't answer, unwilling to own up to how right Julia was. About ninety-five percent of the items in her lingerie drawer—if you could call it that—were of the basic cotton variety. Her work schedule didn't leave time for dating. At least that's what she told herself. It was easier than admitting the truth.

She'd dated a few guys casually between assignments in her early twenties. But something had changed. As her friends had begun to marry and start families, she'd drifted away from them.

Her biological clock should have stopped ticking since

she couldn't have children. Since that hadn't happened, she'd taken far-flung assignments, spending more time on the road. It had been great for her career and much easier than watching the people around her build lives she could never have.

Her gaze settled on Julia's round belly. "So where is Jeff?" she asked, changing the subject away from her underpants. It was odd to see Julia back in their hometown but stranger still that she was so pregnant and here alone.

With some effort, Julia hoisted herself out of the chair and paced the length of their mother's small hospital room.

Vera had been taken to one of several daily physical therapy appointments. The doctor would come in after this latest round to discuss her rehabilitation in more detail.

"He's in South America," Julia finally answered. She stood at the window looking out at the hospital's courtyard, her long fingers massaging either side of her lower back. "He had research to do, and we didn't think it was good to spend the whole pregnancy in the mountains of Brazil. He'll be back before my due date."

"But you won't want to settle in Brevia with Jeff's job at the university. Why aren't you at Mom's? Is it because I was coming home?"

Julia shook her head. "I needed my own space. Mom gets a little overbearing, you know? I'm renting an apartment near downtown. Just temporary, of course."

"That makes sense," Lainey agreed, although something in Julia's tone made her wonder if she was getting the whole story.

"There was nothing keeping me in Columbus with him gone," Julia continued. "I can cut hair anywhere."

"You still work? I thought—"

"A couple hours a week. My blood pressure skyrockets if I stand any longer. Val says I can come back after the baby's born." Julia shrugged. "But who knows where Jeff and I will be by then."

Lainey's mouth dropped open. She clamped it shut before Julia turned around. "You're working at The Hair House?"

Julia glanced over her shoulder and smiled. "It's almost as hard to believe as you in a thong."

"I didn't mean…" Lainey's voice trailed off. Val Dupree had owned "The Best Little Hair House in Brevia" since they were kids. She couldn't picture Julia at Val's any more than she could see her sister in Brevia for the long haul.

She took a deep breath. Julia had only been in New York six months before returning to Brevia that summer. She'd wanted Ethan back, but Lainey had already been pregnant. Julia was so angry she'd left town again as soon as Ethan had offered to marry Lainey.

Lainey didn't know if she had the power to fix all the broken pieces in her relationship with her sister. Since she was here for the better part of the summer, she'd give it her best shot. "Val probably realized how lucky she is to have you," she offered, although it sounded weak to her ears.

"Why?" Julia countered. "Because most of her girls think Marie Osmond is the epitome of high style?"

"Among other reasons."

Julia walked to the chair. "Don't blow sunshine," she said with an eye roll. "You got out and I was sucked back in. Mom's already given me the 'you should have stayed in college' lecture. I messed up. Bad."

The ability to disappoint Vera—at least they now had that in common. Lainey felt a twinge of sympathy, an emotion she'd never associated with Julia. "You had some decent modeling jobs at first. Maybe if you'd had more time…"

"Being voted 'prettiest girl' in your country-bumpkin senior class doesn't count in New York."

Lainey shrugged. "All the 'nicest girl' award got me was

the assumption that I'd say yes to anyone who wanted to cheat off me. I should've been voted class doormat. I was always jealous of you in high school. You were popular, prom queen and had the football captain for your boyfriend."

"Until my little sister stole him away. Nice girl. Yeah, right." Julia laughed, but there was no humor in it. "I wish the voters could've seen that move."

"You'd broken up with him," Lainey said through clenched teeth, bristling at the decade-old accusation. Guilt was one thing, but Lainey only let things go as far as they had with Ethan because she thought Julia had moved on.

"We were on a break," Julia fired back.

"Give *me* a break. You ditched him for the big-city modeling agent. Chewed up his heart, spit it out then ground your heel in it for good measure." The idea that Lainey could have stolen Ethan from her sister was ridiculous. "I was there, remember?"

Julia leaned forward. "I remember. And you're right. Ethan and I were over long before you were in the picture. Still, you did the chewing, spitting and grinding."

"No," Lainey whispered, finally ready to admit the truth. "That was my problem. After you left there wasn't enough of his heart for me to hold on to."

Julia inhaled sharply. "Are you joking?" she began. "Do you know how long he waited—"

The door banged open, interrupting her. Vera's wheelchair rolled into the room, pushed by a strapping physical therapist who looked like he'd just left a biker bar. His bald head glimmered in the fluorescent light, the lines around his eyes etched deep as a dried riverbed as he watched Vera, his gaze filled with rapt adoration.

Even pushing sixty and ravaged by the stroke, Vera radiated energy like light from the mother ship to the opposite sex.

Vera glanced between Lainey and Julia. "Can hear you down hall." She spoke slowly to make her pronunciation clear.

"Sorry, Mom," both women choroused.

"Fighting no good. I need you to help." She took a breath, but the next words she spoke were so garbled Lainey couldn't understand them.

"Don't push yourself," the physical therapist said as he helped Vera back into bed.

He turned, flexing a skull tattoo in Lainey's direction. "Your mom made good progress this morning. Her left leg is about seventy-five percent of its normal strength."

"Stupid right leg," Vera mumbled.

"It'll come," the burly man said with surprising softness as he tucked a quilt around her. "Rest now. You earned it."

Vera smiled at him and Lainey saw color creep up his neck. Her mother could wrap any man around her finger.

Lainey noticed a bright sheen of perspiration across her mother's forehead. Vera used every ounce of strength to get better while Lainey bickered with Julia over ancient history. She was here to help, Lainey reminded herself, not stumble down the rocky path to bad memory lane.

She stepped closer and lifted Vera's fingers. She looked at Julia. "I guess we should stick to discussing the adoption event," she whispered.

"And current local gossip," Julia added. "The kind that doesn't involve our family."

Lainey choked out a laugh at that.

Vera squeezed Lainey's hand. Her eyes fluttered open. "More like it," she said and snuggled deeper against the pillows.

Lainey smiled, impressed but not surprised that even in her condition, Vera Morgan could bend her daughters to her will with a few chosen words. She'd honed that skill for years.

"Heard about your dog?" Vera asked, her eyes concerned.

"Nothing yet."

"Ethan is best. He'll do good."

Lainey nodded. She thought about the care Ethan had given Pita and the tenderness he'd shown to her. A slow ache built in her heart. "I stopped by the shelter office after I left the clinic." She needed to regain control.

"You get the box?"

Lainey pointed to a large plastic storage tub in the corner of the room. "Rest for a bit, Mom. Then we'll go through it."

Julia patted Vera's leg. "I need to go."

Vera's left hand clamped around Julia's wrist. "You stay."

Her tone brooked no argument, although Julia gave it her best shot.

"I need to check in with Val, see if I can pick up some hours if my doctor approves."

Vera's hold didn't loosen. "Later."

"Fine." Vera let go of Julia's hand as she stood. "I need to pee first. It feels like this kid has his heel shoved against my bladder."

Lainey blew out a short breath as Julia closed the bathroom door. She felt her mother's eyes on her. "This doesn't change anything."

"You good girl," Vera said, reaching out to her.

Lainey pushed up from the bed. "I don't know what you expect, but me being here isn't going to make the past go away. I can do my penance this summer, but I can't change what happened. What I did." She couldn't change who she was, how the tragedy had changed her. Forever.

"Good girl," Vera repeated.

Her mother used the same tone Lainey did with Pita. She didn't know whether to laugh or cry. She tucked her hair behind her ear. "We'll go through the plans while you rest," she said, but her mother's eyes had already slipped closed.

Lainey smoothed the quilt again and turned for the big box in the corner.

Work on the adoption event kept Lainey occupied the rest of the day. Julia had stayed at the hospital until lunchtime, the two sisters careful not to let the topic stray from animals needing a home.

The call came in around four o'clock. Her hands shook as she stared at the clinic's number on her cell phone.

"Answer it," her mother said.

She brought the phone to her ear, expecting Ethan's voice.

"Lainey?" Stephanie Rand said. "She's okay."

A strangled sob escaped her lips. "Oh, thank God."

Steph continued, "I don't think you want your undies back, but at least they're out."

"Can I come get her?" Lainey spoke around the lump of tears knotting at the back of her throat.

"We'd like to keep her overnight, just to make sure she's back to normal. You can pick her up first thing in the morning."

Lainey made a squeaky sound she hoped passed for a 'yes' and hung up.

She looked at her mother. The deep understanding in Vera's gaze almost sent her over the edge.

"Underpants," she mumbled, her voice wobbly. "How dumb." Stupid to make everything so personal.

"Go home."

"I'm fine."

"Home," her mother said again, pointing at the door.

Lainey knew she should argue, insist on staying, but fatigue settled over her. She leaned in and kissed her mother's cheek. "I'll be back in the morning." She traced the corner of Vera's lopsided mouth.

"Bring polish."

"What?"

Vera wiggled her fingers in the air. "Upstairs bathroom, bottom drawer. Pink polish, 'Touch of Love.'"

Despite her jumbled emotions, Lainey smiled. "We'll have a mini spa day."

Vera fingered Lainey's hair. "Julia can cut for you."

"I like my hair, Mom." She covered her mother's hand with hers and pulled it away, straightening from the bed.

"Too long. Julia helps."

Her back stiffened. "I'll see you tomorrow," she said quickly and turned for the door. Vera never approved of her hair, her clothes, her makeup—or lack thereof.

Why should it be different now?

Her mother had only one definition of beautiful: blond hair, blue-eyed with a Barbie's unrealistic measurements. Vera had epitomized the look in her day, and Julia was the spitting image of their mother.

Lainey was a chip off the Eastern European block of her father's family with her unruly hair and olive skin. At least she'd gotten her mother's button nose, although it looked out of place set between her almond-shaped eyes and too-wide mouth.

She eyed the hospital exit sign like it was the finish line of the Boston Marathon. When the automatic doors slid open, a wave of aggressively humid air hit her square in the face and she slowed. Everything moved at a snail's pace during a Brevia summer.

"No," she told herself as she unlocked the Land Cruiser and slid behind the steering wheel. She took a few deep breaths and pulled out of the parking lot, determined to hold herself in check.

The heat did not own her.

This town would not bully her.

Her mother could not control her any more.

She forced herself on a four-mile run when she got back

to the house. Better to sweat out her emotions than indulge in another pint of Chubby Hubby.

After a long, cool shower, she slipped into a pair of cotton shorts and a black tank top. She'd spent the previous night awake with Pita, so she now began unpacking her clothes into the same dresser that had once held sets of Garanimals outfits. The shadow of the bed's ruffled canopy fell over her like a weight.

The walls seemed to hum with long-ago conversations and emotions. She couldn't watch television without imagining her father asleep in his faded leather recliner and didn't want to soak in the tub that held the smell of her mother's perfume.

She finally got in her car and drove until she saw the lights of Piggly Wiggly. She didn't need groceries but flipped through magazines, studying the layouts and lighting of the photos, until she felt sleepy.

She bought *Cosmopolitan*, *In Style* and a box of dog biscuits. As she put the bag into the cargo area, something cold and wet nudged her thigh. She spun around.

"Pita." Lainey's heart thudded against her rib cage. She dropped to her knees. "Oh, sweetie. How are you? How did you get here?"

Glancing up, she had a brief glimpse of a dark head before Pita's front paws slammed into her chest. She went over backward in a tangle of arms, legs and dog limbs.

"Easy, girl." Ethan's deep voice cut through the quiet. He grabbed Pita's collar and hauled the dog off her.

Lainey lay flat on her back, legs splayed across the asphalt. Ethan loomed over her, fingers curled around the dog's collar. Under the bright parking lot light, one corner of his mouth kicked up and his eyes danced, sending sparks flying in their deep centers.

"I guess she's better," Lainey managed to say, wheezing a

little as she tried to gather her wits. At least she had the good
sense to close her legs.

"Yep," was his only answer.

"How did you find me?"

He shrugged. "I didn't think you'd want to wait until morning, so I was driving out to Vera's when I saw your car. Not
a lot of fancy SUVs in Brevia."

She lifted a hand into the air. "You want to help me up?"

He cocked his head to one side. "I kind of like you down
there. I imagine you groveling for forgiveness at my feet."

"Fine," she mumbled and looked away. She started to drop
her arm, but he released his hold on the dog and grabbed her
wrist. He hauled her to her feet so fast she stumbled forward
into him. It was like falling against the side of a mountain.

She pushed out her breath, not wanting to inhale his scent,
and tried to step away. He held her close.

"I fixed your dog," he said, his voice rough against her
ear. "I guess you owe me an apology *and* a thank you. How
do you want to settle your debt?"

A hundred wicked images flashed across her mind in the
space of a second. A shiver of anticipation traveled the length
of her body, starting at the top of her head and leaving a trail
of goose bumps from the base of her neck to the tips of her
toes. She shoved away from him and crossed her arms over
her chest, suddenly aware that she wasn't wearing a bra.

His eyes gleamed black as night as he stared at her shirt.

She dug in her heels and blurted, "I already apologized. I
left you the letter. Right after…" Her voice faded as a mur-
derous expression crossed his face. "I thought you would…"

"I burned it."

The words slammed into her with the force of a hurricane.
"Did you even read it?"

He looked away for a few beats then jerked his head. "Before I burned it."

Her eyes widened. She'd poured her soul onto those pages, hoping he'd come after her. She'd spent days in that hotel room in Charlotte waiting for him, wanting to start over and make a life together. Hope had faded into uncertainty and finally a despair that had left her curled on the floor of the hotel bathroom, the blood vessels in her eyes broken from crying so hard.

"Do you know what it took for me to tell you those things? You never…"

"Do you know what it took," he shot back, "for me to stand at the front of that church waiting for you? Half the town watched me get dumped on my wedding day."

Her anger melted away as fresh waves of guilt washed over her, filling her lungs until her entire body ached with it. "I didn't dump you," she whispered.

"Pardon me if I don't get the terminology right. What would you call it? Jilted? Screwed over? Left behind?"

Is that what he thought? That by leaving she'd abandoned him? Maybe he couldn't understand how it had hurt her to watch the pity in his eyes as he'd said he'd still marry her. She'd been so grief-stricken and ashamed, she couldn't face him and the letter had seemed her only option.

If he'd burned the letter after what she'd written, she knew without a doubt she'd done the right thing. All these years later there was no comfort in that fact.

"Things happen for a reason," she said, not believing it. Acid rose in her gut as she forced a smile. "The way I see it now, you should have been relieved. Didn't I let you off the biggest hook in history?"

Chapter Five

She had him there, Ethan thought.

Those were the exact words his buddies used when they'd taken him out to the local bar to get hammered after finding the ring and the note on the bathroom sink in the basement of the church that day.

Ethan, drunk off his gourd and egged on by a friend, had burned it in a bonfire out at Stroud's Run Lake. He'd cursed himself and his wicked hangover the next morning when he'd wanted to read her words again. He wasn't about to admit that now.

"You're right," he told her. "I just wish you'd figured it out before I put on the monkey suit."

"I wish a lot of things, Ethan."

The mix of sympathy and sadness in her eyes grabbed at his gut. He didn't want her sympathy. "You did us both a favor, I guess. I was a lousy boyfriend and would've made a worse husband."

"Did you ever come close again?" she asked, then covered her mouth as if she couldn't believe she'd spoken the words. "I'm sorry. It's none of my business."

He managed a smile. "I escaped the hangman's noose once," he said, drawing out his vowels to sound like a typical good ole boy. "It won't catch me again."

"Oh."

Pain flashed in her eyes. He told himself it was better than sympathy. "How about you? Anything serious?"

She blinked several times then shook her head. "I'm away so much for work. It doesn't leave time for a social life."

"You like all the travel?"

The dog jumped into the back of the SUV, and she patted its head, not making eye contact with him. "It's part of the job. Why?"

"I'd always pegged you for the homemaker type. You know, a couple of kids, carpool, cookies baking in the oven—the whole bit."

"Shows how well you knew me."

"Ain't that the truth."

His gaze fell to where her hand rested on Pita, her fingers trembling. Something inside him stilled. Despite his anger, he wanted to reach out, wipe away the sorrow neither of them could leave behind.

Their eyes met and she snatched her hand away. "I should go."

"How's your mama?" he asked, suddenly not wanting to leave her.

She sighed. "We met with the doctor earlier. She's improving, but it's slow. Her speech is better. Hopefully, she'll come home in the next couple of weeks—once her right side improves. She has a lot of therapy in front of her."

"How's she dealing with everything?"

"She's demanding, prickly, hot-tempered and charming the daylights out of everyone at the hospital."

"Typical Vera."

"Exactly."

"It's not the same at the shelter without her."

One side of Lainey's mouth curved. "Nothing ever is."

Darkness descended over the parking lot. A quarter moon shone overhead and a streetlight glowed a lane over. Shadows covered Lainey's face so he couldn't read her expression.

"Call me if anything changes with Pita."

"Thank you. For everything."

He stepped back as she reached up and pulled the hatch down.

"Sure," he said at the same time the door's edge smashed into her head.

Muttering a curse, Lainey pressed her hands to her head. Pita immediately stood, barked once and pushed against Lainey's shoulder, her tail wagging hard.

She sucked in shallow breaths. Ethan pulled her near as he sat on the raised bumper. "Let me take a look." He pried her fingers away. "How bad is it?"

"Not awful, but I might throw up." She laughed but he heard tears in her voice. "You may not want to be so close."

He didn't get up and she didn't move. "Pita, down."

"How did you do that?" she asked as Pita plopped on her belly.

He clicked on the dim light above the cargo space and tilted her head toward it. "Your mom taught me."

"Figures."

"There's a little blood. Do you have a towel?"

She raised her hands into the light. The tips of her fingers showed traces of red. "Maybe some napkins up front."

"Do *not* try to stand."

"It's really not serious," she said softly. "Feels like slamming a door shut on your fingers." But she stayed put on the bumper.

His gaze flicked to the dog. "You. Stay."

He rummaged through the front seat and found a stack of Dunkin' Donuts napkins and a package of wet wipes under a large camera bag.

When he came back around the SUV, Lainey had covered her eyes with the heels of her hands. He tugged on her outstretched fingers until she raised her head.

"This may sting."

"I saw stars for a minute. I doubt—ouch! Hey…"

He dabbed a wet wipe at the scrape. "I told you." He spread her hair so he could have a closer look. He almost didn't notice how silky the strands were as they slipped through his fingers, how the smell of flowers and honey drifted up as he smoothed down her curls. He bent to examine the cut and held his breath.

"It's not bad," he said. "It doesn't need stitches…"

"You do humans now, too?"

"But," he continued as if she hadn't spoken, "you're going to have a goose egg."

Pink colored her cheeks. "Sorry to snap at you. I feel stupid."

He picked up one of her hands and took out another wipe. Gently he cleaned off the tip of each finger. "It's a good idea to move away before closing an overhead door."

She pulled a face. "I got that. Thanks."

He lifted her other hand and rubbed her fingertips. He marveled at the softness of her skin against his calloused palm, how pale her hands were for someone who lived in the southwest. Her fingernails were just this side of long, rounded at the tips but not painted. She'd kept them short when he knew her and usually stained with ink.

"Why are you being nice to me?"

"What?" He looked down to where her fingers were still laced in his.

A self-deprecating smile softened her mouth. "I know you don't want me here. In Brevia. Most of the town hates me for walking away from you, and the rest think I'm an idiot. No one wants me back."

"Your mother…"

"Needs someone to run the show for her event. I'm cheap labor, and I owe her for not being here the last time she needed me."

He squeezed her hands. "She doesn't blame you for your dad's death. You can't either."

"I can blame myself for a whole host of things that may or may not be my fault." Her brows drew down over her eyes. "Don't change the subject. I want to know why you keep rescuing me."

"Maybe I'm just a nice guy."

She stared at him.

"Or not." It burned his stomach to be so close to her. But here he was like a fly unable to resist the lure of the glowing blue light even when it expected the zap.

He didn't know how to answer her when he couldn't understand it himself. He needed to get away, head down to Charlotte and find a willing woman to scratch the itch that had started under his skin the moment he'd seen her in Carl's Diner. That would be the smart thing to do, the easy way out of a situation that could only end badly for both of them.

He tightened his grip on her fingers and drew her closer. He brought his face so close to hers that he could feel her warm breath against his skin. Still he didn't take her.

It's a test, he told himself. He measured his own resolve, his instinct for survival. *Let's see how much willpower I have, what I've learned in the past decade.* He was smarter now and knew enough to protect himself against the pain that

Lainey was bound to cause him. Seconds ticked by, and he wasn't sure if the pounding in his ears was his heart or hers.

I can do this.

I can let her go.

Her tongue snaked out and traced the seam of her lip. An involuntary gesture, he knew. But as soon as he saw the pink tip he was a goner.

What the hell, he thought and leaned in to kiss her. Just one time wouldn't mess him up that bad.

Ten years disappeared in the space of an instant. She might look and sound different, but Lainey Morgan tasted exactly like he remembered.

She tasted like home.

Lainey felt her eyes drift shut as Ethan's mouth brushed hers. She must have knocked her head really hard or this would never happen.

When a cart clattered nearby, the reality of the situation hit her, and she bolted up then grabbed the side of the Land Cruiser as stars exploded behind her eyes.

"Whoa, there." Ethan stood and steadied her.

"What were we thinking?" she said with a gasp, swatting away his arm. She pointed her finger at him. "What were *you* thinking? Anyone could have seen us."

"Don't start poking me again." He wrapped his palm around her finger and lowered her arm. "There are worse things that could happen."

"Not for me. Not in this town. We can't get involved." She paused. "For a lot of reasons."

His mouth thinned into a hard line. "It was a kiss. I didn't ask you to go steady. We're adults now. Things change."

That's where he was wrong. The jumble of emotions bouncing around her stomach sent a clear message that nothing had changed. "I just can't," she whispered.

"Is your head okay?"

She touched one finger to the scratch. "It's fine. No big deal."

"Put some ointment on it when you get home and call me right away if you get a headache or feel dizzy. I mean it. Anything out of the ordinary."

"I'm fine, Ethan," she repeated.

His hand lifted then pulled back. "Good night, Lainey."

She nodded and he turned and stalked across the parking lot to his truck.

She wanted to call after him but knew it wouldn't do any good. She rationalized the way her skin tingled by telling herself she hadn't had a decent date in over a year.

She was...the words desperate and hard up came to mind. Casual relationships were her forte, but it had become easier not to bother.

She wasn't going to bother now either. Not with Ethan. She had enough complications in her life without looking for more.

"I ran into Lainey the other day."

"Hmm."

"Have you seen her? She looks great—grown up in all the right places."

Ethan took a long swig of beer and studied Tim Reynolds over the bottle. He knew Tim and Lainey had been friends in high school, so it didn't surprise Ethan that Tim had seen her. But it still got under his skin to discuss Lainey in that way. "Did you come here to gab or watch the game?"

Dave Reynolds, Ethan's best friend and Tim's older brother, grabbed a third slice of meat lovers from the pizza box on the coffee table. With his cropped hair and stocky build, Dave still looked every bit the defensive lineman he'd been in high school. "Where'd you see her?"

Tim's wary gaze switched from Ethan to Dave. "She came

into the newspaper office. Press stuff for her mama's event. I guess she's helping out since Vera's sick."

Ethan saw Dave's eyebrows lift. "Did you know, E?"

Ethan took the last swallow from his beer and dropped the empty bottle on the table. "Yeah, I knew." He turned his attention back to the Braves.

"So you've seen her?" Tim asked again.

Tim Reynolds was a persistent little twit, Ethan thought. Maybe that's what made him a good newspaper reporter. Although if he was that good he probably wouldn't have left the *Atlanta Journal-Constitution* to become the editor for *The Brevia Times*.

"I've seen her." He reached for another slice of pizza. "Her dog had some problems."

"Was it weird?" Dave asked.

"It ate a pair of underpants." He turned back to the game but realized both men stared at him.

"What?"

Dave shook his head. "Your job is foul. I meant was seeing Lainey weird?"

To Ethan, weird was the green fuzz that grew on leftovers in the back of his fridge. Seeing Lainey had been like free-falling off a cliff—exhilarating, mind-blowing and scary as hell. He liked his life the way he'd arranged it—simple and uncluttered. His friends accused him of caring more about the animals he treated than real people. That worked for Ethan. He wouldn't let Lainey complicate things again.

He took a deep breath to clear his mind. "It was fine."

"I'm going to talk to her for the paper. A success story piece—someone who actually made it out of Brevia and lived to tell the tale." Tim stood and picked up the empty pizza box. "Plus she's hot, huh?"

"Shut up, Tim," Ethan and Dave said in unison.

"What's the big deal? You said it was fine."

Before Ethan could answer, Dave said, "Hey, Tim, grab more beer from the garage, will ya?"

Tim watched Ethan but answered, "Sure thing, bro." He turned and headed through Dave's kitchen.

"Thanks," Ethan said when he'd disappeared.

"Sorry about that. I'm glad he's back home because it makes my mom happy, but sometimes I wonder how we came from the same parents. Tim can be kind of out there, you know?"

"He's okay."

Dave looked skeptical. "You've always been like a second brother to him—especially after you kept an eye on him in college. I still owe you for that. So how long is Lainey going to be in town?"

"The rest of the summer. She's taken over plans for the fundraiser and adoption fair. It's no big deal."

Dave whistled low. "You worked pretty close with Vera on last year's deal. Is it going to be the same with Lainey?"

Ethan thought about her soft lips under his and how sweet her breath had tasted in his mouth.

Nothing was the same with Lainey.

"We'll see," he said with a shrug. "Seriously, it's no big deal."

"This is me, E. I'm the one who found you knee-deep in take-out bags and beer cans a month after she ran off."

"I survived."

"Barely," Dave argued. "Dude, I thought you might go all Unabomber and hide out in the woods for the rest of your life."

"I was young and stupid."

Dave shoved the last bite of pizza crust into his mouth. "At least you're older now," he said around a mouthful.

"Thanks for the vote of confidence."

Tim came into the room holding three beers. "What's going on?"

"Nothing," Ethan and Dave answered at the same time.

"Whatever," Tim mumbled as he handed each of them a bottle.

Ethan knew Tim felt like the third wheel, but right now he didn't care. He was glad for the quiet. Atlanta came to bat at the top of the seventh inning. Ethan sank against the cushions and watched the Braves try to even the score. Framed photos of his friend's two young daughters and wife filled the shelves around the flat screen.

Ten years ago Ethan had imagined this life for himself—a couple of kids and a wife. He'd expected Julia to be the woman in the pictures cradling his kids. That was how it was done in Brevia. Maybe that's why it had been so hard when Julia had taken off to New York City.

Lainey had brought him back to life. He sure hadn't planned on her getting pregnant the first time they'd been together. Hell, he hadn't even planned on being with her. Dating his ex-girlfriend's sister, that was the lowest of the low. But he couldn't help it—everything about Lainey had drawn him in.

She hadn't gotten pregnant on purpose. He'd known it even with the town trying to convince him otherwise. But it wouldn't have mattered. As soon as he'd found out about the baby, he'd been determined to create a better life than the one his messed-up family had given him. He was going to be the kind of father he'd wanted. The kind who took his kid fishing and not to the racetrack. The kind who grilled burgers on the patio while the kids played in the backyard, not one who sat in the darkened living room while the rest of the family tiptoed through the house, trying not to disturb him.

Ethan had never gotten that chance.

After a few rounds at the bar, guys would still slap his back and toast to how he'd dodged the marriage bullet. He'd smile and raise a glass but he never swallowed. He could not bring himself to drink to the absolute worst day of his life.

He stood, setting his still-full bottle on the table. "I've got a long day tomorrow," he said as he stood, wiping his palms against the sides of his cargo shorts.

Dave stretched his arms over his head. "Me, too. I want to get the walls up on the Perry Park building before Vicki gets back."

Dave owned the largest commercial construction company in the county. His business was thriving thanks to the recent influx of residents wanting to escape to the mountains.

"I drove by last week. At this rate you'll be done by end of summer."

"How's your place coming?"

Ethan shrugged. "I'm hoping to be in by Labor Day."

"I should have a couple weekends to help out."

"I'd appreciate that."

"I can help, too," Tim said as he finished another beer.

"Sure, bud."

Tim's eyes narrowed and his voice grew loud. "That crap with the chain saw was not my fault."

"You cut through my front door."

"The damn thing got away from me. Could've happened to anyone."

Ethan smiled. "You bet."

Tim sprang out of the chair and around the coffee table. "You think I can't handle some stupid power tool." He shoved his palms into Ethan's chest. "Are you saying I'm not good enough to build your high and mighty house?"

"Dude." Dave rose from the couch. "Chill."

Ethan crossed his arms and stared at Tim. The other man's cheeks were red with anger, but his eyes didn't quite focus.

"How many beers have you had?" Ethan asked.

Tim used the sleeve of his T-shirt to wipe the side of his mouth. "A few," he mumbled. "Who are you—my mother?"

Ethan tilted his head toward the front door. "Let me drive you home. You can get your car in the morning."

Tim hesitated then glanced at Dave. "Fine." He wobbled to the front door and let himself out without looking back.

"Thanks for taking care of him," Dave said.

"You'd do the same for me. Hell, you did the same for me. I'm not going to lose it like that ever again."

Dave nodded then settled back onto the couch. "You better get out there. I don't want him taking a leak on my shrubs."

Ethan grinned. "See ya later, buddy."

They didn't speak as Ethan drove toward Tim's apartment in the north end of town.

"Sorry I flew off the handle back there," Tim said, breaking the silence as Ethan pulled to a stop at the curb.

"No worries," Ethan answered, tired and ready to crawl into his own bed.

"I've been stressed at work. Maybe I need to let off a little steam."

Ethan let his eyes drift shut. "I know the feeling."

As Tim opened the door of the truck's cab, light flooded the interior.

"Hey, Tim?"

The other man looked over his shoulder. "Yeah?"

"Even stressed-out, don't start something you can't finish. It'll just cause trouble."

Tim's back went rigid, and Ethan saw his knuckles tighten around the door handle. "Sure thing, E. I got it." He climbed out of the truck and slammed the door shut.

Ethan drove away thinking about how his night had gone to hell so fast. After seeing Lainey in the parking lot, he'd wanted a distraction, and watching the game at Dave's had seemed as good as any. Then Tim had opened his big mouth about Lainey and how good she'd looked. Tension knotted in Ethan's stomach at the thought of another guy looking at Lainey, kissing her the way he had.

Do not go there.

He eased his foot off the gas pedal. This time of night, the only thing he'd run into on the dark road leading to the clinic was a random deer, but he didn't want to take chances. He rolled down the window and let the air calm his boiling blood.

How hard could it be to deal with Lainey for the summer? Hell, he might not see her much. Between the clinic and his house he could stay plenty occupied. He'd pawn off most of his responsibilities for the adoption fair to Steph. Then Lainey would be gone and his life would get back to normal.

By the time he started down the long dirt driveway toward the clinic, he felt more in control. More like the practical man he'd worked to become.

He swung the truck in next to the converted trailer where he currently lived. Something near the door caught in the glow of his headlights. He turned on the brights and leaned over the steering wheel to get a better look. Then realized he was looking directly at a woman's shapely backside. A string of expletives exploded from Ethan's mouth as the figure turned.

In the glare of his lights, she shaded her eyes with her forearm. Still, Ethan would have known the halo of curls that cascaded around Lainey's shoulders anywhere.

She was the last person he'd want to see standing on his front porch this late at night.

At least that's what he told himself.

Chapter Six

Cutting the brights, he climbed out of the truck. In the porch light, she looked as much like a deer in headlights as anything that would have crossed his path.

"What are you doing here?" His voice sounded rough in his own ears.

"I didn't…you weren't…" She whirled around to the front step then turned toward him. "Here," she said, pushing a plate into his stomach.

His hands curled around the sides of it, brushing her fingers in the process. She snatched back her hands.

"It's my way of saying thank you," she said, her voice quiet. "For helping Pita. What happened earlier…well, I don't know exactly what happened." She hugged herself and looked away. "But I still want to thank you. So there. I made brownies."

Ethan quirked a brow. "You bake now?"

"They're from a box," she said with a frown then added, "but they're good. I had one on the way over."

"I see that." He reached forward and with one finger flicked a chocolate crumb from her bottom lip.

Big mistake. Just that tiny contact with her made his insides explode like the night sky on the Fourth of July. Once again, all thoughts of being practical drained from his head.

She looked so beautiful standing in front of him, backlit by the hazy glow of the porch light. She wore a pair of cotton shorts and a faded blue tank top. While some women went to great lengths with hair, makeup and fancy clothes, Lainey never needed to try that hard.

To Ethan, she'd always looked best when she was natural— half awake and curled in his arms in the morning or fresh out of the shower, her hair damp. Or like now with a smudge of chocolate on her face, curls flying around her head.

He lifted one long strand. "I used to love your hair."

She smacked at his hand. "Don't do that."

"What?"

"I can't think straight when I'm near you." She blew out a huffy breath. "You're messing with my mind. I just wanted to give you brownies."

He glanced at his watch. "And you *had* to bring them over at eleven o'clock? It couldn't wait for morning?"

She shifted from one foot to the other. "I needed to get out of the house," she said, not meeting his gaze. "It's too quiet without Mom. Weirds me out."

"Do you want to come in for a bit?"

Her eyes widened. "I didn't come here for *that*."

"I wasn't talking about *that*," he said, exasperated. "A cup of coffee, that's all. Trust me, Lainey, I'm happy with my life just the way it is."

She shook her head. "I'm okay. The drive over here calmed me down." Her brows rose as her chin lifted. "Why are you home so late? Hot date?"

He grinned. "Maybe."

"Who's the...uh...lucky girl?"

His smile widened. "Wouldn't you like to know?"

She huffed again and kicked the toe of her shoe into the dirt. "I couldn't care less."

"Yeah, right."

She rolled her eyes and Ethan felt something he didn't want to name unfurl in his stomach. Damn. This is how it had always been with Lainey—too easy. Long conversations late at night, the quick banter back and forth. She made it too easy to remember how much he liked being near her. Too easy to forget how she'd ruined his life long ago. She was only here for the summer before she left again, taking another big chunk of his heart with her if he wasn't careful.

"Well, thanks for the brownies," he said and started to move past her.

She stopped him with her hand on his forearm, her palm cool against his skin.

"Ethan?" Her voice was hesitant, barely a whisper.

"Yeah?"

"Do you think I can handle everything for the adoption event?"

"What do you mean—"

"I've disappointed my mom so many times. I'm a regular expert at not living up to her expectations. I don't want to mess this up, too."

"Listen to me, Lainey, because I'm only going to say this once. You'll do great."

"Will you help me? I know it's awkward, but I've gone through the files from last year. You worked on every piece. I'm not sure I can do it without you."

He could tell how much it took out of her to ask for help. It was not her nature. Lainey was a giver. That's how it had been for him. When they'd been together all those years ago, he didn't have anything to offer her. But she hadn't cared. She'd saved his miserable life and he'd ruined hers. He couldn't turn his back on her.

"Of course I'll help." He dragged in a breath through his mouth, trying to clear his lungs.

"Thank you," she whispered. She pulled her hand away and stepped back. "Mama's using the clinic conference room as her base of operations, right?"

"Yep."

"I'll be there in the morning. Good night, Ethan."

He waited until she was safely in the SUV before he turned for his door. As far as he knew, no one in Brevia locked up their houses at night. He let himself into the darkened trailer and without turning on the lights, set the plate on the coffee table and sank onto the couch. Josie, the clinic's resident cat, nudged her head against his arm.

He owed Lainey his help, he reasoned. He'd played a big part in the decisions that led to her estrangement from her mother. He knew Vera, like most of the town, had condemned Lainey for going after him. But their attraction had been mutual. She may have had a crush on him before he noticed her, but she never would've acted on her feelings if he hadn't made the first move.

Ten years later, most of the longtime residents of Brevia still blamed her for breaking up small town "Ken & Barbie." Blamed her for that and so much more. His relationship with Julia had been nothing compared to what he'd felt for Lainey. Everyone wanted to help Vera, but Ethan could make it easier by giving Lainey his public support.

He wondered what it would cost him in the end.

* * *

Lainey recognized the feeling of butterflies in her stomach. Each new assignment, whether photographing elephants on their annual migration across the Gobi Desert or grizzlies at the spring salmon runs in Alaska, brought her the same familiar flutter. Would she be good enough, the little wings flapping in her midsection teased? Would she get the right shot?

Invariably, the worry subsided once she picked up her camera. Looking at the world through the lens remained her personal brand of meditation. She saw her surroundings in ways the naked eye missed. Just the feel of the camera's weight in her hands, her finger on the shutter, relaxed her. Made her feel safe.

This morning Lainey didn't have a camera to hide behind. As she walked through the clinic's entrance, her equipment offered no protection from the stares and whispers sure to come.

She felt better after talking with Ethan last night, which set her off balance in another way. Baking brownies was one thing, but what had possessed her to deliver them? In the end he'd promised to support her, a fact that gave her more confidence today.

Several people sat in the waiting area as she stepped toward the reception desk.

"Is Dr. Daniels around?" she asked the young woman seated at a computer on the other side of a large counter.

"He got called out to the Johnsons' farm," the girl said, her eyes on the computer screen. "An emergency with a mare. Is there someone else who can help?" She pushed a few keys on the computer and looked up.

Lainey saw recognition dawn in the girl's eyes. Her small shoulders stiffened and her eyes narrowed. "What do you want with him anyway?" she asked, suspicion laced in her tone.

Lainey's hackles rose and she took a deep breath. "I don't think we've met." She extended a hand. "I'm Lainey Morgan, Vera's daughter."

The girl reluctantly shook Lainey's hand. "I know who you are."

The butterflies in Lainey's stomach multiplied into a full army. *Get a grip,* she told herself. This girl's censure was the tip of the iceberg. She expected much worse from the committee members in this morning's meeting. She'd managed to hide out at the hospital or her mother's house since she'd been in town, only venturing to the grocery store under the cover of darkness. Today she'd finally be exposed to the light and the bright glare of angry feelings that came with it.

Squaring her shoulders, she offered the girl her brightest smile. "What's your name?"

"Brandy Lott. I'm a temp because the regular receptionist has to do office management stuff over at the shelter. We're short-staffed with Vera gone."

"I'm sure everyone is grateful to have you here."

A hesitant look lit Brandy's kohl-rimmed blue eyes. "I don't know. The phones get really busy. I've only been here a week. I still drop lots of calls."

"Happens to everyone."

Brandy looked hopeful. "You really think so?"

Lainey nodded. She didn't think so but was determined to make an ally of this girl. "We're in the same boat. I've got to plan my mom's big event, and I'm totally at a loss. Since you're on the front lines, I'd appreciate any suggestions you have." She paused. "And if there's anything you need, I'm happy to help."

The girl peered over the top of the tall counter toward the lobby. "Actually," she said in a hushed tone, "I had a Big Gulp on the way in. Could you watch the phones while I run to the bathroom?"

Lainey hadn't been behind the reception desk since she'd graduated from high school. "I guess," she answered slowly.

Brandy grinned. "Thanks. I'll be quick as a lick."

Lainey eased around the side of the counter and through the door that led to the front office.

Brandy stood and pointed at a complex-looking phone system. "Just hit the button when the light blinks."

Lainey didn't have time to ask what she should say to the caller. Brandy disappeared through the doorway that led to the back of the clinic.

Within seconds, a green light next to the 'one' button began to blink and a muted ring broke the quiet.

With a groan, Lainey picked up the receiver and pressed the flashing light. "All Creatures Animal Hospital. May I help you?" The phone system may have changed but the words rolled off her tongue easily. She'd answered the clinic's phone every summer and Saturday mornings for most of her teen years.

She forced her attention back to the task at hand and realized the other end of the phone remained silent.

"Hello? May I help you?"

"Lainey?"

Unexpected heat rushed to her cheeks. "Ethan?"

"Lainey," he repeated, his voice rough. "Why are you answering the phone?"

"I got here early. Brandy's in the bathroom."

She heard a muttered curse through the line. "The meeting isn't for another forty-five minutes."

"I know." She sighed. "I wanted time to get my bearings and prepare before the old battle-axes show up."

He laughed, and her resident butterflies took flight again for different reasons.

"Are you nervous?"

"Of course not," she said quickly.

Silence.

"Maybe a little," she amended. "You're going to be here, right?"

"That's why I'm calling." His voice was quiet. "The situation with the mare is more serious than I thought."

"Oh." Her stomach sank.

"You'll do great. Remember the old trick—imagine Mrs. Vassler and her cronies in their skivvies. It's the great equalizer."

Lainey smiled a bit. It was the same advice he'd given her ten years ago before an oral presentation she'd had in one of her art history courses. Back then all she'd wanted was to get through her classes so she could spend time with Ethan. She could not have cared less about how she did on a speech.

This morning mattered. This time she cared about getting it right.

She glanced at the desk. "I need to go. Lines two and three are flashing."

"Be sure to—"

She didn't hear what he said as she slammed down the receiver and picked it up again. She put line two on hold just as an older man leaned over the counter.

"I need to check in," he told her.

She held up one finger then pressed line two, putting them on hold, as well. She looked over her shoulder to see Brandy at the edge of the reception area, Stephanie Rand at her elbow.

"Help," she mouthed silently.

She stood and stepped away as the two women hustled forward. Brandy picked up the phone as Steph spoke to the man across the counter.

A moment later Steph turned and jerked her head toward the back of the clinic. Lainey followed her into the hall.

"What are you doing out there?" Steph whispered.

Lainey blew out a breath. "I have no idea. Brandy had to go to the bathroom," she said by way of an explanation.

"This place isn't a game, Lainey," Steph answered, her voice tight. "It's a much bigger operation than when your dad ran it."

"I'm sorry." Lainey pressed against the wall and put her hands on her knees, letting her head loll forward. Adrenaline and nerves pumped through her body, making her tingle. "I was trying to be nice. To make friends. It would be great if one person in this town didn't turn up their nose the minute I walked into the room."

Steph's tone softened. "Does that really happen?"

Lainey nodded, finding it difficult to speak.

"I don't think it's personal."

Lainey glanced up. "Are you kidding? How is that possible?"

"Everyone wants to protect Ethan. He's a huge part of this community. As much as your dad was back in the day."

Lainey straightened. "It's not a big deal, I guess. I want to have a look around before the meeting."

"I'll introduce you to the staff. Most of them are new to the area."

"So they won't hate me on sight?"

"You're kind of a legend around here."

Lainey groaned.

"Let's see what we can do to make you some new friends."

A half hour later, Lainey stood in an empty conference room, her mind reeling. Growing up, she'd spent so much time at the clinic, but what she'd seen today bore little resemblance to the animal hospital she remembered. She'd met the three other vets who worked with Ethan as well as several technicians.

Everyone had been friendly, and the energy that radiated from the entire building went beyond positive. Even the animals kenneled in back seemed okay with being in their cages. Two different labs with various computers and high-tech surgical equipment took up most of the building's rear. Each of the six exam rooms, including the one she'd been in with Pita, were enlarged and renovated from her days at the clinic.

"Here you go."

Lainey turned as Steph walked into the room and handed her a cup of steaming coffee.

"Thanks." She cradled the mug between her palms and took a sip. "I can't get over how things have changed. I knew the clinic had expanded and about the addition of the shelter. Seeing it firsthand..." She shook her head. "It's amazing."

Steph nodded. "Ethan had a vision."

Lainey propped one hip on the conference table. "I never understood why he stayed. The whole reason he switched from med school to the vet program was because of the baby. Less time in school and my parents could help. Once that burden lifted I figured he'd be long gone."

"He felt a big responsibility to your mom and dad."

"What?" Lainey's brows furrowed. "Why?"

Steph held up her hands, palms open at Lainey's outraged response. "I could be wrong. He was pretty much the reason both you and your sister took off for good that summer. You always loved it here, and Julia might have stuck around after she came back from the big city. Who knows? But I think he wanted to make amends for breaking up your family."

Lainey brought her fingers to her lips. "So Juls and I moved on, and he got stuck paying for all our mistakes."

"I don't think he felt stuck. Not everyone was as hell-bent on getting away from Brevia as you and your sister."

Lainey gave a sad laugh. "All I ever wanted was to spend my life here. I never imagined leaving until the moment I pulled out of the church parking lot."

"You never looked back," Steph countered.

"At what? All my dreams died that day at the hospital." She swallowed against the emotions rising in her throat.

"What about new dreams?"

Lainey forced herself to inhale. "Mine don't involve this town."

"Or Ethan?"

Lainey straightened the pile of papers that sat on the table next to her. "I need to pull it together before this meeting," she said as she stood, reaching into her purse for a tissue to wipe her running nose.

Steph's arms wrapped around her. She turned and hugged her old friend.

"I'm glad you're here."

"You may be the only one."

Steph gave Lainey's arms a tight squeeze. "A bunch of us are going to Cowboys Saturday night. Why don't you come?"

Lainey remembered the neon sign outside the bar she'd seen on her way into town. "Cowboys. Seriously?"

"There's line dancing." Steph grinned. "You own boots?"

"I actually *live* in the Southwest. Of course I own boots."

"Eight-thirty then."

Lainey grimaced. "Steph, I don't—"

A high-pitched "hello" interrupted her.

Five women ranging in age from thirty-five to a hundred and twenty filed in.

"That's my cue," Steph said quickly and walked out of the room, nodding greetings as she left.

"Good morning, Melanie," one of the older women said as she stepped forward.

"How are you, Mrs. Vassler?"

Ida Vassler looked at the group taking seats around the room and then to Lainey again. She'd been a fixture in Brevia since Lainey could remember. Her husband had owned the car dealership out on Route Four, and according to local legend, had left Ida more money than God when he'd died. Money she'd used to wield control over a variety of civic activities—Vera's adoption fair included.

"Frankly, my dear," Ida said in a stage whisper loud enough for the whole room to hear, "I'm a little worried."

Lainey took a step back and did a mental eye roll. "Really?"

"I'm not sure you have what it takes to make your mother's event a success."

"Well...I..." Lainey began but the older woman kept speaking.

"In these tough times, I don't know if I want to put my money behind an event that isn't going to be top-notch." Ida patted Lainey's hand and gave her an insincere smile. "You understand I'm sure."

For the briefest moment, Lainey wanted to run from the room, flee this one-horse town like she'd done a decade earlier. But she wasn't that scared young girl anymore and no one, especially not a leathery old biddy, could scare her off.

Heat flooded her cheeks, but she returned Ida's smile. "It's sad that you'd let your animosity toward me get in the way of helping animals who need it." She squeezed Ida's ample arm. "Mama will be so disappointed."

A buzz broke out in the room. Ida's heavily rouged cheeks turned an unfortunate shade of purple.

"Why you little—"

"I hope I'm not late," a low voice rang out through the commotion.

Ethan's large body filled the doorway. He met her heated gaze and nodded slightly. Relief shot through her.

He lifted a flat box into the air. "I picked up the muffins you asked for, Lainey."

"Thanks." She hadn't said a thing about muffins.

He walked forward, greeting each of the women in the

room by name, the epitome of aw-shucks Southern charm. His accent sounded thicker than normal, his vowels a slow caress.

"I'm not sure I can eat even one." Reaching around Ida, he enveloped Lainey in a quick, friendly hug. "I had a couple of your brownies this morning. They've pretty much spoiled me for anything else." He winked at her. "Was that your mama's recipe?"

"Betty Crocker," Lainey whispered.

He threw his head back and laughed—a deep, rich sound that made her think of warm syrup sliding over a stack of pancakes. Lainey gazed around the room at the starry-eyed looks of every single woman.

Ida's eyes widened as she chewed on the inside of her cheek.

"Did I miss anything?" Ethan asked as he stepped away.

Her skin tingled from where she'd pressed against him, but Lainey forced a relaxed tone. "Mrs. Vassler may not sponsor the adoption fair. Tough economic times, you know."

"Right." Ethan nodded. "How's that guesthouse coming on your property, Miz Vassler?"

"Just fine, Ethan." Ida spoke through clenched teeth.

Lainey made her smile sympathetic. "Luckily, I spoke to a friend of mine at *National Geographic* last night. They want to do a feature on the event for their kids' magazine. I'm sure I could get them to offer a sponsorship."

Ethan let out a low whistle. "Your mother would sure appreciate that kind of exposure."

"But…wait…I didn't say…" Ida sputtered.

"Why don't you sit down, Mrs. Vassler," Lainey said sweetly. "We'll discuss this during the meeting."

The older woman nodded and scurried to the conference table. Ethan held out a chair for her then took a seat, as well.

Lainey picked up the stack of agendas and began passing them out, feeling suddenly like she could handle anything this town threw at her. "Let's get started. We've got a lot to cover."

Chapter Seven

The automatic door at the front of the hospital slid open. Lainey walked out of the sweltering summer heat and into the cool lobby.

Julia stood near the entrance, a cell phone pressed to her ear. A man in blue scrubs tripped over a wheelchair coming off the elevator as he craned his neck to get a better look. Julia could turn more heads seven months pregnant than Lainey would covered head to toe in whipped cream and caramel syrup.

"Are you ready to head up?" Lainey asked when Julia was finished. She bounced on her toes, too exhilarated from her success that morning to indulge long in comparisons to her sister.

"Sure thing. How was the meeting?" Julia dug through her purse, her long hair draped over her cheek like a curtain.

"Pretty good once Ida Vassler pulled in her claws." They turned and walked toward the elevator. "Ethan was there,"

Lainey added quickly. "Probably more as a favor to Mom, but it helped."

"She'll be happy." Julia punched the elevator button.

"Do you think…" Lainey started then broke off when Julia finally met her gaze. "What's the matter?"

The elevator door opened but instead of getting on, Julia whirled and fled down a long hallway off the hospital's main lobby. Lainey followed her into the women's restroom.

Julia stood with her hands gripped on either side of a metal sink. She bent so far forward Lainey couldn't see her face, but in the mirror's reflection tears dripped off the tip of Julia's nose.

"What happened?"

"Hormones," Julia said around a gulp. "I'm fine. I just need a minute."

"Liar." Lainey's voice echoed in the small space. "This has something to do with that phone call. Is everything all right with the baby?" Lainey's heart hammered in her chest, her eyes riveted to Julia's stomach.

Julia grabbed a wad of paper towels from the dispenser and blew her nose. "Are we alone?"

Lainey checked under each stall. "Yes."

"I tried to register for Lamaze class." Julia dabbed at her cheeks.

"So? That's what pregnant women do."

"They won't let me. I don't have a coach."

"You said Jeff is coming when his research wraps up. It won't be long now."

Julia's face crumbled, and she covered it with her hands. "I did a bad thing," she said between sobs.

Lainey wasn't sure what to do. She'd never seen her sister like this. She took a hesitant step forward and reached out to touch Julia's elbow.

"It'll be okay. Once Jeff gets here—"

Julia rubbed her hands over her face. "Jeff didn't go to Brazil for the summer. He took a job there. He's gone."

Lainey's brows drew together. "What about you and the baby?"

"You really didn't get pregnant to trap Ethan, did you?"

Relief skittered across the back of Lainey's neck. She wanted to think it didn't matter that anyone believed her. But it did. It always had. "No. I would never—"

"Well, I did. And it blew up in my face."

Lainey's jaw went slack. "You…why?"

"We dated for three years. I followed him from New York to Boston to Columbus. Anywhere work took him. But he wouldn't commit, wouldn't marry me." Julia's eyes glistened with unshed tears. "I gave him an ultimatum. That's when he told me he'd taken a research position in Brazil. He knew I wouldn't go with a baby." Her smile was sad. "Smooth move, huh?"

The floor shifted under Lainey's feet as her whole world started to spin. "Why haven't you told anyone?"

"Come on, Lainey. I was so mad at you for stealing Ethan. But when Jeff wouldn't give me what I wanted, I figured it worked for you, why not me?"

Lainey shook her head. "I didn't steal Ethan and it didn't work for me. He felt like he *had* to marry me and I couldn't live with that. I couldn't force him into a life he didn't want when he would have ended up with you if he'd had a choice."

"Do you still believe that?" Julia asked.

"Don't you?" Lainey shot back.

"You say he was forced, but he had a choice."

Right. Ethan was one of the good ones. No matter how much he'd hurt her, Lainey couldn't forget she'd brought it on herself. "What are you going to do now?"

"Do they have escort services for baby daddies?" Julia gave a harsh bark of laughter.

"Isn't there someone else?" Fear rose in Lainey's belly as Ethan's face flashed through her mind.

"I was going to tell Mom, ask for her help but—"

"Mom doesn't know?"

"No one knows," Julia said, her voice flat. "You're the only one I've told."

"I could help." Lainey looked around the bathroom, wondering who'd said those words. She *had* looked under the stalls, right?

"You'd do that for me?"

No way. Don't do it. You have to get the heck out of this town. "I can make it work."

"It wouldn't be too weird?"

Getting beamed up by the mother ship was weird. This was downright suicidal. "I know I'm not your favorite person in the world, but if you need me I'm here."

Tears welled in her sister's big eyes. "Thank you."

The restroom door opened and a middle-aged woman walked in, pausing as she caught sight of Lainey and Julia. She raised her eyebrows then shuffled into one of the stalls.

Lainey stepped up to a sink. "Can we get out of here?" she asked, using her fingertips to splash lukewarm water on her face.

Julia nodded.

As Lainey reached for a paper towel, Julia's arm wrapped around her shoulder. "I can't tell you how much you're saving my life right now. To feel like I'm not alone…it means everything."

Lainey hugged her back. She couldn't remember another time when she'd hugged her sister. Not once. It felt strange but somehow right.

The toilet flushed and Julia moved away. "Enough bonding in the bathroom. Let's go."

Lainey punched the elevator button for the third floor,

wondering if she was having some sort of out-of-body experience. She'd just agreed to be her sister's birthing coach. She was going to help Julia with her breathing, calm her nerves. Be there every step of the way. Including the delivery room. The actual birth and the blood. All of it.

Her stomach lurched and not from the elevator's movement. She saw Julia glance at her and tried to keep her features calm. She'd seen a few live births with animals while on assignment, and even that had overwhelmed her. It was too much—having it right in front of her face. It was so…real.

Not a great trait in a nature photographer. She could handle death—watching a pride of lions take down a wildebeest didn't faze her. A cub coming into the world was another story. Too big a reminder of what she'd never have.

How much harder would it be with her sister's baby?

"Are you coming?"

Lainey blinked and saw Julia standing outside the elevator, one hand holding back the sliding door.

She stepped into another hospital corridor. "I brought the nail polish she wanted."

"Ah, spa day." Julia patted her large tote bag. "I have stuff for facials. And my scissors."

Lainey's heart pumped the tiniest bit faster. "Your scissors?"

"Mom told me I'm cutting your hair."

"I don't know…"

Julia shrugged one shoulder. "It's up to you."

"I've worn my hair like this since sixth grade," Lainey said, fingering one long lock.

Julia grinned. "That's sort of the point."

"But it's so curly. What if I end up looking like Shirley Temple? Or maybe you don't remember my third grade picture."

In front of Vera's room, Julia turned. "Give me a little credit, would you?"

"Sorry," Lainey mumbled, still not convinced she needed to change her hairstyle. Then she remembered Ethan's warm hands when he'd held her head and said he'd loved her hair, making it so hard for her to keep distant from him.

She sucked in a breath as sparks danced across her belly. "You're right." She pushed open the door. "Cut it all off."

The smell of cheap cologne and stale beer assaulted her as she walked into Cowboys two nights later. Her fingers fluttered up to rub her bare neck. Although she'd cut almost six inches, true to her word Julia had given Lainey layers that somehow made her typically errant corkscrews relax into soft ringlets around her face. It just wasn't her. Or who she used to be.

Even her clothes felt different. Tonight she wore a sleeveless jersey-knit top and a dark blue miniskirt with a pair of black cowboy boots.

It was only nine o'clock but already a decent-size group of people crowded around the large bar that spanned the length of the room. On the walls, neon beer signs mixed with concert posters for various country singers, mostly Willie Nelson and Toby Keith. A dozen couples two-stepped around the wide wood-plank dance floor to a popular country ballad she recognized but couldn't quite name.

She scanned the crowd for a familiar face, but her gaze caught on an oversize mechanical bull in the corner, surrounded by what looked like a bed of stuffed potato sacks.

"You ever ridden one?" a voice asked close to her ear. She jumped what felt like ten feet then whirled to find Tim Reynolds at her side.

"Geez, Tim. Are you trying to give me a heart attack?" Adjusting her purse tighter against her side, she said, "No,

I've never ridden a bull—mechanical or otherwise. I saw them run once."

He blinked.

"You know, in Barcelona." She forced a smile. "I'm a little out of my element here. You're not helping by staring at me."

"Sorry. I still can't get over how great it is to see you. But where's your hair?"

"Julia cut it." She tried to hide her irritation. Tim had been her friend forever. He'd been the last person she'd seen before leaving Brevia and had been kind to her when she'd needed it most. She'd run into him a few times since coming back but found it difficult to slip into the easy camaraderie of youth. Maybe his time away from Brevia had changed him. Or maybe the change was in her. But something no longer fit.

"It looked better longer, like you wore it in high school."

"I've grown up." She blew out a breath. "It was time for my style to do the same. I travel too much for my job to fuss with long hair."

"I'd like to get out of town more." He took a drink of his beer. "I'm thinking of trying freelance magazine work. Running the paper is great, but I miss digging into research, interviewing sources. Nothing that would take me away too long, but I want the chance to do in-depth reporting. Something that really matters, like the work you do."

"That's exciting." She tried to focus on him while scanning over his shoulder for someone she recognized. "What did you have in mind?"

"Maybe *National Geographic*. We could coordinate a piece together. I'd love to take you out to dinner to get your advice. We have so much in common, Lainey. We always have."

"Oh." She didn't know how to answer. Tim had been a good friend. She supposed the least she owed him was dinner, but something about the look in his eye told her he wanted more than she could give him. "That would be fun," she said, thinking it sounded lame.

He didn't seem to notice. "Awesome. It's a date then."

She shifted under his gaze. "Have you seen Steph? I'm supposed to meet her."

He shook his head. "I want you to know something—"

At that moment a familiar voice rang out through the crowd. "Lainey, over here!"

Lainey looked around Tim to see Steph waving a leopard-print cowboy hat from one of the tables near the bar.

"There she is." Lainey breathed a sigh of relief.

"Great," Tim said, his tone disappointed. "I'll see you later."

Lainey had a vision of Tim walking through the high school hallways alone. He'd had trouble finding his place. She could sympathize now as much as she did then. "A few people from the clinic are getting together," she said on a whim. "Do you want to go over with me?"

His face brightened. "Are you sure? I don't want to be a fifth wheel."

Lainey knew all too well what it felt like to not fit in. "I'm sure."

She wound her way through the people until she found Steph.

"Hey, lady," Steph hollered above the music. "It's Saturday night. Let's start this party." She did a little shimmy with her hips then tugged Lainey into a hug.

Lainey laughed. It was the same line Steph had used every weekend during high school. Exhilaration hummed through Lainey at being part of the mix.

Several groups of clinic staff stood around two tall bar tables. She greeted people and drew Tim forward, making introductions.

"You know Tim," she said, turning to Steph.

"Sure." Steph's eyes widened just a touch. "You need a drink, girl." She grabbed Lainey by the arm and yanked her to the bar. "Are you with him?"

"With Tim?" She laughed. "No. I ran into him when I got here."

"Good. You need to keep your options open."

I don't have options, Lainey thought.

Then Steph gestured with two fingers toward the bartender. "I'm so excited you're here."

"Me, too." Lainey smiled, letting her mind drift from Tim. "Thanks for not holding a grudge that I haven't kept in touch."

"What happened to you sucked." Steph leaned forward to plant a kiss on Lainey's cheek. "I might have flipped out, too, if I'd been in your shoes."

Flipped out? Lainey had never thought of her reaction to events of that summer in those terms. She'd simply left, moved on with her life without looking back.

Or had she? She'd made something out of her professional life, but it was a different story on the personal front. She had a couple of friends at a gallery in Santa Fe, but they were more business associates.

The longest she'd had a boyfriend in the past decade had been about seven months, mostly via phone and email because of her travel schedule. She'd ended it as soon as he'd started talking about the future and a family.

She knew the truth ten years ago. She was far too broken for anyone to want to be with her. She wouldn't take the chance of trusting another man with her heart. *Ever.*

She looked down as Steph pushed a tall glass into her hand. "What's this?"

"A Cowboy Kamikaze." Steph wiggled her eyebrows. "The house specialty."

"I'm not much of a drinker," Lainey said with a grimace, eyeing the frozen concoction.

"Try it," Steph urged.

With one finger, Lainey pushed the paper umbrella out of the way and took a tentative sip from the straw. Smooth, sweet liquid slid over her tongue. "It doesn't taste like alcohol."

"A spoonful of sugar makes the medicine go down." Steph winked. "In the most delightful way." She held her glass aloft. "To old friends and new adventures."

Lainey clinked her glass against Steph's. "To old friends," she repeated.

Both women sucked on their straws then Steph nodded toward the front of the bar. "I can't believe it. Ethan's here."

Lainey's swallow caught in her throat. She sputtered and blinked back tears. "I didn't know he was coming." It was hard to sound casual when she was choking.

Steph thumped on her back. "He usually doesn't—too difficult."

"Why?" Lainey took another drink to clear her throat. "Does he ride the bull?"

Steph laughed. "It's the women. They throw themselves at him."

Lainey's stomach landed with a thud near her feet. "Does he…"

"Ride the ladies?" Steph gave her a meaningful grin.

"Have a girlfriend?" Lainey finished.

"Nope. By now you'd think they'd realize all his time and energy go to the clinic."

Like picking a scab, Lainey couldn't help but continue. "He has to date sometimes."

Steph shook her head. "He's got a long line willing to help relieve his tension, if you know what I mean."

"He wanted a family. His own little football team."

"He volunteer coaches over at the elementary school," Steph countered.

"But—"

"Listen, Lainey, you weren't the only one who was scarred by what happened."

"I never said…" The music changed, drowning out her words.

"I love this song." Steph tapped her foot as Kenny Chesney began to sing about tractors being sexy.

Lainey took another drink only to suck up air from her straw. How had she finished so fast? She blamed her buzzing head on that and not Ethan.

"Come on." Steph pulled on her arm. "Let's dance."

Lainey lifted her empty glass. "I need another."

Steph's eyes widened a fraction before she threw back her head and laughed. "This night is going to be fantastic," she shouted, gliding through the crowd.

Chapter Eight

A muscle ticked in Ethan's jaw as he watched yet another guy gyrate up to Lainey on the dance floor. He'd hardly recognized her when he'd first seen her at the bar. Now he couldn't take his eyes off her.

Stephanie Rand grabbed her and executed some complicated spin to get Lainey away from her latest admirer. Lainey wiggled her hips, curls bouncing around her face as she laughed.

Ethan's gut clenched. She was gorgeous.

He rarely made an appearance at the limited but popular Brevia bar scene. When he'd heard from Steph that Lainey was going to be here, he'd decided to come.

Bad choice.

"I told you she was hot now."

Ethan pushed away from the table and resisted the urge to shove his fist into something as he turned to Tim Reynolds. *She was hot before, you fool,* he said to himself. "You did," he answered, silently counting to ten and remembering his promise to his best friend to look out for his little brother.

Tim put down one beer and picked up another. "I asked her out."

Ethan's beer dropped to the table with a clank. "You did what?" On the dance floor, Lainey twirled and laughed.

Tim took a quick step back. "I didn't figure you'd care. She and I have a lot in common, and the two of you are ancient history, right?"

Ethan leveled a look at his supposed friend then ground out, "Right."

"She's been giving me some big-time signals since she got back."

Over the roar in his ears, Ethan heard the music change to a slow ballad. He didn't care, he told himself. Lainey meant nothing to him. He wanted to erase the debt he felt he owed her. Nothing more. If Tim could help with that, so be it.

Tim rubbed his palms together. "Here's my chance."

Ethan would have stopped him, but a hand clamped down on his shoulder. Paul Thie, the young vet he'd hired earlier this summer, stepped closer.

"Hey, boss," Paul said with his usual mile-wide grin. "This is awesome, huh? Reminds me of a few places in Amarillo."

Paul was a native Texan who'd interned with Ethan the past two summers before being hired two weeks ago. As he talked to the young man, Ethan watched the crowded dance floor. Couples clung to each other, women resting cheeks on the shoulders of their partners. He craned his neck to catch a glimpse of Lainey and Tim. When he finally did, his blood pressure skyrocketed.

Tim held her way too close. The other man's arms snaked around her middle while her fingers rested on the corners of his shoulders. Tim turned her with the music and leaned forward to whisper something in her ear. Her already huge eyes widened a fraction. She shook her head, and they disappeared again as the crowd shifted.

"I'll talk to you later, Paul," Ethan said, not waiting for a response as he strode toward the dance floor.

He elbowed his way through couples until he spotted Lainey's caramel curls. Although the song hadn't ended, she pushed away from Tim, who held tight to her wrist. Ethan practically threw another man into a wall trying to get to them.

"Mind if I cut in?" He tried to keep his voice even. Cowboys on a Saturday night was no place to make a scene. "For old times' sake."

He saw Lainey swallow. "Sure," she answered.

"No way," Tim said at the same time. "Our dance isn't over."

Ethan's mouth thinned. "It's over. *Now.*"

Tim let go of Lainey's arm but didn't step away.

"Remember what I said, buddy." Ethan didn't try to hide his anger. "Don't start something you can't finish."

Tim's eyes narrowed, but he turned away, knocking into several people as he stomped off.

Ethan felt curious eyes on them. Without a word, he put his arms around Lainey. To his surprise, she wrapped her hands around his neck without protest. The warmth of her body melded against his. Her hair tickled his chin as her head tilted closer to his neck. She didn't look at him, which was lucky since his blood was now pumping for a different reason.

"What was going on with you two?" he asked.

She sighed, placing her cheek against his shoulder. His heart caught in his chest at the intimacy of the gesture.

"We were talking about high school and then…I don't know. I think he may be drunk." Her finger traced the side of his jaw. "I remember that scar," she whispered, her mouth so close to his face he could feel her breath when she spoke. "I remember everything about you."

He leaned back and looked into her eyes.

She blinked several times and gave him a lopsided smile. "Are *you* drunk?"

She scrunched up her nose as her smile widened. "I don't get out much," she said with a giggle.

"Holy crap," he muttered. "You're drunk."

Her mouth pulled down at the corners. "Don't be a buzz-kill, Ethan. It's been a rough week. My mama's sick. I agreed to be my sister's birth coach. And I'm missing assignment after assignment because I'm stuck in a town where the only people who don't hate me are just waiting until I mess up so they'll have an excuse to *start* hating me."

"Your Sunday's going to be even rougher once that buzz wears off."

The song ended and the music changed to a fast dance tune. Lainey grabbed both his hands and shook them back and forth. "Wanna dance?" she cooed.

"I want to take you home." He hauled her toward the door.

"Are you putting the moves on me?" she asked, laughing.

He kept walking. "Absolutely not."

She tripped and landed against his back. "Has anyone ever told you you're a real party pooper?"

"I don't think so." He looked down into her face, her generous mouth curved into an irresistible pout, and felt his insides tighten.

He straightened her and put his arm around her waist to steady them both. "How much did you have to drink?"

"Not a lot. Two or three. I think. They were yummy."

She giggled again and he shook his head. "You're a cheap date."

"This is *not* a date," she said as they moved out the bar's front door on to the street. Night had fallen, cooling the temperature enough to make it almost pleasant.

"Tell me about it." He dropped his hand from her waist. "My truck's parked around the corner."

He started down the sidewalk then noticed she wasn't following.

She stood in front of Cowboys' entrance, light from the neon pink sign making her skin glow. She tipped her head to one side and studied him, her expression a mix of confusion and raw pain.

"Would you want to date me?" she asked, her voice so low he barely heard her.

He rubbed his hands across his face. How could he answer that? He'd wanted to marry her ten years ago and spend the rest of their lives together. They both knew he'd offered because of the baby, because that's what a boy from Brevia did when he got a girl pregnant. Who knew what would have happened if fate hadn't stepped in?

"Come on," he said by way of an answer. He held out a hand. "Let's go."

She crossed her arms over her chest. "I don't think…" she started before taking several wobbly steps toward the street. She caught herself on a lamppost before tumbling to the curb.

Ethan was at her side in an instant. "Lainey?"

She hung on to the streetlight like a life raft. "I need to go home," she whispered.

"I know, honey." He rubbed his palm against her back. "I can help you."

She raised her bright green eyes to his, still clinging to the pole. "You won't let me fall?"

"I won't let you fall."

Tentatively, she released one arm.

He leaned forward and wrapped it around his shoulder. "All the way now," he coaxed.

Her other hand slid around the lamppost, and he scooped her up. He heard a chorus of whoops and catcalls from the small huddle of smokers outside the bar.

She squirmed against him, trying to look over his shoulder. "How embarrassing," she mumbled. "I can walk, you know."

"I know," he agreed. "But give your feet a break after all the dancing."

She seemed to ponder that for a moment. "Good idea," she said and dropped her head against his chest.

He walked quickly to his truck, trying not to notice the feel of her rounded bottom pressed into his stomach. He didn't want to remember what it felt like to have her arms curled around him.

At the corner, he shifted her, pulling out his keys. Bending at an awkward angle, he opened the passenger door and deposited her as gently as he could. He reached over her to buckle the seat belt.

He tried to back out of the truck's cab, but she reached up, placing her cool fingers on either side of his face.

"I'm definitely drunk," she said with a lopsided smile.

He held his breath. "Yep."

"You could take advantage of me."

The air drained from his lungs. "Nope."

Her expression turned serious. "I could take advantage of you."

He closed his eyes. "You don't—"

Her mouth touched his and he froze. Her tongue traced the curve of his lips. He didn't move.

"Kiss me back," she whispered into his mouth.

And, God help him, he did.

He pushed his fingers through her short curls and slanted his mouth over hers, pressing her against the truck's leather seat. If ever there was a reminder that she'd left Brevia a girl and returned a woman, this kiss was it.

A very drunk woman.

He broke away, pressing his forehead to hers for several moments until he gained control. Her eyes didn't open, and a slight smile lifted one corner of her mouth.

"Lainey—"

She made a muffled sound.

"Lainey?" he repeated, realizing she was fast asleep.

She wiggled deeper into the leather. He adjusted the seat belt where it cut across her neck and closed the passenger door.

He shook his head and blew out a frustrated breath. "Woman, you are the worst thing ever to happen to my ego."

Lainey struggled to open one eye. She immediately regretted it as bright morning light pounded against her head, frying her few remaining brain cells.

"Owww." She pulled the covers all the way up.

After a few minutes, she tried again, driven by a bone-deep need for water and a handful of ibuprofen. Swinging her legs over the side of the bed, she sat up. The pounding in her head intensified, and she wondered if the percussion session behind her temple might actually find its way out.

A glass of water and bottle of pills sat on her nightstand. She washed down two orange pills with a long drink.

For a moment, she congratulated herself on having the foresight to leave them there. Then memories of the previous night rushed through her mind. Random images of Ethan, his hands on her, his breath on her skin.

She glanced down at the old T-shirt and boxers she wore. She could feel that her bra and underpants remained intact. That was a good sign, right?

Her outfit from the previous night was folded in a neat pile on the dresser. That was bad.

Her eyes shifted to the clock on the nightstand. Nine-thirty. She patted the empty space next to her. No Pita.

A noise from downstairs propelled her to her feet. The dog was used to eating by eight. Lainey couldn't take the chance on Pita getting into something else that would require veterinary services.

She walked down each step trying not to bounce or jostle any part of her body. "Pita," she called as she headed through the hallway. She winced as even that small noise exploded in her head.

In the kitchen she expected to find garbage strewn across the floor or food pulled out of the pantry—definitely not the sight that greeted her.

Ethan stood in front of her mother's old gas stove, stirring what looked to be a skillet full of eggs.

Several shopping bags sat on the tile counter. Pita lay sprawled under the kitchen table, her tail thumping.

Lainey rubbed at the crusted drool stuck to the side of her chin. "What are you doing?" Her mouth felt like it was stuffed with cotton.

Ethan glanced over his shoulder. "You're awake," he said, then turned his attention back to the stove. As if being in Vera's kitchen making breakfast on a Sunday morning was normal.

More than her aching head threw her off balance. She sucked in an irritated breath, but the scent of coffee brewing distracted her.

Following her gaze, Ethan gestured toward the coffeepot. "It's fresh."

She poured a big mug and took a drink. The hot liquid felt smooth on her dry throat. She prayed the caffeine would kick in quickly and tried to get a handle on what was going on in her mother's house. "You don't cook," she said, using her mug to point to the skillet.

"They're eggs, Lainey. Not exactly five-star."

"The only eggs you ever had were sandwiched between a McMuffin."

"I was in med school. No one cooks in med school."

That was one of the things he'd liked about her when they were together—how she'd cooked for him. It made him feel cared about he'd told her.

Lainey had taken the words to heart. She'd made sure the cupboards in her tiny dorm room were stocked with his favorite snacks. Anything to keep him coming around. Even when her soul ached for someone to love her for who she was and not because she made it so easy.

He chopped a handful of mushrooms and dropped them into the pan as the theme from *The Twilight Zone* played in her head. He stirred the eggs and lifted the lid on another fry pan.

"Is that bacon?"

"I thought you could use a greasy breakfast to soak up some of last night's demons," he answered, adjusting a knob on the front of the stove. "I got donuts, too."

"From Three Rivers?" She hadn't had anything from her favorite bakery in years.

He pointed to a box on the kitchen table. "A dozen jellies."

That news made her temporarily forget the strangeness of the morning. "My favorite."

"I remember," he murmured, his attention focused on the stove.

She sank into one of the ladder-back chairs that circled the table, still moving slowly although the coffee had numbed the pain to a dull ache.

Flipping open the cardboard box, she inhaled the sweet, doughy aroma. Her first bite was like returning to heaven and worth the ten-year wait. She licked out a dollop of jelly with her tongue and noticed Ethan watching her, his mouth tipped up on one side.

"Thanks," she said around a mouthful.

"Anytime." His voice was low.

A flush spread from her toes to the top of her head. She rubbed her feet against Pita's soft fur under the table.

"So did we…you know…?" she started, wanting to get the difficult conversation out of the way. She concentrated on the doughnut. "Parts of last night are fuzzy for me."

He set a plate piled high with a perfect omelet and several strips of bacon in front of her.

"Did we get down and dirty?" he prompted.

She glanced up, heat pouring into her cheeks. "These aren't my clothes from last night."

He took the chair across from her. "Let's see," he said, rubbing his chin. "Would that have been before or after you passed out in my truck?"

"What's wrong with me?" she asked with a groan. "I never get out of control."

He tapped her plate with his fork. "Eat your eggs and stop beating yourself up. It's been a crazy week. You let off a little steam—no big deal."

"You're doing it again."

"What?"

"Being nice."

He studied her over the rim of his coffee mug. "It makes me an idiot, I know. But do you want me to stop?"

Lainey couldn't answer that question so she took another bite. Her eyes drifted closed. The omelet was perfect—light and creamy with the perfect mix of veggies and cheese. "This is so good." It tasted familiar. "How did you—"

"Your mom."

Her forked stopped midbite.

He shrugged. "I hung around here at mealtime for so many years, she eventually made me learn a few things. It was a lot better than being with my dad. And since my mom left…"

Lainey thought about what Steph had told her. "Did you stay at the clinic because you thought you'd wrecked my family?"

His shoulders stiffened. She thought he wouldn't answer, but he took another drink then said, "At first, maybe. You know I didn't like med school."

She nodded.

"I was almost grateful for an excuse to drop out. Then after…" He paused. "After you left and Julia was gone, I felt bad for your parents. They seemed shell-shocked by everything."

"That was a big club," Lainey murmured, hoping old bitterness didn't seep into her tone.

"The thing was, I liked working with the animals. I liked helping their owners. Taking care of them—it was good for me."

She thought about his strong hands holding Pita. Lainey had been so consumed by her own loss after the miscarriage, she'd barely considered Ethan's feelings. She'd assumed he felt relief at being released from his obligation to her. Now she could see that healing the animals had helped mend his scars.

He'd gone forward with his life, made a home and place in this community separate from the identity a small-town life thrust on its natives.

She'd moved forward, too, but kept the world at an arm's— or camera's—length away. Familiar resentment clogged her throat as she thought of the relationships she could have, the community and home she might have missed because of that.

"I'm happy for you." She busied herself tearing a strip of bacon into tiny pieces over her eggs.

Ethan's deep chuckle broke the quiet. "You made every meal your own particular combination of flavors. I'd forgotten that."

She shrugged but was surprised he'd ever noticed such a detail about her. "I like to get the perfect bite."

"Your photos are like that."

She thought about how she organized a shot—even on location—setting things up and putting in rocks or other natural props to improve the composition. She smiled. "It's kind of the same thing."

He watched her, his expression unreadable. "You haven't smiled much since you've been back."

Her face grew warm under his scrutiny. "What's with all the groceries?" She pointed to the bags on the counter, grateful for the distraction.

He took another bite and one big shoulder lifted. "You hardly had any food left."

"I live on cereal and Lean Cuisines when I'm at home."

"You loved to cook."

"I thought I *should* love to cook," she said. "I was *that* daughter."

"What daughter?"

A short curl fell into her face as she looked down at her plate. "You know. Julia was the pretty one. I had to…well… have other things to offer."

He sat back in his chair. "I didn't realize you grew up in the 1800s. Did you show potential boyfriends your teeth?"

There were no potential boyfriends, she thought. *Only you.* She stood and picked up both the empty plates, carrying them to the sink. "You don't know how it was to grow up with Julia."

"For what it's worth, I thought you were just as pretty."

Lainey snorted then slapped her hand over her mouth. "That is so not true," she said between her fingers. "No one knew I existed when she was around."

He pushed back from the table and walked over to her, gently prying her hand away from her face. His thumb traced light circles against the tender flesh on the inside of her wrist. A shiver rippled down Lainey's spine. "You were beautiful then and you're more beautiful now." He drew one finger along her bare neck.

She felt herself drift nearer to him, so close she could see each individual bristle of beard that shadowed his jaw.

Without warning, he turned away, grabbing a plastic bag from the counter. "I'll put this stuff away."

Lainey took a woozy step back, pushing her hip into the sink for balance. She bent to offer Pita the last bit of bacon and heard Ethan's mock growl behind her. "Busted," she said, ruffling the dog's ears. "Sorry, doc. Old habits die hard."

"Tell me about it," came his cryptic reply. He put away a box of Cheerios and turned to her. "What do you have planned today?"

Pita stretched and rolled onto her back to give Lainey better access to her soft belly. "I'll go see Mom with what's left of the morning, I guess. Pore over event plans later."

"I'm going fishing out at Stroud's Run. Want to come?"

Her hand stilled, and she felt the gentle rise and fall of Pita's chest under her fingers.

He'd asked the question lightly, as if they'd just be two old friends hanging out. Could that be possible? Suddenly, she didn't relish the long day that stretched in front of her.

"What time?"

He ran his fingers through his hair. "I've been meaning to come by the hospital. Why don't I meet you there around one?"

She nodded.

He took a step toward the door.

"Ethan?"

He glanced over his shoulder.

"Thanks again for breakfast." She wrapped her arms

around her chest, her thin T-shirt not enough protection against the heat of his gaze. "And for last night."

He tipped his head. "I'll see you later."

Chapter Nine

"What are you doing?"

Ethan adjusted the oversize vase of flowers he'd just purchased from the hospital gift shop. Not that he needed to see the woman talking to recognize the voice.

"I'm going to see your mom. What does it look like?" He would have continued down the hall, but Julia blocked his path, her round belly pointing at him like an arrow.

"I'm wondering," she said, a tinge of accusation in her voice, "if you're messing with my sister's head. Again."

Ethan's good mood from the morning dissolved as his temper flared. Because he thought they'd left the past behind and he and Julia were friends. Because he didn't want to admit that he worried about the same thing himself. "Mind your own business, Juls."

"My family is my business. We've had enough heartache to last a lifetime. There's a chance to start over this summer. I don't want anyone jeopardizing that. Even someone as well-intentioned as you, E." The saleslady from the gift shop leaned over the counter to eavesdrop.

He inclined his head. "Do you really want to do this here? You know how much people talk in this town."

A young woman with a baby walked into the gift shop, blocking them from view for a moment. He edged away until Julia grabbed his arm and hauled him across the hall.

She opened a door marked Stairwell and pulled him through.

The heavy fire door slammed shut with a bang. He took two steps away so her stomach wouldn't knock into him. "Jenny Baker," she whispered, "saw you kissing my sister in the Piggly Wiggly parking lot."

He leaned against the metal railing. "Jenny Baker should pay more attention to who her husband is kissing and not worry about other people."

Julia's delicate brows raised then she shook her head. "Don't try to distract me. What's going on with you and Lainey?"

"I don't know. I do know it's between Lainey and me."

"Like you said, this is Brevia. You know the drill." She said quietly, "Leave her alone, Ethan. She deserves someone better."

"How do you know—"

"Come on." She blew out a breath. "Everyone thinks you're the bee's knees, but I know the truth. You let the bus run right over Lainey. We both did." She put her palms on her hips. "I don't blame her for leaving. How else was she going to survive?"

"I didn't mean to hurt her," he argued. Talons of unease crept along his spine. He'd been messed up when he was with Lainey. He'd been messed up almost his entire life. Julia was right—she knew him better than most.

"Neither did I," she agreed. "We were all hurt. I wonder

what would have happened if I'd stayed in New York instead of coming back here that summer, if I hadn't been here the night you found out about the pregnancy."

"It wouldn't have mattered, Juls. You and I weren't going to get back together."

"We know that, but Lainey didn't ten years ago. She thought you were still in love with me. The point is we have a chance to make things better."

"Don't you think I want to help with that?"

"I don't know what you want. What I do know is that she may seem tough, but that girl—the one who worshiped you for so many years—she's still in there. I'm telling you straight up—don't hurt her again."

He wanted to fling the bouquet of flowers in the trash, leave the hospital for someplace where he could think. Where the Morgan women couldn't invade every cell of his body.

Instead, he straightened. "I understand your concern, Juls. I'm not going to hurt her. And right now I'm late to see Vera." He took the steps two at a time, not looking back.

Lainey stepped off the elevator and started toward her mother's room at the same time Ethan burst through the door leading from the stairwell.

He collided into her, the flowers he held tickling her face. His hand reached out to steady her.

"Hey." She smiled, wiping pollen off her nose with one finger.

A scowl drew down the sides of his wide mouth and his eyes were hard as he studied her. "Why are you here?" he practically barked.

She stepped away from him, wondering where the sweet, teasing man from earlier had gone. "Well…it's one o'clock. We're meeting."

"Right." He dropped his hand from her arm.

"Are you okay?" She'd seen that look in his eyes before,

remembered how he'd been after Julia had left all those years ago: angry, frustrated, lost. It tugged on her heart, on the quiet, deep place she'd thought she'd filled with work and travel.

"What can I do?" She didn't want to say the words, didn't want to care. With Ethan she couldn't help herself.

He searched her face for several heartbeats then trailed one finger down her forehead, between her brows, smoothing a crease she hadn't realized was there.

"I'm fine." He took her hand, laced his fingers in hers. "Let's go."

She let him lead her down the hall then drew her hand away when they reached her mother's room.

He frowned, a question in his dark gaze.

"Not here," she whispered and looked away. Before he could argue she stepped forward.

"Hi, there," she called out, making her voice purposely light.

Vera looked up from the book in her lap. Her gaze took in the two of them. Lainey knew this was a mistake, being here with him. Her mother didn't need another reason to judge her.

Vera only smiled. "For me?" she asked as Ethan stepped around Lainey.

"Who else?" He bent to hug her, placing the flowers on the bedside table.

She cupped his face. "How are the animals? Do they miss me?"

"We all miss you."

She patted his cheeks and drew him down to the side of the bed. "Tell me everything. Any new intakes? Who's been adopted?"

Lainey couldn't imagine with his busy schedule at the clinic that Ethan would've had the time or inclination to keep track of shelter business, but he patiently gave Vera a detailed status report.

Her mother listened, asking questions or making comments about certain animals. She handed Ethan a pad of paper and pen from her nightstand, dictating a mile-long list of instructions for him to relay to the shelter staff.

Since Lainey had been in town, Vera had made remarkable progress. Her speech was almost back to normal, although her right arm and leg still didn't function properly.

"Mom, you shouldn't worry about work," Lainey said, coming to stand at the foot of the bed. "The shelter is fine."

Vera turned as if Lainey had just bitten the head off a baby mouse. "Fine isn't good enough, Melanie," she huffed. "The shelter is your father's legacy. It matters."

Lainey struggled to control her breathing. "I know. Your health matters, too."

"I'm being released next week."

"That's great," Ethan said.

"Your leg," Lainey protested. "You can't walk."

"I'll get better at home. They'll give me exercises, and you can drive me to therapy appointments."

Lainey swallowed. "Of course."

"I need to get back to my life," her mother continued, leveling a look at her. "I'm no good to anyone in here."

Lainey's mouth twisted in annoyance. "Is this about the event? I'm not doing enough, right? You're pushing yourself because you don't think I can handle everything."

"It's *my* event, young lady. My reputation's on the line."

"Is it your friends? Do they have a problem with me?" Lainey didn't want to be so vulnerable in front of Ethan, but her fears and self-doubt tumbled forward like a landslide. "I'm doing my best, Mama. If you think you can do better in your condition, have at it. I have about a million places I'd rather be than stuck in Brevia for the summer."

"Do *not* take that tone with me, Melanie Lynne."

Lainey felt her composure begin to crumble. Her stomach burned with old resentment and pain. Then Ethan's large hand wrapped around her wrist.

"Show her the pictures," he said gently.

She glanced down at the envelope still clutched against her T-shirt. "I can't do this," she whispered miserably. "You show her."

Blocking her mother's view, he stroked his thumb against the racing pulse on the inside of her wrist. "Yes, you can."

Just as it had during that first meeting at the clinic, the look in his eyes bolstered her confidence and gave her comfort. She nodded and turned back to Vera.

"I'll be outside," he murmured and pushed open the door.

"What pictures?" her mother demanded.

"I took a few shots of the shelter animals for the website. I thought you'd want to see."

Her mother's chest rose and fell in deep breaths. She took the envelope wordlessly, fumbling with the metal clasp.

Lainey covered her mother's fingers with her own. "I'm sorry I lost my temper. I'm trying my best."

"I know." Vera pressed her head back against the pillow. "The shelter...the animals...they're all I have left of your father, Lainey. I need to be there." Her voice broke. "It's my only connection to him."

Lainey sank down to the edge of the bed. "I know how hard it was with Julia and me gone. If I hadn't left he wouldn't have been so sad and he might have stayed healthier." She wiped tears from her mother's cheeks.

Vera shook her head. "His heart was bad. What happened...his death...none of it was your fault. The heart attack was only a matter of time."

Something went still inside Lainey. She had carried the guilt of her dad's death like a traveling companion. It had gone with her to every destination, wrapped around her like a blanket under the remote skies in Africa, laid down beside her in a tent on a Costa Rican beach. Like the sorrow she felt for the baby she'd lost, she hadn't been able to outrun it or leave it behind.

"When I called…after…" Lainey's voice shook. "When I couldn't get here for the funeral…"

Her mother's face twisted. "I was overcome with grief. I was mad at your father for dying, mad that he hadn't gone to the doctor. I was angry with myself for not realizing how bad off he was. I was mad at you. I was mad at everyone. It wasn't your fault."

Sobs racked Lainey's body. Vera pulled her close and repeated, "It wasn't your fault."

"Oh, Mama. I miss him."

"Me, too, sweetie." Vera leaned back and wiped under her eyes. "I think he's with the baby," she said softly.

"What?" Goose bumps ran the length of Lainey's spine.

Her parents had been with her at the hospital when she'd miscarried, but they'd never discussed the baby she lost. They'd taken Lainey home, tucked her into bed and murmured platitudes about how "things happen for a reason."

Their relief at the outcome of her pregnancy had seemed palpable to Lainey. It had been a slap in the face, caused a rift in her relationship with them that had made leaving easier to bear.

"Your father was so sad for you," her mother continued, grabbing a tissue from the bedside table. "We both were. It makes me feel better to think he's with your baby."

Lainey was filled with a deep sense of…not exactly peace…yet something as freeing. A feeling of calm she hadn't known was missing from her life settled over her like a soft spring rain on the New Mexican mesas. Filling up the dry, barren desert until it once again bloomed with life.

"Thank you," she mouthed to her mother, unable to produce the smallest sound. She wiped her nose and pulled the stack of pictures from the envelope. "Here," she said on a ragged breath.

As her mother looked down, a smile lit her face. She thumbed through the photos, taking several moments to study each one. Lainey walked to the window, gazing out as she worked to steady her heart.

When she turned, her mother watched her with a mix of curiosity and admiration. "These are lovely," she said, her voice trembling. "You've captured their personalities and a bit of their souls in these photos."

Lainey shrugged. "I thought it would help me to get to know them. Besides the website, I'm going to put together a brochure and flyer for the event."

"An excellent idea." Her mother hugged the stack of pictures to her chest. "These are more than photos, Lainey. They're portraits…true art. You have an amazing gift."

Lainey was so used to her mother's disapproval, jumping through hoop after hoop to measure up to Vera's high standards, she wasn't sure how to handle this tender moment. "Thank you," seemed ineffectual, still it was all she could manage.

"May I keep these?"

"Sure."

The door creaked open and Robert, the tattooed physical therapist, rolled a wheelchair into the room.

"Time for your workout," he announced as his gaze took in both Vera and Lainey's puffy, tearstained faces. He shot Lainey a glare before kneeling at Vera's side.

"What's going on?" he asked, taking Vera's tiny hand in his meaty one.

Lainey watched her mother smile at him. Holy cow, she

thought. This might be serious. A smile tugged at the corners of her mouth.

"She brought photos of my babies." Vera tilted the stack of pictures in his direction.

He leaned his shiny head forward. "Tell me about them." His total concentration was focused on Vera.

Lainey backed toward the door. "I'll talk to you later tonight, Mom."

Vera looked around Robert for a moment. "Love ya, honey," she called.

Lainey smiled. It was the first time her mother had said those words in over ten years. "Me, too, Mom."

She closed the door behind her and sagged against it, her eyes drifting shut. Her body felt like Jell-O, weak and almost weightless.

"Hey." Ethan stood in front of her, searching her face.

"I thought you'd gone." Her voice sounded far away in her own ears.

"I didn't know if you'd want to be alone."

She took another breath. "I'm good."

He looked surprised and relieved at the same time. "Do you still want to fish?"

"I do." She stopped when she realized the two words she'd uttered, steeped in meaning for them both.

He only smiled, his eyes crinkling at the corners. "Let's go."

The afternoon flew by in the blink of an eye for Ethan.

He'd packed a cooler with sandwiches, apple slices, chips and cream sodas. Sitting on the dock next to Lainey had made it feel like a gourmet feast. He couldn't remember the last time hanging out with a woman was so easy and exhilarating.

He quizzed her on her work, places she'd visited, adventures she'd had. When they'd been in college he'd been a huge jerk. In their short time together, he wasn't sure if he'd once asked her a question about herself and her interests.

He figured he had a lot to make up for. Maybe he'd deserved to be left at the altar. He didn't know what kind of husband he would have made—pretty bad if his own parents' marriage was any indication.

As the light began to fade behind the trees, Lainey stood and stretched. "I guess we should take off."

He pulled his line out of the water. "I didn't catch anything."

She scrunched up her face. "You didn't try too hard."

"Nope," he agreed.

"My dad always said fishing was one quarter what you caught and the rest an excuse for some peace and quiet."

"Your father was a smart man."

She lifted the blanket. "He would have been proud of what you've done with the clinic."

He shrugged. "I mainly try to stay out of your mom's way."

"I've spent most of my life with that goal." She looked out at the lake as a group of teenagers made their way down the far shore. "You know, I never came here in high school."

He heard a peal of laughter and the thump of rap music in the distance. "Never?"

"This is where the popular kids hung out—the girls with boyfriends. I spent my weekends in Annie Williams's basement, imagining what I'd do when a boy finally brought me here." Her smile was wistful. "It never happened."

"I thought everyone—"

She shook her head, taking a few steps toward the water.

"So who was the lucky guy in your plan?" he asked, trying to keep the conversation light. "Geez, not Tim I hope."

She turned, her eyes bright in the fading light. "*You don't know?* After all this time?" He heard her voice catch. "I'll give you a hint—the boy I dreamed about all through high school didn't know I existed."

Stunned, he could only stare at her. "Lainey, it wasn't like that. I knew you…"

She stood only a few feet away but might as well have been on the other side of the lake. He looked around wildly, desperate for a way to change the subject. His gaze caught on a flash of light through the trees.

"There's something I want to show you."

She glanced over her shoulder and pulled a face. "That's a bad line, even for you."

He grimaced but felt grateful she'd made a joke.

"Come on." He grabbed the cooler and fishing poles and headed toward the parking lot. After dropping the gear into the back of his pickup, he made his way to a small trail that snaked out of the woods.

He paused, waiting for Lainey to catch up as unrealistic anxiety skittered through him. *Pull it together, buddy. This is not a big deal.*

She studied him as she walked to the edge of the parking lot. "You're freaking me out. Should I be worried you're luring me into the deep, dark forest to exact some psycho plan for revenge?"

He flashed her a Jack Nicholson leer. "Do I look psycho?"

"Not reassuring," she muttered.

Grabbing her hand, he started up the path. "Trust me." Her palm felt smooth and warm against his. He liked touching her, like the feeling of connection and awareness that put each of his senses on high alert.

They walked in comfortable silence as shadows cast patterns along the forest floor. The trail was narrow, with thick green foliage creeping close on either side. He'd loved this forest since he was a boy, pedaling his bike miles from his home as often as he could. He'd lost himself in the peaceful stillness of the trees. It had been his sanctuary and escape from the chaos of his own house.

"Didn't your family own some land around the lake?"

"We're on it. I bought it from my granddad a few years ago. This is the place."

He watched her gaze lift, released the breath he hadn't realized he was holding as her jaw dropped.

"It's wonderful," she whispered.

"It's taken a few years. I work on it during weekends, and the clinic doesn't always leave time."

She walked toward the house. "You built this yourself?"

"Mainly," he answered, coming up behind her. He looked beyond her shoulder, trying to see the house with new eyes.

"Can I see inside?"

"The front door is unlocked."

"Show me."

He turned the handle and watched her step across the threshold. A feeling spread through him that this moment was exactly right. As if he'd been waiting to have her in his home. As if she belonged here.

His emotions stirred as she started up the stairs. Her fingers trailed along the wood rail, and his insides grew heavy in response. He followed her through the kitchen and out the French doors onto the deck, his favorite spot.

She leaned forward against the rail. "The view is incredible. You can see the whole lake from here."

"It is incredible." He traced his finger along the back of her neck. The need to touch her pulsed through his entire body.

Her eyes had turned stormy gray again, and in the dim light he could just make out the smattering of freckles across her nose.

"I like you here," he whispered and pressed his mouth to hers. He meant to keep the kiss light. But when he tasted the sweetness of her mouth, all the emotion swirling through him poured out.

He tried to tell her everything he couldn't say out loud. What this moment meant to him, having her in his home. That he was sorry it had taken him so long to realize how special she was.

He'd kissed more than a few women in his life; still nothing had felt like this. Like a piece of his soul was hanging out in the summer air.

When he lifted his head, her eyes were dazed. He knew he looked the same, but if she could see inside… He had to put some distance between them until he could pull his mask back into place.

"I need to check some work the electrician did this week. Are you okay out here for a few minutes?"

The question was clear in her eyes as she looked at him, but to his relief, she only nodded.

As Ethan disappeared inside, Lainey stared across the water at the kids on the other side. She'd dreamed of being part of a group like that when she was younger. A few times her senior year—once Ethan was safely away at college— she'd driven out here with her girlfriends, hiding at the edge of the woods as they'd watched the couples on a Saturday night.

A night like this, where the forest surrounding the lake hummed with the sound of insects and the wind off the water ruffled her hair. She'd imagined him bringing her to the lake, how it would feel to sit near a campfire with his arm around her shoulder.

She'd given up that fantasy years ago.

She wasn't the same lovesick girl who wore her heart on her sleeve. She'd spent too much time living in the shadow of her past mistakes. Now she longed to be whole. To feel like her life and the people in it belonged to her alone.

She rubbed her hands against her bare arms to calm a sudden flush of goose bumps.

"What are you thinking?"

The quiet rumble of Ethan's voice made her jump. She spun and tried to step away. He caught her and pulled her close.

"I can't—" she began then stopped when he covered her mouth with his. Without hesitation, she met his need with her own. She reached up and wrapped her arms around his neck, twining her fingers through his thick hair.

So much for her willpower.

With just a touch, Ethan made her forget all her pain. In its place burned a need years in the making. Suddenly, she was seventeen again and her dreams were coming true in the arms of the man she'd once loved with all her heart.

She dragged her mouth away from his. Digging her fingernails into the wood railing, she concentrated on breathing.

"I need to go home," she said, irritated that she sounded breathless.

His eyes were gentle yet dark as the shadowy woods as he stared at her, but he didn't argue. "If that's what you want."

Chapter Ten

"Are you sure you don't want some place not so busy?"
Ethan asked as he angled into a parking spot. "And with better food." A crowd of people spilled onto Carl's outside patio.

"Everyone but you loves Carl's," Steph said as she climbed
out of the truck. She'd badgered him into taking her to lunch.
Truth be told, he was glad to get a break from his own company. "Best onion rings this side of the Smoky Mountains."

"My arteries are clogging already," he answered. A bead
of sweat rolled down between his shoulder blades. It wasn't
unbearably hot for August and a light breeze tickled the back
of his neck. Why was he suddenly roasting?

Steph didn't notice. "I'll get a table." She took off down
the street as he locked the truck. He'd just finished putting
change in the meter when she reappeared at his side.

"It's too crowded," she said quickly. "Let's go someplace
else."

One last quarter dropped in the slot. "We're here now. Carl

will find us a table. Or we can sit at the bar." He turned to look at the restaurant's entrance. Steph jumped in front of him.

"It's not worth it," she insisted. "We can pick up Chinese and eat at the clinic."

"I put a buck fifty in the meter. What's your problem?" He ducked around her and stopped in his tracks.

A couple was being shown to a table on the enclosed patio in front of the restaurant. Ethan's mouth went dry as Tim Reynolds placed a hand on Lainey's back and leaned close to whisper something in her ear. She laughed and slipped into her chair, gazing at Tim with her sweet, open smile. Her sleeveless black dress hugged every curve on her body—it was the kind of dress a woman wore on a real date.

Anger bubbled up inside him as he took off for the restaurant. Steph hung on to his arm with all her strength.

"Whoa, there, killer," she said.

"Do you see how he's looking at her?" Ethan could hardly see straight for the possessive rage he suddenly felt. "How he touched her?"

"Um, Conan, before you drag her off to your cave, think about how it's going to make you look."

"I don't give a…" He stopped and took a breath. "Fine," he muttered, disgusted that he couldn't put Tim in his place. "We'll play it your way."

"My way? I don't have a way," she protested, tripping in her attempt to keep up with him.

They were almost to the restaurant when Tim noticed them. He leaned forward and spoke quickly to Lainey. She turned as Ethan and Steph got to the table.

"What are you doing here with him?" Ethan asked, his plan to play it cool totally forgotten. Out of the corner of his eye, he saw Tim stand.

"Dude, we're on a date," Tim said. "Do you mind?"

Lainey's chin tilted. "Tim and I need to discuss possible articles to promote the adoption fair. It's a working lunch."

He tried not to let her scent invade his senses. "You print a few pictures of furry animals on the front page. You need a black dress for that?"

Lainey's eyes narrowed. "You're way out of line."

Patrons at other tables looked over, whispering to each other. He wanted everyone in the restaurant to go away, to leave him alone with Lainey. If it was just the two of them, maybe he could calm down—figure out how to make things right. After she'd gone home last night, Ethan had spent hours awake wondering how to show her she still meant so much to him. In his heart, they belonged together. Something about Tim with Lainey wound around his gut and wouldn't let go.

He tried to rein in his fury. "I can pull up stories from previous events—families that have kept in touch about their adoptive pets," he said quietly.

Her expression turned confused, but she smiled slightly. "That would be great."

He couldn't ignore the feelings that seeing her with Tim conjured, but it didn't help either of them to cover his fear with anger. Any man would count his lucky stars to have her on his arm.

What if she realized how much better she could do than him? What if she didn't give him another chance?

He wanted to reach forward and touch the soft strands of her hair. Her dress scooped in front, revealing just a trace of her pale, freckled skin. He noticed a faint blush of pink work its way up from her chest to her cheeks. He couldn't tear his eyes away.

Tim cleared his throat. His trance broken, Ethan glanced at the other man. He wanted to rip Tim's throat out, and it looked like the feeling was mutual.

Steph grabbed his arm. "We should get a table," she said, yanking on him.

He looked at Lainey. Her lashes fluttered down over her green eyes, veiling their expression. It amazed him that her lashes didn't tangle when she blinked, that's how long they were. She wouldn't meet his eyes, but her lips pressed together in a thin line.

Ethan couldn't pretend seeing her with Tim didn't make him want to go ballistic, and he had no intention of sitting down with Steph to watch the whole scene. "I lost my appetite."

He turned on his heel and stalked down the street, not particularly caring if Steph followed. But she scrambled into the seat next to him as he threw the truck in Reverse and slammed on the gas, almost hitting another car as he pulled out.

After a few minutes, Steph spoke. "Ethan, this isn't the Daytona 500. Could you slow down?"

He looked at the speedometer then pulled into the parking lot of Burger Bucket, Brevia's version of fast food.

"I'm sorry, but did you see that?" he yelled. "She was on a date. With Tim Reynolds."

Steph made a face. "I'm not sure what you saw, but they were having lunch. And talking business, for heaven's sake."

"So what? You saw how he looked at her."

"Yeah, well, she looked really good."

"More than good. She looked amazing." He ran his hands through his hair. "What was she doing with *him?*"

"At the risk of repeating myself, they were *eating lunch.* Friends do that. She's been friends with him for years."

He sighed. "The whole scene threw me. The Lainey I knew didn't wear tight dresses and go on lunch dates."

"Maybe you don't know her that well," Steph suggested.

Ethan rested his head against the seat back and closed his

eyes. A picture of Lainey tossing her hair and smiling at another man filled his mind.

"That's obvious." He opened his eyes to clear the scene. "Am I such a first-rate fool?"

Steph smiled. "Is that a rhetorical question?"

"Hell, yes," he answered.

Lainey swallowed against the anger that squeezed her throat as Tim swung his car into the parking space next to her Land Cruiser. He'd met her in front of the newspaper office and driven the short distance to Carl's.

"Are you okay?" he asked, turning to face her.

She tried to smile but couldn't quite coax her mouth into moving. "Sure," she said.

"He's acting like a jerk," Tim said. "He never did deserve you."

"You don't have to say that. I know you two are friends."

He shook his head. "I don't care about Ethan. You're the one who's important to me. Do you understand?"

"I guess." Something about the gleam in Tim's eyes made the hair on her bare arms stand on end. His gaze strayed to her chest. She hadn't purposely worn a dress that could be misconstrued as a come-on. The way he looked at her said she'd made a mistake.

"He can't make you happy—will never give what you want."

Her shoulders stiffened. "What I want is to make the adoption event a success and get back to my life."

"Trust me. We're on the same page."

She wanted to trust Tim, needed people in her corner as she worked on the event. She didn't remember Tim's behavior being so suffocating in high school. Lunch had been uncomfortable, and while she'd blamed that on Ethan's interruption, now she wasn't sure. "Thanks again for lunch. I'll call you next week to confirm the run dates." She reached for the door handle.

"Do you think there's a chance for us, Lainey?"

Her head whipped around. "Excuse me?"

"I'm sorry. I shouldn't have blurted that out." His hands clenched and unclenched in an unnatural rhythm. "You must know how I feel about you. How I've always felt."

"We're old friends, Tim." She cringed at the pain that flashed in his eyes. If there was one thing Lainey knew a lot about, it was unrequited love. "That's all. I don't want to hurt you but…"

"It could be more," he interrupted. "If Ethan wasn't in the picture, if you could forget about him…" He grabbed her wrist and leaned in close. "I don't want to see *you* hurt again." His lips thinned. "He doesn't care about you, Lainey. He never did."

She met his gaze steadily, unwilling to admit how his words spoke to her deepest fears. "Let go of me. Now."

He released her wrist, and she climbed out of the car quickly, slamming the door. He rolled down the passenger window. "I could make you happy, Lainey. I want what's best for you," he said, his tone placating.

"Assign someone else to work with me on publicity, Tim. You need to back off." She turned on her heel and stalked toward her car.

She spent the rest of the afternoon busy with plans for the adoption fair and preparations for her mother to come home, trying to shake off the strange feeling from lunch.

After uploading the pictures she'd taken of the animals to the shelter's website, she'd printed posters to hang in local businesses. To her surprise, once she'd delivered a couple to Carl's Diner and Piggly Wiggly, other merchants called to request them over the next few days. It wasn't as bad as she'd thought to visit with people she'd known since child-hood. Only a couple dropped not-so-subtle digs about Ethan.

The more time she spent with the shelter staff and the animals, the more dedicated she became to making the adoption fair the best this town had ever seen. Not to make amends for old wrongs but because the animals deserved it. So many pets needed good homes. Her heart broke each time a new dog, cat, or even guinea pig was processed into the shelter.

She brought Pita with her to work each morning and found it hard to imagine her life without the lovable mutt that spent most of her time curled in a ball at Lainey's feet.

A few days ago a tiny black Lab pup had been found wandering across the two-lane highway leading out of town. He had no collar and hadn't been claimed yet.

As if she could sense the puppy's need, Pita had followed the wee pup back and forth between the shelter and the clinic. The pup had sniffed and nipped playfully at the older dog, whining incessantly when they were separated. It had gotten so bad that they'd finally moved the puppy's cage into Lainey's office.

Still it wasn't enough. The puppy cried and Pita paced until Lainey opened the cage door. Pita climbed onto her dog bed and the puppy pressed against her belly. Now they were a group of three, and Lainey wondered how her no-strings-attached life had become complicated so quickly.

She glanced at her watch, needing to meet Julia for their first birthing class in twenty minutes. She stood and stretched—tired from hours of work and updating the shelter's website.

As she opened the door of her office, peals of laughter and a few barks rang out from the rear of the building.

She stepped out the back door as Steph's twins, the puppy, and Pita ran by. Joey, Steph's older son, waved from where he stood with Ethan and his mom, watching the game of chase.

Sam, one of the six-year-old twins, stopped when he saw her. "Lainey, your dog's a nut ball," he called as the puppy caught up to him. Pita ran circles around the two, barking happily before joining the pup in covering Sam's face with slobbery licks.

Sam squealed as he rolled on the ground. "Help, help," he yelled, "they're killing me with stinky kisses."

The boy looked happy enough, but kids in distress made Lainey nervous. "Pita, come here." She hurried off the steps. Pita trotted over, and Lainey wrapped her fingers around the dog's collar. "You're not a puppy. You have to be gentle."

"Don't worry," Steph said. "I'm hoping they'll wear him out enough to fall asleep before ten."

Lainey eased her grip on Pita's collar. The dog nuzzled her palm. "He yelled 'help,'" she said weakly, realizing it had been in jest.

Ethan grabbed a football off the ground. "Joey, go long," he called, running toward the center of the yard. "Keep away from the twin terrors."

The boys screamed in delight and gave chase, dogs trailing at their heels.

"I hope a family with young kids adopts her." Lainey made her voice purposely cheerful.

"Puppies are a lot of work but worth it."

Lainey slanted a glance at her friend. "I meant Pita."

Steph turned. "Pita's your dog."

"Not really." Lainey shrugged even as an invisible vice clamped around her midsection. "I can't keep her forever. I wasn't meant to...my job...I travel too much to have a pet."

"And you think you can let her go?" Steph asked, her voice quiet.

"I have to." Lainey blinked several times. "It's what's best."

"Uh-huh," was Steph's only answer. "Go get him, Sam," she cheered when Ethan stole the ball. "Kick his butt."

The six-year-old let out a rebel yell and charged after Ethan. Ethan slowed as the puppy nipped at his ankles and Sam launched onto his back. Ethan went down with an *oof* as Sam, his brother David and then Joey climbed on him.

"Should we rescue someone?" Lainey asked.

Steph shook her head. "Ethan's used to it. The boys are here a lot after school. He always makes time for them." She sighed. "My no-good ex-husband could take lessons."

A thought pricked at the back of her mind. "Joey's eight now?"

Steph nodded. "Starting third grade in a few weeks."

Ten years ago...

She clutched her hands to her stomach and turned away. Her baby would have been nine, only a year older than Joey. She thought about the child she'd lost sometimes, not as often as she used to, but always in terms of small babies. Not a half-grown child with a personality and needs. Hugs and kisses, scraped knees she'd never tend, hurt feelings she wouldn't get to soothe, late-night cuddles she'd never enjoy.

Her vision clouded. Pita was suddenly at her side, nudging against her bare leg.

"Lainey?" Steph's voice was soft next to her ear.

Lainey waved a hand in front of her face. "Sorry. Bug in my eye."

She felt Ethan's eyes on her and met his gaze across the backyard. He stood with David and Sam hanging off him, the muscles in his arms bulging. The deep understanding in his gaze told her he knew exactly what she was thinking.

She made her smile purposely bright. "Don't let him up so easy," she called.

"Hey!" Ethan protested.

The boys gave simultaneous war whoops. Legs and arms went flying.

"I'm okay." She glanced at Steph. "I promise."

Ethan staggered over, the boys holding tight to his legs. "Have mercy on me." The boys giggled.

"Joey. Samuel. David. Off." Steph's voice was gentle but firm.

All three let go, dropping to the ground as the puppy scrambled between them.

"How'd you do that?"

"I read your mom's book." Steph grinned. "Same principle for boys as puppies."

"Chip has puppy breath," Joey whined.

"Chip?" Ethan asked.

David flashed a sheepish smile. "We named him to match Pita."

"Pita. Chip. Cute." Ethan ruffled David's curly blond hair.

The puppy gave Sam a small nip then scampered over to Pita.

"Sorry, Chip." Lainey lifted the fluffy pup, nuzzling its downy fur against her chin. "I need to drop your friend Pita at home." She glanced at her watch. "Yikes. I'm really late."

Ethan scooped Chip out of her arms. "You can leave Pita here until you're finished." His eyes searched hers. "I'm sorry about earlier," he said softly. "I was way out of line."

She nodded. "It wasn't a date."

"Even if it was…" His eyes narrowed. "That's not where you're going now is it? To see Tim? I mean, it's cool, I just…"

"I have a Lamaze class."

Steph's loud snort of laughter drowned out Ethan's response. "You know it's *wrong* on so many levels that you're her birth coach."

"Yeah, well…" There was an awkward silence as Ethan stared at Lainey, a scowl darkening his face and making him all the more gorgeous. She wondered what he was thinking, if the family he'd wanted so badly still crossed his mind.

"I'll be back around seven-thirty."

He nodded. "We'll be here."

She gave Steph a quick hug and high-fived Joey, Sam and David. Despite hitting almost every red light on the way, she was only about fifteen minutes late.

With an apologetic wave, Lainey hurried to where Julia sat by herself at the far end of the room.

"You're late."

"I'm here now." Lainey sank down on the carpet.

"Look at all these happy couples," Julia mumbled as the instructor began her lecture again. "I feel like a complete loser."

"Jeff's an idiot if he's willing to miss this."

Julia flashed a small smile. "Thanks."

Lainey realized she may have spoken too soon as the teacher, Nancy, instructed the coaches to sit behind their partners, legs open. Julia leaned back against Lainey.

"Feel your breath," Nancy told the coaches. "Let the rise and fall of your chest guide the mother in her breathing."

Simple enough, except as soon as Lainey put her hands on either side of Julia's hard belly, she felt a firm kick.

"Holy cow," she said on a gulp.

She moved her hands to a different spot and was rewarded with an even stronger thump, thump, thump. She glanced over Julia's shoulder and saw rippling under the thin yellow T-shirt Julia wore.

She yanked her hands away. "Who's in there—the kid from *The Exorcist?*"

Julia sighed, pushing Lainey's hands back. "Pay attention."

Lainey tried to focus on Nancy's words but continued to be distracted by the movement under her fingers. In her line of work, it was relatively easy to steer clear of pregnant women. Animals were a different matter, but Lainey had never found herself staring wistfully at a tiger's distended stomach.

With the life growing inside her sister literally pulsing

under her hands, Lainey felt a black hole of despair begin to tear open in her own barren womb.

"What is going *on?*" Julia sat up and glanced back.

Lainey let her eyes drift shut for a moment. "Nothing. I'm trying to listen."

"*I'm* trying to match my breathing to yours, which is hard when you're hyperventilating."

"I'm not…" Lainey felt her chest heave up and down. She forced herself to take a deep breath. "I don't know if I can do this," she whispered.

"Please." Julia's chin hitched up a notch. "You're all I've got."

Despite her pounding heart and the sweat beading on her brow, Lainey kept her hands on her sister's stomach. "Turn around then."

Julia swallowed and leaned back.

By the grace of God, the baby remained still for the rest of the class. Lainey concentrated on Julia, on how they would get through her eventual labor.

Once Lainey had her emotions under control, the class wasn't bad. She liked feeling connected. For so long, she'd kept her emotional distance from anyone who wanted to get close. She used her work to build walls around her shattered heart. But even after her heart had healed, she'd still been stuck in her lonely fortress.

They walked to the rec center parking lot after class. It was late, but voices of families enjoying the outdoor pool during the last weeks of summer drifted over the fence.

"So I'm an official coach." Lainey hefted Julia's bag of comfort items to one shoulder and scanned the parking lot.

"Only three more classes to go."

"Three more?"

"Didn't I mention," Julia asked, looking guilty, "that this is a month-long session?"

"No big deal. I'm here anyway." She gave Julia a quick hug.

When Lainey would have let go, Julia held tight. "I'm glad you came back."

Lainey felt her heart expand and pushed away, needing distance. "Where's your car?"

"It had a dead battery. My neighbor gave me a lift." She reached for her bag. "I'll call her to come get me."

"I can take you home."

Julia nodded. "Thanks."

When they got to the SUV, Lainey moved her camera equipment to the backseat.

"Maybe I could take a few shots of you," she suggested. As soon as the words were out, she gave herself a mental head thump. Not smart—focusing her camera on Julia's ripe stomach.

"That would be cool." Julia's tone was wry. "Unless you're asking so you can have proof of how fat I got."

"Give me a break. Eight months pregnant and most women would kill for your hips."

Julia rested her head on the back of the seat. "Jeff liked to remind me that my looks would fade and then I'd have nothing to offer. No brains, no talent, no real skills."

"He did a number on you."

"Maybe. It was an easy line to buy because I already believed it." Julia sighed. "Lord, I was jealous of you growing up."

Lainey glanced over as she pulled out of the parking lot. "That's funny, Juls."

"I'm serious. You were perfect—good grades, honor society, nice friends. You never gave Mom and Dad any trouble."

Lainey snorted. "Until your ex-boyfriend got me pregnant."

Julia dismissed that with a wave of her hand. "Then you left and became this world-famous photographer."

"I'm not exactly famous."

"Whatever. You're in *National Geographic*. People have those things on their shelves forever. My work lasts until someone's next bang trim."

"It's not the same thing," Lainey argued.

"That's my point. You have a legacy. I have a plastic crown from prom."

Emotion bubbled inside Lainey. "You're about to have a baby. That trumps a few magazine layouts in the legacy competition."

"You're only twenty-eight," Julia said. "Not exactly old-maid time. You'll meet someone, try again."

"I won't."

"Who knows," Julia continued as if Lainey hadn't spoken, "I've seen the way Ethan looks at you."

"No." Lainey wrenched the steering wheel, and the Land Cruiser skidded into the gravel on the side of the road.

"What the—" Julia cried as dust flew around them.

Lainey slammed her foot on the brake and threw the car into Park. Her fingers gripped the wheel, white-knuckled, and she kept her gaze trained on the horizon. "I *will not* have a baby," she said, enunciating each word.

"You can't know…"

Lainey spun in her seat, unlatching her seat belt as it cut across her neck. "I do know," she screamed. "I won't have a baby. I can't, Julia."

She expected tears to come but only felt a white-hot burning in her throat.

"I don't understand."

Lainey swallowed to ease her pain. She looked out the window past Julia's shoulder. "There were complications from the miscarriage." She shook her head. "I can't have a baby," she repeated.

Julia's cool fingers wrapped around Lainey's fisted ones.

"I'm sorry," her sister whispered. "What did Ethan say? Is that why you left?"

Lainey pulled her hands into her lap. "I didn't tell Ethan right away. I was too devastated. If he'd looked at me with pity I'm not sure I could have stood it."

"When did you tell him?"

"I left a note at the church. I know it was wrong and cowardly, but I was half crazed at that point. Looking at myself in the wedding dress, I couldn't go through with it. I was wearing white and all I could see was red—the blood—there was so much blood. I knew we wouldn't have stood a chance if he didn't know the whole truth. But I *could not* face him."

"So you ran off?"

"I asked him to meet me at the hotel in Charlotte where we were going for our honeymoon if he could be with me knowing everything."

"And?" Julia prompted.

"He never showed."

A look of disbelief crossed Julia's face. "That doesn't sound like Ethan."

Lainey shook her head. "I'd worshipped him for so long. I doubt we ever had a chance. I tried anything I could to make him happy so he'd forget I wasn't you."

"Did you try being yourself?"

"Yeah, right." Lainey pushed her hair behind her ears. "Mom made it very clear that being me didn't hold a candle to being you. Why would Ethan be any different?"

"You should talk to him."

"No way." Lainey shifted into gear. Her stomach clenched. "I have a life of my own now. What happened ten years ago is old news. I don't *want* another chance."

"Are you sure?"

She thought about how it felt to be with Ethan. Just one smile from him made her whole body light up. But she had to protect her heart. She was incomplete, and there was nothing in Brevia that could fill her.

She pulled up in front of the duplex Julia rented near downtown. "It's the only way."

Chapter Eleven

Ethan heard an engine turn off as an unfamiliar tremor of excitement shivered across his chest.

Pita stood and paced circles near the front door, the fur on her back standing on end. Ethan wondered at her reaction. "It's okay, girl."

A knock sounded and the dog growled softly. Ethan wanted to do the same as he identified the man on the other side.

"Hey, son." Ray Daniels took a drag on his cigarette, dropped it on the makeshift porch and ground it under the toe of his dirty sneaker. "How 'bout a hug for your old man?"

Ethan shifted to completely fill the doorframe. The dim evening light threw his father's face into shadow. Pita poked her head around his knee and growled low in her throat. Good instincts, that dog. "What are you doing here?"

Ray glanced at Pita. "Pick up *another* stray, didya? When are you going to stop with the animals?"

"What do you want, Dad?"

A path of deep and sunburned lines wove a pattern around Ray's eyes. It had been two years since his last unannounced visit. He'd aged badly since then. Late nights, forty years of smokes and a taste for Wild Turkey would do that to a man.

"Are you going to invite your old man in, or is your trailer too good for me?"

Ethan stepped back. "I move into the lake house in a couple of weeks," he said through clenched teeth.

"Got a beer?" Ray asked, opening the refrigerator door. "The photos Lainey Morgan took of the shelter mutts were on the front page down in Charleston." Ray used the corner of the counter to pop the top on a bottle of beer. "I can't believe that little tramp has the nerve to show up here after what she did."

"You should stop talking." Ethan clenched his fists to keep from wrapping them around his father's scrawny throat. "She has every right to be here. Vera had a stroke, Dad. Lainey's been helping her."

Ray hitched one hip onto the counter. "Didn't you learn anything from your mama running out on us? The difficult ones aren't worth the trouble. Are you gonna let Lainey mess with your life all over again? You could've been a real M.D., not some backwoods pet vet."

"I like my job."

"Is she that good between the sheets that you'd go running back? Her sister I can understand. I might have tapped that blonde goddess in my day but Lainey—"

Ethan crossed the space in two steps. He grabbed the bottle as Ray lifted it and threw it into the sink with a clatter. "Get out. Now."

Ray lifted his hands, palms out. "I'm between jobs. Thought I might stick around for the big shindig."

"I don't want you anywhere near here."

"I only want what's best for you, son. And Lainey ain't it.

Trust me, I know women, and that one's gonna mess you up bad," he said with a smirk. "I'm staying with your uncle Tony. He's got room since wife number three took off." Ray walked to the door. "Think about what I said and I'll see you around."

Ethan didn't turn as the door slammed shut. His father in town was a complication he didn't need. He'd almost steadied his breathing when his cell phone buzzed from the coffee table. He picked it up, listened for a few moments and muttered a curse.

"I'll be right there."

Grabbing his keys, he hollered over his shoulder, "Let's go, Pita."

It was the longest ten-minute drive of his life. Lainey had been crying so hard he couldn't understand much of what she'd said, only that she needed help. His imagination went wild imagining what might have happened. He saw her car on the side of the two-lane highway, a shadow in the haze of early evening with the hazards blinking like a lighthouse beacon. He barely pulled to a stop before jumping out of the truck.

The driver's side door swung open, the interior light making her hair glow like a patch of sunlight. "I'm here."

As her head lifted, a shadow of frustration crossed her face. "That was quick." She flashed a smile. "How fast were you driving?"

"Are you okay? Were you hurt?" He scanned her body expecting injuries, took her face between his palms. "Can you focus on me?"

"Unfortunately, yes," she whispered as she shrugged out of his grasp. A minivan rumbled past, its engine drowning out her next words. "I blew a tire," she said when the quiet settled again. "Not exactly an emergency."

"It sure as hell sounded like an emergency."

"I had a bad day. A flat tire was the last thing I needed. I overreacted. Sorry." She narrowed her eyes. "Stop looking at me like that."

"Are you going to tell me what happened?"

"I went over a nail or something. I don't know."

"I mean tonight. With Julia."

Her teeth tugged on her bottom lip. "Nothing. We went to class." She turned to the glove compartment. "I have the owner's manual in here. It tells you how to change a tire."

"I know how to put on a spare," he snapped. He didn't need another dose of attitude after his father's visit.

His life may not have been the one he'd planned, but it worked. Ethan didn't need to think too deeply to get through things. He could leave his feelings and his pain buried, just where he liked them. Being near Lainey made him think about too much that he didn't want to deal with—his past, his shortcomings, his empty life.

He'd thought he could make this summer easier for her and it would right all his wrongs. Assuming he could keep his heart out of the mix was stupid.

His gaze settled on her trembling fingers as she fumbled with the latch for the glove compartment then shifted to her face where color crept into her cheeks, her jaw tight with obvious frustration. He couldn't stand to see her like this.

"Come on," he said and reached in front of her to take the keys out of the ignition. "It's almost dark. I'll take you home and change the tire in the morning."

"Pita—"

He straightened, keys in hand. "Is in the truck. It's not safe to let her out here." As if on cue, a round of muted barking split the night air.

Her eyes squeezed shut for a moment. "I need to get my camera out of the back." Gravel crunched as she climbed out next to him. He reached forward and traced his finger along her jawline, hoping to relieve some of her tension. A shiver ran down her body, and the air surrounding them grew heavy with emotions he thought he'd left safely behind in his youth.

For now he stepped away. He shut the door and near darkness swallowed them. "Get your stuff. I'll be in the truck."

Lainey stood on the side of the road for several seconds before making her way to the back of the SUV. She felt open, exposed and once again attached to Brevia. She'd stayed away from connections that could lead to heartache since she'd left a decade ago. It wasn't the best life, but she knew it and could manage the consequences of her decisions. What she couldn't handle were her mother's expectations, her sister depending on her and the man waiting to drive her home. Even a dog seemed like too much of a burden right now.

She stalked toward the truck and flung her equipment into the backseat. Pita waited with enthusiastic tail wagging. The urge to wrap her arms around the dog's fluffy neck flashed.

No.

She didn't need anyone or anything in Brevia. "Pita, down." Her voice reflected her temper, and guilt immediately coursed through her as the dog flattened itself against the backseat.

Lainey heaved a sigh as she climbed in next to Ethan.

"What's the matter?"

She made a show of digging through her purse. "I'm tired and ready to be home."

His mouth thinned as he watched her. Maybe he wondered if she meant her home in New Mexico or her mother's house. Right now, she didn't know.

He eased the truck on to the highway. Grateful for the silence, she studied the occasional lights of farmhouses out the window and the pale white line at the side of the road. Soon her attention refocused on the man next to her and the dog's soft snoring from the backseat. The companionable stillness only heightened her nerves.

They were at the house in a few minutes. A light glowed in one of the upstairs windows. For a split second, she wished her mother was waiting then cursed her own weakness.

As soon as the truck stopped, Lainey scrambled out, the dog at her heels. "Thanks for the ride," she called over her shoulder, not daring to look back. She needed space. Ethan's door slammed shut as she fumbled with her keys and Pita danced around her legs.

Without switching on the light, she walked into the kitchen. She rested her hands on the table and counted backward from ten, pictured her mother, sang the ABC's in her head, anything to forget the way her body ached.

She didn't move, didn't speak. Only a minute more and she'd be back to normal.

Until he touched her.

Only the brush of fingers against the top of her arm. She waited for him to pull her to him. He continued to trace a light pattern across her skin. Nothing more.

"What are you doing?"

"Trying not to pressure you. To give you space." He paused. "Trying to be the man you want me to be."

"Ethan, I don't know…"

He pulled his hand away. "What do you want, Lainey?" he whispered. "Do you want me to go? I will. You need time? I'll give it to you. But tell me—"

She whirled and pressed her mouth hard against his. She couldn't say what she wanted, but at this moment she knew to the depths of her soul she needed his kiss.

Maybe it was wrong.

Of course it was wrong.

She wasn't nineteen anymore with youth as an excuse to be swept away in the moment. She knew better. Life wasn't a fairy tale, and even loving someone with your whole self didn't guarantee a happy ending.

She didn't care about how this ended. Didn't care if being with him ripped open her heart yet again.

She needed him so much it made her body shudder.

Before she knew it, he'd lifted her shirt over her head. She tried to turn to him, but he pulled her back against his chest. Somehow, he'd pulled off his shirt, too, and his chest hair tickled her bare back.

He lifted one bra strap slowly, kissing her shoulder, then let it fall down around her elbow. She clutched at his arm as his hand cupped her breast. He tilted her face to his and kissed her deeply, catching her moan in his mouth.

"My legs," she breathed. "I don't think…"

He laughed low as he scooped her into his arms.

He carried her up the stairs, his mouth never leaving hers. A shaft of moonlight sifted through the bedroom curtains as he laid her down against the pillows. She watched him undress, as always overwhelmed by his pure physical perfection.

She glanced down at her faded beige bra. "I'm sorry. I would have worn something…you know, fancy, if I'd thought…"

Ethan bent his head and dropped a line of kisses from her rib cage to where the top of her jeans skimmed her hips.

"Do you remember the first time we made love?" he asked.

"Uh-huh." She licked her lips, finding it hard to concentrate as he ran his tongue across her belly button.

"You were wearing a white bra." As he spoke, he pulled the jeans down around her hips. "It had one small bow right in the middle." His eyes darkened to the color of melted chocolate. "Kind of like the one you're wearing now."

If her mind hadn't been so clouded by desire, Lainey might have laughed. She'd been buying the same style of bras for as long as she could remember. At least ten years, apparently.

He tossed her jeans off the bed and skimmed his hands up her legs from her ankles, finally coming to rest on her hips.

His fingers grazed under the waistband of her panties then pulled her down until she was flat on the mattress, gazing into his dark eyes.

"I have never been so turned on by a woman as I was that night."

She closed her eyes and gave into the pleasure of feeling his body above hers. His lips didn't quite touch her, his breath cool as it blew against her hot skin.

"Until now," he whispered.

Her eyes flew open. "Really?"

He smoothed back the hair from her face, cradling her head in his hands with such tenderness tears pricked the back of her eyes.

"Yes, Lainey. Really."

It seemed impossible, but she knew he was telling the truth. Never once could she have imagined he wanted her that much. His desire was liberating.

Lainey gave herself over to her body. She didn't think, didn't analyze. No second-guessing or worrying about how she didn't measure up. They rolled together, a tangle of arms and legs until they finally melded into one.

Later—much later—he pulled her close, settling her back against his chest as he wrapped around her, cocooning her in his warmth. She fell asleep that way and when she woke, his arm was still snug across her chest.

The next several days kept Lainey busy. In addition to the animals at All Creatures Great and Small, adoptable pets would be brought in from shelters as far away as Atlanta. She needed to make sure a plan for housing the animals was worked out in advance. Without Vera, Ethan became the resident expert on animal behavior, so he decided on the best arrangement.

He also made dozens of phone calls to local and regional

businesses soliciting donations for raffle prizes and silent auction items. She'd tried not to be alone with him since the night they'd slept together, her only hope for self-preservation, but couldn't stop her body from craving his touch.

It felt like he could read her mind. He didn't try to kiss or hold her again, but when no one was looking she caught him staring at her, a wolfish smile curving his lips. Every look he gave her was like nonphysical foreplay—as if there could be such a thing.

Lainey took to walking around the shelter several times each hour just to catch her breath. *Get a grip,* she told herself. *It was sex. You've had sex before.* Maybe not for a while and never so good it left a glow three days later.

But still just sex. Nothing more. Nothing at all.

This was day number four, and she felt like an addict itching for a fix. Which may have explained why she was on her fifth lap around the building.

"You're wearing a path in the grass."

Ethan's voice snapped her out of her thoughts. He stood a few feet to her side on the lawn between the shelter and clinic buildings.

She pressed her hand to her heart. "You shouldn't sneak up on a person like that."

"I've been watching you circle the property for ten minutes. I'm starting to get dizzy."

"I needed a break. I think better when I'm moving."

He shifted his weight to one foot and adjusted the ball cap on his head. "What are you thinking about?" he asked, his voice laced with meaning.

She stomped one foot. "You're an egomaniac. For your information, you are not one bit on my mind."

His smile told her he knew exactly what she was thinking. "I have a couple of charts to finish. Do you want to grab dinner later?"

"I'm not hungry." Her stomach growled.

"Thirty minutes?"

"We shouldn't be seen together."

His smile vanished. "Why?"

"People will talk."

He moved in on her so quickly she didn't have time to dart away. "Darlin'," he said, his face inches from hers, "tongues have been wagging about us since you drove over the county line. Why do you care?"

"No one wants me messing with you."

"Are you messing with me?"

She stepped to the side, needing breathing space. "You know my deal. What I can and can't give."

"It's dinner." He flashed a coaxing smile. "What's the worst that could happen? What are you so afraid of?"

"Fine," she huffed, shaking her head. "But as friends."

"With amazing benefits?" he asked, winking.

She picked up a ratty tennis ball from the yard and shook it at his head. "Don't try anything funny. I mean it."

In exactly thirty-one minutes he came to the makeshift studio she'd set up in one of the shelter's empty offices.

He'd showered and changed into dark jeans and a pale green button-down shirt. His smile flashed model white against a tanned face. She pulled her hair from its loose bun.

"Sorry," she said automatically, placing her camera on the worktable. She hooked a leash to the golden retriever she'd been photographing. "I should have changed."

"You look beautiful," he said with complete sincerity.

Her heart turned somersaults in her chest, a clear reaction to the way his eyes followed her. She smoothed her hands over her wrinkled pants. "You need to get out more." She laughed, trying to lighten the mood.

"Only with you." He stepped toward her, so close she could smell the mix of the shower and his own spicy scent. He uncurled her fingers and took the leash from her, his thumb brushing against the sensitive flesh inside her palm.

"I'll put this one away and meet you out front." He turned and the dog trotted behind him as he left the room.

Lainey rested a hand on the table to steady herself. "He's not playing fair," she murmured to Pita. The dog pricked her ears and cocked her head to one side as she watched Lainey from her dog bed.

Lainey turned off the equipment, quickly applied lip-gloss and gave the dog a quick scratch behind the ears. The puppy, Chip, snuggled in the crook of the older dog's neck. "I'll be back soon, you two. Wish me luck."

Pita's tail thumped twice before she buried her nose under Chip's chubby back end.

Lainey grimaced. "I know. Right?"

Chapter Twelve

Ethan took her to the Pinebrook Inn, a popular upscale restaurant on the edge of town. The time flew by as they talked. Ethan seemed to love hearing about her travels, although he admitted he hadn't even made it to the coast in over a year. This man dedicated to his work and the community was so different from the boy she'd known. It was still hard to wrap her mind around the changes in him.

By the time they headed back to the clinic, her whole body itched with anticipation. She wanted more time with him, as much as she could get. A siren wailed behind them, and Ethan pulled to the side of the road as a fire engine raced past.

"Wonder where they're headed."

Ethan eased back on to the two-lane highway. "Could be…" They watched the fire truck take a right turn at the top of the rise. The road that led to the clinic.

Lainey's blood turned to ice. "You don't think…" Her head thumped against the seat as Ethan slammed his foot on the gas pedal. He turned off the highway and raced along the darkened road as she sent up a string of silent prayers.

Before they got close, a bright light shone through the trees. She rolled down her window, and the acrid scent of smoke leeched into the truck, winding its way through every fiber of her being.

"Oh, no," she whispered as they pulled into the clinic's driveway.

Flames licked the night sky above the shelter. Two fire engines flanked the building, which seemed to glow from within. Huge plumes of smoke soared into the air as firefighters sprayed water from long hoses. Lainey felt mesmerized by the scene, as if watching the whole thing in slow motion.

Ethan's harsh voice broke her reverie. "Call Steph," he ordered, handing Lainey his phone as he parked at the edge of the property. "And stay back."

He jumped out of the truck and headed for the shelter. Obviously, his command only applied to her. Her fingers trembled as she pulled up Steph's number.

After Steph promised to call the other vets and staff, Lainey stepped out of the truck. The air was hot, thick with smoke and tiny ribbons of ash. She walked a few paces in a daze as firefighters ran from the building, cages or animals cradled in their arms.

She saw Ethan near one of the trucks, clearly arguing with Sam Callahan, Brevia's new police chief. He threw up his hands then turned away toward a firefighter holding the leash of the golden retriever she'd photographed earlier.

The gravity of the situation hit her. She was watching her mother's dream—her father's legacy—literally go up in smoke.

"No!" she screamed, although no one heard her over the roar of water gushing from the hoses.

She ran forward, scooping a trembling tabby cat out of the arms of a firefighter.

Ethan was at her side in an instant. "I told you to stay back," he yelled over the noise. "It's too dangerous."

She shook her head, her eyes filling with tears, both from the heavy smoke and pure adrenaline. "We have to help get the animals out."

His mouth pressed into a thin frown, but he nodded. "The fire's in back. We have empty kennels in the clinic and barn. Put the cages in my office."

Without a word, she turned and ran toward the clinic. Back and forth she raced, her chest burning from the smoke and heat. She'd come to know many of the shelter animals and whispered words of comfort between coughing fits.

Soon Steph and one of the other vets arrived, setting up a triage unit in the barn's tack room.

As she moved across the property, a tendril of dread crept up her spine, as if she were forgetting something. She walked into the barn and looked around wildly.

Steph glanced up from where she was cleaning a burn on the leg of a black Lab. "You look like you saw a ghost."

Lainey whipped around and tore back across the lawn toward the shelter. The fire was finally under control, although small towers of flame still rose into the sky at the far end of the building.

Ethan walked toward her, arms outstretched. "The kennels are empty. They're all out."

"Pita," Lainey gasped. "Have you seen Pita and the puppy?"

Ethan glanced to either side. "I'm sure she's here. She wasn't locked up. Probably got spooked and took off into the woods. We'll look for her after—"

"No!" Lainey cut him off. "You don't understand. Chip— the puppy—was shut in my mom's office. I brought him in because Pita spent all day outside his cage in the main kennel. I moved his bed from the studio to the office before we went to dinner. She would've never left him."

Ethan looked over his shoulder at the smoldering building, smoke billowing around it like a blanket. "Vera's office was near the back of the shelter."

He used the past tense. The back of the building looked like a mass of charred kindling. A half dozen firefighters clustered around, still spraying small areas of flames.

She sucked in a shallow breath. "No," she repeated.

"Lainey." Ethan reached for her but she ran full speed toward the building. He caught her against his solid chest. When she fought, he wrapped his arms tight around her.

"Let me go. I need to find her. She's still in there."

"If she's…" His voice was rough against her ear. "Nothing could survive that."

"No!" She flailed her arms, but he pinned them against her sides. She couldn't bring herself to imagine Pita in the office as the walls burned around her. Rage and guilt filled her at the thought of the terror the dog must have felt.

"I can't lose her like this. Please, Ethan," she begged, not sure what she was asking. "Please."

He set her away from him, and her shaking legs were forced to hold her up. "Stay here," he commanded. "I mean it, Lainey."

She wiped the back of her arm across her face. "What are you going to do?"

He didn't answer, just stalked to the shelter's front entrance. At least where the door had been before the fire crew bashed it in to get to the animals.

She saw Sam grab Ethan's arm as he got closer. Ethan said something she couldn't hear, pointing at the shelter then glancing back at her. The two men talked for a moment before Sam took a flashlight from one of the other officers standing nearby. Sam nodded at the young deputy then followed Ethan into the building.

Lainey felt an arm curl around her shoulder.

"Steph called me," Julia said softly. "I got a hold of the hospital and told them not to let Mom know. I'm so sorry."

Lainey's eyes never left the gaping hole where Ethan had disappeared.

"How are you holding up?" Julia tried to draw her away. "Where's Ethan?"

Lainey pointed toward the remains of the shelter. "Pita's still in there. He went after her."

Julia went still. "He couldn't have. That part of the building is about to come down."

As if on cue, a terrible cracking reverberated through the night, and the back of the shelter caved in on itself.

"Ethan!" Lainey screamed and twisted out of Julia's grasp. Her lungs burned from the smoke and from trying to gulp in air. One of the firefighters grabbed her as she ran past. She fought against him, struggling with all her strength.

What had she done? Ethan would have never gone into the shelter if not for her pleas.

"Let me go," she screeched. She kicked and scratched at him, anything she could do to wrestle free.

She saw a shadow out of the corner of her eyes. The firefighter released her and she stumbled forward, landing on one knee, her eyes riveted to the front of the shelter.

From the smoke a figure emerged. Ethan staggered out of the building, cradling Pita in his arms. Two firefighters ran to him. One tried to take Pita, but Ethan didn't let go. Sam Callahan came out a moment later, Chip tucked under one arm. Ethan's gaze crashed into hers.

By the time she got close, a crowd of firefighters and emergency workers surrounded him. Lainey pushed people out of the way and threw her arms around his neck. He held Pita but leaned in close.

"Thank God," she whispered and pressed her mouth against his. She didn't care who saw, didn't think about anything except that he was safe.

She felt Pita shift and looked down. The dog's normally fluffy fur was matted and damp. Patches of red skin showed where fur had burned away.

"My sweet girl." Lainey smoothed debris off the dog's head. "Is she hurt?"

"I don't think so, but I'm worried about smoke inhalation." Ethan bent his head on a round of choking coughs.

"Give her to me," Lainey told him. "You need to be checked by the EMTs."

"I'm fine. Just need water." He coughed again. Lainey knew he'd have to be on his deathbed before he let go of the dog.

"Come on." She took his arm. "Sam, can you bring the puppy?"

"I've got her." Julia answered. She stood next to the police chief, her hand on his back as she cradled Chip to her chest.

Harlan Knox, the fire chief, stepped in front of them as they headed for the clinic. "Next time, Ethan, leave the rescuing to us."

"Will do, Chief."

They walked arm in arm. "Since when did you become such a damn hero?" Lainey asked, her voice thick with emotion.

"Since you needed one," he answered without breaking stride.

She lost her footing for a moment before righting herself. "Is she really okay?" Lainey opened the side door. "She's so still."

Ethan maneuvered Pita onto the examination table in

the back room. The dog tried to lift her head, but the effort seemed too much for her. "It's the smoke that's her problem. The whole place was one black cloud."

A small sob broke from Lainey's lips.

He met her gaze, his eyes serious. "I *will* take care of her."

"I know."

Julia came into the room at that moment, trailed by Steph and the young vet, Paul Thie.

"This puppy is shaking so hard I can hear his teeth rattling."

"Yours would, too, if you'd just been trapped in a burning building." Steph reached for Chip but the little dog clung to Julia for dear life.

"Are you ready to be a dog mom, too?" Steph asked. "He's definitely attached to you."

"I think I'll have my hands full," Julia answered but snuggled Chip closer before pulling him off and handing him to Steph.

Lainey saw Ethan glance at Julia, a small smile curving one side of his mouth. She swallowed hard.

"I'm going to check in with Harlan," she said, her throat raw.

"I'll come with you." Julia turned for the door.

They found the fire chief and Sam huddled together near Sam's police cruiser.

Harlan straightened as the two women walked closer. "Where's Ethan?"

"Taking care of my…of the dog he brought out of the building. What's going on?"

Harlan glanced between Lainey and Julia. "I know what this place means to your mother. I'm sorry, girls."

Lainey nodded, but she could tell there was something he wasn't saying. "Do you know how the fire started?"

Harlan shook his head. "We're trying to figure it out—should know more by morning. Are the animals settled?"

"Almost," Julia answered. "Luckily, none of them were seriously injured."

"It's a good thing your mama had that sprinkler system installed. Tell Ethan I'll come by in the morning." Harlan rubbed his forehead as he surveyed the property. "If he has another place to sleep tonight, that would be good."

"He can stay with me," Lainey said then blushed as she felt three pair of eyes on her. "In the spare bedroom at Vera's." She offered Sam a smile. "Thank you for your help with the puppy."

He nodded. "My pleasure." His gaze strayed to Julia. "Let me know if there's anything else."

Lainey and Julia started back toward the clinic. "I think Harlan knows more than he's letting on." Lainey pushed her hair out of her face.

"Don't go looking for trouble," Julia told her with a level gaze. "It will find you all on its own."

Ethan and Steph were still bent over Pita while the puppy watched intently from his bed in one of the smaller kennels.

"Chip is okay, then?"

Ethan looked up. "When we found them, Pita was lying on top of the puppy, shielding him from most of the debris and heat."

Lainey bent her head close to Pita's face. "You are such a good girl," she whispered. Pita licked at Lainey's tearstained cheek. "He's your baby and you are the best mother."

Emotion threatened to overtake her. She straightened, praying she could hold it together.

Julia cleared her throat. "I'm going to check on everyone in the barn and then head home. Lainey, I'll see Mom in the morning."

"I don't want her to know until we find out how bad it really is."

Julia nodded. "I'll do my best."

"I'll walk out with you." Steph turned to Ethan. "Unless you want me to stay."

He shook his head. "Go home now. Paul and one of the techs said they'd stay overnight. We couldn't have done it without you, Steph."

Steph gave Ethan a quick hug. Lainey saw him wince, but before she could say anything, Steph's arms wrapped around her. "We'll fix this," her friend whispered. "We can make it right again."

Julia started for the door. "Get some rest tonight, you two."

"Thanks, Juls," Ethan answered. "You, too, Steph. For everything."

Lainey rounded on Ethan as soon as they were alone. "You're hurt."

He shrugged. "A few scratches, a couple burns. Nothing major."

"You should have let the EMTs take a look."

"I'm fine. I'll finish here, check on the other animals before I go."

She wanted to argue but didn't. He looked exhausted, but she knew he wasn't going to slow down now.

"I'll be fine at the lake house." He kept his attention focused on Pita. "I don't have to come to your place."

She didn't hesitate. "I want you to."

He met her gaze. "Thank you."

"I should be thanking you." One side of her mouth curved up. "Again."

The puppy whined. Pita tried to stand but Ethan held her steady. "He's okay, Pita."

"Can we take her with us?"

"I think she'll be happier here." Ethan picked Pita up off

the table. The dog shook her head and stretched the leg Ethan had bandaged. She limped over to the kennel with Chip and pushed against the metal gate. "Paul can give her more oxygen if she needs it."

Lainey bent and patted the dog's fur, nuzzling her face into Pita's neck. "You want to be with your baby, don't you?"

Lainey wiped at her wet cheeks and ruffled Pita's fur. Her heart clenched with unfamiliar emotions, emotions she imagined a mother could feel putting her young child on the school bus for the first time or watching years later as that grown child left for college.

"Go on, Pita. Stay with him." She gave a self-deprecating laugh. "He needs you more than I do."

Pita watched her a moment longer then stepped slowly into the kennel. She turned around several times and sank to the floor, her bandaged paw stuck out in front of her. Chip scrambled over her back, tumbling to the front of the cage. Pita barked softly and the puppy waddled back, curling into a ball at her side.

Lainey closed the door to the cage and took several deep breaths before standing. "Maybe we can find a home for them together," she said casually.

When Ethan didn't answer, she glanced over. He stared at her, hands on his hips.

"What?" She slammed shut a cabinet door. "She needs a real family, people who will take care of her." A tremor snaked through her body. "Not let her get stuck in a burning building," she muttered.

"It wasn't your fault." Ethan's arms wrapped around her waist. "She needs you," he whispered into her hair. "Just like I do."

She knew she should pull away. Like the fire had engulfed the shelter, her emotions were stripping away the careful defenses she'd built around her heart, burning down her walls until she was left exposed and vulnerable. Instead, she buried her head against Ethan's neck. "I was so scared," she said, her voice raw. "For you, for Pita—of losing you both."

"I'm here." He smoothed his hands along her back. "I've always been here."

The clinic door banged open and Harlan's voice rang out in the quiet. "Ethan?"

"In the back." Ethan dropped a quick kiss on Lainey's forehead.

She sagged against the desk as Harlan walked into the room. "We've done all we can tonight." He rubbed his thick fingers along his neck. "I'll be here first thing tomorrow. Sam, too."

Lainey's head snapped up. "Why will Sam be back? Do you suspect arson?"

Ethan put his hand on her arm. "We'll talk in the morning. Thanks for everything you did tonight."

She nodded. "Yes, thank you."

Harlan turned for the door. "Night y'all."

When it clicked shut, Lainey glanced at Ethan. "Why did you stop me?"

He trailed his hand down her arm and laced their fingers together. "It's almost midnight. Everyone is exhausted. We'll have time to piece it together in the morning."

"You're right, but I don't understand how this happened."

He tugged her toward the hallway, flipping the lights off as he went. "Say it again." He led her out into the darkness.

"Say what?" The smell of smoke still filled the air, burning her eyes as they walked to his truck.

"That I'm right."

She grinned, amazed he could make her smile even after the night they'd had. "If you want, we can take my car. I'll come back in the morning, too."

He squeezed her hand before letting go. "Let me grab a change of clothes," he said and moved toward the trailer.

For a moment Lainey wondered if she was doing the right thing but pushed her doubts aside. After what they'd just been through, tonight she was following her heart. No matter what.

Chapter Thirteen

Ethan stepped into the stream of hot water and plunged his head under the spray. Dirt and grime slipped away, but nothing could wash off the outright terror of watching the shelter he'd helped build burn before his eyes.

The door to the bathroom opened and he pulled his head out of the water.

"Ethan? Is it okay if I wait in here?" Lainey's voice was hesitant. "The house feels too quiet."

"Sure." He opened the shower door just an inch. She'd changed into a pair of pink-and-yellow polka-dot boxers and matching sleeveless pajama shirt.

"There's room in here for two," he said, then cursed himself. The last thing he wanted to do was scare her off.

To his surprise, she answered with a small, "Okay."

His eyes widened.

"I keep thinking of you and Pita, of the noise from the animals trapped in the building. I changed clothes, brushed my hair. The smoke smell is worse than before."

Ethan wiped his face clear of water and looked at her more closely. Her shoulders shook in an obvious attempt to control her emotions.

"I don't know what's wrong with me." She tried to laugh but it came out as a moan. She bent forward. "I can't...stop... crying," she said between sobs.

He threw wide the shower door and hauled her in, pressing her head into his neck. His back took the brunt of the shower spray to protect her from the streaming water. He whispered words of comfort against the top of her head, using a strength he didn't know he possessed to assure her that everything would be okay.

That he would keep her safe.

Always.

It wasn't a promise he could keep. But he'd say anything to calm her, to stop her tears.

When she'd told him about losing the baby, she hadn't cried. She'd looked more miserable than he could imagine, but her eyes had remained dry. He'd had to walk away so he wouldn't break down in front of her, but she'd remained calm.

They may have stayed together for a few minutes or a half hour. At one point, Ethan reached behind him to adjust the hot water knob. Otherwise, he simply held her, offering his strength and support—hoping this time it would be enough to see her through.

Eventually her body went still, but Ethan didn't move. Not until he felt her head tip. He looked down and saw her eyes focused on an area just below his shoulder.

"You're hurt." Her green eyes transformed to smoky gray.

"A couple of scratches. No big deal."

Pressing her soft mouth to his injury, her fingers spread through the hair on his chest.

His eyes drifted shut as a groan escaped his lips.

Her head rose. "Did I hurt you?"

"That feels…"

She trailed more kisses along his chest and the base of his neck.

"…real good," he finished.

"Ethan?" Her voice hummed along his throat.

"Mmm," was all he could manage.

"I'm wearing my pajamas in the shower." She smiled. She looked so beautiful and sexy, water beading on her face and hair.

"I can help you with that." His hands moved to the front of her and fumbled with the fabric-covered buttons, peeling her shirt off.

When she lifted her hands to her breasts, he pulled them away. "You are incredible."

"You, too," she whispered. Her fingers laced through his wet hair, pushing it off his face. She met his gaze, her eyes heavy with desire. "I want you to know I'm yours."

His lungs expanded so fast it made him dizzy. He knew she meant at this moment. But he hadn't realized until now that those were the words he'd been waiting to hear for the past ten years. Maybe his whole life.

Leaning forward, he kissed her. "First things first," he murmured and picked up a bottle of shampoo.

She made a face and held out her hand. "I still smell like smoke, don't I?"

Instead of handing it to her, he poured the thick, pink liquid into his own palm. "Every single inch of you smells and tastes exactly right." He rubbed his hands together then combed his fingers through her curls.

She groaned with pleasure as he massaged his hands against her scalp. The smell of strawberries and honey filled the small space. Lainey closed her eyes and swayed a little as she tipped back her head to rinse out the shampoo.

She turned her head. "I need you," she said against his mouth, her voice hoarse. She spun and pressed into him, wound her arms around his neck so she could bring him closer. "Now."

In seconds, they were out of the shower and into her bed. They stayed together for hours until every part of Lainey tingled. As she drifted toward sleep, Ethan pulled her closer to him, the heat from his body keeping her warm in the cool of the quiet house as he dropped a kiss on the top of her head.

She sighed and snuggled tighter, feeling more at home in his arms than she had any place else in the world.

The next thing Lainey knew, bright sunlight spilled into the room. She blinked several times, and her eyes focused on Ethan. He was only inches away, staring into her eyes with a quiet intensity that made her heart squeeze.

"Morning," he whispered, one side of his mouth pulling up into a crooked grin.

"Did you sleep?" With her free hand, she tugged on the sheet that covered her from the waist down.

"Some." He drew her hand to his lips, kissing each fingertip. "It was more fun to stay awake and watch you."

"That doesn't sound interesting." She yanked on the sheet again.

"Sleeping, snoring, hogging all the covers…" He grabbed the edge of the sheet and flipped it to the bottom of the bed. "Everything you do fascinates me."

"Hey," she protested. "It's cold in here."

He rolled on top of her, his body giving off more heat than a furnace.

She wriggled her hips then laughed when he moaned. "Shouldn't we get to the clinic?"

"It's early," he said with a hoarse gasp. "We have just enough time."

"For what?" Her hands ran down the corded muscles of his back.

"Let me show you," he answered and covered her mouth with his.

Ethan glanced at Lainey every thirty seconds on the way to the clinic until she begged him to stop.

"Do you think it's a sign?" she asked.

"Of what?"

"I wasn't meant to come back."

"It was a terrible accident. End of story."

He saw her swallow and wished he could convince her. The way Ethan saw it, last night had been a sign that he'd been a bigger idiot than he knew ten years ago. Watching the flames consume the shelter, he'd realized the building didn't matter. The animals had been safe and Lainey was by his side.

He'd let her go too easily that day at the church. Let his pride get in the way of going after her, of convincing her they belonged together. Last night he'd realized if he took care of what was really important in his life, he could handle the other stuff no matter how bad things got.

He pulled down the long driveway leading to the clinic. Cars were parked in the grass on either side. A steady stream of people walked toward the property, stepping off the road to let his truck pass.

Lainey sucked in a breath. "Oh, no."

Several men waved to him. "What are they doing here?" he muttered.

"I wanted to keep this quiet," Lainey said miserably. "Figure out how to fix it before Mama found out."

After parking, he went around to Lainey's side and slipped his fingers into hers.

"Don't do that," she said, tugging her hand back. "It'll just give them more to gossip about."

He didn't release her. "Let them talk."

His gaze was drawn to the shelter building. It was hard to imagine heat and flames engulfing it last night. The stale scent of smoke still clung to the air.

In the back of his mind, Ethan could hear the deafening noise of the building crashing in around him. He forced himself to tune in to the sounds of the morning. Tires crunching over gravel, birds from the surrounding forest.

"They're going to think I'm taking advantage of you." Lainey's eyes were wide and vulnerable.

"I'm a big boy."

One side of her mouth curved up. "Don't I know it," she muttered.

He laughed and pressed his lips to hers, not caring if the whole town watched.

"We're all right," she whispered when he pulled back.

"Oh, yeah," he answered. He walked toward the crowd, ignoring the raised eyebrows and stares several people leveled at him.

"Harlan." He approached the fire chief. "What the hell is going on? This place is a three-ring circus."

"Ain't that the truth." Harlan jerked his head toward the clinic. Ethan and Lainey followed him. "It sure isn't making my job easier."

Ethan ran one hand through his hair and muttered a string of curses. "I've got a solution for that. This is private property—my property." He whirled and started down the porch steps.

"Wait." Lainey's hand on his arm stilled him. She turned to Harlan. "What have you found?"

Harlan shifted uncomfortably from one foot to the other. "Nothing's official yet."

Ethan stepped onto the porch, using his size to tower over the short, balding fire chief. "These people are here because of what you're not telling us."

Harlan rested his hands on his wide hips and pushed back off his heels. "As best we can tell, it started in one of the back rooms. Maybe arson."

"How?" Lainey asked.

"A lamp tipped onto a pile of newspapers."

"My studio," Lainey whispered.

Harlan's tone was all business. "We're still working to determine the sequence of events. But…"

Rage exploded inside Ethan like a cannon. "But what, Harlan? What are you trying to say?"

"You think I did it on purpose." Lainey's voice was achingly quiet and devoid of emotion.

"I think it was a careless mistake." Harlan heaved a weary sigh. "But I've heard mumblings from certain individuals." His eyes settled on Lainey again. "People who've been around for a while—who remember you leaving."

Ethan was numb with disbelief. He stood in shock as Lainey walked to the edge of the porch, her back to him, arms ramrod straight at her side.

He focused on Harlan and spoke through clenched teeth. "That is the biggest load of bull I've ever heard and you know it."

Harlan shrugged. "It's no secret she didn't want to come back. This kind of trouble could derail the event, make it easier for her to leave town again."

Ethan gripped the porch railing. "Lainey put her life on hold to help her mother. She's dealt with more garbage from people around here than anyone deserves. Even if she didn't want to come back, you know she'd never do anything to hurt the animals at the shelter." He shook his head, frustration and anger radiating through every pore.

Harlan held both palms up. "Don't shoot the messenger."

"I'm going after anyone I hear talking smack on her."
Ethan pushed one finger into Harlan's meaty chest. "Why
don't you send *that* message around?"

"Fine." Harlan waved his hand toward the crowd in the
parking lot. "What are you going to do about *them?*"

Ethan took a breath and ran his hands through his hair.
"Give me a minute."

With a last look at Lainey, Harlan nodded and walked
down the steps toward the shelter.

Lainey turned slowly when Harlan was out of earshot. Her
eyes were bright.

"I'm sorry—"

"Were you serious?" she interrupted.

"Hell, yeah. I'll get rid of them all." He'd single-handedly
throw every person in this town off the property.

"No." She waved one hand in front of her face. "I mean
what you said to Harlan about me. You believe I'm telling
the truth?"

"Of course."

"There isn't a hint of doubt in your mind?" She took a
step closer, her eyes searching his. "Maybe," she suggested,
"I unconsciously want to sabotage the event."

"That's ridiculous." He didn't understand why she was
talking crazy but a small voice inside him said it was a test.
One he had to pass. "It doesn't matter what anyone says. I
know it. I know you."

She launched herself toward him, twining her arms around
his neck. "You believe me," she whispered.

Suddenly he was transported back to a Sunday afternoon
ten years ago. She'd told him she was pregnant and he'd felt
like an avalanche had landed on top of him. He couldn't
breathe, couldn't get his bearings in the maelstrom of shock
and disbelief.

He hadn't thought she'd done it on purpose. Not until Julia had suggested it at dinner later that night when they'd told their parents.

She'd accused Lainey of trapping him. He'd seen the question in her parents' eyes. For an instant, he'd allowed himself to wonder. She'd looked at him in that moment and he realized now what his doubt had done to her.

He cradled her cheeks between his palms. "I should never have doubted you."

She swallowed hard, and he knew she understood he wasn't talking about today. "It's okay."

"No, it isn't." He placed a soft kiss on her mouth. "I'm sorry. I'll spend as long as you'll let me making it up to you."

He kissed her again. "Let me get rid of these people."

"No." She pulled away from him. "I need everyone together in front of the shelter."

"Are you sure that's a good idea?"

"I have to try to make them understand. Give me a minute to splash cold water on my face."

He studied her but nodded.

Kissing him one last time, she walked into the clinic.

With a deep breath he turned toward the parking lot. "Okay, folks," he shouted. "Listen up…"

Chapter Fourteen

Lainey dug her fingernails into her palms as she walked across the driveway toward the shelter. Maybe the biting pain would help her ignore her pounding heart.

Her mind circled around her last minutes in the office yesterday. She'd turned off the light before leaving, hadn't she? Of course she wanted the event to be a success, no matter the feelings this town brought to the surface in her. She clung to her beliefs as she faced the crowd.

Whispers and murmurs skittered through the group as people spotted her. A volunteer from the shelter reached out as she passed, so numb she barely felt the embrace.

She moved to the front of the large group where Ethan stood with Harlan and Sam Callahan.

The police chief had found her in the clinic just after she'd come out of the bathroom, letting her know the fire had officially been ruled an accident.

"I don't know how the rumors spread so quickly," Sam had said.

"Welcome to life in a small town," she'd answered. Sam had moved from Brooklyn last year, so Lainey knew he still hadn't entirely grasped what life in a community the size of Brevia would mean.

Lainey understood it like the back of her hand. For most of her life, she'd tried to make herself into the kind of girl this town wanted her to be. She'd spent the next chunk running from those arbitrary expectations and her complete failure to meet them.

Today was different. Today she'd move forward on her own terms.

Ethan offered an encouraging smile. "What do you need?"

"I'm good." She tried to return his smile but had a hard time making her lips move. She wanted to relieve some of the palpable tension that hung in the air like heavy fog. "You've… uh…got my butt, right?"

Harlan coughed and Sam turned away as Ethan's eyes widened.

Heat flushed her cheeks. "What?"

His grin spread. "Usually it goes, 'you've got my back.'"

She cringed. "Oops." She felt like a fool but found it easier to smile back at him. "Here goes everything."

She kept her eyes trained on the few friendly faces she spotted.

"Thank you," she began on a squeak then cleared her throat. Although she assumed many in the crowd were here to publically condemn her for any part she played in this tragedy, she was determined to hold her head high. "I can't tell you how much it means to me," she said, her voice ringing out in the sudden quiet, "how much it would mean to my mother to see all of you here today ready to help rebuild what she created."

She saw a couple of older women murmur to one another but continued, "The shelter suffered a terrible tragedy last night. Fire broke out in the room where I've been photographing the animals." She paused for a breath. "For any part I've played in this horrible accident, I'm deeply sorry."

She struggled to remain in control of her emotions. "Miraculously, none of the animals were seriously injured. Something for which Ethan and I—and everyone at the clinic and shelter—will always be grateful." She dabbed her fingers under her eyes. "Several people have suggested the adoption event may not go forward. I'm here to tell you now more than ever, we need to work together to find good homes for our animals."

Confidence blossomed inside her as a number of people nodded. "It will take time and energy to rebuild, but we're going to keep at it until every single rescue pet has been adopted. My father founded this clinic and my mother has devoted her life to making it a success. I'll give every ounce of my blood, sweat and tears to right this situation. However you feel about me, I hope I can count on each one of you to support my father's memory and my mother's life's work and help us move forward. I know that's what they both would want."

Lainey stopped as applause broke out in the crowd. She glanced at Ethan, who gave her a thumbs-up and was about to continue when Ida Vassler pushed her way to the front. Lainey's stomach plummeted as the old woman came to stand next to her.

"I want you to know," Ida said, her severely outlined eyebrows drawn together, "that I'm personally going to donate twenty thousand dollars to rebuild this shelter."

Lainey gasped.

Ida turned to the crowd and wagged a gnarled finger. "And for any of you boys doing seasonal construction work over in

Gradysville—I'll pay double on the weekends so you drag your lazy cabooses here to get this place up and running."

"I'll volunteer for the foreman job."

Lainey looked out at the sea of faces to where Dave Reynolds, Ethan's best friend from high school, grinned up at her.

"I'm sure the ladies' auxiliary will organize potluck lunches on Saturdays and Sundays," Misty Gragg added.

After that, Lainey lost track of the offers of help and supplies. At least a dozen people came forward to hug her. Many more patted her back and pumped her hand, telling her what a good job she'd done organizing the event, how much the posters with the animal photos were making a difference.

"My sister-in-law all the way down in Pensacola saw it in the paper," one woman told her with a wink. "My husband's family thinks he moved to the sticks up here. Now she wants to drive up and find another cat just so she can say she met you."

"My old sorority sisters down in Charlotte want to meet you, too," Jenny Snyder added.

"Meet me? Why?" It made no sense to Lainey. Her mother was the celebrity.

"They're hoping to convince you to take pictures of their animals. My friend, Pauline, is wild about her Pomeranians."

"They're not the only ones interested in you." Lainey whirled as Julia's voice rang out in the commotion.

Her gaze drifted to the wheelchair Julia pushed.

"Mama," Lainey whispered.

Vera stared back, her expression unreadable. A hush fell over the crowd. In the quiet, Lainey was once again aware of the ruined building behind her and the fact that she was likely the cause of it.

She felt Ethan come to stand beside her. His warm hand pressed into the small of her back. She was eighteen all over again, facing her mother and sister across the dining room table, waiting for their anger to pour out.

"I'm sorry," she said softly, taking a hesitant step forward. "I'm so sorry about the fire. I didn't mean—"

"Come here, child." Although she was unable to walk, Vera's speech was almost back to normal. Despite the wheelchair, Vera looked more like herself outside the hospital room. Pale blond hair framed her face, and Lainey could see the shine of makeup on her cheeks. She bore little resemblance to the frail, sickly woman Lainey had come home to.

Lainey wiped her wet cheeks against her shoulder.

"I'm proud of you," Vera said with a smile.

"But I—"

Vera shook her head, cutting Lainey off mid-sentence. "You've done so much for me, for the shelter, for this whole town." She winked. "If I'd have known what a natural you are, I'd have found a way to get you back here sooner."

"The fire was my fault—"

"The fire was an accident," Vera again interrupted. "Accidents happen." She glanced at the crowd that stood watching the scene unfold. "Carol Dakker, are you here?"

A short, chubby woman with teased hair and an unfortunate yellow tracksuit stepped forward. "What can I do, Vera?"

"Remember when you had too many white wine spritzers after the town council meeting last February and drove Mac's Plymouth through the front window at city hall?"

Carol grew noticeably pale under her bottle-bronzed skin. "There was black ice on the road."

Vera snorted. "It was dry as a bone that winter. Janie Baker?" When no one answered, Vera's voice grew louder. "Don't try to hide, Janie. My daughter parked behind your minivan."

A timid voice spoke from the edge of the group. "Sorry, Mrs. Morgan, I didn't hear you at first."

The crowd parted to reveal a young woman with a mousy brown ponytail, vigorously chewing on one nail. Lainey recognized her as the town's librarian.

Lainey did an inward cringe. As much as she hated being judged, she didn't want to see the rest of the town called to the carpet for past indiscretions. "I think they get the point, Mom," she whispered, straightening. "People are here because they want to help rebuild the shelter. It's okay."

"Always too nice," Vera said with a sigh. "The point is everyone makes mistakes." She raked the crowd with a steely gaze. "My daughter—both my daughters—have done as much as humanly possible to help me. To help all of us."

Lainey made eye contact with her sister over Vera's head.

"Wow," Julia mouthed.

Lainey nodded.

"This event brings in people, publicity and revenue that Brevia desperately needs," Vera continued. "I appreciate those of you who have come forward to help. To the rest of you, what are you waiting for? There's work to be done. Vital work."

She paused for a breath and Lainey noticed her mother's chest rose and fell sharply while her hands trembled.

"Mama, don't wear yourself out," she said, resting a hand on Vera's thin shoulder. She looked out at the crowd. "As I said before, we appreciate the concern each of you has shown for the shelter. We hope we can continue to rely on your support as we rebuild All Creatures to its former glory and beyond."

She heard a noise behind her and turned to see Ethan clapping. Sam and Harlan joined him and pretty soon the entire crowd was awash in applause.

"Find me a handkerchief," her mother said. "I don't want my makeup to run."

Julia dug in her bag and pulled out a tissue as a stream of

people came forward to hug all three of them. Lainey was overwhelmed by the words of kindness and support from people she had thought still hated her.

It took almost forty-five minutes for the crowd to disperse after receiving instructions on how they could each help with the reconstruction that would begin in the morning. Vera was clearly tired by the time Lainey, Julia, Ethan and a few core shelter staff members were left.

"Why did you bring her here?" Lainey whispered to Julia as her mother held court with her staff and Ethan.

Julia rubbed her hands over her belly. "By the time I got to the hospital this morning, she'd found out and was already dressed and ready to go. She'd convinced the hospital direc-tor to give her a day pass or whatever you want to call it."

"Is that even legal?"

"Who knows," Julia answered. "Anything's possible with Vera."

"Girls?"

Lainey and Julia both turned.

"I want to see the back of the building."

Lainey heard Julia suck in a breath but Lainey spoke first. "That's not a good idea, Mom. It's pretty awful, and in your condition…"

"Don't tell me what I can and can't do, young lady." She straightened her shoulders. "This is still my operation."

"I didn't say—"

"Ethan, take me to the back," Vera ordered.

He met Lainey's gaze, and she nodded as he stepped for-ward to take the handles of the wheelchair. "You're the boss," Lainey murmured. "I need to find Sam before he leaves, then I'll be around."

"I saw him head over toward the clinic," Julia answered.

Lainey watched Ethan, Julia and her mother disappear around the side of the shelter then turned. Ray Daniels stood directly in front of her. Lainey's heart thumped. She hadn't seen Ethan's father since her ruined wedding day. He'd hated her then for wrecking Ethan's life, and the steely gleam in his eyes told her not much had changed.

She took an instinctive step back. "Does Ethan know you're here?"

"Hell, yes." Ray smirked at her. "We had a cozy little father-son chat the other night. I even met that fleabag mutt of yours. Petey, right?"

"Pita," she whispered, unease curling around her spine.

"Whatever." Ray moved past her and tipped his head in the shelter's burned-out front door. "Ethan knows who's lookin' out for him around here. I ain't gonna let him be jerked around again."

"You never once looked out for him," she answered, holding fast to her temper. "Ethan hates you, Ray."

"Not as much as he hated you, you little tramp."

His words hit her hard, the brutal truth in them making her stagger a step. "He doesn't…"

Ray flicked his cigarette into the shelter's entrance.

"Don't do that," she snapped.

His ugly laugh filled in the silence. "What's it matter now? You took care of this place real good."

A sudden swelling of resolve stiffened her back. "I didn't start the fire."

"Just like you didn't get knocked up to trap my boy." He leaned closer. "You can't fool ole Ray, honey. I know how bad you wanted Ethan. And I know how bad you wanted to stick it to your mama for turning on you all those years ago. I could help, you know." He laughed again. "Maybe I already did."

She pressed her fingers to the sides of her head. "Shut up, Ray."

"Once a lying skank, always a—"

Something flashed in the corner of Lainey's vision and

Ray slammed into the window to the right of the doorway, shattering the already broken glass.

Tim Reynolds loomed over him then turned to Lainey, the wild gleam in his eyes more frightening then Ray's angry tirade.

Lainey stood absolutely still and forced herself to keep her gaze locked on his. Panic rushed through her as he took a step closer.

"I won't let him hurt you," he murmured, his voice a husky growl. "I won't let anyone hurt you."

"What the hell was that for?" Ray straightened, rubbing his jaw.

"Apologize to her," Tim ordered, still pinning Lainey with his stare.

"It's okay, Tim." Lainey shifted her gaze to Ray. "He doesn't matter."

"Screw you, Reynolds," Ray muttered and spit. "I oughta kick your twerpy—"

Tim lunged forward and pushed Ray into the wall. Tim wasn't a big guy but seemed to have adrenaline fueling him. Lainey shuffled to the edge of the building.

Tim squeezed his hand around Ray's throat. "I said—"

"What's going on here?" Sam Callahan walked across the lawn toward them. "Reynolds, get off him."

Tim glanced over his shoulder, thumped Ray's head hard against the wall and let go.

"Sam," Lainey said on a breath. Relief made her knees weak.

He squeezed her arm. "Is everything okay?"

She gave a slight nod. "Ray…was…just leaving."

Sam eyed Ethan's father. "You, too, Tim."

"I need to talk to Lainey," Tim argued.

She shook her head.

"Not a good idea," Sam answered. "Lainey, why don't

you head back with your mom and Ethan? I'll see these two off the property."

"Thanks, Sam," Lainey whispered. Her legs wobbled, but she darted toward the rear of the building. She didn't want Ethan or her mother to see Ray and Tim.

She had time to get a handle on her raging emotions as Vera barked out to-do lists of things needed to bring the shelter back to life. She didn't get angry, didn't shoot Lainey incriminating looks or make snide comments. It was a good thing because Lainey felt like she was walking an emotional tightrope.

"After what I've been through," Vera said, her tone resigned, "I know you can rebuild anything with enough work."

Lainey let out a pent-up breath. "I'll find another place to have the event—"

"We'll have it here." Her mother's tone was firm.

"She's right," Ethan agreed. "With Dave's help, we can get this cleaned up in the next couple of weeks. Maybe even some framing. I'll move out to the lake house so the trailer can be converted to a kennel. The barn and clinic will hold the overflow animals. It'll be good for people coming to see how we're rebuilding."

Lainey nodded, allowing thoughts of the work ahead to drown out Ray's accusations. "I'll do whatever I can to make this up to you, Mama."

"You already are," her mother said and her eyes drifted shut. "Julia, honey, I think I'm ready to go back."

"Do you want me to take her?" Lainey offered.

Julia cast a meaningful glance toward Ethan, who had walked back toward the shelter. "Take the day off," Julia said with a smile. "I've got it covered."

"Okay," she agreed. "I want to finish a few things here and I'll be over this afternoon."

A quiver near Julia's midsection distracted Lainey. "A

wave just rolled across your stomach," she said in a hushed voice, the movement bringing her totally present.

Julia groaned, but her eyes glowed with humor. "He's like a gymnast—turning somersaults, cartwheels—the whole bit."

They'd been to three Lamaze classes, and Lainey had massaged her sister's shoulders, fed her ice chips and rubbed her feet. But she'd actually touched Julia's belly only a couple of times after the first night.

She reached out a tentative hand. "Can I feel it?"

Julia's mouth curved into a small smile. "Of course."

"He's a strong one," Vera said, rolling her chair closer.

Lainey laid her hand on the soft cotton of Julia's pink T-shirt.

Julia's fingers pressed against hers. "He'll perform better if he knows he's got your attention."

"I don't want to hurt him," Lainey whispered.

"You won't."

Then Lainey felt it. A small thud against her palm. She gasped and spread her fingers across Julia's middle. Three more staccato kicks landed on her palm.

Heartache rose in Lainey like a sudden summer storm. She'd thought she'd felt a few flutters before she'd miscarried and had loved to rub her flat stomach like a lucky Buddha.

The doctor later told her she was probably experiencing indigestion. *Indigestion.* He might have been trying to ease her sorrow but had only succeeded in making her feel like a fool on top of everything else. She couldn't tell the difference between a baby's movement and gas pains. How pathetic was that?

The baby inside of her sister was so vitally alive. Julia's every pore burst with life. Lainey felt like a recovering alcoholic watching someone drink a rare, priceless wine. When alone, she didn't miss what she couldn't have, but seeing someone else enjoy it made her soul ache.

She shook her head, forced her mind to clear. "It won't be long now, buddy," she said to Julia's stomach. "You hold out a few more weeks."

"Longest of my life. Are you ready, Mom?"

Lainey bent and kissed her mother's forehead. "I'll see you later."

Vera placed her hands on Lainey's cheeks. "I'm proud of you," she said.

"Thank you, Mom. For everything." She watched Julia wheel Vera over the grass toward the parking lot.

Ethan placed a hand on the small of her back. "Dave's going to meet me here after lunch to figure out the best way to start rebuilding. Do you want to grab a bite in town or at your place?"

"Do you ever wish you were a dad?" The words whooshed out on a rush of air. When would she learn to leave well enough alone? "I need to understand why you don't have a family. I know you wanted kids."

"That was ten years ago. Wants and needs change." He looked away, began to pace in front of her. "Maybe I said that because I couldn't stand how sad you were after you lost the baby. Look at my old man. He was one helluva role model. Maybe I wasn't meant to be a family man."

She studied him. He was different than Ray in every way possible. "You'd be a great father."

His eyes widened in shock before his mask slammed back into place. "How about you?" he countered. "Why haven't you settled down?"

"My job…" she began.

"That's crazy," he interrupted. "You'd find a way around your work with the right guy."

If only that were possible, she thought. She said simply, "I don't like commitment."

He studied her. "I don't believe you."

"I'm not asking you to."

He rubbed one hand over his face. "We're quite a pair." He walked to her, cupped her face in his palms. "I want to be with *you,* Lainey. Only you."

"Me, too," she whispered and let him draw her closer.

In the quiet, the gentle rhythm of her breath calmed his own heart as her chest rose and fell against his body. The soft breeze played with strands of her hair, tickling his neck as they drifted around him.

"I can't stand to hurt you," he whispered.

"You won't," she murmured.

He wondered how she could be so sure. He'd caused her so much pain years ago. They'd hurt each other.

"I have to move clothes to the lake house. Let's get carry-out and take it out there, away from everyone."

"I can't. I told Ida I'd come over to discuss her donation. That woman has more strings than a circus tent."

"Later then," he said, rubbing his lips across her temple.

"My mom isn't coming home until tomorrow." She almost giggled as she said the words. She felt like a teenager again, but this time she had the boy she'd always wanted. "I could come out for the night."

He lifted her off her feet in a tight hug. "Hell, yeah, you could."

Chapter Fifteen

Rain came down in steady sheets by the time Lainey left Ida's several hours later. She didn't have an umbrella but was too tired to care as the downpour soaked her T-shirt.

She walked into the kitchen—some food, a shower and quick nap high on her to-do list. One good thing about being so exhausted was it made her too tired to think about the extra work she'd have to do to get the event back on track.

Well, almost too tired.

She took a box of cereal from the cabinet and opened the fridge. Between the milk and the orange juice sat a cardboard carton and a plastic salad container.

No note, but an order form was taped to the side of the carton. "Pad Thai, no sprouts, small salad" was written in handwriting she didn't recognize. Pad Thai had been her favorite forever, but she couldn't get it in Brevia. The name of a restaurant from a neighboring town was stamped on the box.

She looked around, not sure what she expected to see.

Would Ethan have driven forty minutes just to get her take-out? A smile spread across her face as she grabbed a fork and dug into the noodles, not bothering to heat them first.

It was the best food she'd ever tasted.

When the phone rang a few minutes later, she picked it up on the first ring. "I can't talk, I'm busy chewing." She laughed into the receiver.

"Lainey? Is that you?"

She recognized the voice and swallowed hard. "Sam?" It wasn't good if the police chief was calling her at home. "Sorry. I thought you were someone else."

"Lainey, listen," he interrupted. "I'm at Memorial North. Your sister's here. They need you to come in...."

"What happened?" Her stomach lurched, the noodles threatening a repeat appearance. "Is she okay? Is it the baby?"

"Car accident. She's all right." He paused. "I'll stay until you get here."

"I'm on my way." She clicked off the phone and reached for her keys.

The rain had turned to a light mist as she pulled on to the highway. She used her cell phone to dial her mother's room but got no answer. Memorial North was situated between Brevia and its closest neighboring town. It was bigger than the local hospital where her mother was but not a critical care center, which reassured her. Anything really serious and Julia would be in Charlotte.

Still her heart thumped wildly as she pushed through the doors under the Emergency Room sign.

She approached the information desk. "Julia Morgan? I'm looking for my sister, Julia."

The woman behind the counter checked the computer. "Exam Three," she answered. "Second door on your left."

Lainey walked quickly down the hall then stopped in front of Julia's room. The steady beep that monitored both Julia's vitals and the baby's heartbeat echoed through the door. She hesitated as memories washed over her.

When she finally stepped into the room, her breath caught. A large bandage covered Julia's forehead above her left eye while a dark purple bruise shadowed the skin underneath. The rest of her face looked pale.

Julia's eyes narrowed when the door opened. "You called her," she said with a moan. "I told you not to call. I'm fine."

Lainey's gaze flicked to the end of the bed. Sam stood there, his arms crossed across his chest, concern and frustration warring in his features.

"You are *not* fine," he told Julia. "Just stubborn."

Lainey watched the two of them stare at each other, wondering if she was interrupting a private moment. Sam turned to her. "She's going to be all right. A few cuts and bruises. The baby's fine. She'll need a ride home. Even if she could drive, her car was totaled."

"Piece of junk," Julia muttered.

Lainey shook her head, frustrated she couldn't follow the conversation. "What happened? Julia, you don't look fine."

"I need to get back to the station," Sam said, glancing at his watch. He placed a hand on Julia's leg. "Let me know when you're ready for something new. I've got a buddy with a used lot over in Ft. Thomas."

Julia rolled her eyes. "I think I can buy a car on my own."

Sam smiled. He stepped over to Lainey. "Go easy on her," he whispered. "She's more shaken than she's letting on."

Julia humphed. "I can hear you."

"Gotta go." With a last glance at Julia, Sam walked out the exam room door.

Lainey's eyebrows rose. "What was that all about?"

"Nothing. That guy may be hot, but he's too much of a stinkin' choir boy for my taste."

Lainey heard the catch in Julia's voice. It scared her more

than she wanted to admit to think of Julia in danger. She'd come to see her sister in a new light since returning, to finally feel connected to her family. She sat on the edge of the bed. "Start at the beginning, Juls."

"It wasn't my fault. It was the rain. And my tires. They should have been changed a thousand miles ago, but I don't have the money. I came around the corner on Whitton's Hill. You know how tight it is?"

Lainey nodded.

"There was a pool of water and the car hydroplaned."

"There's a huge hill on that bend," Lainey interrupted, shocked at the scene Julia described.

"I went over it. The front of the car kind of folded across my lap. Thank God I could reach my purse and my cell phone still worked."

"Did you get a hold of Mom?"

"No." Julia pressed her head against the pillows on the bed and closed her eyes. "She was napping when I left. I didn't want to bother her."

A nurse came into the room, cutting off Lainey's response. She walked to the bed and unhooked the monitor. The room went quiet. "Ms. Morgan, you're free to go. You have a follow-up appointment scheduled. An orderly will wheel you down to the front. Pick up the discharge orders at the desk on your way out." The nurse glanced at Lainey then back to Julia. "Do you have a ride home or should I call a cab?"

"A cab would be—"

"She has a ride," Lainey interrupted and gave her sister's hand a small squeeze. "I'm going to pull the car around to the front."

"Thanks, Lainey." Julia swung her legs over the side of the bed. "I'll be waiting."

Lainey had taken only a few steps down the hall when

Ethan came around a corner, looking as frazzled as she felt. He pulled her into a quick hug then moved back.

"Jake Maguire told me he towed Julia's car, that it was totaled." He struggled to catch his breath. "Is she okay? What about the baby?"

"She's fine. The baby's fine." Lainey resisted the urge to lean into him again. "In fact she's just been released."

"How are *you* doing with all of this?"

She tried to smile but couldn't force her mouth to move in that direction. "Shocked. Relieved. Running on pure adrenaline."

Ethan searched her face, and while she was pale and her eyes tired, she actually seemed to be holding up pretty well given all she'd been through recently. When he'd heard about the accident, he'd worried not only about Julia but also how Lainey would be affected by the possibility of trauma to the baby. He knew a situation like this could bring back memories of the loss they'd shared.

He wanted to wrap his arms around her, reassure her in any way he could, but this wasn't the right time or place. He watched her draw in a slow breath. "Do you want me to stay?" he asked.

Her eyes darkened until the irises were dusky green. She reached up and her cool fingers stroked his cheek. A simple touch from her could send him over the deep end.

She stepped away. "You should go. It'll be easier with the two of us."

He smiled despite his disappointment. "Once a complication, always a complication."

Lainey swayed toward him then straightened. "I know you want to do the right thing. We all do. But this is so new. I'm going to pick up her paperwork and get the car. I'll call you later. Promise." She kissed his cheek and turned toward the nurses' station as he walked away. She didn't glance back, too afraid she'd surrender to the impulse to run after him and melt into his arms.

A nurse came barreling out of the exam room, almost running over Lainey. "Get in there," she barked, hurrying down the hall. "Your sister's gone into labor."

"No," Lainey whispered. In a daze, she returned to the room. Julia met her gaze as another nurse cleaned up a puddle of liquid from the floor next to the bed.

"My water broke," Julia said with an apologetic laugh. "I bent down to pick up a shoe and…"

"It's okay, hon." The nurse straightened, a wad of crumpled towels in one hand.

"I'm not ready. It's not time…the baby…"

The nurse patted Julia's leg. "We'll get you moved up to Maternity and the doctor will see you. Everything will be okay."

"No," Lainey repeated, louder. Her world tilted off-kilter. *Okay. Okay.* That one word haunted her. Stars danced before her eyes and she licked her dry lips.

The nurse turned. "Are you the sister?"

Lainey stared.

"The birth coach, right?"

Lainey forced herself to nod.

"It's a good thing you're here," the nurse told her as she slipped past. "She needs you now."

With the nurse gone, Lainey stepped farther into the room. She opened her mouth to speak, but Julia's face contorted, eyes shut tight as she bit down on her lower lip.

A contraction.

Lainey recognized it but couldn't remember a single thing she'd learned in the birthing classes. Her mind went blank as she watched obvious pain wash through her sister.

As she remembered her own pain.

A moment later Julia's eyes opened again. Her mouth trembled. "Is it really going to be okay?" she asked weakly.

Lainey swallowed and nodded. She used the fear in Julia's eyes to push away her own anxiety. As overwhelmed as she felt, she wouldn't let Julia be alone at this moment. She had a chance now to make something right, once and for all.

She came forward and pushed a sweaty strand of hair off Julia's face, smoothing her fingers across her sister's skin. "We're going to get through this together," she said.

Tears welled in Julia's eyes. "Are you sure? Because—"

"I'm sure. The nurse was right. Everything's going to be okay." She dropped a quick kiss on Julia's forehead. "Better than okay, Juls. You're about to become a mother."

Ethan had walked out of the hospital feeling more alone than he could remember. He'd never been close to his own family.

He'd spent most of his time at the Morgans', happy for Vera to feed and fuss over him. He tried to remember Lainey at that age. She didn't talk to him a lot, always seemed to have her nose buried in a book. Or maybe he just wasn't paying attention.

He picked up Chinese takeout and drove out to the lake house. Flipping on the television, he dropped to the couch, ate and dozed off.

A noise sounded from the floor below several hours later. Ethan stood and wiped his mouth on the back of his sleeve. The last thing he needed was a random bear or raccoons nosing around his trash.

He started down the steps but stopped midway. "Lainey?"

"Hey," she said. "Sorry to show up without calling."

Ethan barely registered her words. Her scent trailed up to him, overriding his senses until he was dizzy with need. He tried to steady his heart, to think of something normal to say. Something to make her stay in Brevia longer than this summer—maybe even forever.

She gave him a questioning look. "If I'm here at a bad time…"

"No," he said quickly. He realized he was blocking her way up the narrow staircase. "Come on up."

He grabbed the remote and flipped off the TV then tried to straighten newspapers and magazines on the coffee table. He picked up his half-empty Chinese carton and moved it to the kitchen counter, next to a stack of crusty dishes.

"I came to say thank you for the pad Thai." She crossed and uncrossed her arms, looking both uncomfortable and adorable. "It's my favorite."

"I remember," he said with a grimace. "I just can't figure out why. Give me good ole kung pao any day."

"That's why I appreciate it so much."

A wave of pleasure washed through him. Funny how doing something nice for her made him feel ridiculously happy.

"I also wanted you know Julia had the baby."

Ethan felt like he'd taken a hard right to the jaw. "What?"

"I went back to the room." Her eyes widened. "Her water broke. Everything went so fast and then—"

He didn't know what to say, how to react. He studied Lainey but couldn't read her expression. "What happened?"

A dazed grin broke across her face. "I have a nephew, Ethan. He was determined to meet the world today. Julia barely had time to push. And Charlie is perfect."

"Named after your dad."

Lainey nodded. "Ten fingers, ten toes. The loudest cry you've ever heard. He's perfect," she repeated in a whisper.

"Congratulations, Aunt Lainey. I'm happy for her. For both of you."

Her head cocked to one side. "Do you ever think about the baby we would have had?"

He stumbled a step.

"If we have a chance," she said with a sigh, "we need to talk about our loss."

His pulse began to thump. He cupped her face in his hands. "I think about that summer—the baby. About what would have happened. About you being my wife." He kissed the tip of her nose. "I only care about our future, Lainey." He forced himself to continue. "Do we have one?"

Her breath caught.

She wanted to answer *yes*. Isn't that why she'd come here in the first place?

She'd meant to drive straight home from the hospital and hide under the covers but instead found herself here. She needed to crawl into the safety of Ethan's arms.

To lose herself in him.

But did they have a future?

This was the time when she should lay everything on the line. Familiar fear rushed through her.

She'd spent so long condemning herself; she couldn't bear to talk about her inability to have children and risk seeing that same judgment in Ethan's eyes. Of being rejected by him again.

Instead of answering, she touched her lips to his. She breathed him in, wrapped her arms around his neck and held on tight.

He didn't disappoint. His kiss was deep, hungry, demanding. Like he was trying to prove something. His desire for her went beyond pure lust or the familiarity of old lovers. He was urgent, desperate and she matched his need.

"You're making me crazy." He laughed into her hair. "I have about as much control as a teenager."

As she drew back and looked deep into his eyes, she had

no doubt that the longing she saw reflected there was only for her.

"Control is overrated," she whispered with a smile.

"I want this forever," he whispered then pressed his mouth against hers before she could answer. "You are the best part of me, Lainey." He led her to his bed as he kissed her forehead, her cheeks, the line of her jaw. "You make me a whole person."

"I love you with every part of me," she whispered. "I always have."

They breathed into each other, melding together until she wasn't sure where he stopped and she began.

She could feel his heart thundering in his chest, matching the pounding of her own. They stayed wrapped tightly together, taking and giving pleasure for hours. When Lainey heard the hiss of sprinklers outside the window, she finally glanced over at the clock.

"It's almost eleven. I should go." Even as she said the words, he nestled her against him.

"Stay."

Little tingles of awareness spread down her spine. "I need to get up early to see Julia before work."

"I'll set the alarm."

She propped her elbows on either side of his chest and looked at him. Could she trust him with her heart again? She was afraid if she had to take another emotional pounding, she might not survive it with her soul intact.

"Please stay with me tonight."

"Yes."

As his mouth claimed hers, her doubts faded away like the moon in the first light of morning. Maybe they were still there waiting to resurface when darkness fell again, but for now his kiss was like the bright sun, warming every part of her.

* * *

Lainey had left Ethan on the lake house's deck with a steaming cup of coffee, a kiss and a promise to meet later that morning.

She'd called her mother on the way to the hospital and after visiting her sister and nephew, she finally pulled herself away and made it to the clinic around noon. She'd called Ethan's cell phone but got voice mail, so left a message she'd pick up sandwiches on the way over.

In a million years, Lainey would have never guessed she'd have such a hard time leaving Julia and Charlie, even for a few hours. But from the moment her new nephew had wrapped his little hand around her finger, she'd been a goner. She hadn't even minded changing his dirty diaper.

Nothing about Charlie or the maternity ward made her revisit her own pain. She stayed totally focused on the present moment, grateful for new life and her chance to be a part of it.

Which may have explained why she'd lost track of time. Vera had called three times. She was being released later that afternoon and was chomping at the bit to meet her grandson. Lainey planned to pick her up when she left the clinic.

As she pulled down the driveway, an ominous feeling settled in her stomach. It was Sunday, but staff from both the clinic and shelter were supposed to be working so they could open on Monday. The parking lot was empty.

She climbed out of the Land Cruiser, holding the takeout bag high as Pita came bounding around the side of the clinic, Chip in hot pursuit.

"Hey, you two." Lainey used her free hand to rub her fingers under Pita's collar then gave the puppy's head a soft pat. "Where is everyone?"

The dogs snuggled together on the dog bed behind the receptionist's desk and she made her way toward Ethan's office, breathing a sigh of relief when she saw his dark head bent over his desk. She pressed a hand to her chest where her heart was beating like mad. Why was she so freaked out?

"This place is like a ghost town," she said as she stepped into the doorway.

"I sent everyone to lunch." He looked up and the anger blazing in his eyes stopped her dead in her tracks.

"What's the matter?" She couldn't imagine anything worse than the fire, but she'd never seen him look that way.

"Why haven't you settled down?" His voice was void of emotion.

She clutched the paper bag tighter against her stomach but kept her gaze level with his. "I told you I don't want that kind of commitment." She forced herself to laugh. "Although now I'm officially a doting aunt."

"Liar." Ethan stood abruptly, sending the chair flying as he leaned on the bookshelf behind him. He felt off balance and didn't know how to right himself. He wanted her to do it for him. Prayed she'd offer a logical explanation. He jabbed one finger at the newspaper spread across his desk. "Tell me the *real* reason you don't want a family."

She stared at him as if he'd lost his mind. "Ethan…"

"How could you have written something like that after everything that happened this summer?"

"Write what?" She leaned over the desk, turning the paper toward herself. Her mouth formed a shocked *oh* as the color drained from her face and her long fingers—the same ones that she'd run across his back hours earlier—dug into the bag she held against her stomach.

He snatched up the newspaper and shook it near her face. "Is this what you were doing at lunch with Tim—having him help you create some sort of manifesto? You got the entire town to trust you and then blamed everyone for how you left. This is how I have to find out the truth of that summer—with your open editorial to the community?" He tried to keep hold of his anger. He couldn't let her see how much she'd hurt him. Again.

Her head shot up. "I didn't write this."

"Who else would have known these details?"

"I don't know."

"Why didn't you tell me?" Ethan paced to the corner of the room and back again. "'Decade-old tragedy shapes photographer's life and career,'" he quoted from the editorial's headline. He'd read the piece so many times he had most of it memorized. "That day in the hospital, after the miscarriage, you knew you couldn't get pregnant again. *You knew.*"

Chapter Sixteen

As Lainey nodded, Ethan felt his stomach hit the ground like a lead balloon. "I told you we could try again and you said nothing."

"I couldn't disappoint you," she whispered.

"Disappoint me?" he bellowed. "How much of a jerk was I? I got you pregnant, you end up infertile and you're worried about *my* disappointment? You didn't even cry. I was about to lose my mind, and you were comforting *me*. All the while knowing you'd never have another chance. Did it ever register that I should have been making *you* feel better?"

"That wasn't how it worked for us." She gave a strangled laugh. "You wouldn't have wanted me without the baby involved. You were fulfilling an obligation and we both knew it."

Why didn't anyone in his life think he was capable of handling something difficult? Was he such an emotional screwup that he couldn't be trusted with anything serious?

He'd thought Lainey saw more in him, but apparently he'd been wrong.

"You were still willing to marry me?" he asked, his voice hoarse.

"It's why I left the church. I couldn't go through with it—like I was tricking you. You had to know, to be able to make the choice of whether you could still be with me. After you got the note, I thought—"

"Stop talking about the note," he shouted. "Your note didn't tell me a thing except that you made a mistake. That being together wasn't worth the trouble it would cause either of us." He crossed his arms over his chest. "It's the same thing now, isn't it? You don't think a relationship with me is worth fighting for."

"I didn't say that." She wiped at her eyes as Pita and the puppy came into the room and crouched at her feet. "And the note…I asked you to meet…you were the one who didn't want me…." Her voice broke off. "You never came."

"Came where? I was at the church for four hours waiting, hoping you'd come back. If I'd meant anything to you, you'd never have left. You'd have stuck it out with me. I didn't care what anyone said. I wanted you."

"But you didn't love me. You never once said it, and I'm sure you didn't feel it."

"What are you talking about? I was standing at the altar."

"Because you felt responsible," she said on a ragged breath. "I wanted you to love me." She paused then added softly, "I still do."

He wanted to tell her that he did, that sometimes when he saw her it felt like his heart was going to burst from how much he loved her. But he didn't. He couldn't say it then, and he wouldn't now. No matter how he felt, she was leaving. She'd made that clear in her editorial. He wasn't going to try to stop her just to be kicked in the teeth one more time.

Pita stretched out her nose and pushed against his hand. His pain was so great he couldn't even take the comfort she offered and he shooed her away.

Lainey's voice cracked. "What if you'd known?" She looked at him, her eyes hollow and desperate. "What if you knew about me then?"

"You never gave me that chance."

"I tried, Ethan." She hitched her chin a notch, as if daring him to contradict her. "What about now?"

He forced himself to look at her, to keep his gaze as hard as his heart. "You didn't trust me, and I can't trust you."

Her shoulders stiffened. "That's not fair."

"Don't talk to me about fair. You've made me a laughing-stock in this town for a second time." He slammed his hand down as anger coursed through him. "You get to waltz in and out of here, but this is my life, Lainey. My home."

She swallowed. "What if I want to be a part of it?"

"It's too late," he told her, his voice icy cold. "I don't want you. We had a good run this summer. I can't make you happy, and I'm not interested in trying. You did me a favor ten years ago, and I'm returning it now."

"That's why you didn't come after me, isn't it? That's why you're doing this now. It's all about you and how much you can't afford to give." The dogs circled her legs as her voice rose.

"Call us even." He forced his mouth into a smug smile. "I guess we both got lucky to figure it out."

She sniffed and rubbed her hands across her cheeks. "Some luck, Ethan."

She turned on her heel and stalked out of his office and probably out of his life for good—Pita and the puppy following in her wake.

After sitting in his office for who knew how long, Ethan

heard noise from the hall, but no one came in, probably afraid of being chewed out.

It had taken him years after Lainey jilted him to walk through Brevia without people looking at him with pity in their eyes. He'd had enough pity to last a lifetime when his mother had run off. The second dose of it had about pushed him over the edge. He'd sworn never to open himself up again. Then Lainey had come back and he hadn't been able to help himself.

He finally came out to oversee a meeting with the staff. He kept the tone light, making sure no one could see the way the pain burned a hole in his stomach.

Checking on the animals and arrangements to open the clinic and shelter the next morning took up most of the afternoon. He was on his way to the lake house when an urgent call forced a detour to the hospital.

He made it to the fourth floor in minutes, taking the stairs three at a time.

"Shh," Julia whispered as he came to a screeching halt at the foot of her bed. "Charlie just fell asleep."

"What's going on, Juls? You said it was an emergency."

Her smile was slightly abashed. "I didn't think you'd come otherwise."

"You're right." Ethan closed his eyes and took a deep breath. "And now I'm leaving before—"

"Don't worry. Lainey took Mom home. She won't be back until I'm discharged tomorrow."

He straightened and studied Julia. She was propped on a collection of pillows, wearing a pajama top with red lips puckering up all over it. In her arms, she cradled a small bundle wrapped in a blue blanket. Ethan could just make out a tuft of dark hair peeking from the center.

He took a hesitant step toward the bed. "That's the baby?"

Her smile widened. "His name is Charlie."

"I know." He peered closer. "Congratulations." Ethan studied the wrinkled, red face that looked more like Yoda from Star Wars than an actual human. "He's...uh...cute."

Julia didn't seem to notice his hesitation. "He's amazing," she said on a sigh.

"Sure." He was out of his element. Kittens and puppies he could handle, real babies not so much. "Julia, why am I here?"

She gazed at him. "You read Lainey's letter in the newspaper?"

"Didn't everyone?"

"What happens now?"

"Lainey and I are through. I won't be taken for another ride." Ethan felt frustration rising inside him and struggled to keep his voice low. "I'm not that much of a fool." He turned for the door.

"Wait."

Something in Julia's tone stopped him. "What?"

"You love her, right?"

"It doesn't matter," he repeated.

"You two were meant to be together. It's the same now as it was ten years ago."

He turned slowly. "Love isn't the answer to everything. You of all people should know that."

She held out the bundle. "Hold him."

His mouth pressed into a thin line. "I don't think—"

"Just for a minute, Ethan. He won't break."

Ethan took the baby from her arms. As delicately as he could, he settled Charlie into the crook of his arm. The baby squirmed and one fist shot into the air. Ethan used two fingers to nudge it back down under the blanket. He was amazed at how soft Charlie's skin felt. At Ethan's touch, the baby opened his eyes for a second, yawned and worked his jaw before settling back down to sleep.

Ethan felt his mouth curl into a smile. Charlie still looked like Yoda, but his magical baby charm was having an effect. "I'm happy for you, Julia," he said without taking his eyes off Charlie.

"This is what she lost."

Ethan's head shot up.

"It wasn't just the miscarriage," Julia continued, her tone soft. "She not only lost that baby, but she knew she would never have the chance again. She was eighteen, Ethan."

"Why didn't she tell me? I could have…"

"What? What could anyone have done for her?" Julia looked out the window. "She listened to everyone telling her how it was for the best—you were both too young. I wasn't the only one who thought she'd trapped you."

"I said we could try again." His eyes drifted shut as he remembered the emptiness in her eyes that day at the hospital.

"Talk about salt in a wound."

"I didn't know."

"Would that have changed things?" Her gaze settled back on him. "Would you have still married her?"

"I did that to her. I owed her."

Julia's smile was sad. "Not exactly the basis for a happy marriage."

"How was I supposed to know if I was in love? It was all so quick and crazy. There wasn't time to figure anything out." He sank down on the edge of the bed, the baby tucked in the crook of his arm. "In my experience, love doesn't count for much. It didn't make things right for my parents. Or for us."

"But what about Lainey?"

"She made me feel whole, Julia. I know it was wrong. You'd just left and she was your sister," he said. He turned, willing her to understand.

"It's okay," she prompted.

"I was happier in those few months with Lainey than I'd ever been before…"

"Or since?"

"Until this summer." He sighed. "It's too late now."

"Come on, Ethan. Hasn't this summer shown you it's never too late?"

Charlie let out a small cry and squirmed. "That's my cue," he said and deposited the baby back into Julia's arms.

"I'm sorry I lured you here under false pretenses," Julia said as she settled Charlie on her shoulder.

"No, you're not."

She grinned. "I don't want to see you mess up again."

"You're one in a million."

"Don't I know it," she said with a laugh. Despite Julia rubbing his back, Charlie's cries got louder. "He needs to eat," she announced. "So unless you want to see my supersized boob—"

Ethan gulped and held up his hands. "I'm leaving." He leaned forward and gave her a quick kiss on the head. "Thanks, Juls."

Outside the closed door of the hospital room, Lainey pulled back as Ethan bent over her sister. With tears almost blinding her, she stumbled down the stairs to the hospital's main entrance. She made it outside and around the corner before her legs gave out. She sank to the concrete, her back pressed against the side of the building.

Her mother had wanted takeout from the Italian deli near the hospital, and Lainey had decided to make a quick stop to see Charlie one more time. She'd peeked into the rectangular window to make sure the new mom and baby weren't asleep.

What she'd seen had almost killed her: Ethan snuggling Charlie while Julia looked on, a serene smile plastered on her face. It was the exact scene she'd pictured for herself. At least until that summer when everything had changed.

So what if Ethan and Julia both told her they didn't have

feelings for each other? Julia needed a daddy for her baby and who better than Ethan to fit the bill?

Once Lainey was gone, it would be only a matter of time before the two of them came together. They belonged to-gether—beautiful, happy, *whole*. She couldn't give Ethan the family he craved.

She should have never come back to Brevia in the first place. She didn't belong here and never would.

With a trembling hand, she balanced on the wall and picked herself up. Taking a tissue out of her purse, she blew her nose hard and started toward the parking lot. She had food to pick up and a life to reclaim.

A life that didn't involve Ethan Daniels.

Four days later, Lainey zipped her oversize duffle bag closed.

"Are you sure about this?" her mother asked from the doorway.

"I have to go, Mom." She sank down on the side of the bed. "The Kittlitz's Murrelet is almost extinct. The fact that they found one with a nest—I can't miss the opportunity to get the photos." Pita nudged her head into Lainey's lap. Her fingers brushed across the dog's soft fur.

"You have to confront Tim. If you didn't write that edi-torial, who else could it have been? And how did he know about what had happened to you?"

"I'm not sure—the envelope I gave him that day at the church was sealed. It doesn't matter anymore. Maybe Ethan showed him my letter. I was mad at first, but now I don't care." Lainey sighed. "If it was Tim, he did me a favor. Ethan and I could never have made a future together with the past still between us. He doesn't trust me and probably never could. I thought he understood what I did, but he was so angry. I just need to get out of Brevia."

"But you'll be back for the event?" Vera prompted.

"No. I have another assignment." She met her mother's worried gaze. "I left detailed instructions for the staff and volunteers, and I'm going to make the final calls from the airport."

Vera pursed her lips. "What about Pita?"

Tears pricked the back of Lainey's eyes. "It's probably better if I'm not here when she's adopted—"

"Adopted?" Vera's tone turned harsh. "She is *your* dog. You can't desert her."

"That wasn't the deal," Lainey said quietly, too wrung out to offer much of a fight. Pita glanced up and whined. Lainey felt her heart start to crack open and tried to think rationally about the whole situation. "I can't keep a dog with all the travel. It's too much responsibility. I'd only ruin it."

"She needs *you,*" Vera repeated. "And she's not the only one."

"I can't do this." Lainey stood, jostling the dog off her lap. She looked at her mother, willing her to understand. "I'm sorry."

Ethan slammed the door to his office and threw a stack of files onto his desk.

He whirled around as the door opened again. "What?" he yelled.

Stephanie Rand ducked as if he'd physically thrown something at her. "What's wrong with you?"

"Nothing."

"Doesn't look like nothing. And the way you've been grumping at everyone the past few days, it sure doesn't sound like nothing."

"We've been swamped." He ran his hands through his hair. "The event's in two days and we've got animals coming out of the woodwork. That's all."

"Have you seen Lainey since the weekend?"

"No," he ground out. "She hasn't been around here."

"Can you blame her?"

He leveled a look at her. "How is this my fault?"

Her lips thinned. "Tim Reynolds is a jerk. I get that he's your friend and you needed to share all that stuff with someone, but for him to publish that junk and pass it off like Lainey wrote it—"

"Hold on a minute." He crossed his arms over his chest. "What makes you think Lainey didn't write it? Tim couldn't have gotten the information from me. I didn't know most of it until I read it in the paper."

"She told me she had nothing to do with it, and I believe her. She has no reason to lie." Steph's eyes narrowed. "And you have a pretty sad memory, Ethan. I saw the note she left the day of the wedding. Maybe she should have told you in person, but she was too scared of your reaction." She leaned back against the door and sighed. "I picked her up at the hotel when you didn't come. She was a total wreck. I think waiting and wondering made it worse for her in the end."

"I'm sick of hearing about the stupid note, Steph." He stepped behind his desk. "I got a half piece of paper with a few typed sentences on it." His eyes drifted shut as he remembered the words that had ruined his life. "'It's not worth it,' she wrote. 'I don't need you and I don't want a life with you.'" His eyes snapped open. "Doesn't get much clearer than that."

Her jaw dropped. "Where did you get the letter that day?" she asked softly.

"Tim brought it to me. She'd left it at the church."

"Her note didn't say that. And she didn't leave it. She gave it to Tim—sealed so no one but you would read it—and asked him to deliver it to you."

He stood, pressure building in his lungs. "What are you talking about?"

"Her note was handwritten, Ethan. I know they had a type-writer in the church office, but she didn't use it. She explained everything about the complications from the miscarriage. She thought you were only marrying her because you'd already committed to it and if she'd told you about her infertility you'd feel responsible for that, too."

"Of course I would have."

"She didn't want that," Steph said, shaking her head. "She didn't want to trap you."

"I made the choice."

"She wanted you to choose her for her, not because of an obligation. She got a room in Charlotte. You were supposed to meet her there. If you didn't come, she'd know you didn't want her."

"That's not what the note *I* read said."

Steph looked confused. "I saw her write it, Ethan. She handed it to Tim. The only explanation is that he typed a different letter and switched them. But why—"

"No!" He pressed his palms on to the desk. It made him sick to think what Lainey must have gone through when she'd left. What she'd believed about him, how alone she'd been. No wonder she'd never settled down. He could imagine how his rejection had haunted her. He didn't know if he could have made it better that day, but he sure as hell would have tried. "Tim left town. I stopped by the paper yesterday. The receptionist told me he went to Atlanta for a few days."

"You guys are—were—friends." Steph shook her head. "I know it was mainly because he's Dave's little brother, but changing the note is plain evil. Why would he have done that?"

Ethan shrugged. "I have no clue, but you better believe I'm going to find out."

"I don't know why Lainey hung out with him," she said, her eyes narrowing. "He always looked at her kind of moony."

Steph paused. "Like the way she looked at you. Maybe he was in love with her the whole time."

"I have to talk to her. She thinks—" Ethan scrubbed his hands over his face. A small glimmer of hope emerged out of the dark shadows of his heart. Lainey hadn't deserted him all those years ago. At least not like he'd thought. She'd wanted him. Maybe she wanted him now....

"She's gone."

"Gone where?"

"She left for Alaska this morning," Steph said apologetically. "She called on her way to the airport. A photo shoot with birds or something."

"The event is this weekend."

Steph lifted her palms in the air. "She told me she worked out the details with Vera before she left and delegated all the outstanding stuff. She's going to have her cell phone with her."

"She ran away again," he muttered.

"Maybe she didn't feel like she had a choice."

He didn't want to hear excuses. "We all have choices. Some people make bad ones." Ethan let disappointment begin to rebuild his defenses. He'd wanted to believe in Lainey. He'd held back his heart, blamed himself for the distance between them. Screw that. She wouldn't stay and fight for their relationship. If that was how little she cared, why should he be any different?

He sank into his chair, forcing his hand steady as he reached for a stack of papers. "I've got to work on these charts."

"I'm sorry, Ethan," Steph whispered and walked out the door.

Chapter Seventeen

Lainey scrambled up the loose rocks on the side of the mountain, deep in the Alaskan wilderness. It had taken her almost twenty-four hours to get to the location, and other than a few hours on the plane between Denver and Anchorage, she hadn't slept since leaving Brevia. Normally, a few minutes in nature were enough to put her in the zone, but she couldn't shake the slightly sick feeling in the pit of her stomach.

She pulled the parka she'd bought in the Denver airport more tightly around her. After the heat and humidity of North Carolina, she felt especially sensitive to the cool, crisp air of the Awapia National Forest.

She waved at Tom Roper, the reporter from *National Geographic* covering the story. He lifted a hand but scowled and continued his cell phone conversation.

"How do you get coverage out here?" she asked as she approached.

He pocketed the phone. "It's satellite." He pressed his fingers to his temples. "Listen, Lainey, I'm sorry to make you come all this way, but I think it's a lost cause."

She looked around. "What's the problem?"

He pointed to a tall pine tree jutting off from a ledge across the valley from where they stood. "Take a look," he said, handing her a pair of binoculars.

She pushed her hair behind her ears and trained the lenses on the pine tree. Adjusting the focus, she studied a medium-sized nest made of twigs and mud midway up the tree and buried deep in the branches. "It'll be a tough shot," she said, lowering the binoculars and scanning the area. "But not impossible. If I can set up near the—"

"It's not the right bird," Tom interrupted.

"What?" She raised the binoculars again. A red-feathered head peeked out of the nest. "It looks like the pictures you faxed me."

Tom shook his head. "The bird is right. The babies aren't."

"I don't get it."

"The story was the Murrelet, which is on the verge of extinction, having a nest full of eggs."

"Right," she agreed, not following his logic.

He grabbed a book from on top of the backpack that sat near his tent opening. "This is its nest." He pointed to a picture of an oval-shaped mass of leaves and grass. "That," he said, inclining his head toward the pine tree, "is a warbler's nest with baby warblers in it."

She squinted against the bright sunlight and stared at the tree. "Then why is a Kittlitz's Murrelet with the wrong baby birds?"

"Apparently, birdbrained isn't just a figure of speech. The stupid Murrelet doesn't seem to know it's not hers."

"Where's the warbler?"

"Who knows?" He shrugged. "Fox food probably. But that

Murrelet isn't going to help population issues by feeding warbler chicks. Those birds are a dime a dozen up here."

Lainey raised the binoculars again and focused on the pine
tree. The nest looked empty until a flash of red came into
view. The Murrelet landed on the edge with a small insect
clamped in its beak. Three tiny brown and white heads poked
up, all clamoring for the morsel. The Murrelet dropped the
insect into one waiting beak and took off again.

Lainey's mouth went dry and her skin tingled. "That's
the story."

Tom stared at her. "There is no story."

"How many times do you find deserted nests?"

"Enough."

"How many times do you see an animal or bird adopting
orphaned babies?"

He shaded his eyes and turned toward the pine tree. "You
don't."

"But we are." Lainey pulled her backpack off and dug
through it for her camera. "I don't know why the Murrelet
isn't laying her own eggs." She attached a telephoto lens to
the end of her camera. "But I can tell you it's amazing to
watch that bird's determination to have a family of her own.
It's a miracle. And I'm not the only one who will think it."

Tom nodded slowly. "I get it."

Lainey sighed. "Me, too. Finally."

By the time Ethan pulled his truck into the driveway at the
lake house, it was close to midnight. The adoption fair was
tomorrow, and he'd spent every waking hour for the past few
days at the shelter getting things ready. He knew the event
would be a success by the phone calls and emails they'd already received from people interested in adopting. He also
knew that Lainey deserved most of the credit for the way she'd
organized volunteers and publicized the event.

The anger that had crowded out every other emotion when he'd discovered she'd left again had been replaced by a dull ache in his chest whenever he thought of her. She'd once again become the North Star in his life, and the pain of losing her was no easier to bear the second time around. Especially knowing it could have been different ten years ago and wondering if he could have changed the outcome this summer.

Even his dream home seemed empty without her in it. That first night, he'd come close to throwing every piece of furniture into a huge bonfire when her smell seemed to linger in each room. As if he could burn away her memory.

He climbed the front porch steps slowly then noticed that the door stood wide open. It was one thing to joke about burning his stuff, another to have it stolen. He raced into the house but stopped short at the sight of a cigarette glowing in the darkness. "Dad," he murmured.

"I hope you don't mind I stopped by to check out the new pad." Ray took a pull from his beer bottle. "I have to admit you did a pretty fine job with it."

Ethan dropped his keys to the coffee table and crossed his arms over his chest. A run in with his father was the last thing he needed. "Couldn't resist a good gloat?"

Ray flashed a self-satisfied grin. "I'm not one to say I told you so, but—"

"Save it." Ethan turned toward the kitchen. He hadn't eaten since having a Pop-Tart this morning. "I've got a big day tomorrow and need some sleep."

"What's Lainey's connection with Tim Reynolds?"

Ethan pulled a carton of leftover kung pao out of the fridge. "They went to high school together. I don't know. Isn't Brevia one big screwed up family at the core?"

"Why do you think she told him all that stuff?"

"*I* don't think she did."

Ray gave a gruff laugh. "I can't see you laying your soul bare to Dave's twerpy little brother."

"I guess Tim switched the note Lainey left for me for a different one, the one I actually read." Ethan scrubbed his palm across his face. "What's it matter now?"

"It might if you knew the whole story. I'm heading down to Florida in a couple of days. Maybe you want to help your old man out with some gas money? I can make it worth your while."

Ethan hissed out an angry breath. "The only time I see you is when you need something, Dad. I'm done being used. By anyone."

"You may not feel that way if you hear me out. How much do you remember about Dave and Tim's mother?"

Ethan turned, fork in midair. "She was kind of a train wreck. Drank a lot, string of loser boyfriends after their dad left town." His eyes narrowed as unease pricked his spine. "Why?"

"Diane Reynolds was a firecracker in her day. She waitressed at the bar where a few of us hung out. Right about the time she and her husband separated and your mom and I were on the skids. Things happened."

"What kind of things?"

Ray wiggled his heavy eyebrows. "Crazy things, son." He whistled low. "Like I said, she was a firecracker."

"You cheated on Mom with Dave's mother?"

"Your mother was one foot out the door already."

"I thought she left because being a mother was too much to handle. You let me believe it was my fault."

Ray shrugged. "Who knows what would have happened if it had just been the two of us. We had some good times at the beginning, your mom and me."

Ethan tossed his food into the garbage can and the fork into the sink, his appetite gone. He'd spent years believing that he was the reason his mother had deserted them. It had shaped so much of who he was—his inability to trust people, to be vulnerable. He'd never wanted to risk that kind of pain again.

"Does Dave know?" How could his best friend of almost two decades not tell him something like this?

"I don't think so," Ray said then grimaced. "Tim is another story. He walked in on us along with his dad. I guess there had been talk of a reconciliation, but our little deal ended it. Diane made him promise not to tell you or Dave. I guess he kept his word. The divorce went through right after that."

Ethan felt his jaw drop. "No wonder Tim hated me. All those years of pretending things were fine when he knew you'd destroyed his family."

Ray jumped to his feet. "Destroy is a mighty strong word, Ethan."

"That's what you did. You destroyed their family and in turn, Tim took his revenge on me. And Lainey got hurt in the process."

"I didn't think—"

"That's always been your problem, but it doesn't fly as an excuse." Ethan felt his world tilt. All those things he'd never said, he'd never let himself feel…

He took a step toward his father and pointed to the front door. "I'm not giving you a penny tonight or ever again. Leave. Now. And this time don't come back."

"I'm helping you here. I didn't have to do this. You're picking a skirt over your own flesh and blood?" Ray asked as he walked to the door, his voice a little desperate. "Think about it, son."

"We're done, Ray. No more unexpected visits, no more phone calls when you're between jobs. We're done." Ethan slammed the door on his father with no regrets.

* * *

Lainey parked her rental car almost a quarter-mile down the road from the shelter then walked with a steady stream of people headed for the adoption fair.

Stopping midstride, her heart filled as families and couples came down the driveway leading dogs or holding cardboard boxes with new pets they were taking home. She recognized some of the animals, and while it was bittersweet to see the ones she'd come to love leaving, her heart swelled to see them going to true homes.

She'd been so scarred by the miscarriage and its aftermath, she'd believed she wasn't worthy of the role she wanted most in the world. But biology didn't make a person a mother or create a family—only love could do that. There were many, many children in the world who needed homes, who needed the love that Lainey now knew she could give.

"Lainey!"

She turned at the sound of her name.

"I knew you'd come back," her mother said, still limping as she hurried across the yard while Julia followed behind. "Do you know we've doubled the amount of adoptions from last year?"

Lainey turned to her sister. "Where's Charlie?"

"He's napping in the shelter office. Ida Vassler's with him. Turns out the old battle-ax has a soft spot for babies."

"Do you feel okay, Mom?" Lainey asked. "You're not over-doing it?"

"I feel better than I have in years. This is exactly what your father would have wanted to see." Vera took a deep breath. "It's all because of your work."

Lainey glanced at Julia. "Everyone pitched in to make it a success. The shelter and clinic staff, Julia, Ethan…" Her voice trailed off.

"What happened in Alaska?" her mother asked softly.

Lainey's throat clogged with emotion, but she only shrugged. "The usual. I took some pictures, met with—"

"What really happened?" Julia interrupted. "When you left, it didn't seem like you'd be back at all, let alone for the event. Your message yesterday only said you'd be here and we needed to talk. I imagine there's a pretty good reason."

It had been a whirlwind week, and Lainey was running on pure adrenaline at this point. Not exactly the clear mindset in which she'd prefer to have this conversation. But one thing she knew for certain: no more running away. She'd face whatever challenges life threw at her head-on with no regrets. She swallowed and began, "I want to apologize to you both."

Her mother waved a hand. "We're moving forward, Melanie. No need—"

"Mama." She wrapped her hand around Vera's fingers and squeezed softly. "There is a need. I need to say this." She looked at her sister. "To both of you."

Julia nodded. "Go ahead, Lain."

"First off, I'm not sorry I fell in love with Ethan or about my time with him. If I could have picked a different man I would have. But that's not how the heart works." She took a breath. "What I *am* sorry for, Mama, is that I felt inferior to Julia and was so scared of disappointing you and Daddy that I didn't stick it out and make things better back then. I always thought I was the odd girl out. I didn't measure up to you or Juls and what a woman should be—"

"That's ridiculous, Lainey." Her mother shook her head. "You—"

Vera stopped as Julia clapped a hand over her mouth. "Let her talk, Mama. For once in your life, let someone else finish a thought." She kept her hand over Vera's mouth until their mother finally nodded. Julia flashed a self-congratulatory smile at Lainey. "Continue, please."

That tiny moment of levity made all the difference to

Lainey. These women were her family, and she could tell them everything she'd needed to say for so long. "After I lost the baby, the doctor told me about the scarring and how it meant I wouldn't be able to get pregnant again. It pushed me over the edge. I already thought I didn't deserve Ethan, and it was like the universe giving me a sign that I was so messed up I wasn't even fit to be a mother."

Tears welled in her mother's eyes.

"I should have told you," Lainey said quickly before Vera could speak. "I was ashamed of who I was, and it felt like part of my punishment should be to carry the burden alone. By the time the wedding day came, I knew I couldn't keep the secret from Ethan. But it felt like if I said the words out loud it would make it too real. So I left the note. It was cowardly, and I don't blame him for his reaction to it then or now."

Julia took a step forward. "Ethan never read your note, Lainey. Tim Reynolds switched yours for a couple of lines about you wanting to end things."

"What?" Lainey whispered as her jaw dropped. "Why?"

"I'm not totally sure, but you need to know Ethan didn't desert you the way you thought."

Lainey tried for a moment to wrap her mind around that concept then shook her head. "It doesn't change the facts. *I deserted him*. All of you. If I'd had the courage to face him on our wedding day, there wouldn't have been any confusion. I don't know if I deserve a second chance with Ethan after what I put him through, but I owe him an honest conversation about my feelings then and now. Like you said, Mama, it's time to move on. Whether or not I can have children biologically doesn't make me damaged goods. I've let my sorrow define me for too long. I'm making a change starting today. I want a family, and I'm going to have one. I want both of you and Charlie to be a part of my life. This summer has shown how much you mean to me and how lonely I've been. I just hope it's not too late."

She looked at Julia who smiled then pulled her into a hug. "I have a lot to make up for, too, little sister. We'll be all right. Charlie needs his favorite auntie to spoil him rotten."

"Absolutely," Lainey agreed.

They both turned to Vera.

"Am I allowed to speak now?" she asked with a small smile.

Lainey grimaced. "Of course."

Her mother took both Lainey's hands in her own. "I'm proud of you, Lainey. For what you did this summer and the changes you're making. If my stroke is what brought you back here, then I'm thankful something good could come from it. You'll be a wonderful mother." She paused and wiped at her eyes then added, "I want lots of grandkids."

The three women hugged as more families with dogs trailed by them. Lainey heard her name spoken and looked up to see Tim standing near the clinic's entrance.

"How dare he show up here," Vera whispered on a hiss of breath.

Julia's shoulders stiffened. "I'll kick his butt into next week."

She took a step toward Tim but Lainey tugged her back. "I should talk to him. I need to know what happened at the wedding and why he published all that garbage under my name."

"All you need to know is he's a scumbag," Julia argued.

"He's part of this. Another challenge and I'm going to face it."

Julia studied her then nodded. "Come on, Mama. We'll check on things at the shelter. Lainey, we're right around the corner if you need anything."

"Your sister can be kind of scary when she wants to," Tim said when they'd gone.

"She wants to protect me."

"Since when?" he answered with a scoff. "We were alike—no one in our corner. The way I remember it, the only person who protected you was me."

Lainey frowned. "Is that what you call switching the note, Tim? The editorial exposing my personal business for everyone to read? That's exploitation, not protection. I came back here to make amends, not more enemies."

He took a step closer to her, running one hand through his thinning hair. "Don't you understand? I did those things for your own good. You need to get out of this town. You're better than Brevia. Definitely better than Ethan Daniels. He's just like his father."

"Ethan is nothing like his father, which is not the point. You had no right to interfere in my life."

"I did it because I loved you. I still do. If you hadn't been so obsessed with Ethan, maybe you would have noticed. I hated to see how sad you were when he hurt you. It made me crazy when everyone in town turned on you. I'd never do that, Lainey. We want the same things in life. I could travel with you. We'd see the world together if you'd only give me a chance."

He reached out and Lainey took a step away. What he'd done was wrong and unforgivable. "You don't show you love someone by manipulating them, Tim." She crossed her arms over her chest. "I thought we were friends. I trusted you. You abused my trust in the worst way possible. Not to mention the pain you caused Ethan and the rest of my family. There is no chance for us and there never was. Whether or not Ethan is in the picture doesn't change that. Stay away from me and out of my life, once and for all."

His jaw dropped. "You can't mean it."

She started up the clinic steps. "I have nothing more to say to you, Tim," she called over her shoulder.

She made it to the front porch just as Tim grabbed her arm. "Let me explain," he yelled, yanking her back. "I can make you understand."

As she tried to pull away, her shoe caught on the last step and she tumbled into him. "Get your hands off me," she hollered as his arms wrapped around her, too angry to care about the small crowd of people that had gathered in the front driveway to watch the spectacle.

"Please, Lainey—"

"Let her go, Reynolds."

Lainey caught a glimpse of Ethan filling the doorway of the clinic just before Tim pushed her away. Off balance, she dropped onto all fours in the grass.

"Stay out of this, Ethan. It's between Lainey and me." Tim's voice sounded petulant.

"There is nothing between the two of us," she snapped, standing up then grimacing as she tried to put weight on her ankle.

Ethan's gaze met hers, and she could see him read the pain in her eyes. In an instant he was in front of Tim, practically lifting him off the ground by his shirt collar. "If you've hurt her, I'm going to—"

"It's okay," she said quickly, placing a hand on Ethan's chest. The last thing any of them needed was another public scene.

"Tim, what the hell is wrong with you?" Dave Reynolds elbowed his way through the cluster of people.

Ethan gave Tim a solid shove then came to stand next to Lainey. "Get him out of here, Dave."

Tim swatted at his brother's hand. "You think he's your best friend, Dave. But you don't know the things I do. What his old man did. Ethan isn't so high-and-mighty. He's cut from the same cloth."

"I do know," Dave said, temper flaring in his eyes. "I know

about Ray and our mom. It wasn't Ethan's fault. We were all kids when it happened."

"Everyone knows his mother left town because she didn't want to be saddled with a family. If it wasn't for Ethan, maybe his dad wouldn't have come sniffin' around Mom. Maybe she and Dad—"

"You need to shut your trap." Dave grabbed the back of Tim's neck and pulled him through the crowd. "Before I do it for you." He looked toward Ethan. "I'm sorry, man. About everything."

Ethan gave him a small nod.

"You too, Lainey. I wish I could make it up to you."

She swallowed and tried to offer a reassuring smile. "It's okay, Dave."

"Show's over, folks," Ethan called out as Dave disappeared into the crowd. "Nothing more to see here." He looked down at Lainey, his eyes dark. "We need to talk."

She nodded then winced as she put weight on her ankle.

"You're hurt."

"It's fine," she said quickly. "Just twisted it a little."

Ethan cursed under his breath and gathered her into his arms. He climbed the steps of the clinic and maneuvered inside, not putting her down until the door was safely closed and they were alone.

"I know you probably hate me more now," she said quietly, focusing her gaze on a place just past his shoulder. "The things Tim published in my name were awful, and instead of facing the problem, I ran off again. I'm sorry I didn't stay, then and now. I was wrong—"

He covered her mouth with his, cutting off the rest of her sentence. A sliver of hope began to grow in her, blooming into something more when she pulled back and met his gaze. She saw the same love shining in his eyes she knew was reflected in her own.

"You don't hate me?"

"I could never hate you." He smoothed his palms over her cheeks. "As much as I wanted to—tried to—I've always loved you, Lainey. All those years you were gone, it was like you'd taken a part of my soul with you." He pressed another kiss to her mouth. "I'm half a man without you. You make me whole."

"The infertility made me feel like part of me was missing. Even you couldn't fill the empty space. How could I expect you to accept me when I wouldn't accept myself? I know I can't give you the family you've wanted—"

He shook his head. "What I want is you. You're all I've ever wanted."

His words made her heart soar. "I want you, too, Ethan. I want us to have a family. Together." She paused to catch her breath as emotion clogged her throat. "I should have talked to you earlier, been honest from the start. I love you so much. I can't imagine my life without you in it."

"You never have to." He pulled her down the hall toward his office. "I want to show you something."

She leaned on him as they walked, his fingers warm and sure laced in hers. He picked up a stack of papers from his desk and handed it to her.

Her eyes widened as she looked over the brochures and books on adoption. She jerked her head up. "You'd be willing to consider adoption?"

He smiled and pulled out a slip of paper with a boarding pass printed on it. "I was leaving for Alaska tonight. I let you get away once and didn't plan to repeat that mistake. It doesn't matter to me whether you give birth or we find a child who needs us as much as we need him or her. I want to see you hold our child in your arms, Lainey. I want to grow old with you, take our grandkids to Disney World. I want a life with you."

"I was such a fool." She struggled to catch her breath. "For so long I thought I was being punished—I didn't deserve to be a mother." When he reached for her she shook her head. "It was an accident, Ethan. I realized that in Alaska. I finally understood my life is what I make of it, not something that happens to me." She smiled through her tears. "And I want to make a life with you."

He drew her to him and caressed her mouth with his. She gave herself up to the pleasure of his touch until a thought pierced the edge of her mind.

"Oh, no!" she yelled, pulling back.

His eyes were dark as he looked at her. "What is it?"

"Pita," she whispered. "I told Mom to put her on the adoptive animal roster. And the puppy, too. I thought they'd be better without me, but I need them. Pita and Chip belong to me. To us." She whirled for the door. "What if they're already gone? I have to get them back, Ethan."

He grabbed her arm. "Come on."

Instead of turning toward the front, he led her down the hall to the back. "There's no time, Ethan. I need to—"

He opened the door to one of the empty exam rooms and flipped on the light switch. Pita trotted out with Chip trailing behind her and sniffed at Ethan.

Lainey gasped and the dog charged at her, tail wagging in an ecstatic greeting. She dropped to the ground and wrapped her arms around Pita's neck while the puppy dashed over to cover her with enthusiastic kisses.

"I never put them with the other animals. They're yours, sweetheart. Always have been."

Straightening, she hugged him as Pita and Chip pranced around them, yipping wildly. "Just like you?" She rained kisses across his face.

"Just like me," he agreed. "You're still the one, Lainey. You always will be."

She sighed and rested her head on his chest. "Are you sure you're ready for this?"

"I've been waiting for this moment for ten years."

"Better or worse, Ethan. I'm here for good. Forever."

His mouth grazed over hers. "Forever," he agreed.

She'd found her place in the world and couldn't imagine belonging anywhere else. She lost herself in his kiss once more, knowing she was finally home.

* * * * *

HOT-SHOT DOC COMES TO TOWN

SUSAN CARLISLE

To Mom
For all your love and support

Susan Carlisle's love affair with books began in the sixth grade when she made a bad grade in math. Not allowed to watch TV until she brought the grade up, Susan filled her time with books. She turned her love of reading into a passion for writing and now has over ten medicals published through Mills & Boon. She writes hot sexy docs and the strong women that captivate them. www.SusanCarlisle.com.

CHAPTER ONE

THE flash of red in the parking space directly in front of the Benton Clinic door caught Dr. Shelby Wayne's attention. Great, this could only be the bad-boy doctor her uncle had told her to expect, and over six hours late.

Squinting, she looked through the dusty plate-glass window at the slick convertible sports car on the other side. As far as she knew, no one in that area of western Tennessee had a car nearly as fine as the one now almost blocking the door. This was big-truck not fancy-car country.

Babysitting her Uncle Gene's most recent personal project wasn't her idea of a good time. But needing help at the clinic so badly meant she couldn't send him back to Nashville. Still if she could get two weeks' worth of free medical help out of it, she'd bend over backwards to accommodate her uncle. Maybe if she played her cards right she could convince the doctor that his skills would be better utilized in Benton than where he was currently working.

If she wanted the clinic to remain open, she'd have to find some help soon.

She glanced at the clipboard for the name of her next patient then scanned the packed waiting room for Mrs. Stewart. It would be a waste of time to try to get the attention of the sweet little grandmotherly woman with a hearing problem over the din in the tiny room. As she walked towards Mrs.

Stewart the people waiting quieted, and all eyes turned to look out the window.

Shelby watched, along with everyone else, as the expensive-looking loafer touched the pavement. In one athletic movement a man slipped out of the low car. His gaze met hers through the window. Her breath caught in her throat. His piercing look made her wonder if he could see secrets she'd kept hidden. He gave her a slight nod of acknowledgement.

His gaze traveled back and forth along the line of stores in the mostly abandoned strip mall. If it hadn't been for the brief twist of contempt marring his looks he would've qualified for the term "dangerously attractive".

How dared he act as if Benton was beneath him? After her husband Jim had died, continuing to live and work here had been the best decision she'd ever made. Her parents had encouraged her to move back to her home town to practice but she'd decided Benton was where she belonged. It was where she and Jim had chosen to make their home. Benton had supported her a hundred and ten percent as she'd grieved. Each person had their own little quirks but they all had a big hearts. Here she felt secure.

The new doctor still held the room's attention as he stepped to the door and pulled. The front of his car rested so far over the sidewalk that it wouldn't allow the door to open far enough for him to enter.

Shelby couldn't stop the twitch of her lips as she checked a chuckle. He was making a notable first impression on the locals sitting in the waiting room. Everyone in town would be enjoying this story by bedtime. That was one of the great things about living in a small town, though it could also be the worst. Everyone knew everything. When you had a tragedy your friends and neighbors were there to support you, but when there was a good story to tell they spread it.

The man snarled and murmured a sharp word under his

breath. Turning, he took three quick strides back to the driver's door, opened it and slid behind the wheel with the same grace as when he'd alighted. Leaving one leg hanging outside the open door, he started the car. The windows of the clinic vibrated slightly as he backed the vehicle up until the entire sidewalk could be seen. As quickly as he'd started the car he shut off the engine, got out and slammed the door.

His long strides brought him towards the entrance of the clinic again. The only indication in his demeanor that he might still be annoyed was the jerk he gave the clinic door.

Shelby smiled but not too broadly so that he wouldn't think she'd been laughing at him. "You must be Dr. Stiles. I was expecting you hours ago."

"Are you Dr. Wayne?"

She offered him her hand. "I'm Dr. Shelby Wayne."

He shook her hand. "With the name Shelby I had expected a man. Taylor Stiles."

His clasp was firm. Warm and dry. Not the dead-fish handshake she'd anticipated from the fancy-dressed, showy-car-driving, big-city doctor.

"Sorry to disappoint you," Shelby said with a hint of sarcasm.

"If you two young people are through putting on a show..." Mrs. Stewart looked pointedly at Taylor Stiles "...and making nice, would one of you mind seeing about my sciatica?"

Taylor blinked in surprise. As if on cue, the room erupted in noise as though the curtain had closed and the play was over.

Shelby cleared her throat. She loved the outspoken and to-the-point woman. "Uh, yes, Mrs. Stewart. You're next." Shelby handed the clipboard to Dr. Stiles. "Call the next patient under Mrs. Stewart's name and put him or her in room two." She pointed down the short hallway. "I'll be in after I see Mrs. Stewart."

Dr. Stiles's dashing brow rose a fraction of an inch but he accepted the clipboard. Apparently he wasn't used to taking direction. His deep baritone voice called little Greg Hankins's name while she guided Mrs. Stewart to exam room one.

"Kind of snooty, that one, but still mighty handsome," Mrs. Stewart remarked as she took a seat in the chair in the room.

"Um, I guess," Shelby said as she flipped through the seventy-four-year-old's chart.

"I could tell by the look on your face you noticed it too. Doc Shelby, you have to start living again. It's been three years. Your Jim is dead, not you."

A stab of pain came with that frank statement about her husband. There had been nothing she could do when she'd reached the accident. Despite not being far behind Jim in her own car, his truck had already been wrapped around a tree when she arrived at the scene. Nothing she'd done had stopped his blood from pooling in the mangled metal. The sight, the smell… She'd retched. Three years later she could at least do everything in her power to honor his memory by keeping the clinic open any way she could. The people of Benton she loved so much needed the medical care and she needed the security of knowing she was needed.

"Now, Mrs. Stewart…" Shelby smiled "…I'm supposed to be taking care of you, not you seeing about me."

"Well, missy, I think you don't want to see about you, so I'm just going to have to."

Shelby took a deep breath and let it out slowly. "Why don't you let me examine you, then we can work on me?" Adjusting her bright pink stethoscope in her ears, she placed the disk on the woman's chest.

"All you think about is this clinic. Maybe with Dr. Kildare here you can have a little fun for a change," the old woman groused.

"Dr. Kildare?"

"Yeah, he was one of those handsome TV doctors before your time. That new doctor makes me think of him. All tall, dark and handsome."

Shelby laughed. "Mrs. Stewart, you're outrageous." Mrs. Stewart's youngest son had to be older than Dr. Stiles. "You don't even know him and I really don't either. Anyway, he's only going to be helping out for a couple of weeks."

"Yeah, but you could have a little fun for a while. You're not dead. So stop acting like it."

Shelby patted the woman's arm. "For you I will try, I promise."

Without a doubt he had messed up this time. There had been no talking the judge out of his decision. Community service in a rural area. His lawyer had cautioned against arguing with the judge but Taylor had tried anyway. If he didn't have such a lead foot, he'd still be in Nashville in his nice modern trauma department instead of in a town like Benton. He'd run from a town similar to this one years ago and had never returned.

Taylor lifted the large-for-his-age two-year-old boy up onto the metal exam table. *Where in the world did you go to find a piece of medical office equipment from the 1950s?*

Thump, thump the table responded in rebellion as the boy's heels hit its side.

It was a sturdy table, Taylor would give it that.

The thin, frail mother carefully placed a brown bag she'd been carrying on the floor. She reminded Taylor of how his mother had looked when he had been a child, work weary and sad.

"So what's wrong with Greg?" Taylor looked at the boy's mother while keeping a hand on the wiggling child.

At one time he'd been like this little boy, dirty and wearing hand-me-down clothes from the church thrift closet. The sharp bite of memory froze him for a second. He pushed it aside. He hadn't dwelled on his dysfunctional childhood in years and he refused to start again today.

"I think he has something in his nose. We'll wait and let Doc Wayne take it out."

The mother doesn't trust me. Taylor didn't like that. He was the one with the knowledge who worked in a well-respected hospital, who had managed to get out of a nowhere town like this one, and she questioned his abilities. Turning away as if to get something, he gathered his patience.

Taylor faced the mother again. "Well, why don't I just take a quick look, okay?" Taylor forced his best smile for the mother then sought the otoscope that should have been hanging on the wall. "Uh, excuse me I need to find a light."

"There's a flashlight in the drawer." The mother pointed to the metal stand beside him.

Taylor pulled the drawer open and found what he needed, including plastic gloves. He checked inside the boy's nose. "There it is. In his left nostril. A lima bean, I believe. Do you mind if I get it out? Dr. Wayne will be busy for a while."

"I guess it'll be all right," the mother said without much enthusiasm.

"Let me find—"

"The big tweezers thing is in the jar on top of the stand," the mother said in a dry tone.

"So how often has Greg been in with this type of problem?" Taylor asked as he reached for the instrument in the outdated clear sterile jar.

"This is the third time in two weeks."

"Really. That often?" Taylor nodded his head thoughtfully. "Greg, you just lean back and hold still. I'll have that old bean out in no time," he said sternly enough so the boy would do as instructed but not so harshly as to scare him.

The bean slipped out with a gentle tug and Taylor dropped it into the trash can, along with the gloves.

"Okay, young man, you're done here." Taylor picked up the boy and set him on his feet.

As if Taylor had pushed the button of a doorbell, the boy burst out crying then wailing. His slight mother hefted the child into her arms. "Shu, what's wrong, honey? Did the doctor hurt you?"

Great, now she's making the kid afraid of me.

"Sucker, I want a sucker," the child demanded between gasps.

Over the noise, Taylor asked, "Has Dr. Wayne been giving Greg a sucker each time she's taken something out of his nose?"

The woman nodded.

"Greg," Taylor said firmly, gaining the boy's attention and shutting off his tantrum. "If you don't put anything in your nose for one week then your mother will bring you by to get a sucker. Do you understand?"

The boy nodded his agreement and plopped his filthy thumb into his mouth.

"Good. See you next week."

As they exited the room the mother handed Taylor the brown sack she'd been carrying with extra care. "Your pay."

"Uh, thank you."

As the mother and child walked back down the hall toward the waiting area, Taylor unrolled the top of the bag. Nestled inside were six brown eggs. He crushed the top of the bag. He could remember his mother not being able to pay the doctor and bartering her house-cleaning services for medical care for him and his siblings. Of all the places the judge could have sent him, why did it have to be here?

"Where's my patient?" Dr. Wayne demanded as she looked around him into the room.

"He's gone."

"Gone where?"

"I examined him, and he's left."

Her shoulders went back, her chest came forward. He would've taken time to enjoy the sight if it hadn't been for her flashing gray eyes.

"That's not what I instructed you to do."

"I'm a doctor. I treated a patient. End of story."

She didn't say anything for a few moments. The blood rose in her face. More calmly than her appearance indicated she said, "We need to step into my office."

Turning, she walked to the end of the hallway. Apparently it wasn't until she reached the office door that she realized he hadn't moved. She glared at him.

Not appreciating being treated like a school child being called to the principal's office, Taylor resigned himself to putting up with her bossy ways for the time being. The judge had stated in no uncertain terms—clinic or jail.

"Coming, Dr. Wayne," he said, loud enough to be heard but with zero sincerity.

After he'd entered the office, she closed the flimsy door behind him. "Dr. Stiles, you will *not* come into my clinic six hours late and start doing as you please. If you'd been here on time I could've instructed you in the clinic protocol."

Straight chestnut hair that touched the ridge of her shoulders swayed as she spoke. Taylor would describe her as cute in a college co-ed sort of way. Her practical black slacks and white shirt did nothing to move her up on the looks scale.

"These are my people. I won't have you showing up for two short weeks and taking over. I cannot, will not, have you here for God knows what reason and let you destroy the trust I've built with my patients. I expect you to follow my instructions."

Who did this woman think she was, talking to him that

way? Taylor carefully set the bag of eggs down on the desk. Turning his back to it, he placed his hands on the edge of the desk and leaned back.

"Doctor," he said, with enough disdain to make the word sound like he questioned whether or not that was the correct term. He took pleasure in watching the thrust of her breasts indicating her indignation as his barb struck home. "I won't be relegated to being your nurse. I'm the chief trauma doctor of a major hospital in Nashville. I can assure you that there will be few, if any, problems you see in this small, backwards clinic that I'll need your handholding for.

"I don't like being here any more than you obviously like having me. But what I can tell you is that I'm a good doctor. By no choice of my own, your patients are also *my* patients for the time being. Now, I suggest that we get back to that room full of people you're so concerned about."

Her mouth opened and closed. A sense of satisfaction filled him at having so thoroughly shut her up. Based on the last few minutes the next couple of weeks wouldn't be dull.

The infuriating doctor was calling his next patient before Shelby gathered her wits enough to follow him out of the office and down the hall. She'd never before forgotten about having patients waiting. It was a source of pride that she'd always put them first. Not even here a day and this egotistical doctor her uncle had sent had scrambled her brain. How was she supposed to survive the days ahead while having the likes of him in her face?

Who did he think he was talking to? The Benton Medical Clinic was hers. Her and Jim's dream. She'd make it clear later this evening who was in charge. For now she had to admit the high-handed doctor was right, she had patients to see.

The afternoon wore on and the most contact she had with

Dr. Stiles was when they passed in the hall. It was narrow and their bodies brushed when they maneuvered by each other. For once she regretted not insisting that the landlord let her and Jim change the already existing partitions and make the hallway wider. Before they'd converted it to a medical clinic, the space had been an insurance company office without a large amount of traffic in the hallway.

The first time they passed each other her body went harp-string tight as a tingle rippled through her. She pushed it away, convincing herself it was a delayed reaction to being so irate with him. The next time he was too close was when he looked down at her with his dark steady gaze and said, "By the way, where's the nurse?"

"Don't have one. I have a teenager who's usually here but she's out sick today."

"Really," he said in astonishment. For a second she thought she saw admiration in his eyes. She wasn't sure why it mattered but she liked the thought that he might be impressed by something she did.

When he left her she felt like she'd just stepped out of a hot bath—all warm from head to toe. Thankfully she managed not to cross his path again.

Enough of those thoughts, Shelby scolded herself as she knelt to clean juice from the linoleum. The juice had spilt when a child had thrown a cup. Using a hand on her knee for balance, she pushed up and brushed her clothes off. Instead of her uniform of slacks and shirts she wished she could wear cute sundresses to work, but having to be the cleaning crew meant that wasn't practical.

She looked at the bright red car parked front and center of the door. Despite the fact the cost of it alone could finance the clinic for weeks, maybe months if she was thrifty, she'd love to climb into it and let her hair blow in the wind. Forget all her cares for a while. With a deep sigh she picked up the window cleaner. The trouble was, all her concerns would still be right here waiting. It was her responsibility to see that the clinic remained open.

Footfalls on the floor tiles drew her attention. Shelby moved out of the way so the last patient of the day could leave. "How're you, Mrs. Ferguson?" she asked the barrel-round woman with the white face.

"I would've been better if you hadn't been too busy to see me," she grumbled.

"How's that? Did Dr. Stiles not take good care of you?" The man was going to be out of here tonight if he'd upset Mrs. Ferguson.

"I don't like strange doctors looking me over," she groused.

Relieved there was nothing more to her concern than that, Shelby watched Taylor approach. As Mrs. Stewart had remarked, he was good looking but Shelby was more interested in his abilities, and those she couldn't question. He'd held up his end of the workload, she'd have to give him that. Most of the patients had been unsure about seeing him but had cautiously agreed when they'd been told how long they'd have to wait to see her. Most had given in and decided to let Taylor examine them. But there was a little part of Shelby that liked knowing she was their first choice.

"Dr. Stiles will only be helping out until the end of the month."

"Good," Mrs. Ferguson said, as she shifted her oversized bag on her ample hip. "Then things will get back to normal around here."

"So, are you two ladies talking about me?" Dr. Stiles came to stand beside them and flashed Mrs. Ferguson a grin.

Was there no end to the man's ego? "No." The word came out harsher than Shelby had intended, making her look guilty of doing exactly what he'd accused them of.

The twinkle in Taylor's eyes told her he knew it too. "Mrs. Ferguson, why don't I walk you out?"

She gave him a startled look. "Uh, I guess that would be all right." The woman clutched her purse in her sausage-sized fingers and shuffled towards the door.

Shelby made a swipe with the glass cleaner as she observed Taylor helping Mrs. Ferguson into her car. A summer breeze lifted the deep waves of his brown hair as he strolled back toward the clinic. Would it be soft and silky to the touch?

Shaking her head at thoughts like that, Shelby rubbed extra hard at a spot on the glass. It had been an easier day having Dr. Stile's help but she couldn't afford to get used to it. He wouldn't be there very long. Regardless of what good help he'd turned out to be, he made her angrier than anyone she'd ever known. She'd have a talk with him tonight and set the ground rules. This was her and Jim's clinic. She was in charge.

Shelby had stepped outside to wash the other side of the window by the time he'd reached the door. She glanced at him.

"Crusty old bird and a heart attack waiting to happen," he said, running a hand across his chin dark with stubble.

Suddenly she noticed the shadowy circles under his eyes. He looked tired. "I know. I've talked to her until I'm blue in the face. But she just can't bring herself to give up the carbs."

Shelby sprayed the window and began making circles with the rag. From the reflection in the glass she could tell the sun was turning pink in the western sky above the rolling hills and lush foliage of summer. She had to hurry or she wouldn't finish before she could no longer see.

"I'm bushed. I understand you have a place where I can stay," Taylor said as he pulled the door open.

"Yeah, but I have to finish up here before we leave."

"Don't you have a cleaning service?"

"Sure I do. Sometimes Carly, my receptionist, if she doesn't have a date. Which she almost always has." She glanced at him. He stood with his hands in his pockets and his head slanted in disbelief.

"Surely you don't do all the cleaning after seeing patients all day."

"Dr. Stiles—"

"Taylor. After hours I believe we can call each other by our first names."

Somehow it seemed petty not to agree. "Taylor, this is a state-supported clinic. And that may not last. Funding's tight and I have to constantly prove need. I'd rather put every dollar available into patient care."

Taylor looked through the glass at the room with the water-stained ceiling and mismatched chairs crowded against the wall. Shelby's voice spoke with pride but all he saw was a sad, needy place that he couldn't leave soon enough. It represented all that he had gladly left behind. He couldn't get back to his sparkling state-of-the-art hospital too soon. With a resigned breath he said, "Where do you keep the cleaning supplies?" He might as well help if he planned to get some sleep any time soon.

"Why?"

"I thought I'd help."

"I've got it."

Really, she was such a control freak that she even had to do all the cleaning? "It'll go twice as fast if I help."

"You're right. Stuff's in the closet in my office."

Taylor walked down the hall to the office and pulled the bucket full of cleaning materials out of the closet. The plastic pail was the same type his mother had carried when she'd cleaned people's homes. She had worked six days a week and even that hadn't always kept him and his two brothers in clothes or put food on the table. His drunken father...

"If you'll give me that, I'll do the restroom. I don't want you to mess up those pretty shoes," Shelby said.

"Oh, that's already happened. Little Jack Purdy threw up on them hours ago."

She wrinkled her nose. "Sorry."

"All part of the job. I'll sweep. Then can we get out of here."

"Yeah, I'll come in early and set up the rooms."

Was there anything she didn't do?

Thirty minutes later Shelby locked the door behind them and pulled the strap of her satchel over her slim shoulder. "Follow me."

He backed out of the parking space and was waiting before she'd made it to the ancient black pick-up across the three-row parking lot. He watched as Shelby pulled herself up into the truck. She was a petite woman, but she had a strong backbone to make up for any weakness she might have in other areas. A pit bull had nothing on her.

The whine of Shelby's starter refusing to co-operate and her hand hitting the steering-wheel told him he needed to offer her a lift. Taylor pulled in front of the truck. "Need a ride?"

She leaned out the open window. "Yeah, much as I hate to admit it."

"Is that riding with me you hate or that the truck won't start?"

"Both." She gave him a dry smile and climbed out of the truck, hefted her bag over her shoulder and came around the car.

He'd had no idea what to expect when the judge had ordered him here. He would've never imagined in a million years he'd find someone so smart, stubborn and surprisingly fascinating hiding out in some tiny 'burb in the middle of nowhere. Why was she here?

Taylor leaned across and unlatched the passenger door. Stretching farther, he pushed the door open. "Give me that." He pointed to the bag. Shelby handed it to him. "What've you got in this?" He put it in the space behind them.

"Charts." She slid into the low seat.

"You're taking work home? You've already put in, what? A twelve-hour day and now you're going to do paperwork. Don't you have a life?"

"The clinic is my life."

He gave her a long look. "I can see that."

She narrowed her eyes and said, "By the way, tomorrow please park away from the door. Leave the closer spaces for my patients. Some, like Mrs. Ferguson, can't walk very far."

He put up a hand. "Okay. I've been adequately rebuked. Which way?"

"Out of the lot and then to the left on the main road. My house isn't far."

That figured. She wouldn't live too far from her precious clinic. The only thing he'd ever been single-mindedly focused on had been getting the heck out of a town just like the one he was in now. Medicine had been the vehicle he'd used to achieve that goal. His lips twisted. Ironically, it had also been the vehicle that had brought him back.

"Turn to the left just past the white two-story house. My house is the third one on the right."

He pulled into the tree-lined street with perfect houses and immaculate lawns. The neighbors were out in the coolness of the evening. Two couples stood talking to each other while kids played nearby. At another house a man mowed his grass.

"True suburbia," Taylor murmured.

"Yes, it is and that's why I bought on this street. I wanted to live where neighbors spoke to each other, helped each other. Where children could play and be safe."

His stomach clinched. The scene she described was everything he'd ever dreamed of as a kid. Slowly releasing a breath, he pulled his car into the paved drive Shelby indicated. The house was a red-brick ranch style with a two-story detached wooden garage and stairs running along the outside.

"You'll be staying there." Shelby pointed at the garage when he turned off the car engine.

"I'm staying here?" If working in the makeshift clinic wasn't bad enough, staying in this homey neighborhood might kill him. "With you?"

"You're not staying *with* me. I rent this out. It just happens I don't have a tenant right now."

Things had just got more interesting.

She glanced over her shoulder to the neighbors watching from across the street, then turned to him and grinned. "You've already started the neighbors talking. We don't often see cars like this in Benton."

"I guess you don't." Taylor felt his lips thin. He didn't like being talked about. He'd spent his youth being the topic of gossip, being made fun of. At least these people weren't talking about him in relationship to the town drunk.

Her smile had disappeared by the time his gaze met hers. "You know, if you don't want people to notice you then you might try not living so extravagantly." She opened the door and climbed out, picking up her satchel.

How had she read him so well? Were his feelings that obvious? He'd spent years learning to hide them. How had this woman he known mere hours been able to see through him?

Taylor stepped out of the car and slammed the door, facing her. "Extravagantly?" His voice rose. "I'll have you know I work hard for what I have. I can afford this car and I don't have to justify it to you or anyone else."

"Little touchy, aren't you?" she replied with a noticeable effort to keep her voice down.

"Everything okay, Shelby?" a deep voice called.

Taylor glared at the man who had crossed the street to stand at the end of her drive. Small towns never changed. People were always in your business.

She walked a few steps toward the man and waved. "Everything's fine, Mr. Marshall. I'm just showing Dr. Stiles where he'll be staying while he's in town."

Taylor went to the trunk of the car, popped it and grabbed his suitcase.

"Okay," Mr. Marshall said. "We'll see you at the block party, won't we?"

"Sure. Looking forward to it."

"Bring the new doctor along if you wish. We'd like to meet him."

Taylor certainly hoped that she wasn't planning on him attending any party. The Arctic would become a beach before he'd attend any social function around here. He'd made himself into an arts and opera guy. Benton didn't even have a movie theater, from what he could tell.

Shelby turned, her gray eyes flashing, her tone tight with control. "Don't you ever raise your voice to me again where my neighbors can hear. They worry about me."

She motioned towards the garage stairs and headed that way. "You'll not come here and upset them or create fodder for talk at their dinner tables. For some reason I don't understand, Uncle Gene thinks I'm a halfway house warden for bad-boy trauma doctors." The last few words were said more to herself than to him.

So, Shelby didn't like being the talk of the town any more than he did. Maybe they had more in common than he'd given her credit for.

CHAPTER TWO

SHELBY dropped her bag on the bottom step of the stairs that ran alongside the garage.

"Since you don't want to be a topic of gossip any more than I do," Taylor said calmly, "maybe you should just agree to disagree about my car."

With great effort Shelby pushed down the temptation to say something. Having a public argument would certainly give her neighbors and friends a good tale to tell.

"Just what did you do to get on Uncle Gene's bad side?"

"Uncle Gene?" he asked in a puzzled tone.

"Judge Gene Robbins. He's my uncle," she said as she started to climb the stairs.

"So that's why I'm here." The words were little more than a mumble, as if he was contemplating the meaning of life. After a moment he commented, "We've had a few legal dealings. Nothing special."

Shelby stopped and looked down at him. What did he mean? Was he an ax murderer? No, her uncle wouldn't send anyone to work with her who wasn't a decent person.

Taylor's look moved slowly up from where his focus had been, on her bottom. Heat filled her cheeks. It had been a long time since a man had noticed her and made his appreciation so obvious. She and Jim had been an item since childhood, leaving little room for another man to show interest. The men in Benton had never approached her in anything other than friendship since Jim had been gone. In truth, she'd not given them a chance. She couldn't take the chance of losing someone she loved again.

Shelby hurried up the stairs. Taylor was here to help in the clinic and that was all. On the landing she opened the door to the apartment.

"You don't lock up?"

Turning round, she found Taylor too close for comfort. Standing on the small landing that made her a step higher than he, Shelby was almost at eye level with him.

From there she could see the tiny laugh lines that radiated out from the corners of his eyes. Apparently he wasn't always the hypercritical person his body language indicated he was. His eyes were brown with small flakes of gold.

The twist of the corner of his mouth brought her attention to his firm, full lips. She blinked.

"Doesn't your husband tell you to lock the doors?" he asked.

"I'm a widow."

"I'm sorry." He sounded like he meant it.

"I am too." She turned away from the sincerity in his eyes. The sadness that usually accompanied thoughts of Jim was suddenly not as sharp.

Shelby hadn't missed the look of displeasure on Taylor's face when he had entered the clinic or when he'd seen the working conditions. She'd also not missed the expression of disgust when he'd realized she drove an old truck. His knuckles had turned white on his steering-wheel when he'd pulled onto her street, as if he didn't like her neighborhood. Did he think that living here was beneath him? Or was it that she rubbed him the wrong way?

"How does your family feel about you being away from home?" she asked.

"No family." He made it sound like he liked it that way.

Entering the one-room apartment, Shelby moved to one side to prevent any physical contact. He made her feel nervous and she was never nervous around men. After dropping his bag on the floor, he looked around the place.

Shelby's gaze followed his. A full bed with her grandmother's hand-quilted blanket dominated the room. There was a small refrigerator-stove combo in one corner. A two-seater table with chairs sat in front of the double window that looked out onto the back of her house. A braided rug, sofa and chair finished off the living area. A bathroom took up the other corner. She was rather pleased with her decorating efforts. It made a cute place for one person to stay.

"I think you will be comfortable here," she said with a smile full of pride.

He didn't agree or disagree. Instead he picked up his bag, carried it to the bed and began unzipping it.

"Not up to your usual standards, I'm sure," she mumbled.

Taylor pulled clothing out of his bag, his back to her. "You don't know me well enough to know my standards. Now, if you'll excuse me, I'm going to get a much-needed shower and go to bed. I've been up almost twenty-four hours."

"What? Why?"

"Because I had to handle an emergency last night. A boy had been hit by a car. I didn't get out of the hospital until ten this morning and then I had to drive straight here or *Uncle Gene* would've been unhappy."

So that's why he'd been late. Why hadn't she noticed he wasn't just tired, he was exhausted? As a physician trained to observe the human condition she should've known. Had she completely missed it because of her strange reaction to his nearness?

Now she felt small and petty. Why hadn't he said something? She could've given him directions here. The clinic had been running with just her for three years and she could've certainly made it through another afternoon. Instead, Taylor had gone to work, never giving the patients or her any indication he was drained. His perfect bedside manner had never faltered. For that, he'd earned her admiration.

Taylor began unbuttoning his dress shirt.

Shelby headed for the door but turned back when she reached it. "One more thing about the clinic…" Her gaze went to where his hands worked the buttons open.

"Yeah?"

His shirt parted, revealing a broad chest lightly covered with dark hair. Her gaze rose to meet his. One of his dark brows rose quizzically.

Heaven help her, she'd been caught staring. Shelby drew in a quick breath. "Uh, do you mind keeping your clothes on until I'm gone?"

"Actually, I do. Can't whatever you have to say wait?"

Was she losing her mind? She didn't stand around in half-naked strangers' rooms. Holding her ground, she gave him her best piercing look. "No. I need to make a few things clear before tomorrow."

"Go ahead. I guess I can't stop you," he said as he shrugged out of his shirt and let it drop to the floor.

"Although I appreciate your help today, it needs to be clear to the patients that I'm in charge. I make the decisions. I determine what the patients require. I will not have you changing routines I've worked hard to implement. Is that clear?"

"So, to make it short and sweet, you're the boss."

Put that way, he made her sound like a shrew. That didn't sit well. "It's just that—"

He put up a hand, halting her words. "I've got it. Now, if you'll excuse me, I'd like to get some shut-eye."

Departing, she carried the feeling she'd been the one reprimanded. "The clinic opens at eight sharp," she said over her shoulder.

"I'll be there."

Taylor woke to threads of early morning sunshine through the window. He'd slept well, whether from exhaustion or because this simple room had offered him a good mattress he didn't know.

Shelby had been right. He didn't think much of the apartment but on second look it did have a rather homey feel. It was a great deal nicer than what he'd had growing up. To even have a bed to himself would've been considered high living.

He glanced at the electric clock on the bedside table. It said seven twenty-eight. The woman would have his hide if he didn't turn up on time this morning. He couldn't take a chance that she'd inform her Uncle Gene about his tardiness. More time he couldn't do.

Ten minutes later, freshly shaven and dressed in khakis, a knit shirt and loafers, he opened the door and almost stepped in the tray sitting on the stoop. There he found a Thermos of coffee, toast and a boiled egg. He smiled. Maybe the caustic doctor was feeling a little guilty about how she'd treated him when he'd been late. Apparently she wasn't all vinegar.

He checked the time. If he didn't get a move on she might chew him out again. Grabbing the Thermos and egg, he closed the door behind him and hurried down the stairs. Knocking on the back door of her house, he received no response. She must've found a ride to work. If she wasn't at the clinic when he got there, he'd hunt for her.

As Taylor walked across the parking lot towards the clinic, Shelby came out. "Coming in under the wire, aren't you, Doctor?" Her voice was full of censure as she worked the key until the deadbolt was drawn into the door to open the office for the day.

"I said I'd be here, and I'm here. And good morning to you too, Doctor. What time did you show up?"

"I've been here an hour or so. It usually takes me that long to set up for the day."

"I knocked to see if you needed a ride."

"I walked. Bert said he'd have my truck fixed this afternoon."

Taylor held the door for her to enter ahead of him. "You walked? I would've brought you if you'd woken me."

"You were tired. Walking isn't a problem. I do it pretty regularly. I'm safe enough and it's good exercise."

A couple of people who'd been waiting around outside came in behind them.

"Thanks for the breakfast." He showed her the egg and Thermos.

"No problem. Those'll have to wait, though. We've patients to see."

Her no-nonsense statement went along with her functional attire of navy slacks and white V-neck T-shirt that showed a hint of cleavage. Despite her simple attire, it couldn't hide the shapely curves of her body. Her waist was small enough that a man's hands could easily slip around it.

She'd pulled her hair back but at the nape it was too short to capture. The only flash of color was a bright neon-pink stethoscope hanging around her neck. Taylor followed her to the desk, where a blonde teenage girl sat, drumming a pencil and chewing gum.

"Carly, this is Dr. Stiles. He'll be helping us for the next couple of weeks," Shelby said as she picked up the sign-in clipboard.

Taylor nodded to the girl.

She looked up. He watched her eyes widen. She shifted, then straightened in her chair. "Hey." She flipped her long blonde hair behind her shoulder. He'd never thought of himself as vain, far from it, but he did know when a female appreciated his looks.

"Carly, do you think you could find Ms. Cooper's file? And get rid of the gum." Shelby turned to him, "I'll see Ms. Cooper since this is a check-up."

Carly didn't move. He didn't know why but he wished Shelby would have the same reaction to him that Carly did. Other than that one unguarded moment when he'd been unbuttoning his shirt, she'd acted as if she had no idea he was male. It intrigued and disappointed him. Simple admiration from Shelby would be hard earned.

"I'll call Dr. Stiles's patient for him," Carly said as she dropped her gum into the trash can at her feet and gave him a toothy smile.

"Will I be using exam one?" he asked Shelby.

"That'll be fine."

Her words were said so tersely that he glanced at her. What was her problem now?

For the rest of the morning he had little time to ponder what might have upset Shelby. The waiting room stayed full no matter how efficiently he tended to the patients or how simple the cases were.

Where Carly's reaction to him had been an ego booster earlier in the day, it had become borderline comical by midday. He noticed that she saw to all his patients, showing them to their exam room, asking him if he had everything he needed or if she could get him something to drink. All of it was nice but it was in direct contrast to how Carly treated Shelby. Carly offered her no assistance.

When Taylor asked Carly about that she shrugged in a typical teenage dramatic fashion and said, "Oh, Dr. Wayne likes to do everything herself."

Of course she does.

By lunchtime Taylor couldn't help but admit that he'd put

in a pretty hard morning. The little clinic was plenty busy. The mundane work sucked him back to another time. Each patient reminded him too much of the people he'd known growing up.

There was the kid with the cough that never disappeared, like Mike Walker's. He'd been in Taylor's third-grade class one year but wasn't there the next. Or others, such as old man Parsons, who'd had no teeth and had chewed tobacco until his gums were diseased. Or Mrs. Roberts, who might've been pretty at fifty, but with too many children and a sorry husband had looked like she was seventy.

Taylor would do his time and get back to where he belonged, where memories weren't darts being thrown at him constantly.

Around noon the egg he'd eaten in bites between patients was gone. He was glad to see that the crowd in the waiting room had dwindled. Maybe they would let him and Shelby have some lunch before every seat was filled again.

"Where do you get a good burger in this town?" Taylor asked as Shelby approached the front desk.

"There's a burger place on Main," Carly offered.

"We can all go. I'll buy," he offered.

Shelby gave a negative shake of her head. "I have paperwork to do. And someone may come in." She slipped a chart into the file cabinet.

Really? The woman couldn't even stop long enough to go out for a quick bite of lunch?

"I want to go. Can we ride in that cool car of yours?"

Taylor wasn't sure he wanted to be seen riding around town with the very young girl beside him but there was no choice because he had no idea where the burger joint was and he was starving. "Can we bring you back something?" Taylor asked Shelby.

"No, I have a pack of crackers in my desk."

"Okay." He shrugged. "But I bet a burger would be a lot better." He looked at Carly. "Come on. Show me the way. I guess I should learn my way around town."

Shelby pulled out the drawer of her desk and reached for the package of crackers but didn't pick them up. She would've been satisfied with them if Taylor hadn't mentioned a burger.

She popped the top of her diet drink and stared off into space. The sounds of Carly's high-pitched giggle and Taylor's deep rumble came from the front. It grew louder as they walked in her direction.

Taylor stopped and let Carly enter Shelby's office before him. "We decided to go through the drive-in and pick up something. We brought you a burger. Before you argue, I owe you for breakfast and the place to stay."

Carly's eyes widened with surprise. "You're staying at Doc Wayne's?"

"Yeah." Taylor pulled one of the spare chairs closer to the desk with his foot.

Carly looked from Taylor to Shelby and back to Taylor.

No telling what the rumor would be if she didn't clear this up now. "He's staying in my garage apartment."

"Oh, I thought—"

"I know what you thought." Shelby said in a tight voice.

Already this man was disrupting her life. Carly would have that information spread far and wide by the end of the day.

Maybe Uncle Gene could have sent her someone else less... She couldn't think of the word. Intrusive? Disruptive? Attractive?

Taylor sat down in one of the two folding chairs that suddenly appeared child-size beneath his large body and started digging through the paper bag in his hand. He acted as if he took his meals in a tiny, shabby office every day. It didn't take long for Taylor to act like he belonged. Carly took the other chair and he handed her a burger wrapped in paper before his hand slipped into the bag again. Pulling out another burger, he offered it to Shelby.

When she hesitated he said, "Take it. Don't act like you don't want it."

Shelby wished that wasn't the truth. She reached for the offered package. By the time she'd eaten a couple of bites of hers Taylor had already finished his first burger and was searching the bag for another.

The tinkle of the bell hanging on the door sounded.

"Doc Wayne! Doc Wayne!"

The urgent cry made Shelby stand and head towards the door. Taylor had hurried out and was moving up the hall by the time she stepped from the office.

The metallic smell of blood reached her nose before she saw the bright red drops on the floor. It seeped through the rag wrapped around Mr. Hardy's arm. Shelby's stomach rolled like a boat on a stormy sea, making her wish she hadn't eaten.

She mentally braced herself. She could do this.

"Sir," Taylor said, "I'm Dr. Stiles. Come back to the exam room and we'll see what we've got here."

For once Shelby was glad to have Taylor take over. When the injured man, in his mid-fifties, gave her a questioning look she said, "He's a trauma doctor. You're in good hands."

Shelby believed those words. Was it because of the way Taylor led with confidence or because of the quality of care she'd seen him provide? Either way, it kept her from having to deal with the blood.

"Carly," she called, "get out a suture kit in exam one. Now." She turned to the pale-faced woman left standing in the waiting room. Shelby took her arm and led her to a chair.

"Wait here, Mrs. Hardy. We'll let you see him as soon as we can."

Shelby headed toward the exam room. "Carly, get Mrs. Hardy a drink and sit with her. She looks a little shaken," Shelby said as she passed the girl in the hall.

In the examination room, Taylor gingerly unwrapped the rag from around the man's arm. Stepping to the table, she asked, "Mr. Hardy, what did you do to yourself?"

"I was cutting a limb off a tree that'd been damaged during the storm last week. Darn chainsaw kicked back and got me."

Shelby took a fortifying breath as Taylor revealed the gnarled flesh on Mr. Hardy's forearm. She'd never been a fan of blood to start with but after seeing so much of Jim's pouring from his body, her aversion to it had become worse. Red liquid continued to slowly drip onto the white cloth covering the table. "Looks like it got you three times before it let go," Taylor remarked as he examined the man's arm. "I don't see any bone damage."

"Do you mind if I have a look?" Shelby asked, stepping forward. Cases like these were her least favorite but she'd learned to deal with them because she was usually the only doctor available. She wouldn't let this know-it-all doctor make her look weak in front of a patient who would be hers long after he'd gone home.

Taylor shifted to the right so she could have a better view. Shelby gently rotated the arm. "Does that hurt?" Her stomach chose that moment to make a Waikiki surfing wave. She hoped her face didn't give away to Mr. Hardy and Taylor how awful she felt.

"No," the middle-aged man said.

She gently eased the man's arm down on the table. Her hands trembled and she tightened her jaw, willing her throat not to spasm. If she focused on what she was doing, she could get through it. She had before and she would again. "Well, I don't see any damage past the skin, which is good news. We just need to get you stitched up."

Something made her look at Taylor. He was studying her too closely for her comfort. Seconds later a look of realization entered his dark expressive eyes then surprise.

"Dr. Wayne," he said, his tone all business, "do you mind if I do the suturing? It's my expertise and I don't see many chainsaw injuries where I'm from."

A sense of relief washed over her. She looked at Mr. Hardy questioningly.

"I don't mind. Just need to get it done. My wife's already mad 'cos I got blood all over her freshly mopped kitchen floor."

The bell on the door sounded and Carly spoke to someone. "If you have this," Shelby said to Taylor, "I'll go see this other patient."

Taylor glanced up at Mr. Hardy, "We're good here?"

The man nodded agreement. Shelby left as Taylor untaped the suture kit.

Over an hour later Shelby stood beside the front desk ready to call her next patient. She watched as Taylor saw Mr. and Mrs. Hardy out with instructions to return in a couple of days.

Taylor approached the desk and stepped close enough she could smell the soap on his skin that she'd placed in his bath. "We need to talk."

A shiver ran up her spine. "Is something wrong with Mr. Hardy?"

"Your office," he said in a low voice.

"You don't order me around."

"Do you really want to broadcast our discussion to the entire county?" He turned his back to the handful of people in the waiting room. "I don't think you want people to know their doctor's little secret."

Her stomach dropped. He wasn't going to let what he'd learned pass without comment. She entered the office ahead of him. He came in and closed the door.

"What've you got to say that can't wait until after our patients are gone?" she demanded.

Taylor leaned causally against the door, crossing his arms over his chest and one foot over the other, a slight grin on his lips. "Interesting, a doctor who can't stand the sight of blood," he stated in complete amazement.

"I'm a general practitioner. I don't have to deal with blood to do my job well," she huffed.

"I guess you don't. But you must've had a devil of a time getting through emergency rotation in med school."

She looked him directly in the eyes. "I worked through it."

"Yeah, I could see how well you're working through it in there with Mr. Hardy." He had to admire her fortitude. She looked as if she was determined to do what had to be done, even at a cost to herself.

"You won't tell, will you?"

He wished he could tease her and make her think that he would but her wide-eyed, pleading look softened his heart. "Your secret is safe with me."

"You know, I would've stitched up Mr. Hardy if you hadn't been here. Wouldn't have enjoyed it but I would've gotten it done. Patients with major injuries don't normally come to the clinic. His wife refusing to drive outside Benton is the only reason they stopped here. Otherwise they would've gone straight to Nashville or Jackson."

"Either one of those places is around a hundred miles away."

"I know. Mr. Hardy could've gone into shock before he got there."

Shelby gave him a grateful look that made him feel heroic. "I appreciate your help."

The frustration she felt over her weakness shone in her large gray eyes. The desire to take her in his arms and re-assure her that she wasn't failing her patients flooded him. Taylor resisted the urge. Shelby wouldn't appreciate him not-ing her flaw any more than he'd already had. He shrugged. "I'm glad I was here too. The old man required a number of stitches."

Taylor had actually found Mr. Hardy's case interesting. Chainsaw accidents weren't common inside a metropolitan area. To his surprise, he'd enjoyed talking to the tell-it-like-it-is man. Straightening, Taylor prepared to open the door. "I did some of my finest work. He'll have scars but nothing as extensive as they could've been."

"Well, I'm glad it worked out for you *and* Mr. Hardy," Shelby said in a mocking tone.

She made it sound as if Taylor had caused the accident so he could show off his skills. At least that sad expression had left her eyes. He ignored her remark and asked, "So what's the plan when I'm gone?"

"The plan is to go on as I have been and look for a doctor who's trained in emergency medicine. Someone willing to work here at least part time."

"Well, it won't be me. I'm going to do what's required. Then I'm gone. Don't be getting any ideas."

"I don't have any ideas about you one way or another. Uncle Gene said he was sending me some help for a cou-ple of weeks. The minute I met you I knew you wouldn't be staying long."

He didn't understand why that remark annoyed him. He didn't like her thinking she knew him that well. "Why?"

"Well, let's see," she said with a sassy bob to her head, "car, clothes, attitude. All are a dead giveaway."

He'd covered his past well. Had worked hard at it. Tay-lor stepped closer, stopping just outside her personal space.

Her eyes shifted with apprehension. He made her nervous and he liked it.

Leaning down to her eye level, he said, "You of all people should know that appearances aren't always how things are." He paused. "For example, a doctor who hates the sight of blood."

A knock on the door punctuated his statement.

"It's standing room only out here," Carly called.

"Maybe you'd better go do what you have to do," Shelby said in an ice-cold voice as she moved past him to hold open the door.

Taylor spent Wednesday morning seeing patients, only able to snatch a quick lunch before the afternoon influx of people into the waiting room. Despite working in a small-town clinic, he was still keeping large trauma center hours. It amazed him that Shelby had managed to hold it together without help for so long. She had to be mentally and physically exhausted. The clinic was definitely a two-person set-up, and three would be better.

Late that afternoon, Taylor trailed behind his latest patient as he left. Going to the front to call his next one, he was pleasantly surprised to find that there was no one else needing attention. Shelby was busy giving Carly directions and shifting through papers at the same time. The picture had become so commonplace it seemed like he'd been working at the Benton Clinic for ever. It amazed him that he didn't feel more like an outsider.

He and Shelby had only spoken a few words to each other the entire day. For some reason, he'd missed their sparring. If nothing else it brought a little spark to the backwater town, something to challenge his mind.

The bell on the door rang. The peace hadn't lasted long enough for him to even say something that would aggravate Shelby. A girl of around sixteen with large, gloomy eyes and long blonde hair entered looking as if she'd like to turn and run. She wore a simple dress covering too much of her body for the warm day. The girl hesitated as the door closed behind her.

Shelby must have realized that the three of them looking at the girl was intimidating because she stepped forward and offered her hand. "I'm Dr. Wayne. Can I help you?"

The girl nodded but didn't make eye contact.

"Come this way." Shelby led the teen down the hall.

Ten minutes later Taylor entered the small lab area to find Shelby facing the counter, gripping it so hard the veins on the top of her hands stood out. She kept her head down.

He closed the door. "What's wrong?" he asked, keeping his voice low and stepping closer. "What's happened?" He didn't try to keep his concern out of his voice.

Shelby's actions seemed out of character. Even when blood had been an issue she'd hung tough, but now…

"Nothing." Her tone said differently.

"Something's obviously wrong. Let me help."

She turned so quickly that she caught him off guard. Her eyes glistened and her face was drawn with misery. "Really? You think you can help," she muttered. "I have an unwed pregnant teen in there…" she gestured toward the door across the hall "…who's terrified to talk to her parents. When she does find the courage to tell her family about the baby she also has to explain to them that she has a venereal disease. So just how can you help with this?"

Her bold stare said he couldn't fix this no matter what he did. As much as he hated to admit it, she was right.

"I can't help her but I can help you." He gathered Shelby into his arms. What was he doing? Nurses, other female doctors had been upset in his presence and he'd never hugged them. Something about Shelby made him want to comfort her, help her with her problems. Be there for her. He winced.

That was something he couldn't do. How had he become so involved in her life so quickly?

She resisted, remaining rigid against him. "Please let me go."

It pricked his ego that she wouldn't consent to his comfort, but he schooled his face not to show a reaction. He did as she asked and stepped back, missing the contact immediately. "Would you like me to talk to the girl?"

Shelby shook her head. "No, that's my job. She's scared enough without me sending a man in to discuss this. She lives in the county above us and wanted to go where she wouldn't be recognized. Someone told her that there was a female doctor here."

"In this day and age she's hiding? Afraid to tell her parents? The teenage girls I know are proud to be unwed and pregnant."

"You have to remember that there're still strong moral standards in this area. Everyone knows everyone. Has an opinion about everything."

Taylor was well aware of how those concepts worked.

Shelby continued, "Her parents, she says, aren't going to be happy or accepting." She moved past him. "I'd better go give her the news."

He placed a hand on her shoulder and her gaze met his. "Shelby, I wish I could do more than say I'm sorry."

She gave him a weak smile. "I am too," she said, before squaring her shoulders and knocking on the door to the exam room across the hall.

Her heart was too big for her own good. For once, Taylor thought that Uncle Gene sentencing him to the clinic had been a good thing. It had allowed him to be there for Shelby today.

The girl left the clinic thirty minutes later with a gentle pat on the shoulder from Shelby and the reassurance that she'd be there if the girl needed her. Shelby said not a word as she passed him. She entered her office and effectively closed everyone out.

After preparing the clinic for the next day, Taylor knocked lightly on the office door. "You ready to close up?"

"You go on. I'll see you in the morning."

She needed space and wouldn't appreciate him insisting she leave. He really shouldn't care. All doctors ran into cases that got under their skin. The problem was that Shelby cared too deeply. For the girl. For her all her patients.

Who took care of her?

Hours later, Taylor rolled over in bed and looked at the bedside clock for the umpteenth time. It was well past midnight.

Where was she?

With a sense of relief that amazed him he saw Shelby's headlights flash across the wall of the apartment as she pulled into the drive.

She worked far too hard, felt too much. The clinic, for all he could see, was her life. She took no down time. In his opinion it wasn't healthy. She needed to slow down or she'd be the one needing a doctor. He knew of few doctors who worked harder than Shelby.

He didn't want to care. No matter what happened he refused to get involved but with every day he stayed in Benton it made it more difficult to keep his distance. First it had been Mrs. Ferguson, then Mr. Hardy and now he was stressing about a workaholic tyrant of a doctor who lived in a one-red-light town. Heck, he didn't really know how to care. He'd certainly not gotten an example of how that worked from his family. Could he have picked a more foreign emotion?

The way Shelby's big gray eyes looked stormy when she was mad and turned soft and sad when she worried over a patient pulled at him. Even her sharp tongue didn't squelch his anxiety for the turbocharged woman.

Reassured Shelby was safely home, Taylor rolled over and punched his pillow, knowing he could now find sleep. He'd no idea why it mattered to him what she did. Shelby had been fine before he'd arrived and she'd be fine after he left.

But who would be there for her when she needed a shoulder to lean on next time?

CHAPTER THREE

THURSDAY evening Shelby pulled into her drive well after dark. She'd stayed late at the clinic to finish some charting. Now her plan was to spend the next few hours working on grant applications. She had to find some long-term help for the clinic soon or the state would shut it down. Taylor had made it abundantly clear he wouldn't be the answer to her problem.

The old truck rattled to a stop when Shelby shut it off. She regarded the sports car in front of her. She'd always liked nice cars but her parents were supportive but practical people who didn't encourage that type of extravagance. Shelby couldn't really see herself ever owning such a fancy vehicle. She was the wrong type of doctor, in the wrong area of the world, to even drive one. Still, a girl could appreciate a nice ride.

A movement in the garage window caught her attention. Taylor stood silhouetted there. He wore no shirt and was talking on the phone. Shelby's attention was riveted to his wide shoulders that tapered to a trim waist. Sliding down in the seat, she hoped he wouldn't see her and think she'd already gone into the house. His pants rode low on his hips. He must work out. A lot. She'd say his efforts were worth it.

Frustration welled within her. She had no business even noticing him. There could never be anything real between them. She had to keep reminding herself of that. He wasn't staying and she refused to care then be hurt when he left. She'd barely lived through that pain before and she couldn't do it again.

Taylor put a hand above his head and stretched. Shelby sucked in a breath. Good heavens. Her heart went into overdrive. Ignoring him was going to be much more difficult than she imagined. The tingle of desire that had lay dormant since Jim's death had returned, heating her from the inside out, catching her by surprise. She needed to go into the house. Stand under the air-conditioning vent. Her reaction to this well-built man was way over the top.

How would she get inside without looking like she'd become a peeping Tomette? She grinned. At least she hadn't lost her sense of humor even though she'd lost her mind. With relief, and disappointment she didn't want to examine, Taylor moved away from the window.

Gathering her bag, she opened the truck door and slid out. Closing the door with less force than usual, she accused herself of being silly. This was her house, her drive, her neighborhood. Seeing Taylor Stiles's chest from a distance wasn't that big a deal. She'd even seen it up close. As a doctor she'd seen all kinds of half-naked men.

Yeah, but chests as fine as Taylor's were few and far between. Great. Now she was starting to think like Carly. Lifting her shoulders and standing taller, Shelby walked to the back door. Why hadn't she left the porch light on?

"I was wondering how long it would take you to get out of the truck."

Shelby jumped, dropping her bag. "What're you doing, sneaking up on me?"

"I wasn't sneaking. I came down the stairs like I always do. Your mind must've been on something else."

Thankful for the shadows, she didn't want to contemplate

what her mind had been on and she certainly didn't need him to see the guilt covering her face.

"I wanted to speak to you a minute," Taylor said.

Shelby retrieved her bag. "Could we make it quick? I'm really not up for some long discussion right now. All I want is a sandwich and to get to bed early."

"Why don't you get that sandwich while we talk?" He followed her up the steps. "I wouldn't mind having one too."

She reached inside and flipped on the light switches for the kitchen and the outside. Glancing around at him, she was relieved to find he'd pulled on a T-shirt before coming out to meet her. "Do you make it a habit of inviting yourself into people's homes? To meals? Anyway, I thought you finally agreed to go to Vinnie's with Carly and her boyfriend. I heard her begging you to go."

"That was hours ago. I've a pretty big appetite."

Suddenly hers was gone. Her mouth went dry. Her mind was going places it shouldn't. That she didn't want it to go.

"Shelby?"

"Huh?"

"Aren't you going inside?"

Shelby opened the screen door and entered the kitchen, dropping her bag in one of the kitchen chairs. Taylor followed her.

"Hey, I still didn't say you could come in."

"Awe, come on, Shelby. Have pity on a hungry man with nothing in his pantry. Share a sandwich."

With a sigh, she said, "Okay, one sandwich and tell me what you need, then you're out of here."

The large family kitchen shrank, taking on a more intimate feel with Taylor in it. To cover her unease, Shelby gathered the sandwich fixings. Having Taylor in her home made them seem like more than colleagues. Maybe friends? In just a few short days. Could a woman be just friends with someone who exuded all-male sex-appeal as Taylor did? No, she needed to protect herself. He'd never settle here and she'd never be someone's two-week stand.

Placing the bread, ham, cheese and condiments on the table, Shelby poured two glasses of iced tea. She set Taylor's glass before him, taking special care not to touch him. Taking the chair opposite him, she reached for the bread. Her hand circled the mustard bottle at the same time his did. His fingers brushed across hers. Their warmth against the coolness of hers made her shiver. She let the bottle go but Taylor's touch lingered.

"Ladies first," he quipped, going after the cheese instead.

A sense of disgust filled her. She was acting like a ninny and he wasn't even affected. After her meltdown the other day, he probably wasn't surprised by the way she acted.

Taking a sip of tea, she carefully set the glass down and finished making her sandwich. She'd never let him know that even his casual touch rattled her. She took a restorative breath and said, "So what do you want to talk about?"

"I was wondering if the clinic is open on the weekends. I have a date for the opera in Nashville and need to know if I should cancel it."

It shouldn't have surprised her that Taylor might have a love interest back home but until then she'd not given it any thought. He'd said there was no family but that didn't mean he didn't have someone special waiting for his return. One he obviously missed. A girlfriend. The prick of rejection caught her unawares. Why should she feel that way? There wasn't anything between them.

"The clinic's open on Saturday from eight to noon. After that the weekend is yours. I'll expect you there at eight on Monday morning sharp."

"Yes, ma'am. Do you know how often you use the word

'expect'?" he asked around a bite of ham sandwich. It wasn't said as a putdown but more as a conversational question.

"I don't use it a lot," she said with a huff.

"Yeah, you do," he said nonchalantly as he looked over her head. "Nice pictures."

A swell of pride filled her at his compliment. "They were some of my husband's favorites." She'd been able to capture the essence of her subjects in the photos, showing the truth of what life was like in this rural area.

"His favorite photographer?"

"You could say that. Me."

"Really? You took these?" Taylor stood, moving closer to study the two lines of framed photographs, six pictures in all. "You really caught what the subjects were feeling. I'm impressed."

"Thanks." A warm glow filled her at his compliment. "Those are really old. I don't have time to take pictures now." She picked up her sandwich.

"Why's that?" He took his chair again, propping his elbows on the table and giving her his full attention.

Her hand tightened on her sandwich. Having his intent look focused on her made her feel self-conscious. "Well, I have the clinic to run."

"So what's the deal with the clinic? I'd think you could have your choice of positions anywhere you'd like."

Shelby pushed away the plate holding her half-eaten sandwich. "I want to work here. The clinic was our dream."

His brows rose. "'Our'?"

"Mine, and my husband's." To her surprise the stab of pain she normally felt when she spoke of Jim wasn't as strong as it had once been.

Taylor prompted, "So you and your husband started the clinic?"

"We grew up together. Jim wanted to be a doctor and I

did too. So we decided to go to medical school together and work where we were needed the most, which was here. It might be a small town, but it needed medical help and we could provide that, *wanted* to provide that."

"Well, I'm glad there are doctors like you because I couldn't do this."

"Do what?"

"Live here."

Her chair made a scraping noise as she pushed away from the table. Indignation and the need to defend Benton welled up in her. She stood and picked up her plate. "I can appreciate that Benton might not be for everyone but I happen to love living here. I love the town square with our wonderful old courthouse. I love the shops and the fact that the store owners call me by name when I go in. I love that we have no traffic!" She looked pointedly at him. "What I don't appreciate is people coming here and insulting it."

"I'm not insulting your precious town," Taylor said, following her. His arm brushed hers as he placed his plate in the sink.

A ripple of awareness went up her arm and ran through her body. She stepped out of reach, not liking the out-of-control feeling she had when he was near.

"I'm just saying living here isn't for me," Taylor continued, as if nothing had happened.

For him, she guessed it hadn't. "You know, I think it's time for you to go. I'm going to call it a night."

Taylor stepped to the door. "I'll see you in the morning."

At the slap of the screen door closing, loneliness filled her. The large country kitchen suddenly seemed cold and empty. She had enjoyed sharing a meal with someone. It was nice not to go into the house by herself and to have someone with whom she could discuss her passion for photography.

She sucked in a breath. Being around Taylor made her feel

like a desirable, interesting woman. To everyone in town she was "Doc" first and foremost. Until Taylor had arrived, she'd had no idea she missed being thought of as a person. She had to stay alert, think sharply to keep up with him. It was invigorating on a number of levels to have Taylor around. Even if the man made her temper flare faster than anyone else could.

He'd hardly been there four days. She had no doubt that she would miss him when he left. And leave he would.

"Greg, what're you doing here again?" Shelby asked in bewilderment when she walked into the waiting room to call her next patient on Friday afternoon. "Surely he hasn't stuck something else up his nose?" she said, looking at the boy's mother for confirmation.

The mother shook her head slowly.

"His ear?" Shelby asked with a note of disbelief surrounding her words.

The mother gave a negative shake of her head. "The other doctor told us to come back."

"Dr. Stiles?"

"Yeah."

Shelby couldn't imagine why Taylor had asked Greg's mother to bring him in if there was no reason. Other than the propensity to always put things where they didn't belong, Greg was a healthy child, too healthy, in fact.

"I'll let Dr. Stiles know you're here." She didn't like the fact that patients were now coming in to see Taylor. They had always been her patients. He wasn't staying around long and she didn't want the community to start relying on him. She didn't want to start to count on him.

Shelby went to her office where she'd left Taylor minutes earlier completing some paperwork. They'd taken to rotating time behind the desk to get their charting completed. Taylor opened the office door as she prepared to enter and she walked right into him.

"Whoa." His hand circled her waist and pulled her against him to stop her from falling.

A larger-than-average guy, he seemed even more over-powering close up. With her nose pressed against him, she smelled like soap and a unique scent. It surrounded her, drawing her to him.

A low rumble filled his chest. "If you're not careful you're going to fall at my feet."

Putting her hands on his chest, she pushed away. His chuckle reminded her she was still in his arms. "If you'd let me go, I could stand."

He did, and she rocked back and gained her footing, unsure if she was off balance because he'd been holding her or because he'd let her go so quickly.

"Were you looking for me?" he asked, as if he thought she'd been on a personal quest.

"I was, but only because you have a patient. Greg, the boy whose nose you removed the bean from, is here. His mother said they were to see you. Did you tell them to come in for a follow-up exam?"

"I did ask them to stop by."

"Why?"

"Come with me and you'll see." He allowed her to walk ahead of him up the hall.

If she'd had patients waiting she would've argued that she didn't have time for show and tell but for once the waiting room was empty, something that happen more often now that Taylor was helping out.

Even the time she spent working at home had gotten shorter. Taylor had been in town less than a week and he was already having a big impact on her life. He was efficient and thorough, and some of the patients were starting to warm up to him. When they came into the waiting room, Greg popped down from his mother's lap and ran to Taylor. "I good. Sucker." Greg tugged on Taylor's well-pressed slacks.

Taylor pulled something out of his pocket before squatting down on one heel, which brought him close to eye level with the boy.

Holding out a sucker, Taylor said, "Greg, you were good. You didn't stick anything in your nose for a week. Now, if you want another one you have to be good for two weeks. I won't be here but I'm sure Doc Wayne will give you one." Taylor looked at her for confirmation.

Something about Taylor not being there when the boy came back caused a catch in her chest. Pushing the thought to a back drawer in her mind, Shelby nodded and said to Greg, "I'll have it waiting for you. But you can't put anything in your nose or ears."

The boy nodded, unwrapped the sucker and popped it into his mouth, his cheeks going chubby with his wide smile.

The mother nodded her thanks, took the boy's hand and headed for the door. With them gone, Shelby turned to Taylor. "How did you know?"

"As soon as I removed the bean he started begging for a sucker. I asked his mother if you gave him one every time you removed something. She said yes and I knew something was up.

"Greg was stuffing his nose full in order to come here and get a sucker. I made a deal with him that if he didn't do it again then I'd see that he got one. I know how bad they are for the teeth but one thing at a time. You can wean him off them."

"It was a nice call. I should've caught on."

"Don't beat yourself up. You can't do it all perfectly. You have a lot to see about here. Greg's fine and now you know.

Just keep weaning him off. Soon it won't be a problem. Let up on yourself."

"I still should have realized what he was doing. Thanks."

"You don't have to sound like you're in pain when you say that."

She gave him a wry smile. "It's a little excruciating to admit I missed something so simple."

"You'll get it next time," he said, going to the reception desk.

Later that evening at closing time, Taylor said, "Hey, Mr. Teems gave me coupons for a free ice cream down at the Cream Castle. Why don't we all go and get a banana split after we close?"

"I've got a date. Got to go," Carly said, picking up her purse.

He turned to Shelby.

"I don't think so."

"Oh, come on, Shelby. Do something a little spontaneous for a change. All that paperwork will be here when you get back. I'll even help you."

"I still don't think so. And I don't need your help with my paperwork."

"Look, have pity on a stranger in town. I'm not even sure how to get there. I told Mr. Teems I'd stop by."

"Still—"

"I know you missed lunch because I did. Let's make this our supper."

"Well, put like that…"

"Great. I'll drive."

Even though she'd been hard to convince, it didn't take her long to get her purse, lock up and climb into his car.

"Which way?" He backed out of what had become his usual parking space.

"The best way to go is out to the bypass. Turn left out of the parking lot." She leaned her head back and closed her eyes.

She had to be worn out. He was. "Bypass? This town isn't large enough to have a bypass."

"They built it when the talk started about building a lake."

"Lake?"

"Lake Benton. The hope is that it'll bring business to this area. It'll be another couple of years, though, before there's water."

"From what little I've seen of the area, it could use it." He glanced her way. Her hair blew around her face. She looked totally relaxed. Something he'd rarely seen.

"It can. Most of the young people are leaving because there're no jobs. Make a left at the next light," she said, just loud enough that he could hear her over the wind. For the first time she'd not growled when he'd said something negative about the town, a sure sign she was tired.

"The Cream Castle is a mile down on the right." She indicated after he'd driven another mile.

He pulled into the gravel parking lot. They got out and walked to the window of the white building with the bright red awning. "One vanilla ice cream cone and one banana split with the works," he told the teenager at the window. "I used to work in a place like this when I was in high school."

"Really? I would've thought from looking at you that you would've spent all your time on the football or baseball field, being a star."

"Couldn't stay out of trouble long enough," he said flatly.

His words held a bitterness that surprised Shelby. The skinny teen with the earring pushed Taylor's huge banana split toward him and handed her the cone, stopping further questions.

Taylor took a seat on the bench of the cement table next to the building. He must have seen her hesitate and look towards the car because he said in a voice that wouldn't consent to an argument, "No way are we carrying this in my car. You can take a few minutes to enjoy." He dug a spoon into the bowl of nuts and chocolate sauce. "Mmm. Good," he said as he pulled the plastic spoon from his mouth.

"So you've found something in this town you like," Shelby said as she sat down and gave her ice cream a long lick.

Taylor's gaze lifted to meet hers. "I've found a few things."

If she wasn't careful, the ice cream in her hand would melt all over her fingers from the heat surging through her. Just as quickly his concentration returned to his ice cream. Was she reading something into what he'd said? Imagining things? Nothing was going to happen between them. He was just flirting. "What's Mr. Lambert's story?"

Shelby blinked. His question out of the blue caught her by surprise. The eighty-year-old man had refused to see Taylor earlier in the day, insisting that Shelby was the only one he would allow to take care of him.

"Some of the people around here are very set in their ways. He's lived in the same hollow a few miles out of town his entire life. He's tough. Been a logger since he was a boy. You wouldn't believe the house he lives in. No indoor plumbing. Animals living inside in the winter." Shelby shuddered. "It took me almost a year before Mr. Lambert would let me see him. It wasn't until he hurt his hand and his daughter came to get me that I ever took care of him."

"You do house calls?"

"When I have to. You know, it may be hard for some of the patients to relate to you because your clothes and shoes cost enough to feed their entire family for a year."

"There's nothing wrong with liking nice things."

"No, there isn't. Don't get me wrong, you look great—"

"Why, thank you, Shelby."

"That's not what I meant. I just think some of the older

patients might find you less, uh, intimidating if you maybe wore jeans and tennis shoes."

"Would you find me less intimidating?" His look bored into hers.

Somehow this conversation had gotten off track. "You don't intimidate me," Shelby said with as much conviction as she could muster.

His spoon fell into the empty plastic tray with a clunk, and he leaned back as if in deep thought. "I'm not sure you're telling me the truth, but that's beside the point. I also think it might surprise you just how much I know about how people around here think."

"Really?"

"Yes, but we need to be getting back. I promised to help you out with that charting."

"That's okay, I can manage it."

"I know you can. But I'm going to help anyway."

Shelby rubbed her hand along the seat of Taylor's car as they rode down the road a few minutes later. "You know, this is a nice car."

"Now, that wasn't that hard to admit, was it?"

She laughed, "No I guess it wasn't. I do love riding with the top down."

The sound of a police siren pierced the air.

Taylor's sharp word made her wince. He slowly pulled off onto the shoulder of the road and turned off the engine. His jaw muscles jumped and his hand shook almost imperceptibly as he leaned across her to reach into the glove compartment. She wouldn't have noticed if he hadn't been so close. "I'll handle this," he said gruffly. "I know I wasn't speeding," he said, more to himself than to her.

The deputy hadn't even approached the car yet and Taylor was angry. It seemed over the top. "Maybe you just have a taillight out?" Shelby suggested.

He glared at her. His look prevented her from offering further comments. "No hick deputy's going to give me a ticket for doing nothing," he mumbled as he pulled his wallet from his hip pocket and dug for his license.

"Hey, Shelby, I thought that was you," the deputy said from where he stood beside Taylor's door.

"Hi, Sam." Shelby smiled up at the man.

Taylor gave her an odd look before switching his attention to the deputy. Holding out his license and insurance information, Taylor looked even more exasperated when the deputy didn't immediately take them.

"I don't need those. I just wanted to see if Shelby's planning to bring her famous carrot cake to the block party."

A look of confusion then disbelief washed over Taylor's face. Shelby had to work to keep a straight face. "I hadn't planned to but since you asked I'll be sure to bake one. By the way, this is Dr. Stiles. He's working with me for a couple of weeks."

Sam looked down at Taylor. "Nice to meet you, Doc." His attention didn't linger but returned to Shelby. "I do love your carrot cake."

"Sam, that's so sweet."

Taylor's facial expression turned to complete disgust. Her grin grew. *And he thought he understood small towns.*

"We have to go. Sam. See you Saturday."

The palm of Sam's hand double-thumped the top of the car door. "I look forward to it."

Taylor started the car and pulled out onto the road. She had the impression he wished he could spin gravel and roar off, but instead he moved into traffic as if he was learning to drive.

"Just what was that all about?" he asked, his voice full of wonder and irritation.

"You heard. Cake and the block party."

"Do the cops around here regularly pull people over to discuss a party?" He gave her an incredulous look.

Shelby shrugged. "I guess when they want to. What's the big deal?" He shook his head as if trying to make sense of an abstract painting. She leaned forward enough to see his face. "You really were afraid that you were being stopped for speeding." She made no effort to hide her amazement.

His eyes remained on the road and he didn't answer.

She continued to watch his face. Her eyes narrowed. "What aren't you telling me?"

He glanced at her. "I've had a few speeding tickets."

"How many is a few?"

"Enough that your uncle sent me here instead of to jail."

She gave a low whistle and grinned. "So-o-o, that's what Uncle Gene meant when he said, and I quote, 'He needs to slow down for a while.'" She giggled.

"It's not funny, Shelby."

She giggled again. "Oh, yes, it is. So this fancy car is a police magnet."

"Sometimes I was on the way to an emergency," he said indignantly.

"Really?" She drew the word out.

"There might've been a few times when I exaggerated a bit. Someone checked, and dear sweet Uncle Gene decided to throw the book at me." His top lip curled as he said the last few words.

Shelby slapped her leg and howled with laughter. "So your lead foot got you sent to me." She gave his shoulder a friendly shove. "Uncle Gene has always been creative in his rulings."

"He outdid himself this time," Taylor grumbled.

For some reason, Taylor's obvious agitation tickled Shelby's funny bone. "What're you? Sixteen?"

Taylor pulled the car into his parking space next to her truck. "Now you're really making fun of me."

She laughed. "I'm sorry." Tears filled her eyes.

"Doesn't sound like it."

Shelby couldn't stop the merriment that continued to roll up from deep within her belly. She'd not laughed like this in years.

"It's not that funny," Taylor said, turning to look at her.

"I'm trying to stop but I can't help thinking about your face when you found out you'd been stopped because of a cake." Her laughter bubbled over again.

"Okay, that is kind of funny." His chuckle intertwined with her giggles. "Now I think you've had enough fun at my expense. If you don't stop…"

"What're you going to do?" She pointed at him. "You should have seen your face."

Another peal of mirth escaped her.

"Okay, that did it." Before she realized his intent, he'd grabbed her by the top of her arms and pulled her towards him. His mouth came down to cover hers.

Her laughter caught in her throat. His lips were firm, warm and confident. A red-hot flow of desire went through her. She didn't move. His mouth shifted to the side, finding a more secure place, sealing her mouth completely with his. For moments of pure bliss her world was nothing but Taylor's kiss. He pulled away and her eyelids fluttered open seconds after his hands no longer held her.

"I told you to stop."

She stared at his lips. "You did." Even to her own ears she sounded wistful. "I'll try to remember not to laugh at you again."

"That would be a good idea, unless you want more of the same."

"I don't." With effort she made the words sound sharp in the hope that it covered her true reaction. She couldn't make more of the kiss than it was. He was just trying to stop her from laughing at him, that was all.

"We'll see about that, but for now I think we should go in and get started on that paperwork." He stepped out of the car and Shelby followed more slowly.

She loved her husband. Missed him, but she'd never felt the fire with him that she'd experienced during Taylor's kiss. A shiver skated through her. If she had that kind of reaction to one playful kiss from Taylor, what would it be like to be on the receiving end of one of his seductive ones?

It was Saturday afternoon and Taylor's foot lay heavily on the gas pedal of the car. He was driving too fast but he couldn't get past the thought of what he had done yesterday evening.

God, he'd kissed Shelby and he desperately wanted to do it again. What had he been thinking? That was the problem, he hadn't been thinking. He'd reacted. The kiss had been far too short, far too cautious. He wanted to experience Shelby meeting him kiss for kiss, explore her wonderfully sensual mouth. He'd been hurt as a kid by laughter and ridicule but hers had made him want to join her. When he'd been a middle-school student, laughter at his expense had been an everyday occurrence. With her, he found he could appreciate the humor also.

But to kiss her. It only complicated things.

That he didn't need or want. He didn't even know how to give what Shelby would surely demand. He'd never been on the inside of a functional relationship. His parents' marriage certainly hadn't been a sterling example.

Shaking his head and lifting his foot a little, he slowed the car. As always Shelby had been efficient and business-like at the clinic that morning but there had been a change towards him. He should've been glad she wanted to remain at arm's length but he didn't like the idea one bit and he wasn't sure why.

It'd been a relief to say, "I'm out of here. See you Monday morning."

Shelby had nodded her understanding without looking up from the chart she was studying. Her giving him the cold shoulder irritated him.

What she thought of him or, for that matter, what the other hick people in this nothing town thought didn't matter. He had one more week to serve and he'd be out of there, never to think of any of them again. Right now he was getting some time away from Benton and Shelby and he planned to make the most of it.

The outskirts of Nashville were coming up quickly when his cellphone rang. It was his date for the evening, telling him she wasn't going to make the opera after all.

Taylor continued his conversation as he watched a state patrolman turn around and get behind him. The speedometer on the sports car let him know that he wasn't over the limit. At the next exit Taylor pulled off the interstate. With relief, he watched the patrol car go on down the road. All he needed was to be caught in town speeding. That would really make "Uncle Gene" irate. With no one expecting him now, he decided to play it safe and head back to Benton. He didn't need to take a chance on being sentenced to more time at the clinic.

Would it really be that bad to be stuck in Benton longer? With Shelby?

CHAPTER FOUR

SHELBY loved the quarterly block parties. She had little time to socialize and she made a point of joining these. They were an opportunity to connect with neighbors and one of the best parts of living in a small town.

She adored living in Benton and didn't understand Taylor's aversion to the town. Carly thought he was the best thing to come along since texting. To her surprise, she herself had nothing to complain about where his professional skills were concerned but she shouldn't learn to rely on him as he wasn't going to stay. It was a shame because the next doctor might not relate to her patients as well as Taylor did.

Some of the people had been slow to warm up to him but that was changing. If she did have an issue, it was that she had this unexplained attraction to him that made her feel uneasy. But the feeling of comfort and contentment at being surrounded by people who cared about you and watched after you washed over her, easing away her troubles.

Shelby swished her hips more than necessary as she carried her plate loaded with food to the folding chair she'd brought from home. The occasion not only let her leave the clinic problems for a while but gave her a chance to wear one of the sundresses she had hanging in her closet. The light-weight fabric with the tiny rosebuds brushed against her skin, making her feel very feminine. Something she hadn't experienced in a long time. At least, not until Taylor had come rolling into town.

He'd managed to make her feel warm, soft and womanly more than once, but she shook her head. She had no business thinking that way about him or his kiss. He was off with another woman. Taylor had no real interest in *her*. She was just the doctor he had to put up with until he'd done his time and could go home.

She sat with her neighbors in a lawn chair under a large oak tree to eat her meal and listened to their chatter. The saying "lonely in a crowd" flitted through her mind. Nibbling at her food, she placed the half-eaten meal on the ground. Leaning her head back against the top of the chair, she closed her eyes and enjoyed the warmth of the sun on her face. And drifted off.

A rustling noise nearby woke her. She lifted her eyelids, rolled her head in the direction of the sound and straightened in the chair. "What're you doing here? I thought you were in Nashville."

Taylor grinned. "And hello to you too." He took a seat in the empty chair next to her.

He looked completely at home in khaki shorts, knit shirt and leather sandals but his demeanor still screamed cosmopolitan man. Among her neighbors Taylor stood out but she had no doubt he would in any crowd. He was the type of man who drew attention and admiration.

A tingle flitted through her. She was happy to see him. Maybe too happy. "Why're you here, Taylor?"

"Mmm. Plans changed." He took a bite out of a fried chicken leg.

She lowered her voice. "I didn't think this was your idea of a good time. Too small town."

"It's not. I was pulling into the drive and Mr. Carter flagged me down. Said you were down here. He insisted

I come too. I gave in." His shoulders rose and fell. "Heck, I've got nothing better to do." He bit into the chicken again.

"Please don't hurt their feelings."

"Are you implying I don't know how to behave?" His skin drew taut across his strong jaw. Had she made him angry?

"You've made it clear on more than one occasion that you think you're too good for Benton," she whispered.

"I might not want to stay here for ever, but I do know how to be sociable and gracious when I have the right incentive."

"Incentive?"

His eyes bored into hers and then dropped to her lips. A flash of heat sped through her. Warmth pooled low in her belly. She wrapped her arms around her waist. Was he trying to coerce her into another kiss? Or more?

"Yeah, I wanted to see if the cake that the cop with the crush on you likes so much is that good." At the whoosh of her breath, he grinned. "Did you have something else in mind?"

"I did not. The cake's inside. Help yourself." She pointed in the direction of the door into the house from the carport.

Taylor stood and offered his hand to her. "Why don't you show me?"

Mrs. Nettleboom, the elderly lady who lived across the street, walked up. "Well, Dr. Stiles, I see you found her."

"Yes, I did. Thank you for pointing me in the correct direction. I was just telling Shelby how much I'd enjoy having some of that cake I've been hearing about." The woman nearly preened under the grin Taylor gave her. "The deputy over there…" he nodded in the direction of a group of men "…thought it was good enough to pull us over to ask about."

"That sounds like little Sam. He loves Shelby's carrot cake," Mrs. Nettleboom cooed. "He always requests that she bring it. Always makes sure he cuts an extra piece to take to the station the next day."

Taylor looked at Shelby and smirked. "He does, does he?"

"Honey," the woman said to Shelby, "go on and take this nice young man in and get him a slice."

Shelby feared she was well on her way to having a sugar stroke from listening to their conversation. The only way to put an end to it was to do as Mrs. Nettleboom instructed.

Ignoring his offer to help, she picked up her plate and stood. He trailed close behind her as she walked up the drive. She dropped her plate into the garbage beside the door and entered the house. "The desserts are in the kitchen."

The counter space was covered with cakes, pies and sweets of all kinds. Shelby waved her hand. "Help yourself. The plates and plastic forks are on the table," Shelby said.

The cozy kitchen suddenly didn't feel large enough for both of them. Taylor's presence filled the area, pressing against her. She needed to leave.

His hand gently circled her forearm, making her start. "Which one is yours?" he asked, much too close.

Shelby paused. His fingers slipped along her skin and away. "It's the cake on the blue plate over there." The touch had been casual but there was nothing ordinary about her body's reaction.

"You're not going to have any?"

"Not right now. Maybe later." She circled past the kitchen counter and headed out the door, grateful for the breeze that blew outside.

Had the kiss made her skittish? Taylor couldn't imagine strong, willful Shelby being intimidated by him or anyone else. She apparently didn't even trust him long enough to stay in the same room with him. He didn't like that at all. Taking the kiss back wasn't possible, even if he wanted to and he didn't. Instead he could only think of kissing her again but this time like she deserved to be kissed. Long, sweet and deep.

He ran his fingers through his hair. The last few days they'd worked together had been nice. The cases had been interesting and he found he liked working beside someone who so obviously cared about her patients and their feelings. Something he'd not always experienced in a large hospital.

He'd messed up with that kiss and he didn't know how to fix it.

Taylor cut a large slice of Shelby's cake, put it on a plate and carried it outside. Shelby wasn't visible anywhere. As he headed toward his chair the old insecure feeling of not being accepted made his stomach clench. He gained control by reminding himself that he was no longer the kid of the town drunk. No one here knew his secret. Instead he was a doctor and a well-respected one.

Still, he was surprised when Mr. Carter called, "Hey, Doc, come have a seat with us." Squaring his shoulders, he said, "Sure," with more enthusiasm than he felt and took the open place at the table.

Taylor filled his fork with cake and put it in his mouth. Taking a moment to savor the sweetness, he said, "You're right. It's great." He lifted his utensil in the direction of Shelby's boyfriend cop, who was seated across from him.

"Yeah, Shelby has many talents," the deputy said, grinning at Taylor.

"Don't mind him," Mr. Carter said, nudging the younger man in the ribs. "He's had a crush on her for ages, but she won't even look his way."

Lightness replaced the twinge of possessiveness in Taylor's heart. That baffled him. He and Shelby didn't have that kind of relationship. Their relationship didn't warrant jealousy. Yet, as illogical as it was, the pang had still been there.

Mr. Roster, a thin, white-headed man, said, "We're glad you're here to help out our Shelby. She works too hard. I know she has appreciated having you around."

Taylor wasn't so sure about that. "I'm only going to be at the clinic for another week then I'm headed home."

"You're not staying?" a man from the other end of the table asked. "We thought you might decide to make it permanent."

"No, this was only a temporary assignment." Taylor slid the last bit of cake off his fork, wishing he had more. Shelby certainly had other abilities besides caring for people and photography.

The conversation changed to the construction of the new dam that would create a recreational lake and what the town might expect from the influx of people. As for whether or not there would be a big change, the jury seemed to be out. Taylor listened, offering little input. The lake wasn't his worry. He'd be long gone.

When there was a lull in the conversation he looked around and asked, "Where did Shelby go?"

"I saw her heading around the side of the house. She had her camera," Mr. Roster said, before returning to the conversation with the others.

Minutes later, Taylor excused himself and strolled in the direction Shelby had gone. Children's laughter and the soft tinkle of Shelby's amusement told him he'd headed in the correct direction. Going through the gate of the chain-link fence, he found Shelby snapping pictures of a young girl as she glided back and forth on a swing set. A group of middle-school boys played baseball nearby.

Taylor leaned against a tree and watched. Encouraging the girl to continue swinging, Shelby moved around, taking pictures from different angles. Her dress blew around her legs in the light breeze, accenting her shapely behind. Occasionally, Shelby gave the thin strap of her dress an impatient push up her slim shoulder from where it had slipped. Taylor smiled. He liked seeing her relaxed, the worry lines on her face gone. She deserved an easier life but he wasn't the one to give her that.

The entire scene looked like a Norman Rockwell painting. Taylor had never really identified with images of Rockwell's homespun family life, because his own childhood had never been anything near resembling the pictures. Shelby brought that hometown feeling to life right in front of his eyes. He bet her photos would turn out to be wonderful. Unfortunately, she became so uptight around him he doubted he'd ever be invited to see them.

"You're dumb."

"Yeah, nobody likes you."

The ugly words took a moment to work their way through Shelby's concentration on the picture's subject.

"Everyone hates you."

Taking the viewfinder away from her eye, she turned to where the boys crowded around the smallest boy.

Before she could intervene, Taylor stalked past her. She'd been so absorbed in finding the right shot she'd not realized he stood nearby. He went to stand behind the child the others faced and placed his hand on the boy's shoulder.

"Now, what's going on here?" Taylor's gaze fell on each individual long enough so that they each looked at their feet instead of at Taylor. "Well?" he demanded in an even voice but giving the word a sharp edge.

A boy's head rose. "He always messes up. He doesn't know how to play."

"I see. And you do everything you try right all the time?"

The boy rubbed his bare foot back and forth in the dirt. "No, but—"

"Exactly. So why don't you let me and…?" He looked down at the boy in front of him.

"Charlie," the boy murmured.

"So why don't you let Charlie and I be a team and play against you guys?"

"That wouldn't be fair," a heavyset boy in the group complained. "You're big."

"No more than it's fair when three people gang up on one. How do you think you would feel? So why don't you guys try to play something that Charlie might be good at?"

Taylor looked at Charlie again.

"I'm pretty good at basketball," he said in a stronger voice than he'd used earlier.

"Great," Taylor said. "I saw a hoop in the driveway next door. Why don't you guys head that way?"

"I don't really like basketball," the leader of the group said.

"Why's that?" Taylor asked.

"Because he ain't any good at it," a tall, thin boy offered.

Taylor said nothing but look pointedly at the leader.

"Come on, guys. Let's go find a ball," the boy finally offered.

Shelby watched in amazement as the group walked past her on their way out the gate.

"Lauren, honey," she told the girl she'd been taking pictures of, "I bet your mother's looking for you. It's getting late."

The girl ran behind the boys towards the front of the house.

Taylor stood rigid, staring off into the distance. His breaths were coming shallow and fast as if he fought a demon. What was going on?

"Taylor?"

She received no response.

"Taylor?"

As if coming out of a trance, he looked at her but without really seeing her.

"You okay?"

"Oh, yeah, sure." A look of recognition flickered in his eyes.

"What you did with those boys was impressive. Did you get a child psych degree along with that MD?"

Taylor visibly relaxed, regaining his causal manner. "Nothing to it."

He might say that but she knew better.

The green light of fireflies blinked around them as they walked back along the sidewalk toward her house.

"Was the block party as bad as you thought it would be?" Shelby asked.

Taylor gave her a sideways glance. "I never said it was going to be bad."

"You sure acted that way."

He stuffed his hands in the pockets of his shorts. "It wasn't exactly what I'd expected."

"How's that?"

"I didn't think your neighbors would be so accepting of me. It has been my experience that small towns are pretty close knit. Don't let people in who don't fit their idea of acceptable. Shall we say judgmental?"

"Really?" she remarked, enjoying the soft breeze and the ruffling of Taylor's shirt against his body. "I grew up in a small town and I thought we were a wonderfully supportive group of people."

"Apparently you lived on the right side of the tracks." The words had a raw-edged roughness to them.

She searched his face. "What's that supposed to mean?"

He glanced at her. "That not everyone has such great memories of living in a small town."

"Why don't you just come on out with it? Quit beating around the bush."

He looked around the street as if he was searching for

something. The words, the right way to say them or the answer? She wasn't sure which.

Her fingertips touched his forearm briefly. He was warm, firm and all male.

"We aren't that different in some ways." He stated his words slowly. "I grew up in a town much like this one but in Kentucky."

"Really? I never would have guessed."

"And I had no intention that you ever would. It isn't something I share."

"Why not?" She didn't try to keep her astonishment out of her voice.

"I've worked hard to put that time, that place behind me." He stopped short, turned and looked at her.

"What happened?" she asked quietly.

His eyes turned stone hard then he stalked ahead. Shelby jogged to catch up, her sandals making a slapping noise against the concrete and her camera bouncing against her side from where the strap hung over her shoulder. When she came alongside him he began talking but didn't slow his pace.

"If you must know, I'm the son of the town drunk and the kid who used his fists to prove his worth." He snapped the words like gunshots.

Shelby slowed, stopped and watched as Taylor stalked off. It didn't surprise her that Taylor hadn't noticed she was no longer panting beside him. He'd slipped into his past.

By the time she'd reached her back door, he'd entered the apartment and effectively shut the world and her out.

At mid-morning on Sunday Shelby sat at her kitchen table, paying her personal bills as well as the clinic's. A knock at the door interrupted her concentration. Before she could move, the door opened and Taylor's head appeared.

"Taylor!" Shelby let out a squeak and pulled her lightweight robe over her thin gown. "You can't just barge into my house uninvited. I'm not even dressed."

"I knocked." His look traveled to her bare toes and slowly upwards until his gaze met hers. There was a twinkle of appreciation in his coffee-colored eyes. "Nice outfit."

Heat zipped to her cheeks. He had a way of making her blush and she was entirely too old for such silliness. "What do you need? I'm trying to get some work done."

"You know, it would be nice for you to be happy to see me just once."

She was glad to see that his bad mood from the day before had disappeared. She huffed.

He grinned. "How about showing me around? Maybe take me out to where they're building the dam for the lake?"

"I don't know. I've tons of paperwork to do." She waved her hand toward the table where the bills were stacked. "There might be an emergency and I'll be needed."

"And there might not be. You work too hard. It's not healthy. You need some down time to be ready for your patients. Besides, you'll have your cellphone with you."

Why this sudden interest in Benton, and the lake? She'd been surprised to see his car still parked in the drive this morning after the way they'd parted the evening before. She'd expected him to spend his day off far away from Benton. But she didn't plan to ruin his cheerful mood by quizzing him about his past now. "Okay, I guess this can wait."

"Get dressed. I'll wait." Taylor pulled a chair out from under the table, sat and propped an ankle over his knee.

He looked at home in her house and that disturbed her. He'd only been there a week and already he seemed like he belonged. It had been too easy to get used to having him around. When he left, which he'd assured her he would, she'd be on her own again. If she let him into her life there would be heartache and that she wouldn't chance.

Given little choice and beginning to look forward to spending time away from her mundane responsibilities, she headed to her bedroom to change. It would be nice to spend a day having fun, something she didn't often do.

She returned dressed similarly to Taylor in cut-off jeans, a T-shirt and sandals. He looked less like the slick, fashion-plate doctor and more like a regular guy out looking for adventure. She liked this newer version. This one she understood better. He smiled at her and her hand trembled as she pushed a stray strand of hair behind her ear.

"Come on," Taylor said impatiently. "Don't forget your camera," he said over his shoulder as the door slapped into place.

"Stop telling me what to do," she called after him in a playful voice, even though she was grateful for the reminder. She hadn't thought of taking her camera. At one time it had been as attached to her as her skin, though life and the clinic had pushed photography way down on her priority list. With a sudden feeling of liberation she picked up her case and followed him outside.

He opened his car door.

"Hey," she called, "if you want to really see the area, we need to go in my truck. The bottom of that car might not survive the back roads."

He gave the small battered truck a dubious look but slammed his car door shut. "Is there enough room for my legs in that thing?"

"You'll be fine."

Shelby slipped behind the wheel and couldn't help but grin as she watched Taylor settle in beside her. He overwhelmed the small interior. And her too. For once, she wished she drove a larger vehicle.

As she shifted into reverse, the back of her hand slid across his bare knee. The gears made a grinding sound as she found the correct slot. She glanced at Taylor. His mouth lifted slightly at the corners. She took special care that her fingers remained on the top of the gearshift instead of gripping it with her hand in order to avoid touching Taylor's knee again. She put the truck into first gear.

Pulling out onto the highway, she said, "I'm surprised you're interested in sightseeing."

"Not so much interested as bored. There's not even a movie theater in this town."

"We have some culture." She refused to become defensive.

"How's that? The cultures at the clinic?"

"Funny. No, we have a museum."

"What kind?"

She grinned. "The Benton Historical Museum."

"Figures."

His low chuckle rippled through her like water over stones in a brook. She wanted to hear that sound again. He'd relaxed somewhat since he'd arrived in town. Even the lines around his eyes had become less noticeable.

Shelby slowed for the car in front of them to make a turn. She looked at him. "You know," she said causally but with meaning, "for someone who insisted I show them around, you're not being very nice."

He gave her a lopsided grin. "I'm sorry. I'll keep my snide remarks to myself. So why did you and your husband decide Benton was the place to start a clinic?"

"Because this county qualified for state assistance and we thought it would be a great place to raise children."

Shelby winced. After his admission yesterday, he wouldn't be impressed by that plan. Thankfully the road she'd been looking for came into sight. She made a left turn.

"Where're we headed?"

"I thought you wanted to see the lake. Also there's a spot along here where I'd like to get some pictures. The last time

I made it out this way the light wasn't right. Today it looks perfect. I won't be long."

"I've got nothing but time." He ran one tan arm along the back of the seat, his fingers falling inches above her shoulder.

When she changed gears, the tips of his fingers brushed the top of her shoulder. Super-sensitive to each touch, she was thankful when she found the place where she could ease off onto the grassy roadside. "There's an old house in the woods here. I'll snap a few pictures and be right back."

"I'll come with you."

"It's pretty rough walking."

"Please, don't insult my manhood," he said in disgust as he opened the door and climbed out. Shelby followed suit, finding the path that hunters or animals used and following it into the stand of pines.

"I had no intention of besmirching your manhood." She certainly couldn't find anything to complain about in that department.

"Besmirching?" he said with interest. "I couldn't tell you the last time I heard that word used."

She glanced back at him. "Just because I live in a small town doesn't mean I don't know how to use big words."

"I was besmirched my entire childhood. Somehow using that word doesn't make it sound so bad."

She gave him a look of understanding and walked on. Taylor stayed close behind. She glanced back and found him sure-footed and confident as he walked over the pine-needle-padded track. He'd obviously done this type of hiking before.

"This area used to have head-high gullies. We'd play in them as kids. We'd show up at my dad's truck red from head to toe, covered in dirt."

"What caused the gullies?"

"Erosion of the farmland during the thirties and forties. *Grapes of Wrath* type stuff. A forester who knew what he was doing bought up the land for almost nothing and planted pines. Now you can hardly tell there was ever a dip in the land."

"What's he doing with the land now?"

"When the trees mature they'll be harvested and turned into pulp for paper and the land replanted. You know the renewable resource—trees."

"Yeah, I remember that old slogan. Just never saw it in action before."

Taylor was much more interested in watching the sway of Shelby's hips than hearing an environmental report. However, the more she talked the longer he had to enjoy the enticing view.

They'd not gone far before entering an open area. In the middle of a knoll stood a tumbledown shack built from clapboard that had mellowed to a pale gray. The porch, which extended across the entire front, listed on the right corner. A large oak tree stood off to the side, its limbs offering shade to half the house. Wildflowers grew in the knee-high grass surrounding the area.

It looked much like the house where he'd grown up, sharing a cramped bedroom with his two brothers. He refused to revisit those morose memories. The day was too pretty and he had too lovely a woman with him to let ugly thoughts spoil it. Last night had been difficult enough. He wouldn't let his emotions show like that again.

Shelby moved around, leaning one way and another then squatting as she brought the camera to her eye. He had no idea why she was so interested in taking pictures of the sad reminder of what had been. He spent every minute of his life trying to forget a place like this one.

When Shelby stepped onto the porch he headed towards her. "I don't think that's a good idea." His overprotective reaction surprised him. He usually let people do as they pleased. Fear that Shelby might get hurt disturbed him on a level he didn't wish to explore.

"I'm just going to stand here." She brought the camera to her face again. "I do know what I'm doing."

"Never doubted it," Taylor said, and went to lean a hand against the one post of the porch that appeared stable.

Taylor found he enjoyed discovering each new facet of Shelby's personality. She continued to surprise him daily. That aspect of being forced to be in Benton had turned into an interesting pastime. He tested the porch post for sturdiness then leaned his shoulder against it as he continued to watch her.

Standing, she stepped back a few feet. He straightened and she said, "No, don't move. I need to get a contrast in these. Something living and breathing."

With her camera still up to her eye, she continued to step back. He settled against the post again.

"That's great."

Click, click.

Shelby was totally engaged. She treated taking pictures just as she did working at the clinic. With complete absorption and focus. What would it be like to be on the receiving end of that focus? Was she just as intent and conscious of detail when making love?

Ooh, that wasn't a thought he should be having. Their plans for their lives diverged, not converged. She was the perfect house, perfect yard, and perfect family kind of person. He had no concept of that kind of life. It was like a fairy tale to him. He shifted, looking in the direction of a noise coming from under the trees.

"Stop right there," she ordered.

"What's wrong?"

"Nothing. It looks great."

Minutes later she breathed a sigh of satisfaction, suggesting she'd gotten all she wanted. Again he was thinking of things he had no business contemplating.

"I'm ready if you are."

Mind out of the bedroom, Stiles!

They made their way back to the truck. Just as they were preparing to cross the ditch bordering the road a yelping sound came from the weeds.

Shelby moved toward the sound, bent down and straightened out her hand. A tiny, deathly thin dog with matted hair sniffed at her fingers. "I hate it when people just throw animals out. I can't imagine what kind of person does that."

My father.

Shelby picked up the dog.

"What do you plan to do with him?" Taylor asked.

She turned to him as if he was suggesting they commit murder. "We can't leave it here!"

"I wasn't suggesting that we do. I was just wondering what you were thinking. Keeping him?"

"I'll just take him home and clean him up. Then see if I can find a home for him."

"He looks like he might need to see a vet."

"I'll see about that tomorrow. There's an old blanket behind my seat in the truck—would you get it?"

Did she take home every stray animal she found? In many ways he was one, and she had taken him in. "Sure."

He returned with the blanket and handed it to her. She wrapped the panic-stricken animal in it, bringing the dog close to her chest. "It'll be all right, little one. I'll take care of you," she cooed. She said to Taylor, "We're almost at the lake. I'll show it to you and then we'll head home and take care of this cutie."

Cutie. There was nothing cute about the sad little animal. For a brief second Taylor was jealous of the puppy and the attention it was receiving.

"Would you mind?" She indicated that she'd like him to hold the dog.

Taylor reached out for the bundle. He looked down at the dog, and the mixed-breed mutt with one floppy ear and wiry hair looked at Taylor as if he was his savior.

"He seems to like you." Shelby smiled at Taylor.

He grunted a response. He'd always wanted a dog as a boy. His father had said no more than once and the last time had been with the back of his hand. Taylor hadn't asked again. When he'd been in college and later working he hadn't had time for a dog so he'd never considered getting one. He ran a finger along the head of the confused little animal. Maybe it wasn't too late for him to make a change in his life and have a dog?

CHAPTER FIVE

SHELBY steered the truck along the windy tree-lined road until it sloped sharply downwards. Ahead lay a wide open area. It was level and clear of trees, with two unmaintained roads intersecting at the bottom.

"What do you think about the lake?" she asked.

"Where's the water?"

She smiled at Taylor's incredulous tone. "The dam's down the road a couple of miles. It'll take a few years to fill."

Shelby shifted into reverse.

"Hey! What're you doing? Aren't we going to drive across?"

"I don't think so. We're really not supposed to be this far down the road."

"Come on, Shelby. Live a little. I don't think the only doctors for miles around are going to be sent to jail for driving across a dry lake bed."

Taylor had managed to make her sound silly. With a huff of resignation Shelby changed gears. She eased the truck into terrain that would soon be under water. They rocked and bumped over the uneven road where heavy equipment had crossed.

"You don't like driving through here, do you?" Taylor asked.

Had it been that obvious that it unnerved her? She needed

to work on schooling her emotions or he'd learn things she'd rather keep hidden. Like her fear of caring too much for him, or her dread of being hurt. "There's something spooky about knowing that I should be under eight feet of water. I know it isn't rational but it makes me nervous. Maybe it's from watching old earthquake movies or something."

Taylor chuckled. "Interesting. So you're afraid of blood and dry lake beds."

She glanced at him. "What're you doing? Keeping a record?"

"I just find your little quirks intriguing." He grinned at her.

"Quirks? I don't have quirks."

"Okay. Foibles."

"Foibles! That makes me sound like I'm eighty."

A guffaw of Taylor's laughter filled the cab of the truck. "You know, it's fun to tease you. You blush every time."

Taylor's smile only grew wider at her huff of dismissal. He enjoyed the pink color on her cheeks that wasn't disappearing. Had a woman ever been more desirable? Had he ever wanted to kiss one more? With great effort he kept his hands to himself. Slowly she eased the truck down into the lake bed. His smile grew.

They had reached an area where the narrow road intersected another. Shelby concentrated on downshifting, veering to the right faster than necessary but correcting before the truck went off the road. She was really spooked by being on the lake bed. The road sloped upwards as they traveled farther to what she thought of as dry land. Taylor delighted in the sight of Shelby's chest rising and falling with her sigh of relief.

"Glad to be back on shore?" he quipped.

She snarled, her upper lip in a mock look of displeasure. "Funny. Very funny."

Shelby was adorable. He couldn't remember spending a

more enjoyable afternoon or one when he'd felt more sexually frustrated. The dog whimpered in his lap.

"We need to get him home. Feed him," she said, as much to herself as to Taylor.

We. It surprised him that her use of the word didn't disturb him. He kind of liked the sound of it. He'd been on his own so long that it was nice to be included, even if it had to do with a stray dog. Her kind of *we* he'd like to be a part of. If he knew how.

They were back out on the highway and headed towards town when Shelby pulled off in front of a small country store.

"I don't have anything around the house to feed him. I'll be right back." She climbed out of the truck.

A couple of grizzly looking men sat against the wall of the building, their wooden chairs leaning back on the back legs. From their appearance they could've been the same two guys who had hung out in front of the general store in Taylor's hometown. Men like these, he was sure, spent their days talking and spitting, and knew all the gossip in the county. Unfortunately, his family had provided much of the gossip back then.

The only time Taylor had ever seen one of those men move off the porch had been when he'd been around ten years old. A group of boys had followed Taylor into the store. When he'd caught them stealing they'd cornered him in the candy aisle and threatened to say that he was the thief. He had been preparing to fight when Old Man Carr, one of the men sitting out front, had stepped into the aisle and said, "Hey, you boys break it up."

The boys disappeared in seconds, leaving Taylor to stare up at Mr. Carr. "Sometimes it looks like life is ganging up on you," the old man said in a gravelly voice. "I hear you do good in school. If you use them smarts, you'll never have to worry about fighting boys like them again."

Those words had stuck with Taylor and he'd taken them to heart. He'd decided that he could make something of himself because of that old man. His had been the few encouraging words that an angry, rebellious boy had needed to hear. The ones that had dared him to dream, made him think his life could be more than battles and disillusionment.

Shelby came out of the store with a skip in her step and a smile on her face. That look would be something Taylor would definitely miss when he left.

Opening the door of the truck, she handed Taylor a small paper bag and climbed in.

"That stop sure made you happy." Taylor shifted the dog in his lap and put the bag on the floor between his feet.

"Yeah. I used to walk to an old general store much like this one. It always makes me feel good here."

"Same with me."

"You did?"

"Yeah, we even had the same type of old men hanging around out front."

She chuckled. "I think they just come with places like this."

Taylor glanced back at the men as Shelby pulled the truck onto the highway. Maybe so, but he wasn't sure that they all came with a Mr. Carr. No matter how hard Taylor worked at it as they wound their way back home, he couldn't seem to leave that part of his life behind.

Shelby stopped the truck in her drive and turned the engine off. She reached over to take the puppy.

"He's sleeping. I'll hold him until you get his food ready." He cradled the dog in the crook of his arm as he opened the passenger door. "You get the food." He kicked the truck door closed with his heel.

In the kitchen, Shelby emptied the can of puppy food she'd

bought into a bowl. Taylor set the puppy down. He wandered around the floor on weak legs.

"Come here, sweetie," Shelby placed the bowl on the floor. The dog tentatively approached the food. "Good boy," she cooed.

"You know," Taylor whispered, "if you talked to me like that, I'd do whatever you asked."

Her head jerked up. She glared at him. "You're making fun of me again."

A few seconds went by with the only sound coming from the dog eating with gusto.

"Maybe a little bit. But I can't help myself. I love your reactions. Like now. If looks could kill…" He looked down at the dog. "You know, this ragamuffin isn't the only one who's hungry. Is the burger joint open on Sunday?"

"No."

"You got anything I could fix us a meal out of?"

"I think I have some hamburger meat in the fridge."

"Great." The look on her face said she'd not planned to have dinner with him. He ignored it. "I'll cook while you see about the dog."

"You asking or telling?"

"More like suggesting."

"Only because I'm hungry too will I accept your suggestion. The frying pan is under there." She pointed to a lower cabinet then picked up the little dog with the now rounded belly. "I shouldn't be long."

Shelby returned with a wiggling puppy in her hands as she dried him off with a towel. Taylor stood at the stove, flipping burgers. There was something nice about having a man cook for her.

"How'd the bath go?" He turned in her direction when she entered. "Looks like you might've had one too." Taylor gaze didn't meet hers. Instead it was focused further south.

His eyes had darkened, grown intent. She'd not had someone look at her like that in a long time. Jim had loved her. She'd never doubted that, but he had never regarded her with the same intensity, the same longing that Taylor showed now.

A river of heat flowed swiftly and sweetly through her, making her heart do the two-step. She glanced down and found that a large wet spot covered her breasts. Spinning round, she covered her embarrassment as well as her reaction to his regard. With a couple of quick rubs, she set the puppy on the floor and returned to her bedroom.

"You don't have to change on my account," he called. "I was enjoying the view."

Closing the door to her bedroom with a firm click, she sat on the bed and put her hands over her hot cheeks. She'd blushed more since Taylor had ridden into town than she had in her whole life before that.

She re-entered the kitchen in a dry shirt, to find the table set and a platter of burgers and buns front and center. It was good to have the kitchen used to prepare a real meal. She didn't cook often, it wasn't for just one.

"Got any chips to go with these burgers?" he asked.

Obviously those few heated moments earlier hadn't affected Taylor but they'd set her well-ordered world spinning.

"In the refrigerator freezer."

"The freezer?" he asked incredulously.

"Keeps them fresh. I'm not around enough and the chips go stale."

She sat in her usual chair while Taylor found the chips.

"You work too hard." The bag rattled as he opened it and stuck his hand in.

"How so?" Her tone betrayed the small spike of irritation igniting in her stomach. It had been years since someone had commented on the way she lived her life. She didn't think he knew her well enough to be making such a statement.

"Early to the clinic, staying late, no time off, no longer doing your photography. Do I need to go on?"

Who did he think he was to be saying something like that to her? "I don't need you telling me how I should live."

"I'm just making an observation." He bit into a cool chip, making a loud crunching sound. "I don't think anyone could make you do anything you don't want to."

"It sounded like an accusation to me."

"I didn't mean for it to. I just think you need to take better care of yourself."

"Do you make it a habit of cooking for people and then telling them how they need to live their lives?"

He cocked his head, saying nothing for a moment as if in deep thought. "No-o-o." He drew the word out. "I don't think I've ever done it before." He sounded astounded that he had this time. "I guess you're just special that way."

The puppy chose that moment to nose around their feet. Taylor scooped up the small ball of fur in his large hand. With a long index finger he stroked the small head between the ears. The puppy snuggled into his lap. The contrast between the broad-shouldered man and tiny trusting animal captured her whole attention.

What would it be like to be on the receiving end of a tender touch from this man?

Taylor was running late the next morning. He hurried to the car. He stopped short in the humid air when he saw that Shelby's truck was still parked behind his car.

Something must be wrong. He'd been there a little over a week and Shelby had always been gone by the time he'd left for the clinic. He loped to the back door and up the outside steps. Shaking his head to think she didn't lock her doors, he pulled the screen door open and called, "Shelby?"

Listening, he heard a movement from the direction she'd

gone the night before to change her shirt. He'd almost lost control when she'd returned from bathing the dog all wet and flushed, an enormous smile of pleasure on her face. He'd felt like he'd been sucker-punched, she'd been so beautiful.

Only by sheer willpower had he managed to make light of the situation. As soon as their meal had ended, he'd left before he did something he'd regret.

Now he headed to the bedroom that he'd been so tempted to find last night.

"Shelby, where are you?" His heart picked up speed as his concern increased. Why wasn't she answering?

A low whimper came from the room at the end of the hall and he went in that direction. If the puppy was here, Shelby would be nearby. Slowly pushing the bedroom door open, he called, "Shelby, are you okay? Can I come in?"

Receiving no response, he stepped farther into the room. The dog tried to climb out of the box next to the bed. Taylor lifted him into his arms. "So what have you done with Shelby, boy?" He rubbed the dog behind his ears. The puppy licked at Taylor's fingers as he looked at the bed. The only thing that might be Shelby was a large lump under the light blanket.

"Shelby, are you under there?"

Slowly the ball in the center of the bed began to move.

Relief filled him. At least she was alive. "What's wrong? It's past time to be at the clinic."

A groan and then "Oh, no" came from beneath the covers. Shelby pushed the pastel pink blanket back enough so that he could see her face.

Her hair went every direction as if she had been tossing and turning most of the night. A pale face and bloodshot eyes told him she was sick.

Taylor sat on the edge of the bed, the dog in the crook of one arm. "Shelby, you look awful." Maybe that wasn't the best example of his bedside manner but her misery took him by surprise.

"Get out. I'll get dressed and see you at the clinic," she said in a weak voice.

"How long have you been ill?"

"Since around midnight."

Her glassy-eyed look tore at his heart. "Ah, honey, you should've called me."

If she hadn't looked so pitiful, he would've laughed at her expression of disbelief. It had never occurred to her to call him for help. That hurt. He wouldn't let himself examine why it was significant.

"It's just a stomach virus. All I need is a shower and I'll feel better."

Taylor didn't move from the bed.

"Please leave."

"Are you sure you can make it to the shower without help?"

"I can take care of myself."

"Okay. I'll take Buster to the kitchen and feed him."

"Buster?" She looked at him in question.

"Yeah. I can't keep calling him 'Dog.' You yell if you need help."

He was confident she wouldn't be doing that no matter how terrible she felt. Shelby wouldn't admit any feebleness, to him or anyone else.

Taylor pulled the door shut but remained in the hall until he heard the shower running. He'd see that Buster got his breakfast then come back to check on Shelby.

By the time he returned, the water was no longer running. He knocked on the bedroom door but received no reply. Pushing it open, he didn't see Shelby. "You okay?" Still nothing. Going to the door of the bath, he knocked lightly. He couldn't take a chance that in her weakened state she'd fallen.

An unintelligible murmur came from the other side of the

door. Concern overriding any other thought, Taylor didn't wait for an answer before going in.

Shelby sat on the edge of the tub wrapped in a towel, with her wet head against the aqua tile wall. She had taken a hot shower by all the steam floating near the ceiling. Her illness and shower combination had zapped what little energy she'd had left.

"Let me dry your hair and then I'll get you back into bed." Under any other circumstances that would have been a suggestive statement.

"I can do it. Just leave me alone."

"For crying out loud, Shelby, just this once accept some help. Now, you sit right there while I see about your hair." He pulled a towel off the holder.

"Give it to me. I'll do it."

Taylor looked at her meaningfully and briskly rubbed her hair with the towel. "Where's your hairdryer?"

After a long moment she pointed to the cabinet under the sink. *Stubborn woman.* Taylor quickly retrieved the appliance, plugged it in and sat down beside her. Being a novice hairdresser, this job was way outside his comfort zone but he'd do his best. He turned on the dryer and directed the air flow towards her head. His fingers gently ran though the wet strands, separating her hair into sections.

"Lean against me so I can get underneath." Giving her no opportunity to argue, he guided her head to his chest.

She rested against him but never completely relaxed. Didn't the woman ever think she could use someone's help? As her hair dried it became warm silk flowing through his hand. Could anything be sexier? He rubbed his cheek against the glossy cloud.

He turned off the dryer. She slowly sat up. Did she ever let go? Stop being obstinate? "Shelby, honey, you need to get dressed."

She looked at him weakly. He stood and put the hairdryer away. On the corner of the vanity he found a lacy gown that would have made his blood sizzle had circumstances been different. With it suspended on his index fingers by the tiny straps he asked, "You need help with this?"

"I can do it," she said, sounding stronger than she looked.

Relief filled him. And disappointment. It would've been difficult to treat her as a patient if her luscious body had been on display. Still, it would've been his chance to see what he'd been daydreaming about for days.

He stepped into the bedroom but didn't completely close the door between them. Fear that she might fall kept him close. When she opened the door he scooped her into his arms, cradling her close.

She made a weak movement of protest. "Put me down."

He tightened his arms. As if she had no more energy to fight, she accepted his care and settled against him. "I assure you I have no intention of taking advantage of a woman when she's sick. I like my women willing and able, and obviously you're neither. So quit being so uncooperative. The sooner I have you tucked into bed the sooner I can get to the clinic."

"I need to go to work." She resisted his hold again.

"Not today you don't."

"But—"

"There's no but. I'll take care of the clinic. You need to rest."

"You can't tell me what to do."

"I can and I am. Doctor's orders."

"I have patients to see."

"Really, Shelby. Be reasonable. You don't want to give your patients whatever you have."

The fight left her. No matter what, she thought of her patients first, even before herself.

Taylor placed her on the sheets. Her short gown left an

enticing amount of leg showing, forcing him to suppress a groan. He'd always remained a professional when taking care of a patient but seeing to Shelby was testing his restraint. For the first time he was having a difficult time keeping his actions and reactions strictly professional.

He pulled the floral sheet up, concealing the silken skin that his fingers itched to touch. He needed to leave before he did something she wouldn't appreciate and he'd regret.

Brushing her hair away from her face, he said, "I'll take Buster with me to the clinic. We'll be back to check on you at lunchtime."

Shelby feeling miserable made him feel the same. Taylor stopped at the door to the hall and looked back at her. Her breathing had already become steady and deepened.

Never before had Taylor resented his work but this time he wished he could spend the entire day sitting beside Shelby, nursing her back to health. The tiny dynamo had slipped into a corner of his life where he had never let another person go.

Shelby rolled over and looked at the clock on her bedside table. Eleven. She couldn't believe she'd slept the morning away, even though she'd been up most of the night. It had been a long time since she'd felt so wretched.

The clinic!

She flipped the covers back and sat up. Her head spun. Lying back, she flung an arm over her eyes. In the four years the clinic had been open, she'd not missed a day of work. As horrible as she felt physically, it killed her to know that she had patients needing to be seen.

No, Taylor was there. He was taking care of her patients.

Doing her work. Seeing that the community had medical care. She'd not relied on anyone in years, and she had to depend on him, of all people. She fought the rising panic the thought brought to her. The person who swore he was leaving as soon as he could, and she had to trust him.

Removing her arm from her eyes, she slowly sat up. Her stomach rose and fell in protest. Maybe if she ate something she'd feel better. Placing a hand over her stomach, she made her way to the kitchen. She was standing on her toes taking the soda cracker box off the top cabinet shelf when the door opened. With a squeak she dropped the box. "Don't you know to knock?"

Taylor entered, carrying the dog. "I thought you'd still be in bed. From the look of things you should be."

"Thanks for making me feel better." She retrieved the box and placed it on the counter.

"I'll say I'm sorry if you'll promise to dress like that for me when you feel good."

Trying to overlook his statement, she said, "Hey, shouldn't you be at the clinic instead of here? What if someone comes? I'll get dressed."

"Relax, I left a note that I'd be back at one. You know you can train people to come to the clinic during the hours you set, don't you? You need a lunch hour. Your number is on the door if there's an emergency. Otherwise they can wait."

She couldn't ignore the heat of desire that became evident in Taylor eyes, which stopped further argument from her. His eyes had turned dark and daring. He put Buster down and stepped toward her. The dog's tail wagged as he found his food bowl.

Not expecting anyone to come into her house unannounced, she'd not put on a robe. Now she stood in front of Taylor in her thinnest, shortest gown. She was just short of naked. By the way he was looking at her she might as well have been. "A gentleman would turn his back and let me get something to cover up with," she said with as much authority as a queen as she headed toward her bedroom.

"A gentleman would but I've never been accused of being one," he called.

Shelby returned to the kitchen to find Taylor pouring something into a small boiler. Surprisingly, sparring with Taylor had made her forget about her stomach troubles. Now it complained more from hunger than a sour feeling. "What're you doing now?"

"I brought you lunch. Home-made chicken soup," he said as he stirred the soup.

"Home-made? When've you had time to make chicken soup? You did open the clinic, didn't you?" Her voice held a note of alarm.

"Yes, I've seen patients this morning. Mrs. Stewart came in to have her sciatica checked and asked where you were. To make a long story short, she said she'd make some chicken-noodle soup."

"With her leg problem, you asked her to make soup for me?"

He did have the decency to look contrite. "I didn't ask. She volunteered. I thought her soup would be better than something out of a can."

"That's sweet of her."

"Now sit down before you fall down while I get this heated."

Once again Taylor was busy preparing a meal for her. Jim had done little if any domestic work during their marriage. His total focus had been the clinic. Much like how it had now become her sole interest.

It hadn't taken Taylor the "I'm leaving town as soon as I can" man long to feel comfortable in her kitchen. He moved around the room with easy grace, finding the utensils and bowls with ease. Somehow it seemed natural, even reassuring to have him there. It was nice to have someone taking care of her. She'd almost forgotten how it felt.

Sitting in a chair, she picked up Buster and brought his face up to hers. "So what've you been doing all morning, little guy?"

"He spent most of the time in a box in your office. The rest of the time he spent eating. He can really put it away."

She settled Buster in her lap and he fell asleep. "That's what happens when you've been starving. You never seem to get enough." Kind of like she couldn't seem to get enough of Taylor's attention. Oh, that was heartbreak waiting to happen.

Taylor's gaze met hers. Did he think she was talking about something else?

When had she become so self-sufficient that she no longer needed a man in her life? She hadn't realized until recently that she'd been starving for a man's notice. Her days were spent giving others care but no one had taken the time to be concerned about her. Until today. Until Taylor. It was a heady feeling she'd miss when he left. The man was slipping in under her defenses.

Taylor placed two filled bowls on the table, and pulled the box of crackers out from under his arm. He went back and returned with two large glasses of iced tea.

"I don't know if my stomach can handle all this," she said, looking at the full bowl of soup.

"You need to eat something or you'll get dehydrated."

Dipping her spoon into the liquid, she put it in her mouth. "Mmm. It tastes wonderful."

"Kind of a hot meal for the middle of the summer but I thought it might make you feel better."

"Thanks for doing this. It's really nice of you."

He shrugged. "Not a problem. Least I can do for my landlord."

A prick of disappointment touched her. So he was just being nice because she'd given him a place to stay for a couple of weeks. Had she been hoping for more? Pushing that disconcerting thought away, she asked, "Who did you see this morning?"

"Mr. Rogers came in with a cough. Mrs. Smith had plantar fasciitis. Mark Myers has a bad cold. The usual stuff."

"Did you do an X-ray of Mr. Rogers's lungs? Rule out pneumonia. He's eighty-five."

"I took good care of him." Taylor put down his spoon, sat back in his chair and looked straight at her. "I thought by now you'd quit questioning my abilities. Have I given you any reason to doubt me?"

She reached over and placed her hand on his forearm. The heat of him seeped into her. "I'm sorry. You didn't deserve that. You've done excellent work while you've been here. And I don't know what I would have done without you today."

Taylor rubbed the pad of his index finger across her cheek. "I bet that was hard for you to admit. I'm glad I was here to help." An emotion similar to shock crossed his face, as if he was surprised to hear himself utter those words. She was certainly surprised by them. It was the first time he hadn't acted like he had his car headed out of town.

His attention centered on her fingers as they trailed off his arm. Suddenly the large kitchen had turned small and intimate. The air between them vibrated with awareness. She returned to eating with a great deal of effort and concentration. Taylor stood and went back to the stove to refill his bowl.

"I'm feeling better. I should get dressed and go back with you."

Taylor wheeled around from the stove. "For someone so intelligent, you have some of the most bizarre ideas."

"I don't have bizarre ideas!"

"Do you honestly believe that you have any business at the clinic this afternoon?"

"Yes, I do. It my clinic. My responsibility."

"You're human. You got sick. Maybe even, despite how

horrible the thought, you might one day like to take a day off."

"What I'm I suppose to do here? I'm feeling much better."

"How about something you enjoy? While I'm here, take advantage of me. After I'm gone it may be a while before you get more help." He returned to the table with his bowl in hand.

Shelby hated to admit it but he was right. She loved her work at the clinic but it had consumed her life. It had been wonderful to spend yesterday outside, taking pictures, she'd even liked Taylor's company. It had been the first real leisure day she'd taken since Jim had died. One that wouldn't have happened if it hadn't been for Taylor's insistence.

"I'd better get back," Taylor said, scooting his chair back having finished his meal. "Mrs. Ferguson is on the schedule for a blood-pressure check so I'd better be there to help her in."

Shelby smiled. The old woman wouldn't be happy to learn that Taylor would be caring for her again.

"What?" He stood and started stacking the used bowls.

"Just thinking you might be taking a liking to us."

"I just might be," he said, soft enough that she looked at him. "Some more than others."

His intense stare made her wonder if she was starting to run a fever.

"You're kind of growing on us too," she murmured.

He leaned toward her.

"Don't get too close. You might catch what I've got."

His mouth moved closer. "I'll take my chances."

She placed a hand on his chest, stopping him. "I don't think this is a good idea."

"You're probably right," he murmured as his arm came around her. His hand settled low on her back and he pulled her against him. "But I've wanted to do it for too long to stop now."

His lips were dry and firm as they met hers. At first he tested and teased. This kiss was nothing like the first one. It was different than any she'd ever experienced. So tender it could've been her very first kiss. She moved forward, resting against him, soaking up the heaven that was being in his arms.

The squeal of an animal in pain pierced the air. She jerked back. She'd stepped on Buster's foot. Taylor's hands dropped away. The warmth and security of being next to him disappeared.

Taylor picked up the dog. "I get a chance to kiss a beautiful girl and you get in my way."

Beautiful girl. Taylor thought she was beautiful.

"Are you feeling well enough to have Buster for company this afternoon?" he asked, placing the dog on the floor again. "He wasn't as well behaved this morning as I had hoped."

"I think so." She forced herself to sound normal after that earthquake of a kiss. "We could both use a nap, I'm sure."

"Wish I could stay and join you," he said in a suggestive voice, along with a long passionate look, before abruptly turning and stepping through the screen door and letting it slam behind him.

How had he managed to reduce her to having a schoolgirl crush in only seven short days?

CHAPTER SIX

SHELBY woke from her nap feeling much improved. Bathing again, she dressed and styled her hair. With a surprise she realized that it had been nice to get some rest without worrying about the clinic. For at least today the concerns of the clinic had been Taylor's and that was a freeing feeling. She could too easily get used to not carrying all the burdens in her life.

Now she sat at her desk, with Buster asleep on a towel beside her. She'd love to spend more afternoons this way. Pushing a button on her computer, she brought up the pictures she'd taken the day before. She clicked on each individual photo in the rows of small squares. With one tap a photograph of Taylor standing causally in front of the shack filled the screen.

Even his picture made her blood hum. He was a handsome man with high cheekbones and a strong jaw. That she was well aware of already. His well cared-for appearance contrasting against the dilapidated building made him the focal point of the photo. He captivated her by simply looking into the camera.

Thoughts of his kisses made her heart break the speed limit. She shouldn't let that happen again. It would be too easy to let him into her heart. But what then?

She clicked through each picture. It wasn't until the picture where he'd looked directly at her that the veneer slipped.

There his vulnerability became visible. No doubt he'd not meant for that particular part of his personality to show. Aware of his need, she longed to soothe him.

"Hey, what're you doing?" Taylor interrupted her thoughts.

Shelby squealed, her hand going to her chest. "For heaven's sake, Taylor, are you trying to scare me to death?"

"I thought for sure you would've heard the door slam."

Buster made a whimpering sound and Taylor picked him up.

"So, I see you're feeling better. What are you up to?"

"Just looking over the pictures I took yesterday."

"Mind if I see?"

He pulled a chair up before she could respond. "Scoot over."

Now he was entirely too close for her comfort. She went back and began clicking through the photos. The house and surrounding landscape had turned out perfectly. Taylor made noises of appreciation and interest in his throat. A soft, warm feeling washed over her at each of his responses.

She leaned back in the chair and put her hands in her lap.

"What about those?" he pointed to the last row of pictures.

"They're just more of the house."

"I'd like to see them also."

With a resigned sigh she put the cursor over the first picture. His face popped into focus.

He moved nearer and gently pushed her hand off the mouse and continued clicking. "Why didn't you want me to see these?"

"I don't know. I thought they might make you feel uncomfortable."

"Why? You're an excellent photographer. Didn't you think I would like them?"

She shifted in the chair because of both his earnest question and him being so near. "I wasn't sure." Did he not see what she did?

Taylor stopped on the one where he'd been watching her, really watching. He studied it for a long moment before he sat back and said, "You have a real talent. One you should be sharing with the world."

She huffed.

He smiled. "Okay, at least this part of the country. You should see about setting up a show." His eyes widened and he lightly slapped his leg. "You know, it would be a great way to raise awareness and money for the clinic. Bring reality to the need for clinics like Benton's."

"I don't think so. I'm not that good and I certainly don't have time to prepare for something like that. The clinic has to come first." She leaned back.

"That's the point." He leaned toward her, his eyes earnest. "You could help the clinic while you're also taking care of yourself. You need to get away from work some."

Rolling her chair away from the computer and Taylor, she stood and faced him. The stab of anger and something else she wouldn't name rose again in her stomach. "I don't need you telling me what to do. If you're so interested in helping, maybe you should commit to staying here and working at the clinic indefinitely, or at least until I find someone to replace you."

Taylor stood, looked at her from across the room. "I've made it clear that I can't do that. I'm only here because your uncle gave me no real choice. Stop trying to drag me into something I want no part of!"

"Is it can't or won't? What would be so awful about having to live here for a little while longer? You seem to be doing fine. And people are starting to like you."

"Enough pushing!" he snapped, and headed out the door.

* * *

Taylor normally didn't care when someone was aggravated with him. After years of living with his father's drunken tirades, he'd learned to tune out people's negative emotions. Regardless of that discipline, the tension between Shelby and himself was starting to get to him. For some reason, her happiness mattered.

Why it was important he couldn't comprehend. He never let anyone get close enough for their feelings to affect him one way or another. He wished he could give her what she wanted but he couldn't. Making his life in Benton wasn't possible. Was he even capable of having a positive relationship with someone?

He'd worked too hard to gain his self-respect, and the respect of others. Now if people were talking about him, it was because of his skill as a doctor, not because he was the brainy son of the town drunk. This tiny town brought back bad memories and he refused to live with them even for Shelby's sake. Still she pushed against that well-established barrier he'd built to protect his emotions. That wall was swaying. He was afraid that if she continued to shove, the partition would fall. Then he'd be vulnerable to a pain greater than any he'd ever known.

Carly knocked on the office door, drawing his attention away from his turmoil. The paperwork he'd been trying to catch up on during a lag in patients that afternoon might have to wait.

"Yes?"

"You have a patient. I put him in exam one," she said.

"Thanks. I'll be right there."

As he opened the door of the exam room, he glanced at the chart for a name. "So, uh, Bill, what seems to be wrong?"

He looked up to find a boy of around ten sitting on the exam table. He was battered and bruised about the face and one sleeve of his shirt had been torn. One knee was badly skinned and the other was openly bleeding. A small trail of blood went down his shinbone.

The boy had been in a fight. He'd not been the winner. Taylor knew the blank look in the boy's eyes. Had seen it in the mirror countless times. Torment gripped Taylor like a strap squeezing his chest.

"What happened?" Taylor had to work to keep his voice steady.

"Some boys at school beat him up," said the haggard-looking mother standing beside the exam table.

"Tell me what happened," Taylor said as he gathered supplies. He would do what his training had taught him to do for now. Later, he'd try to forget.

"It has been an ongoing problem. Some of the boys won't leave him alone. They tease him. He won't let me talk to the kids' parents. Doesn't want me to talk to the teachers. Then this happened." The woman looked at Taylor with tearful eyes.

Taylor knew the feeling well. He'd been hit a number of times before his mother had found out. He wasn't sure his dad ever had. "The school authorities know?"

"Yes, they sent us here." She thrust a paper at him. Taylor glanced at it and set it aside.

"If this continues I'll have no choice but to contact the police."

The boy's eyes widened. Fear filled the blank look that had been in his eyes. Taylor wouldn't be the one giving the report. He was only going to be there a few more days.

Taylor finished examining the boy, relieved there were no broken bones or internal bleeding, then applied bandages to his knee. "You'll need to keep ice on that eye. Twenty minutes on and twenty minutes off."

The mother nodded.

"Now I'd like to speak to Bill for a minute, if you don't

mind?" he addressed the mother, while forcing a smile to reassure the boy. Smiling was the last thing Taylor felt like doing. One little boy's troubles had transported him back to days in his life he'd like to forget.

The mother stepped outside the door and Taylor pulled the chair up in front of the boy. "Bill, I know how hard this is for you because I was once you. I fought at school too. But a man told me that if I did my best in school I could one day be better than all the boys who gave me a hard time. I did work hard in school and it gave me a chance to go to college. There I slowly became proud of myself, liked myself, and that made me stronger than those boys who had always been mean to me.

"So stay in school and make the best grades you can. One day you'll be stronger than those boys picking on you too. Knowledge is power. You never know, one day you might even be their boss and tell them what to do." Taylor pulled one of the leftover coupons out of his pocket. "Now, go get yourself an ice cream."

The slightest smile came to Bill's lips and the sadness disappeared briefly from his eyes.

Minutes after the boy and his mother left the clinic, Taylor stalked out to his car, climbed in, put the top down and headed out to nowhere in particular. He just had to get away. Find some way to ease that band of pain.

That kid's fearful, beaten and disillusioned look tore at his gut. Taylor had worked hard to put those same horrific emotions behind him. That was a sham. All it took was one boy in one small town to make them return with a vengeance. He was still an inmate in the prison of his past. A childhood wasn't something he could make vanish. Somehow he had to learn to live with it or he would never be free of it.

* * *

Shelby searched the driveway from the kitchen window to see if Taylor had come home. Where was he? Surely he wouldn't have left town without saying goodbye, even if they'd had a disagreement.

She hadn't seen him all afternoon and the clinic was slow but even then they should've crossed paths. Finally she asked Carly if she'd seen him.

"He walked out with the little boy who'd been beaten up and his mother. I saw him get in his car and leave."

Taylor hadn't returned to the clinic by the time she'd locked up and his car hadn't been in the drive when she'd arrived home. He'd made it clear he wasn't interested in socializing with people who lived around here, so she couldn't imagine that he'd stopped at the local bar or was at a church event. Those were the only two places open in town that evening.

Now it was going on midnight and he'd still not shown up. Worry made her stomach tense. What had happened to make him leave so abruptly? To stay away?

She turned the light off over the kitchen sink to see more clearly. A misty rain fell and the red car hadn't returned to the drive. Had Taylor been in an accident? Was he in a ditch somewhere? He had a track record of driving too fast. What if he had skidded off the road and no one had seen him do it? A flash of Jim's car wrapped around the tree burst into her mind, but she shook off the image. As perturbed as she'd been with him for leaving without telling anyone, she still wouldn't want anything bad to happen to him.

A double beam of light skimmed across the glass. Shelby's heart rose and fell. The light straightened and then was extinguished. Taylor was home. Relief flooded through her and she was left with a nervousness that could only be the aftermath of fear.

Now she could go to bed.

Picking up the bed she'd bought for Buster, she walked through the dark house to her bedroom. Placing the sleeping dog on the floor beside her nightstand, she took one last look out her back window at the garage.

Taylor stood at the window with the dim glow of a light behind him. His normally strong shoulders were hunched, his head down and hands shoved into his pockets. His body language was in complete contrast to the one she'd seen the last time he'd stood there. He looked like a man totally isolated from the world. Taylor was in pain. Everything about him screamed it.

His head rose and he looked in her direction. She held her breath. Did he know that she was watching him? He ran a hand through his hair and turned away.

Shelby slipped under the bed covers. She should be exhausted but sleep eluded her. What was going on with Taylor? She rolled over, hugging a pillow to her. Would he be there in the morning? She needed to know for the clinic's sake. If she was truthful, she needed to know for herself.

Unable to stand it any longer, she tossed the sheet off and stood. Pulling on shorts and a light sweatshirt over her shorty gown, she headed for the back door. When Buster whimpered, she scooped him up.

Light still burned in Taylor's window. The gentle rain turned heavier as she crossed the short distance to the steps. It began to pour as she climbed the stairs. She knocked on the door of the apartment, her head down against the deluge. She cradled Buster closer as her hand went up to knock again. Before knuckle met wood, the door swung open.

Taylor stood there in nothing but navy slacks. They hung on his hips and were zipped but not buttoned.

"Shelby, what are you doing here?"

Before she could respond, he took her by the upper arms and pulled her out of the rain. She stood inside the door while he stalked to the bathroom and returned with a towel. "Give him to me." He reached for Buster, swapping the towel for the dog. As she dried her head, Taylor placed the dog on another towel on the floor.

"I just wanted—" she started.

"This isn't a good time for a lecture about how I should be more considerate of the clinic," he snapped. His mouth drew into a tight line and he stood with his hands fisted at his side.

"I—"

"You need to leave, Shelby. Just leave me alone."

She couldn't. Shelby stepped toward him, her wet hair hanging in ropes about her head. The sweatshirt lay heavy with water across her shoulders.

"Let me tell you something, Taylor Stiles. My being here has nothing to do with the clinic." She stepped closer, poking her index finger into his chest. He remained immobile but his eyes narrowed. "I've been worried about you." Another poke. "Afraid you'd had an accident." Another poke. "I'm sorry I wasted my time."

At the next poke Taylor grabbed her hand and pulled her to him. She slammed against his chest. His mouth lowered, taking control of hers. Strong arms circled her waist, lifting her. His mouth eased, shifted and took possession more thoroughly. Heat flooded her, pooled low in her middle, making her tingle with longing.

Her hands skimmed across the warm skin of his chest over the strong column of his neck, before wrapping around it. Taylor felt strong, secure, steady. Something she'd missed for so long. She leaned into him.

His tongue teased the seam of her lips and she opened for him, inviting him in. He swept her, teased her, and parried, asking her to play. Tentative at first, she joined him eagerly.

Taylor took the kiss deeper. One of his hands moved to cup her bottom, bringing her closer. Gradually he eased the kiss and his hands moved to grip her waist. He let her slowly slide down him. The evidence of his desire stood hard and prominent between them. When her feet touched his floor, he pushed her gently away.

"You should go."

This strong, intelligent man was a suffering soul and she had a soft spot for suffering souls. She couldn't leave him when he needed someone.

"No." She stood on trembling legs.

He moved to stand at the window, staring out into the night. She came up beside him, lifted a hand to touch his back.

"Don't," he growled.

She pulled her hand away. "Taylor, you need to talk."

"I want to do something more than talk with you." His voice carried a gritty sound of need.

"I know," she said softly. "I'm here. Please tell me what's wrong. You're scaring me."

Taylor hung his head. No one had worried about him in so long. He'd never allowed himself to dream that Shelby might. Could he explain his feelings to her? Would she understand? Dared he think she really cared?

Her fingertips were like points of fire on his skin when she touched his back. Gently the palm of her hand came to rest flat on him and moved in a soothing pattern.

"Tell me what's wrong. I want to help." Shelby continued her tender caress. "What happened today? Why did you leave?"

As her hand moved across his skin he felt his muscles relaxing, his breathing slowing.

"The kid that came in today had been bullied at school." *Just say it and get it over with then she'll leave.* "That was me. I was the kid of the town drunk. Which gave them a lot of material. As a little kid it was a daily occurrence until I started defending myself. That led into fights and escalated into rebelling against everything and everyone. It became a big ugly circle of pain. One that I don't want the kid I saw today to live through."

The movement of her hand faltered for a second. Her calming movement started again with more pressure from her fingertips. Her arms encircled his waist, her face coming to rest against his back. Dampness touched his skin. Shelby was crying for him! When had anyone cried for him?

He turned and enveloped her in his arms. Her face rested against his chest. She snuggled into him as if she wanted to absorb his pain. "Sweetie, don't cry. That was a long time ago."

"I'm crying for that boy that had to live with so much heartache."

He pulled her more securely against him. Her arms around his waist squeezed him closer. He'd never felt more humbled. This woman who had experienced great loss and worked herself almost beyond what was humanly possible was crying for a little boy she hadn't even known. What had he done to deserve her concern? Some of the pain of being an outsider with no one who really cared about him slowly seeped from him.

"I've seen kids in the ER numerous times who'd been beaten but none got to me like this boy. I've kept my childhood issues closed off for years, pushed them away as I focused on first med school then my career. I didn't even bring them out to examine when I had no family at my graduations, or spent my holidays alone. It just was. I accepted that. Until today, when they just came boiling out. I had to leave, take some down time. I'm sorry if I left you in the lurch."

He sucked in a breath at the soft touch of her lips on his chest. Seconds later, the brush of her mouth against him made him forget the past and concentrate fully on the here and now. Shelby was in his arms.

Her hands began to travel over his back, stopping to knead before moving on to explore another spot.

"Shelby? Do you know what you're doing?" His breath spurted unevenly against her hair.

"Mmm... Comforting you?" She nipped at his skin and his manhood stiffened.

Hands on her shoulders, he pushed her far enough away to meet her gaze. "I'm not interested in your pity. Admit it, you want me."

His skin rippled across his back as she trailed her fingers down to his waist and up over his pecs to his neck.

Standing on tiptoe, she stretched upwards. "I thought I was making that clear."

"I want to hear you say it."

"I want you," she whispered over his lips before they met his.

Need, strong, bottomless and more frightening than he'd ever experienced, filled him.

What was she doing? Shelby had never been the aggressor in lovemaking. But Taylor needed her. That little boy in him who'd lived daily in misery and the grown man who'd overcome so much touched her heart. She grieved for the boy and hurt for the scarred man.

He met her tentative kiss with one of fire, consuming her. His tongue entered, demanded. She accepted and gave. Fanning her fingers though his hair, she pulled his head closer. Heavenly, hot, hungry moments later his lips left hers to skim along her cheek, leaving butterfly kisses behind. His mouth traveled down her neck. She shivered.

"We need to get this damp shirt off you," he murmured against her neck as his hands went to the hem of the garment.

She raised her hands above her head, allowing him to slip

the shirt off. He dropped it to the floor and pushed her shorts over her hips and down, leaving her standing in her gown.

His index finger followed the line of lace that covered her right breast to where it ended at her cleavage. Her nipples puckered in response. His finger moved to tease the nipple of her left breast. A quake of delight ran through her.

"As much as I like this little slip of clothing, I know I'll like what's under it so much more," he said in a low gravelly voice that made her tremble.

Before she could respond, she stood naked before him.

"Mercy, you're beautiful." He bent his head and took her nipple into his mouth. His tongue teased and tugged just as he had done with his kisses. Her center melted, ready for him. There was an excitement to being in Taylor's arms that she'd never known existed between a man and a woman, despite her years of happy marriage. He moved to her other breast, giving it the same undivided attention. She shifted toward him, sliding her hands over his shoulders to prevent herself falling.

He chuckled lightly. "Like that, do you?"

Putting her hands on each side of his head, she encouraged him to meet her look. "I do, but I think before we go any further you should turn off the light. We've probably already given the neighbors the show of a lifetime."

He reached over and clicked off the floor lamp, leaving only the light from the bathroom, which prevented them from being in total darkness. Taking her hand, he led her towards the bed.

"What about the bathroom light?"

"No, I want to see you. I don't care what the neighbors know."

She didn't either. What she cared about was him.

He pulled the bedcovers away and she sat on the bed, tugging his hand to encourage him to join her. Instead of coming with her, he resisted, letting go of her hand. She scooted back, watching in fascination and anticipation as he unzipped his slacks and let them drop to the floor.

Taylor was all proud male, his desire evident. For her. There was a potent power in knowing she had such an effect on him.

Placing a knee on the edge of the bed, he leaned over and kissed her. She reached for him. He came down but instead of covering her, as she wanted, he lay on his side, his head supported by a hand. What began as a protest turned to a sharp intake of breath when he trailed his free hand over her hip bone and followed the curvature of her waist upwards.

She quivered as he continued his exploration by tracing the arc of one breast before tugging gently at a straining nipple. He then focused his attention on her other breast that ached for his devotion. Her breath came roughly and raggedly. Heat filled her, making her squirm.

"I love the way you respond to me," he said with a voice full of wonder. He lifted and tested the weight of her breast before his hand moved lower across her stomach.

"Taylor, please," she said, rolling her hips towards him.

"Please. I like the sound of that word coming from you."

"Don't tease." She pushed his shoulders to the bed and straddled him.

"Imagine you wanting to be in charge." His chuckle rumbled low in his chest but held a note of excitement. "This time I think I'll enjoy it."

She came up on her knees then bent to give him a wet, hot kiss, letting her breasts graze his chest. The moan of a man teetering at the edge of his limit filled the air. She smiled against his lips and he took control of the kiss.

His tongue circled her mouth, asking and demanding and tempting. One of his hands fondled a breast while the index finger of the other hand found her center. His finger slowly entered her, retreated and went deeper the next time. She gasped, absorbed the pleasure and begged for more.

Shifting, Taylor rolled Shelby over onto her back and followed her. She boldly met his gaze and offered herself.

The woman in his arms was killing him. She kept such a tight rein on her world yet she was so sweetly, and without reservations, offering her beautiful body to him. What had he done to deserve his dreams coming true? He reached for his wallet on the bedside table, found the small packet and covered himself.

Returning his focus to Shelby, he watched her expressive dove-gray eyes go from yearning anticipation to contemplation to exhilaration as he sheathed himself within her heat. Her eyes slowly closed. She whispered his name and he smiled. He thrust deeper and she met him with a lift of her hips in acceptance. His world rocked, never to be the same again.

Kissing her tenderly while giving her the pleasure she craved, he found his own but at the same time lost his heart.

Later Taylor lay back, pulling the warm sleeping Shelby more snugly against him. He didn't regret making love with Shelby. How could he? It was the closest to heaven he'd ever been.

Yet what had he done? This wasn't a quick fling. This was the real thing. The thing he'd thought he'd never have, could never have. He still couldn't.

Shelby had said she and her husband had moved to Benton with the idea of having a family. Could he offer her the same? What kind of father would he be? He had no experience in that area. Worse, he'd had no example to follow. Was it possible for him to move beyond how he'd been raised? Surely he could do a better job of parenting than his father? Anyone could.

But what he was confident of was that Shelby would accept no half-measures. She desired a family—had told him that was her dream—and would settle for nothing less than a lifetime.

It wasn't yet light outside when Shelby woke to an arm heavy across her waist and a hand cupping a breast. A shock-wave of contentment ran through her. Taylor didn't even have to be awake for her body to react to him being near. It had been a long time for her, and Jim had been her only one, but Taylor had loved her with such tenderness and so thoroughly she'd never felt a moment of apprehension. Her pleasure had seemed to be his only concern. She shifted slightly and the hand pulled her tighter against the solid wall of maleness behind her.

"Don't," his husky voice whispered against her ear, before his mouth lightly tugged at her earlobe. "Too nice here."

She rolled over and kissed him. "I'm not going anywhere. Just getting more comfortable."

The reality of the hurt she'd opened herself up to washed over her. She may not be going anywhere, but he'd be leaving soon. And it might kill her when he did. He'd only been there a short while but he'd managed to ingratiate himself so undeniably into her life, her heart that she might not recover from the loss.

"What's wrong?" Taylor asked, propping his head on a hand and looking down at her.

Had she made a movement or sound betraying her distress or was he so cognizant of her emotions that he sensed what she was feeling? If the latter was the case, she'd have to work hard to keep her thoughts from being transparent. She had to distract him. Was there more to his story than he'd told her?

"I was just wondering…" she trailed her hand across his chest and kissed a spot over his heart "…if you'd tell me about yesterday. What happened?"

Taylor flopped backwards on the bed and looked up at

the ceiling. When she moved closer, he put an arm loosely around her. She sighed. He wasn't pushing her away.

"Do you really want to hear all the ugly details?"

She pulled the sheet up over them and then placed her head on his chest. His heartbeat was steady beneath her ear but the tension in his body said there was nothing calm about him.

"Where did you go?" she whispered.

"Just around."

"You drove around for eight hours."

"Yeah."

Shelby barely heard the word it was said so softly. She sat up, bringing a corner of the sheet up with her, covering herself. Her movement left much of Taylor exposed to her view. Heaven help her, he was gorgeous. As much as she enjoyed his body, she still needed to understand him. She wanted to help him through whatever was hurting him. At least she could give him that before he left.

"Please tell me why."

He took a deep breath. His body shuddered as he released it. "I've already told you more than I've ever told anyone else."

"We all have something negative in our past. Why is it a secret?"

"Not a secret, just not something I enjoy talking about."

"I would like to understand."

"It wasn't the best time in my life."

She placed a hand on his forearm in encouragement. The muscles under her hand jumped.

"I was the youngest of the town drunk's three sons. My mother worked herself into an early grave cleaning houses and whatever else she could find to do to keep clothes on our backs and food on the table. She died when I was sixteen."

"I'm so sorry, Taylor." As if he hadn't heard her, he continued. His eyes seemed to focus on the gloomy night outside.

As if lost in his memories, his voice became a monotone. "The kids at school were particularly cruel. The teachers tried to help. But there was nothing they could really do. I was too angry. If I'd been a jock it might have been better but I stayed in so much trouble I never qualified for any school team. The only thing I had going for me was that school was easy for me."

She reached out to him, began to say something.

He pushed her hand away. "No. I don't need your sympathy. I've moved on. I have a completely different life now."

It stung that he didn't want her comfort. What he didn't see was that he hadn't really moved on. His past still controlled him. He still saw himself as that ne'er-do-well child he'd been told he would be.

"Are your father and brothers still living?"

"I heard that my father died while I was in college. I've not talked to my brothers in years. When I left for college they were on their way to becoming my father. I got my chance to get out of town and I've not been back." Bitterness surrounded each of his words.

"So what gave you your chance to leave?"

Couldn't he see that it was cathartic for him to be letting go after years of holding the disappointment and hurt inside? Glad she could be there for him, she waited.

"An old man telling me to use my brains instead of my fists made the difference. I did. My high-school counselor noticed me, knew my background, saw my grades and helped me with scholarships to college."

He said the last statement with a finality that said she shouldn't ask any additional questions. Instead, she wrapped her arms around his waist, settled her head on his chest and hugged him close. She wanted to absorb his painful memories, make them fade.

Long seconds ticked by before Taylor returned her embrace. Gently he rolled her over and brought his lips down to hers, letting her warmth push the coldness of the past away.

CHAPTER SEVEN

TAYLOR lightly rubbed his cheek against Shelby's soft hair as she lay nestled against his shoulder. He watched as the pink of the new morning edged the top of the large oak tree in her neighbor's yard. Having Shelby in his arms and a beautiful sunrise was the perfect way to start any day.

He'd learned early to accept what life dished out. This time he recognized that making love with Shelby had been a mistake. A wondrous, soul-touching mistake. He couldn't return to a town like the one he'd grown up in. He'd worked too hard to get out. No matter how much he cared for Shelby or how much he was needed here as a doctor, neither were strong enough to entice him to call this place home. He wouldn't break his promise to himself.

Shelby deserved better than what he could give her. She needed someone beside her who shared the same hopes and dreams. Who knew how to be a husband. A father. He wasn't that person. In the long run he'd only make her unhappy. He didn't want to live his life always on guard. No, small-town life wasn't for him.

The woman of his dreams shifted against him and leaned her head back. His gaze met her misty gray one. She blinked twice.

"Hi," she whispered, with a sweet smile on her lips.

"Hey, there." Unable to resist those lips, he kissed her

lightly. The knowledge that this sexy, exciting and generous woman had given herself so totally to him made his heart swell with pleasure yet at the same time caused it to ache. He couldn't keep her.

"Shelby, we need to talk."

She tensed in his arms then pulled away, rolling to the side of the bed. The sheet dropped away, leaving an enticing view of her back and the curve of her well-rounded behind. The desire to run his hand along those smooth curves made his fingers flex against the sheet.

"I'm not interested in an uncomfortable morning-after discussion."

He grabbed her wrist, stopping her from standing. She didn't turn to him. "Shelby, I wish you'd look at me."

She half turned but didn't meet his eyes.

"You know nothing can come of this. I can't stay in Benton," he said quietly. "Just as I know you can't leave."

"That's a cop-out but I'm a big girl. I understand. I need to get ready to go to the clinic now." She stood and started dressing.

The tempting view of her naked body made him want to pull her back against him and kiss her until she forgot about the last few minutes. But her jerky movements as she pulled on her sweatshirt said she wouldn't tolerate being touched.

He'd hurt her. She had a right to be hurt. And it had been the last thing in the world he'd wanted to do.

When he'd needed someone, she'd been there. She'd given herself. Even cried for him. What had he done? Used her.

Slipping out of bed, he started gathering his clothes. The silence in the room hung as heavy as humidity in the hot southern summer. He wanted to go to her, reassure her, tell her all she wanted to hear, but he couldn't lie.

Disgust brought a sour taste in his mouth. He'd fulfilled

the prophecy of his youth. He'd amounted to nothing when it mattered to someone he cared about.

"I'll see you at the clinic," she said as she closed the door on her way out.

She sounded too calm. As if she'd already relegated him to something in the past with no intention of ever giving him another thought. The urge to punch something flared in him.

Buster whimpered at his feet. He picked the dog up and scratched his belly. He'd finish out his time at the clinic. That he had no choice about but he'd try to keep his relationship with Shelby strictly professional. For both their sakes.

The tricky part was he couldn't think of anything more difficult to accomplish.

Shelby had thought her days long and stressful without help at work but they'd been nothing compared to what this morning brought. The tension between her and Taylor made working together almost intolerable.

The situation must be bad if Carly, a teen totally focused on her own world, asked what was going on. Shelby shrugged. "Nothing." A totally ineffectual lie.

Carly's nose wrinkled in disbelief. "Right."

"We need to get back to work."

"It had started to be fun to work here. You smiled and laughed," Carly mumbled as she logged into the computer. "Now even Dr. Stiles is all about work. You two need to try some of that adult advice you're always handing out."

The door opened with a jingle of a bell.

"That's enough, Carly," Shelby said repressively.

Mrs. Ferguson waddled towards them.

"Hello, what can we do for you today?" Shelby asked as she mustered a smile she'd didn't feel.

"I'm just stopping by to see that Dr. Stiles. He insisted I come by to have my blood pressure checked again."

"Do you want me to do it or would you rather see Dr. Stiles."

"I guess I might as well see him, since he's the one that told me to come in," Mrs. Ferguson said gruffly.

It seemed Shelby wasn't the only one who was starting to take a liking to Taylor.

"Carly, please let Dr. Stiles know that Mrs. Ferguson is here," Shelby said.

The girl didn't try to hide her surprise. Shelby had instructed her after the first day when she'd fallen all over herself to help Taylor that her job was to stay behind the deck.

The phone rang and Carly hesitated, looking at Shelby questioningly. "You get the phone. I'll find Dr. Stiles."

In reality, Shelby didn't have to hunt for Taylor. She knew where he was. She'd been aware of his movements all day. Her body hummed with the thought of him. She'd never given herself so totally to a man.

He'd taken what she'd offered but he'd freely given in return.

She wasn't angry with him, disappointed if anything but even that wasn't rational. He'd done nothing to deserve either of those responses. Did she really think that one night of passion would make him change his mind? She'd been the one who'd gone to his apartment. If she was angry with someone it should be herself. She'd created her own heartache.

The door to what was now their shared office stood open. Taylor had managed to carve out an area on the desk for his own pens and personal items. It amazed her that she'd so easily permitted him space. This room was her sanctuary, the door she closed on the world. Not even Carly came into this room freely. Stepping into the doorway, she found Taylor sitting behind the desk, staring off into space. Was he thinking about their discussion this morning or their lovemaking during the night?

"Taylor, Mrs. Ferguson is here." It didn't even bother her that the older woman was now more his patient than hers.

His gaze met hers. "Shelby—"

"Mrs. Ferguson is waiting." She didn't trust herself to say more when all she wanted to do was to walk into his arms and beg him to change his mind.

Shelby stepped into the lab. A minute later her body sent out a signal that Taylor stood nearby. Her hands shook as she placed the slide under the microscope.

"You can dodge me all you want," he said so softly he had to be standing right behind her, "but we will talk."

Twenty minutes after he left, she was preparing to call her next patient as Mrs. Ferguson came up the hall escorted by Taylor. The older woman stopped beside Shelby and placed a hand on her arm. "Honey, my kids have decided to give me a birthday tea this Saturday afternoon. I'd like you two to come." Mrs. Ferguson looked first at her and then at him.

Shelby glanced at Taylor. "I don't know if Dr. Stiles can make it. His work will be done here but I'll be there."

The words sounded catty even to her ears. She regretted them the second they were out.

Taylor's eyes narrowed, his brow wrinkled.

"Oh, are you leaving so soon?" Mrs. Ferguson's focus shifted to Taylor, oblivious to the stiffness between him and Shelby. "I had so hoped that you might decide to stay with us. I know Dr. Wayne has appreciated your help at the clinic. You'll be missed."

A flicker of shock entered his brown eyes and turned to a sparkle of pleasure. His face eased. He smiled at Shelby but spoke to Mrs. Ferguson, "I think I can hang around long enough to enjoy your birthday party."

"Good. It's being held in the church fellowship hall. Dr. Wayne can show you where to go. Now I must be going."

"I'll see you out." Taylor said, cupping the woman's elbow.

"I do love the personal touch I receive from my doctor," Mrs. Ferguson twittered.

Me, too.

Taylor finished his last charting chore and pushed the chair back from the desk. He and Shelby had swapped roles. Instead of her being the one to stay late, it was him.

As soon as it had been time to close the door for the day, she'd announced she was leaving. He was glad she was finely taking some time for herself, yet he knew it was also to put some space between them. He'd asked her to see to Buster. At least that had put a slight smile on her face. Taylor had gone home during lunch to check on the dog, but he needed to be let out to play that evening.

Refusing to spend another day like the one he had today, he had to clear the air between him and Shelby. He'd spent far too much time thinking about her and not enough focusing on his patients. He was grateful there hadn't been an emergency.

Even if he managed to get the stubborn, willful woman to listen to reason, could he keep his hands off her? Right now his body craved her touch, her warmth.

There were no lights on in or around her house when Taylor turned into the drive. Shelby's beat-up truck parked in the drive told him she was probably home. Maybe she'd gone to bed early? Was she out on a date? That latter question made his stomach clench. He didn't want Shelby seeing anyone, but he had no right to demand she didn't.

He walked toward his apartment and paused when he saw the dark form of Shelby sitting a couple of steps up on the stairs.

"Hi," she said so softly he almost missed hearing it above the noise from the night creatures talking to each other. "I've been waiting for you."

His heart fluttered. How he wanted her, wanted things to be right between them again.

"I need to apologize," she said in a steady, firm tone.

This wasn't what he'd been hoping for. By her tone of voice she wouldn't be sharing his bed tonight. How like her to meet the problem head on, though he didn't appreciate being considered an issue she had to solve. Being her knight in shining armor was more to his liking.

When he sat on the step below hers, she shifted her feet to one side to give him room. The riser was so short that one of her knees rested against his shoulder.

Having her touch, even in the slightest of ways, gave him a feeling of belonging. Something he'd not realized he missed so profoundly until then. "You don't owe me an apology. We're two intelligent, consenting adults who spent the night together," he said. The untruth of the description screamed *You are so wrong* in his head seconds after he'd uttered it. It may have been the truth with other women in his life but not Shelby.

She wasn't just any woman. Shelby was *the* woman. The woman he could never make happy.

Her knee tensed against his shoulder. He'd hurt her—again.

"I understand. I'd just like to say I'm sorry for my very unprofessional remark in front of Mrs. Ferguson about you not staying for the party. It was uncalled for."

"Apology accepted."

She stood. "Well, I do appreciate all the help you've given me while you've been here."

"You're welcome." Their relationship had taken three giant steps backwards. Now they were talking to each other like they had when he'd first arrived. He didn't like this new stalemate. Could they ever recover the easiness they'd once known?

"Shelby—"

She walked down the stairs to the pavement, turned and looked back at him. "I'm tired and we both have a full day tomorrow. I've got Buster. Goodnight, Taylor."

He couldn't see her very well in the night shadows but the wistful tone in her voice came through loud and clear. A yearning to reach out and pull her back into his arms gnawed at him, but he couldn't let himself do it. He knew what hurt and rejection and wishing life to be different could do to a person. Adding to Shelby's pain wasn't something he was willing do.

Shelby made it just inside the kitchen door before tears slid down her cheeks. Until she'd said Taylor's name she'd believed she'd held herself together pretty well. The shake in the last syllable had given her away.

She'd tried to play the adult game of sex with no strings. She'd lost. She'd fallen and fallen hard for a man who refused to be a part of the town she'd made a pledge to. One she couldn't break. She and Jim had made a commitment to Benton to provide medical care. She'd promised Jim the night he'd died that she'd uphold their pledge, keep their dream alive. If she broke that vow, she'd be dishonoring Jim's memory and everything she had spent the last few years working towards. To have Taylor in her life, he had to embrace the town of Benton too, and all it meant to her. In that tug of war, she wouldn't win. Taylor's childhood fears were stronger than his desire for her.

Heaving a sigh, she found her way to her bedroom and undressed without turning on the light. The full moon that had risen over the trees shone brightly enough that she didn't need to switch on a lamp.

She couldn't resist the urge to look out the window at the apartment. There was no light on but she knew with all her being that Taylor stood there, looking down at her. A tingle ran though her, leaving a path of longing deep and sharp. If there was a silver lining in their whole mixed-up relationship it was the knowledge that he seemed as out of sorts as she.

With the faintest of movement the connection was severed. Taylor was going to bed without her.

Some time later, a banging at her door brought her out of her fitful sleep.

"Doc Wayne! Shelby!" a frantic voice yelled.

"I'm coming," she called.

Flipping on the lamp, she went to the closet and found her robe. Jerking it on and tying the belt, she made her way to the front door.

The beating and shouting continued. "I'm here. Hold on a minute," she called, turning on the porch light and opening the door.

"Sam, what's the problem? Why didn't you call me instead of waking the whole neighborhood?"

"The station tried but got no answer. They sent me."

She been so tied in knots after talking to Taylor that she'd left her phone on the kitchen table instead of taking it to the bedroom.

"What's going on here, Deputy?" Taylor asked from behind Shelby. She turned, her nose making contact with his bare chest. She glanced downwards to find him dressed in nothing but red plaid boxers. She groaned.

"We didn't mean to wake you. I can handle this," she hissed.

"I wasn't asleep." Taylor's deadpan tone said he was having as rough a night as she.

He must have seen the patrol car drive up, realized there was an emergency and come in through the back door. No matter why he was there, his appearance in her house to Sam and soon to the entire town it would look like they'd been sleeping together. She couldn't worry about that now.

Turning back to Sam, she saw the slight smirk on his face that confirmed her fears. "What's happened?" she asked the deputy in her most professional voice.

"There's been an accident on the Hartman farm. Something to do with a tractor. You're needed out there."

"I'll get dressed and get my bag. The ambulance service has been notified?"

"Yeah, but they're out on another run. They'll meet us there as soon as they can."

When she turned around Taylor was gone. She wasted no time wondering where he was off to. Instead she concentrated on the emergency ahead. She dressed in record speed in T-shirt, jeans, and tennis shoes, pulling a light jacket off a peg by the door. She also snatched up the emergency bag she kept stocked for these types of occasions. Reaching her truck, she found Taylor waiting with his own medical bag in hand. He took her larger bag and placed it in the back before then taking to the passenger seat.

As she climbed behind the wheel she said, "You don't have to come."

"Do you really think I'd let you go alone?" He sounded disappointed that she might think he would not do his duty. "We're a team," he said firmly.

What he'd left unsaid was "until the end of the week."

A little later Taylor stepped out of the truck onto the well-worn gravel of the drive circling in front of the farmhouse. The lights around the house blazed and a couple of large late-model trucks were parked off to the side. A police patrol car sat in front of the main door.

A middle-aged woman and a girl of about fourteen hurried down the steps trailed by a large dog. Sam, the deputy, followed them and came to stand beside Shelby.

"Dr. Wayne," the woman said, panic filling her voice, "I'm so glad to see you. Bob's leg is trapped."

"Trapped by what?" Taylor asked.

"Mrs. Hartman, this is Dr. Stiles. He's a trauma doctor from Nashville here helping me."

The woman nodded curtly and quickly turned her attention back to Shelby. "The tractor."

Shelby looked toward a large structure behind the house that had to be the barn. "Where is he?"

Mrs. Hartman pointed off into the distance. "Down in the bottoms near the river. He was trying to get in some last-minute bush hogging before the rain set in." Her words rushed together as she spoke. "He didn't come in at dark. I sent our son, John, to look for him. He found the tractor jackknifed. His dad is pinned in. John's down there with him right now. That private ambulance service is off on another run. It'll be awhile before they get here, and even then I'm not sure they can handle this. That's why I called you."

Sirens sounded in the distance. Shelby glanced at Sam. "Volunteer fire department," the deputy said. She dipped her chin in understanding.

"We need to prepare for shock, maybe puncture wounds, a break at the least," Taylor told her.

She nodded in agreement. "Mrs. Hartman, we're going to need blankets and towels. Is there someone who can show us where to go while you gather them?"

"My girl, Jenny, will take you."

"I'll wait for the fire department," Sam said.

The girl ran to a four-wheel flatbed vehicle with two seats. Taylor sprinted to the truck to retrieve the medical bags and met Shelby and the girl. "I'll sit on the back," he called. Shelby's look questioned his choice but for once she didn't argue. He climbed on and scooted on his bottom along the metal platform until his back was against the seats.

Jenny had the vehicle moving by the time he and Shelby were settled. They traveled through an open gate and into the darkness. As they left the yard behind the ride became bumpier. Due to the rough terrain, Taylor had a hard time telling where they were going or what the land looked like, with the beam of the headlights darting up and down. He had to hang onto the low metal bar to keep from sliding or falling off the flatbed.

"How far?" Shelby asked.

"Ten minutes," the girl said, before shifting into a higher gear and throwing them all sideways as one wheel hit a bump. Behind the two women, Taylor grabbed again for the metal bar. They traveled into the night as the all-terrain continued its slow, steady pace over the rough terrain.

With no real idea about what to expect, he could tell from Shelby's look earlier this wasn't going to be an easy case. The fact that they'd be working in the pitch dark wouldn't help.

Shelby glanced at him. Even in almost non-existent light, he could see her apprehension. He squeezed her shoulder gently. Was she worried she couldn't handle the situation? Or the blood?

Being a small-town kid, he had no experience with farms or farm equipment. His nerves were strained at the thought of what they might encounter.

They rode in silence for a while, following a track through the field and into a stand of trees. While fording a creek, they listed heavily to one side and then to the other as they rode over large rocks. He braced himself with both hands on either side of the vehicle to manage the sway. Using a leg, he was able to stop the med bags from sliding off.

"What kind of vehicle is this?" he asked the girl in a voice loud enough to be heard over the motor beneath him.

"An army mule."

"Mule?"

"It's some kind of World War Two thing."

Minutes later they came out of the woods and crossed a large field, approaching the scene of the accident. The only light present came from a four-wheeler's headlights pointed in the direction of the tractor.

From what he could tell, the tractor was an antique. It had a long body, with dual wheels close together in the front and large, head-high ones at the rear. Didn't these people own anything from the last decade?

One of the large wheels rested in a wide, three-foot ditch while the front wheels hung in the air. Behind it at a right angle was the bush hog pressed against the other back wheel. Sandwiched between the two pieces of dangerous equipment was Mr. Hartman.

"We're going to need to get more light down here," Taylor said.

"Neighbors are on their way with more four-wheelers." Even as Jenny said the words Taylor heard the whine of the vehicles. The girl pulled to a stop and he jumped off the mule, grabbing both bags. He paused long enough to see that Shelby had climbed down safely.

"Jenny, you go back and get those blankets and towels. Tell your mother to call the neighbors and to get a couple of tractors out here. Hurry back."

The girl hesitated.

"Your daddy's going to be fine," Shelby said, standing on tiptoe to reach over and touch the girl's shoulder across the passenger seat. "You can help him best by helping us."

How like Shelby to not only take care of the patient but the family as well. In the big emergency room where he worked, he often never saw the family. The social worker did all the consoling.

"Shouldn't this be the EMTs' job?" Taylor asked as he and Shelby made their way over to the accident.

"Yeah, it would be if we had EMTs. We have a volunteer fire department and a private ambulance service. Nothing more. I'm the EMT on the rare cases like this."

A boy of about eighteen stood and came towards them from where he'd been sitting next to the injured man.

"John, I'm Dr. Wayne and this is Dr. Stiles. We're here to help your dad. We're going to get your father taken care of." At her reassuring words, the boy's shoulders relaxed.

He led them to where Taylor could see the man half lying, half sitting on the top of the bush hog, his body twisted in an unnatural position. Shelby fell to her knees beside the farmer. Taylor set the bags down and sat on one heel. Quickly, Shelby found a flashlight in the emergency bag.

"Mr. Hartman, you've managed to get yourself into quite a pickle this time." Shelby's bright tone played down the desperate situation. The man could lose his leg, possibly his life. "This is Dr. Stiles," she continued.

"Glad to see you, Doc," the man said weakly.

"Sorry it's under these circumstances." Taylor moved in close to Shelby as she shone the flashlight indirectly over Mr. Hartman's face. The man was already deathly pale. Pain lines circled his mouth.

"We're going to get you out of here as soon as we can. More help is on the way. While Dr. Stiles and I have a good look and listen to you, why don't you tell us what happened? Start with how long you've been here."

Taking the cue, Taylor reached for his own small bag, pulled out his stethoscope and began to listen to the farmer's heartbeat. It sounded thin but steady. His breathing sounds were what really concerned Taylor. They were rapid and shallow. Had he broken some ribs as he'd gone down? While Taylor worked, Shelby pulled out a small penlight to check the man's eyes. She then took his blood pressure.

"Been here since sunset." He paused, taking a breath.

"Got too close to the ditch. Heard a noise. Sheer pin rattled loose. Tried to put spare in. Knew better. Stepped between the tractor and bush hog..." He paused, exhausted.

"Dad said that the ground below the right back tire gave away," John offered. "The tractor slid into the ditch, jack-knifing the bushhog. He tried to jump backwards but didn't get his leg out in time."

"Well, that's quite a story, Mr. Hartman. You'll have something to tell your grandchildren one day," Taylor said, looping his stethoscope around his neck. "Where do you hurt?"

"I can't feel my foot."

"Can you wiggle your toes?"

The man shook his head.

Shelby glanced at Taylor. His face mirrored her concern. Did they share the same worry that the blood supply might be cut off to the lower part of Mr. Hartman's leg or, just as troublesome, that there a possibility he could be bleeding to death?

"John, sit with your father. I'd like to talk to Dr. Wayne," Taylor called. The boy came closer. "We'll be right over here if you need us."

Taylor quietly pulled Shelby out of their hearing. "I'm anxious about him bleeding out without us realizing it because we won't be able to see it. I'm going to try to get a look at his leg." Taylor pulled his stethoscope off.

"How're you going to do that?" Shelby asked, her voice raised an octave.

"I'll lie on the ground and stick my hand under the bush-hog and feel for his leg. If I can't do that then I'll feel on the ground for blood."

"Okay. I'll check his leg from above."

Taylor stuffed his stethoscope into his bag. Going down on his belly, he reached beneath the bush hog, searching for the man's leg. His fingertips brushed cloth that was wet and sticky. Stretching out as far as he could, he felt up and down the leg. It was bleeding but not as much as Taylor had feared.

Scooting back, he got to his feet. Shelby came to stand close beside him. "He's bleeding but not badly, considering," he said for Shelby's ears only. "The trick is to get pressure applied as soon as we can move the bush hog to prevent hemorrhage. The secondary concern is that he may lose the leg from loss of blood flow to the feet. When the ambulance does arrive, it isn't going to make it back here. We're going to have to figure out how to take him out ourselves." He looked around. "Where's that help?"

"They should be here soon." As she said the words an army of headlights came out of the woods and headed across the field.

"Thank God," Taylor whispered under his breath.

As two tractors that were part of the fire department, along with Mrs. Hartman and Jenny on the mule and several neighbors on their four-wheelers, arrived, Shelby returned to monitoring Mr. Hartman's vitals.

Taylor morphed into trauma doctor mode and began giving orders. He asked Sam to oversee the positioning of three of the four-wheelers on the other side of the ditch so that their headlights focused on the tractor and bush hog. Noise from all the engines was almost deafening in such a small area but Taylor's voice could still be heard over the din.

"John, I need you to swing your four-wheeler around to the right." The boy went running to follow Taylor's order.

A natural leader, Taylor had no trouble getting the people to respond as if they'd known and trusted him for ever.

Jenny and Mrs. Hartman appeared inside the circle of light and brought Shelby the blankets and towels. While she worked to reassure Mrs. Hartman that her husband would be fine, Taylor continued directing four-wheelers. He told two of the newly arrived drivers that he wanted them on that side of the ditch so that light would be coming from as many different angles as possible.

Shelby felt a sense of pride as she listened to Taylor organize the operation. His abilities to manage people and keep a level head in a crisis were outstanding. The man had special skills that would fit well into the community. Too bad he wasn't interested.

Rolling up a towel, she placed it under Mr. Hartman's head then covered him with a couple of blankets, tucking them in securely to hold the warmth in and slow down shock. She hoped they weren't too late to prevent it. If they couldn't get him out soon, he might die of it. He needed to be on his way to a hospital.

As the men on the tractors wrapped chains around the wrecked vehicle and attached another chain to the bush hog, Taylor instructed them on how to pull in order to minimize the damage to Mr. Hartman's leg.

Discussion broke out about the best way to perform the maneuver and Taylor interrupted the conversation, making it clear what had to be done and how otherwise Mr. Hartman could be injured further. Once again, Shelby was grateful to Taylor. Would the tough farmers have given her as much respect as they were now giving Taylor? With everything set as Taylor had ordered, and the driver of each tractor understanding his duty, Taylor approached her.

"My plan is for us to move the tractor and bush hog enough for us to assess again before we pull Mr. Hartman out. Do you agree?"

"I agree. Before the pressure is completely released we need to know how to handle it and where the bleeding is coming from. My only concern is if anything shifts when we examine him again, we might do him more harm."

"I've thought of that but I don't think we have a choice."

Shelby nodded her agreement.

She went back to Mr. Hartman. "We're getting ready to pull you out. It shouldn't be too much longer now."

The injured man did little more than grunt.

"Okay, everybody, stand back." Taylor shouted to be heard over the roar of the tractors. Shelby moved away but not so far that she couldn't be back to the farmer's side lightning fast.

"Slowly," Taylor yelled. At tortoise speed, the tractors pulled in opposite directions. The wheel of the tractor pinning Mr. Hartman shifted. Shelby sucked in a quick breath, held it. Was Taylor's strategy going to cause more damage? Seconds later the bush hog moved slightly.

Mr. Hartman let out a moan of pain. Shelby rushed to him, going down on her knees. "Hold your positions, guys," Taylor shouted to the tractor drivers, then joined her.

"He's passed out," Shelby said.

"It'll probably be better for him this way. It's going to be painful when we lift him," Taylor said, and Shelby couldn't disagree.

"I'm going into the ditch and underneath to see what we've got before we pull him out."

"That's too dangerous." She grabbed his forearm. "Is it really necessary?"

"I think it is. I'll be fine. The tractors aren't going anywhere. Hand me the flashlight." She did as she was told. Taylor moved to leave and she grabbed his hand. "Please be careful. I don't need you hurt too."

He squeezed her hand, then went to the edge of the ditch and sat on his butt before sliding down on it and disappearing into the gully.

"Get out of the light!" Taylor demanded from below.

She looked across the ditch to see one of the teenagers walking over to another four-wheeler.

"Hey," she hollered. "You're in the light."

The boy quickly stepped out of the way.

"That's better." Taylor's voice was muffled, telling her that he was moving farther under the tractor.

Shelby held her breath. As her imagination took hold she pictured the chains breaking, the tractor falling, Taylor being pinned underneath.

With enormous relief she watched Taylor climb out of the ditch. He came to stand beside her and offer his hand. She took it and he helped her stand.

Mrs. Hartman rushed by them to take Shelby's place beside her husband.

"We need to talk a sec." He led her out of the ring of light, where the two of them could speak without being overheard. "He has a puncture wound high on the left thigh. A smaller one on the right. We're going to need to pull him out quickly and apply pressure immediately.

"I know how you feel about blood and I hate it that there's no other way, but you're going to need to see to the wounds and stop the bleeding."

"I'll do what has to be done."

He ran a fingertip lightly down her cheek. "That's my girl. I never doubted it."

CHAPTER EIGHT

SHELBY searched through the emergency bag until she found plastic gloves. Next she pulled out the containers of four-by-four gauze bandages and broke the paper seals. With them stacked firmly in her hand, she nodded to Taylor that she was ready. Taking a cleansing breath, she prepared herself, refusing to let him or her patient down.

Taylor reassured her with a smile then motioned the largest-looking guy over and said, "I'm going to need your help lifting Mr. Hartman. When the tractors release him, on my mark—pull. You understand?"

The man nodded and Taylor looked directly at her.

"I'm ready." Shelby stood as close to the machinery as she dared, out of Taylor's and the man's way, and waited.

Taylor put his hand in the air, waved and the tractors moved in unison and in opposite directions. He placed his hands under Mr. Hartman's armpit and low on his back, showing the large man how he wanted him to pull Mr. Hartman out. When the man matched Taylor's hands, he shouted "Pull!" Seconds later the farmer was out and Shelby was kneeling beside him, applying pressure to the bleeding wound. She ignored the roll of her stomach. She must do whatever it took to save Mr. Hartman's life. Her and Taylor's patient.

Taylor hollered, "Hold." The tractors halted as he and

his helper laid Mr. Hartman on the bush hog. They adjusted their position before moving the injured man to a blanket that Jenny and her mother had placed on the ground. Across from her, Taylor remained on one knee and applied a bandage to the smaller wound, securing it.

"You got that?" He waited until she looked up.

"I'm good." Until her patient was out of her care, she had to be.

"I'm going to check for other injuries then we'll pack the wound and then splint." With efficient movements he ran his hands down Mr. Hartman's legs and up again. "Mr. Hartman, can you hear me?"

The man's groan affirmed he'd regained consciousness.

"Can you feel your toes?"

The man gave them the smallest of nods. Relief rushed through her as she returned Taylor's smile. "Great. Let's get this leg splinted and get him to a hospital," Shelby said.

"Yes, ma'am," he said in a whoosh of released breath.

He grabbed her bag, located the splints and handed one to her. Carefully and quickly they wrapped the leg, making sure the four-by-fours were securely in place.

"Jenny," she called, "pull the mule up alongside your dad." To Taylor she said, "We need to get blankets laid out on the back of the mule. This is going to be a painful ride out for him."

Taylor followed her instruction unquestioningly. Just as she'd followed his earlier. They'd switched roles, each finding their niche. She'd never experienced this type of rapport with any other doctor, not even with her husband. She and Taylor seemed to know what the other was thinking. They worked together as a smooth and skilled team.

He directed Jenny to where she needed to be and then she and Taylor saw to the padding.

"We need to keep him as level as possible," Shelby said,

and turned to one of the volunteer firemen. "You brought a board, didn't you?" The lack of light made it difficult to see and she'd been too busy to search beforehand.

"Right here, Doc," one of the men called, pulling the wooden backboard towards her.

"Okay, guys, I need us to get on each side of Mr. Hartman and put our arms under him as far as you can. On three—lift."

As the men lifted, Shelby supported Mr. Hartman's head. She made a mental note to include a neck brace in her emergency bag. Once the injured man was on the mule, she and Taylor rolled towels and placed them along the man's legs and neck to stabilize them. Jenny gave them a couple of industrial straps and they used them to secure the backboard to the mule. Mrs. Hartman climbed into the passenger seat. "He's going to be fine, Mrs. Hartman."

"Okay, Jenny. Dr. Stiles and I are going to ride in back with your father. Go slowly and the fewer bumps the better." Before Shelby could finish the sentence, Taylor had lifted her up onto the mule. Their gazes met for a second. She found her seat then he went around to the other side and climbed on.

There was little space for them to sit and it wasn't going to be a comfortable ride, but it would be much worse for Mr. Hartman. As they bumped and rocked along, Taylor grabbed her arm when she threatened to fall off. A tingle went through her, then it was gone when he let go. After the third time he held her hand across the barely conscious man's chest. Mr. Hartman groaned as they went but never woke fully. She was grateful for Taylor's steadying support.

Taylor's hand was gritty and rough from the dirt caked to his fingers, but she didn't care. They were warm and reassuring around hers. His touch said he would take care of her. She liked that feeling.

The trip seemed never-ending. It was a relief to see the

house lights in the distance. When they finally made it to the drive, the ambulance was waiting. As soon as Jenny stopped the mule, Taylor hopped off and came around to her to assist her in getting down. She'd been in one position for so long her legs were stiff.

"Walk around a second to ease your legs and I'll see about getting Mr. Hartman unloaded."

Shelby followed his advice and was soon able to help with getting Mr. Hartman situated in the ambulance. Mrs. Hartman gushed her thanks then climbed into the passenger seat for the ride to Nashville.

Taylor had instructed the ambulance men to take Mr. Hartman to the hospital where he himself worked, saying he'd call ahead and let them know they were coming.

"I need a phone. I left mine at home. It probably wouldn't get any service out here anyway," he said to no one in particular.

"You can use ours in the house," Jenny offered.

As the sun was coming up after a long night, Shelby watched Taylor walk towards the house. Those wide shoulders of his were solid, sure, and strong enough to lean on.

Taylor had finished his call then cleaned up in the bathroom Jenny had indicated on the way to the phone. He was headed back outside when Shelby's laughter drew him down the hallway of the old, two-story house. He liked hearing that soft ripple of sound. She didn't make it enough. Those notes led him to a huge family-style kitchen.

Shelby stood amidst volunteer firemen, tractor drivers and the kids who had been on the four-wheelers. They were all laughing and talking loudly as they filled their plates with food.

A woman Taylor had seen only briefly earlier came up beside him. "I'm Bess, a friend of the Hartmans. Mrs. Hartman told us to take care of everyone. To give you her thanks for saving her husband's life. We've prepared breakfast, so help yourself."

The group stopped talking and waved him forward to envelop him inside. Taylor hesitated before stepping forward to stand beside Shelby.

A few patted him on the back while others told him how impressed they'd been with the job he'd done. Treating him as a hero, they insisted he go first. He filled his plate with eggs, bacon and the most delicious-smelling home-made biscuits. Being accepted into a community was an alien experience but wholly wonderful.

He took a seat down at the family-style table. Shelby smiled widely as she took a seat across from him. Her eyes sparkled as she chatted with those around her. He was glad to see no visible lasting effects from Mr. Hartman's trauma. The blood hadn't prevented her from doing what had to be done. Picking up his fork, he started on his meal. He was ravenous for nourishment and for Shelby.

Shelby watched from under half-raised lids as Mr. Abernathy, a particularly boisterous, middle-aged farmer, shook Taylor's hand vigorously and invited him to go hunting. She grinned. Taylor faltered a second, before replying, "Thank you, sir. I'd like that." Taylor looked at her as if perplexed by all the camaraderie.

Shelby chuckled. When the man walked away she said to Taylor, "I guess you'll be back to hunt in the fall." That little boy who had always stood on the outside had been accepted into the fold. She just hoped he realized it.

As they ate, Taylor was peppered by questions about himself from the men and teens sitting around the table. At first he showed little enthusiasm for answering their questions but with some encouragement he became part of the crowd, even entertaining them with anecdotes.

Taylor called the hospital after finishing his meal and reported to the group that Mr. Hartman was in surgery and doing as well as expected. Taylor received high fives all round, which he acknowledged with a grin on his face. He had a wonderful smile.

Her heart swelled with the goodness of life as she looked around the table. These people were neighbors and friends who cared about one another. They'd worked together the night before to help Mr. Hartman and now it was time to celebrate their success. Taylor was smiling broadly and he seemed much happier and more at ease with himself than he'd been when he'd first come to town. She enjoyed the opportunity to visit with everyone outside the clinic. It's a shame it took a tragedy for her to socialize more with her community. She was going to do better in the future.

Finally, knowing they'd stayed long enough, Shelby said to Taylor, "We need to go. We should've been at the clinic an hour ago."

Taylor gave her a dubious look but said his goodbyes. The others mumbled their own need to leave and followed them out. The sun had risen high enough that the area they'd traveled in the dark was clearly visible. Looking at it made her realize that she didn't want to repeat that adventure again any time soon.

When they reached the truck Taylor said he'd drive and she'd gladly agreed, climbing into the passenger seat. "You know the way?"

"I believe I can make it," he said, as he got behind the wheel.

"Isn't it a beautiful day? I love this country." She looked at the low mountains creating the farm valley and the green fields butting up against them.

"Yes, beautiful."

Taylor's low tone filled with wonderment made her glance at him. He was looking at her. Her gaze met his and held. *He thinks I'm beautiful.* A fuzzy, pleasurable sensation trickled through her. Taylor believing that made her believe it too.

He leaned toward her, itching to kiss her, then glanced out the window at the others mingling in the yard and sat up. "Come on, Dr. Wayne. You've done a good night's work and I need to get you home."

"The clinic—"

"First things first. We both should clean up."

She rested her head against the back of the seat and closed her eyes. "We had a pretty amazing night, didn't we?" she murmured. "I guess you're used to that type of thing but I don't see it often. Mr. Hartman was a trouper. I hope he recovers quickly. You were great, by the way."

Taylor smiled. Shelby had been on an adrenalin high and now she'd crashed. She snored softly beside him. When her head drooped, he reached over and guided it to his shoulder. A gentle sigh of acceptance blew warmly over his bare arm as she snuggled into him. Resentment for the gearshift filled him. It didn't allow him to put his arm around her. He'd never given much thought to the benefits of a bench seat in an automobile until he'd met Shelby. He wanted her soft, warm curves next to him as much as possible.

When he pulled into the drive, Shelby roused enough to know they were home. "How come I'm so out of it and you don't seem to be tired?" she asked in a sexy, sleepy voice that made him wish to hear it every morning.

"I keep these hours way more often than you do. My body's used to it."

"I need to get it together and get to the clinic." She shook her head lightly.

"You go on and get a bath. Have a good nap and I'll handle things at the clinic this morning."

"You know, Dr. Stiles, you're starting to make yourself

indispensable," Shelby said, climbing out of the truck and walking toward her back door.

He chuckled. "I'll take that as a compliment."

Taylor hustled to his apartment and changed clothes. He'd get a bath later. He arrived at the clinic to find Carly behind the desk, fending off patients unhappy because no one had been there to see them. He saw to the patients and told Carly to start calling to reschedule appointments already on the book for that afternoon. He also asked Carly to stay until after lunch in case anyone showed up and to ask them to come back the next day. After that she could post a sign on the door to call him in case of an emergency and take the afternoon off.

A few hours later, Taylor exhaled in pleasure as he stood under the hot flow of water from the showerhead. Done, he stepped out naked into the cool of the air-conditioned room and slid beneath the sheet on his bed. The wish that Shelby lay warm and compliant next to him followed him into welcome sleep.

The thud of the door being pushed too far and the stomping of bare feet across the wooden floor snatched him from his dream. Shelby, dressed in a long T-shirt, glaring at him from above brought him fully awake.

"Why didn't you wake me? I trusted you to see to the clinic. It's after two o'clock and no one is there!"

That was his Shelby. All fire and brimstone.

He reached for her, capturing her before she could step away. With a short whoosh she landed on top of him, squirming. The smell of sleep and wild flowers tickled his nose.

"Stop wiggling, Shelby."

"Then let me go!"

"No, because I want you to listen to me."

She struggled against him. His body reacted by going to full attention. Heaven help him, he had no control around her.

"I'll listen. Just let me go," she snarled, putting her hands on either side of his head and pushing upwards. She glowered down at him.

The arching of her back brought her pelvis into more intimate contact with his swelling masculinity. "I don't think you will. Anyway, I like you right where you are." He flexed his hips.

Her eyes widened as if they had registered what she did to him. She brought her chest down to his but remained stiff against him. The only indication of her desire was her fingers curling into his shoulders. He nuzzled her neck, his lips traveling upwards to find the sweet spot behind her ear. She exhaled and turned her head slightly, giving him better access. He smiled. He had her attention now. Slowly she melted against him, purring her pleasure. He wanted her desperately, and he would have her.

Taylor moved his mouth upwards to whisper in her ear, "Listen, my little she-cat, Carly and I changed the afternoon appointments only, and she stayed until noon. I told her to take the rest of the day off and put a sign on the door to call us if there's an emergency."

He flipped her quickly onto her back, bringing his hips against her with a purposely suggestive flex. "Can you tell how much I want you, my little she-cat?" His mouth found hers.

She met him kiss for searing, slick kiss. She held his lips to hers, opening for him. All the fight and fury of earlier had been turned into red-hot passion and promise. One of her hands came up to circle his neck.

Her other hand made bold strokes over his body, exploring every dip and crevice. When her small hand pushed the sheet away and brushed over his straining manhood, he almost shattered.

Taylor pulled her hand away and captured it below his

on his belly. "I'm thinking one of us has on far too many clothes."

"Mmm, and one of us has just the right amount." She placed a kiss on his shoulder and smiled as the low rumble of his chuckle vibrated beneath her.

"I believe in equality," he murmured, as his hand moved under her shirt, pushing it up and over her head. His hand found her breasts. He bestowed devotion on them that made her womb contract with escalating hunger. In short order, he saw to it that her underwear found the floor.

"Now this is fairer," he murmured as he rose over her.

Shelby waited with anticipation, acceptance and an aching desire to be his again. There was no clinic, no obligation to Benton, nothing but Taylor and how he made her feel. She pulled his lips to hers as he entered her. Once again she was his.

Later, Shelby woke to the sky turning dark blue in the east and her head supported on Taylor's firm, comfy chest. His hands were clasped possessively around her waist. She'd slept the afternoon away in Taylor's arms and she'd never felt more contented.

"Hey, there. I was starting to wonder if I needed to kiss sleeping beauty awake." Taylor's deep voice rumbled from just above her. "Not that I'd mind."

"I think that would be a rather nice way to be woken up." She lifted her face. He took her hint and his lips found hers.

A long pleasurable minute later he pulled his mouth from hers and said, "I'm hungry. How about we go out for a meal?"

"Like a date?"

He shifted onto his side and looked down at her. "Yeah, a date. The kind where I come to the front door."

She couldn't remember the last time she'd been on a date. Maybe she never had. She and her husband being childhood sweethearts had meant they had attended school and church functions together, gone to college and med school, but she couldn't remember Jim ever asking her out on a real date. They had just gone places together. She liked the idea of being thought special enough to be asked out by Taylor.

She wanted this date to be memorable. It would probably be their one and only. Despite the passionate hours they'd spent in bed, nothing had really changed. Their differences weren't about Benton. They went deeper than that. Taylor couldn't move beyond his uncertainties and memories and she couldn't leave her obligations, face her own fear of change. Taylor would go back to Nashville and she'd remain in Benton. She wanted to snatch as many happy moments she could before then. After Taylor left life would go on, but it would be sadder and lonelier.

"I don't know if the neighbors can stand you showing up at the front door again. The last time you were in your boxers."

He grinned. "This time I'll make sure to have all my clothes on."

"I rather like the red plaid number."

"Then I have to make sure to wear them again for you some time." He gave her a playful swat on the behind. "So, do you want to get a bite to eat with me or not?"

"Thank you, that sounds nice," she said primly and properly. He chuckled. Something he was doing more often these days. She'd become fond of hearing that nice, easy-rolling sound. He had a wonderful laugh, one he should use often. She'd commit it to memory and pull it out late at night. She put on a bright smile. "I'll go get ready."

He ran a hand over her bare hip. "We have a few more minutes before you need to do that."

"How did you know about this place?" Shelby asked Taylor as they were being seated at a restaurant table with a crisp white tablecloth.

"I called Mrs. Ferguson and asked her advice."

"I bet she wanted to know why you were asking."

He grinned. "She did. I told her I had a date and needed advice on somewhere special to go. She said that she thought you'd enjoy coming here."

"Once again there are no secrets in Benton." She picked up the menu.

"Did you think there would be?"

He sounded much more resigned to that idea than he'd been in the past. "I guess not. I've heard of this place but I've not had a chance to try it."

"That figures."

She pursed her lips and narrowed her eyes. Taylor reached across the table and took her hand. "I shouldn't have said that. I don't want us to fight. Let's just enjoy our meal."

After the waiter took their orders and quietly moved away, Shelby said, "I feel guilty about not going to the clinic today. That's two days in the same week. I've never done that before." She looked into his warm brown eyes. "I did enjoy my afternoon, though," she said quietly.

He gave her the smile of a man who knew he'd satisfied his woman. "Why, thank you, ma'am. I believe that's the third compliment you've ever given me. I'm honored." She longed for more afternoons like the one they'd just shared but knew there was little chance of that.

"I didn't realize a smooth-talking, fast-driving, handsome doctor from the big city needed to have his ego stroked regularly."

"I think that there's at least one more compliment in there somewhere. My, with four so close together, you really make me feel special."

"Like you don't have people telling you you're wonderful all the time. Mrs. Ferguson all but melts at your feet now."

His lids went to half-mast over his darkening eyes. "That's not the same as having you say it."

She shivered with the longing Taylor evoked in her, something only he could do. "Am I that bad?"

"Yeah, in some ways. It's been pretty hard to coerce a smile out of you at times."

She gave him a bright smile she didn't really feel. "Better?"

"Perfect." He leaned over and kissed her too slowly to be appropriate in a public place but she didn't push him away.

Their meal was outstanding and Taylor turned out to be a dream dinner companion. She wasn't surprised. Over the past couple of weeks she'd found fewer of his traits to criticize.

While they ate local catfish, she and Taylor discussed their likes and dislikes from movies to books to politics. Shelby was pleased to find that they often agreed even on their food.

The only divide between them was that he hated living in a small town, couldn't see beyond his childhood memories to appreciate the good qualities. And that gulf was Grand Canyon wide, because Benton was her haven—her place of safety and security after Jim's death. But Shelby shoved those thoughts aside. Just for this one night she wanted to enjoy being with him and not have to think of tomorrow.

They were leaving the restaurant as Roger and Mary Albright were coming in. Shelby stopped to say hello. Taylor's hand rested possessively on her waist. When she tried to step away, he pulled her more securely against him, making it clear that they were out for more than a friendly meal.

"Well, hi, Shelby," Mary simpered as her gaze fell on Taylor. "And you must be the Dr. Stiles that we've been hearing so much about."

"Taylor Stiles," he said as he nodded to Mary and shook Roger's hand. "Nice to meet you both."

"We've heard all about what happened last night from Mildred Miller. She says you were heaven sent." Mary's focus remained on Taylor.

"I don't know about that." Taylor's lips curved into a small smile. He glanced at Shelby.

More like Uncle Gene sent.

"Dr. Wayne did an excellent job also." Taylor gave her waist a squeeze.

"Well, I'm sure the Hartmans were glad you were both available," Mary said smiling in too syrupy a way for Shelby's taste.

Was Mary making a veiled reference to the fact that Taylor had turned up wearing nothing but his boxers at her front door? Shelby had no doubt that Sam had told that story more than once.

As if Taylor knew where the conversation was headed, he said, "It was a pleasure to meet you both." He nudged Shelby in the direction of the door.

"That woman's the biggest busybody in town," Shelby said when they were outside on the way to the car.

"I suspected as much," he said in a flat voice. "I'm familiar with her kind."

"I guess everyone has spent their day getting caught up on us." She resigned herself to the fact that she and Taylor would be the hot topic in the town until something new and equally titillating replaced them.

"No doubt."

She glanced at him. "You okay with that?"

"That's just how small towns are. I've accepted that the good goes with the bad. The Hartman neighbors were wonderful to us last night. When I leave I can be assured that people are looking after you. That's a good thing."

They'd reached the car and Taylor held the door open for her, so with her heart in her mouth Shelby asked him directly. "Have you learned enough to consider staying for a while longer?"

"We've already covered this subject more than once." Taylor closed the door.

They remained quiet on the ride home. Apparently her optimism that their teamwork as doctors, their compatibility in bed and the fact they'd enjoyed a nice evening together hadn't changed his mind.

He pulled into the drive and turned the car engine off, leaving them in darkness. She really should have changed the bulb in the porch when it blew yesterday.She pulled on the door latch, preparing to get out. Taylor reached across and took her hand. "Wait." The shadows falling across his face accented the serious lines.

"I had a nice time. Thank you. But I'm tired and would really just like to go in." Shelby pulled her hand away, reaching for the handle again.

"Shelby, come with me to Nashville." His voice sounded as if this was a sudden thought that he'd just blurted out. "There are plenty of practices looking for another GP as partner. You're a great doctor. You'll have no trouble finding a position."

"I can't do that."

"Yes, you can. I'll help you find someone to take over the clinic. I'll even agree to work a Saturday a month for a while."

"No. This is my home. My community depends on me. I can't just pull up and leave."

He took both of her hands in his, encouraging her to face him. "Shelby, I realize and I think you do too, that what's between us is special. I don't want it to end. If you won't come with me then we'll just have to meet when we can. You come to Nashville or we can meet somewhere between there and here. I want to see you."

With a heavy heart she gave a shake of her head. "It would

never work. Long-distance relationships are hard under the best of conditions. Our schedules alone work against us. The clinic has to be my priority."

"Above everything, and apparently everybody." His words dripped sarcasm.

"What do you mean by that?"

"The clinic is your entire life. You need to stop hanging onto that dream you had as a child. You use this town, your job as a shield against the world, being hurt. Me. It's as if you are afraid to live your life. You have to let go, for your own good. You've convinced yourself that Benton needs you when it's really you that needs Benton. You're so caught up in safeguarding yourself from any pain or loss that you can't think of anything else. Can't let go. Certainly not for me."

"Are you about through?" She pulled her hands from his.

"Not yet. You can't take care of everybody else and not take care of yourself. Before long you'll have nothing left to give to anyone. What was your dream at one time? Yours alone? I bet you can't even remember."

"You seem to have all the answers for me but what about yours? You're running from your past. You hide it behind that well-respected profession you picked. All those fine clothes and the fancy car but you still carry those little-boy scars of not being good enough."

He shook his head.

"You don't believe me? Tell me, when was the last time you spoke to anyone from your home town? When's the last time you spoke to one of your brothers? Visited them?"

"That has nothing to do with us."

"It has everything to do with us. You've come to Benton and found a place where you can belong and you don't know what to do about it. Now you're scared that you might really form lasting relationships, invest in others' lives. That terrifies you because it would mean letting go of that security blanket of bitterness you carry around.

"You even refuse to see that the people of Benton like and accept you just as you are. They haven't asked you to prove yourself. What you can't see is that you're the one not accepting them." She waved trembling hands.

"Look what you have accomplished," she continued, her voice no longer gentle. "You're a doctor. And a darned good one. You've come to town and made friends. People like you. Here you could make a real difference. Here you've found that acceptance you've searched so hard for but you push it away."

Angry words hung heavily between them before Taylor asked in a tight voice, "Are you done? I see that you didn't have the same trouble with the psych rotation that you did with emergency."

Despite being unable to see his face well, Shelby had no doubt that his jaw was clenched piano-string tight. She'd hurt his feelings. Something she'd not intended to do. Still, she'd said things he'd needed to hear. She reached for him. "Taylor—"

"Look, I think we should just call it a night," he said, sliding out of the car.

She was already out and closing the door by the time he'd made it around to help her. If she didn't hurry inside she'd break down in front of him. Something she fought against doing.

He didn't touch her on the way to her door and they didn't speak. Taylor waited at the bottom of the steps, making no move to stop her from going in. She closed the door with a finality that made her heart break. She watched out the window through watery eyes as Taylor slowly climbed the stairs to the apartment.

How was she going to survive the next two days with him so near and them miles apart at the same time?

CHAPTER NINE

SHELBY arrived at the clinic earlier than usual on Saturday morning. She might as well be there as in her bed, willing her mind and body to stop thinking about Taylor. Her plan was to get some work done but that wasn't happening. She understood loss, had experienced it acutely, but Taylor's departure today was a deeper pain than she'd ever known.

Pushing the folders on the desk away, she crossed her arms, laid her head on them and closed her eyes. The stiffness in her shoulders remained no matter how often she'd rolled them, searching for relief. Taking a deep breath, she released it gradually, hoping the oxygen would clear her mind. Nothing could ease the despair that the next few hours would bring.

She'd feared this would happen. This horrible suffering was the reason she'd worked to keep Taylor uninvolved in her life. But it hadn't worked. He'd found a stronghold in her heart. She should've protected herself better. She would from now on.

Taking another deep breath and releasing it, she said, "Keep the connection friendly. Don't start to care. Do whatever it takes to survive."

Yesterday she'd given serious consideration to calling her uncle and bragging about Taylor, encouraging the judge to give him a day and a half's amnesty. That would at least allow the pain to be quick and sharp instead of the lingering ache she now carried. She hadn't called but only because she hadn't been able to stand the thought of Taylor leaving any sooner than scheduled. That made no sense. She'd become irrational. Her emotions were all over the place.

She and Taylor had made it through the workday Friday with little interaction. Because the clinic had been closed the afternoon before, they'd had little time to eat lunch, much less talk. Still her desire for him had simmered, threatening to burst into flame if he'd given her even the slightest touch.

She'd stayed in her office doing paperwork until her normal departure time. Hidden out, if she admitted the truth, until Taylor had left. He'd said a polite goodnight as she'd locked the door for the day. When she'd left, she'd gone to the grocery store for some much-needed staples and dog food, not trusting herself not to run into Taylor at home. She had decided to keep Buster. With a living and breathing thing around when she came home, it wasn't nearly as lonely.

To cheer herself up, she decided a haircut was in order. Plus, it would keep her away from the house until bedtime. Taylor had managed to stop her from going to her own home. Her haven. She'd become fragile where he was concerned. Her greatest fear was that she'd climb the stairs to the apartment and ask him to take her into his arms.

Enough of those thoughts. Sitting up, she pushed her clinic office chair back and went to the restroom. She studied her face in the mirror. Her eyes were bloodshot from crying and no rest. She couldn't show up looking like this to Mrs. Ferguson's tea. Turning on the cold water, she let it run until it was ice cold before splashing it in her face.

As she patted her cheeks dry, footsteps approached in the hall. She'd know those anywhere. Taylor. Pushing her hair back into place, she took a deep breath.

Opening the door, she found him propped against the wall,

his head down, shoulders slumped. His head rose. He gave her a direct look, studying her. That warmth that smoldered within her any time he came near began to bubble. The disks of darkness under both his eyes testified to the fact he'd not been sleeping any better than she had.

Her fingers spasmed with the need to pull him to her and make all that misery disappear. If she allowed that one show of weakness, she wouldn't be able to stop herself from begging him to stay. That she couldn't do. He had to want to be here or they'd never find happiness. Above all, she wished for him to be happy. Even if it wasn't with her.

"Shelby," he said longingly, as he straightened and stepped toward her.

She put a hand out, stopping his advance while being careful not to make physical contact. "Please don't." The need to feel sheltered in his embrace warred with her need to protect her heart from further pain.

"I'm sorry for those things I said," he said gently.

"I'm sorry for what I said too. How you live isn't my business."

He flinched but recovered quickly. "Can't we just start over?" his chocolatey eyes pleaded. "At least be friends."

"We are friends." With a firm resolve that Shelby would've never guessed she possessed, she said, "I think that's all it can ever be between us." She couldn't keep the melancholy out of her voice.

Taylor stepped toward her. She moved away, meeting the wall behind her. He didn't touch her but he stood close enough that she smelled the citrus of his shaving cream and the scent she knew so well. She took a deep breath, committing that aroma to memory.

"I don't want to go with this...uh..." he searched for the right word "...thing between us," he finished.

"Look, we just want different things. I can't leave and you

can't stay. It's as simple as that." But saying the words made her realize that it was so much more.

"You make it sound so final."

"Taylor, you've never led me to believe anything but that you'd be gone after your time here was over. You've been nothing but honest, so you have nothing to feel guilty about."

He moved nearer but didn't touch her. Close enough that if she inhaled deeply her breasts would brush his chest. "Come on, Shelby," he whispered in a raspy voice. "Reconsider my offer. We're so good together."

"I can't."

"Why?"

"Because I want things you can't give me."

"Like?" His breath brushed across her cheek.

Her gaze met his piercing one. "I want to work here, live here, raise a family here."

"Does it have to be all or nothing?"

"For me it does."

His hand gently cupped her cheek. "I'm sorry you feel that way. We could be so good together." His fingers caressed her skin before they fell away.

Taylor's words rang in her ears as he walked toward the front of the building.

At noon, Taylor logged out of Shelby's computer for the last time and pushed the chair back from the desk. Massaging his neck with his hands, he prepared himself for the next few hours. He had to return to Shelby's apartment and pack then attend Mrs. Ferguson's birthday tea. After that, he'd put Benton in his rearview mirror for good.

He'd already checked in with the hospital and learned he was scheduled to work the next morning at seven. He was pleased with that information because he was ready to return to the busy emergency room. There he would just practice medicine, not get involved in people's lives.

"Uncle Gene" would expect him to appear in court in the next day or so. Taylor was sure the judge would be calling Shelby for a report on how he'd done during the last two weeks. Would she let on to Uncle Gene that they had become more than colleagues? He didn't think so. He was completely confident that what happened between him and Shelby on a personal level wouldn't help his cause with the judge.

Taylor checked his watch. There was just enough time to pick up his dress shirt from the cleaners, get back to the apartment, shower and change, and pack before party time. He'd asked Carly for directions to the church, planning to leave town directly from there. He didn't even try to ask Shelby if she'd like to ride to the party with him. He already knew what her answer would be.

An hour and a half later, he came down the stairs with his bag over his shoulder. Shelby's truck was sitting out on the street. She must be inside, getting ready to attend the tea. The temptation to knock on her back door was only prevented by his better judgment. Hadn't they already said everything they needed to say?

Taylor opened the trunk of his car and tossed his bag in with more force than necessary. He stayed seated behind the wheel of the car for a moment before starting it and backing out of the drive. He'd never be required to come back here again. Mr. Marshall, the neighbor across the street, smiled and waved from his mailbox. Taylor returned the greeting then glanced at Shelby's house. What was he hoping? That she'd be looking out the window for a glimpse of him? His heart said he was leaving more than an unmade bed on this tree-lined street.

Minutes later he pulled into the parking lot of a small white clapboard church with a red-brick addition on the back. There were few cars in the lot. He'd made a point of coming early so he could be on his way back to Nashville before it got too late. He followed what looked like a family walking in the direction of the annexe. One of them carried a beautifully wrapped present.

Heck, he'd forgotten all about a gift. He'd just have to send one later. Maybe flowers.

He bet Shelby liked flowers. Were daisies her favorite or roses? Those thoughts were taking him nowhere.

He adjusted his tie. The irony that he had come full circle didn't escape him. He'd not worn these clothes since he'd arrived in town. Each day he'd become more casual in his choice of clothing. That morning he'd dressed in a T-shirt and cargo shorts to work the few hours at the clinic. Now he was back in his city clothes. He pulled at his collar.

Entering the fellowship hall, he was greeted with smiles by a couple of patients he recognized. Mrs. Ferguson, sitting in a wing-back chair at the end of the rectangular room, holding court. Children surrounded her dressed in what had to be their Sunday finest. They must be her grandchildren.

A young woman wearing a bright blue dress with large pink flowers on it approached him. "You must be Dr. Stiles. By my mother's description, I'd know you anywhere. She has nothing but high praise for you. I'm so glad you came."

Taylor smiled. Mrs. Ferguson's daughter might not look a great deal like her but she certainly had the old woman's personality. "Yes, I'm Taylor Stiles. Thank you for inviting me."

"Do help yourself to some food and tea." She indicated a long table covered in a white cloth across the room.

"Thank you, I will. But I'd like to speak to your mother first."

"She'll be glad to see you. She's so disappointed you're leaving."

He nodded, grateful that a couple entering the room caught the woman's attention.

Mrs. Ferguson smiled brightly as he approached and made

an effort to stand. "Please don't get up," he said, taking longer strides to get there before she could rise. "It's your birthday and you have the right to act like a queen today."

The woman giggled, her heavy jowls swinging. "I'm so happy you came."

"I wouldn't have missed it." He took her hand and grinned down at her. He liked the old bird. He would miss her.

"I can't talk you into staying with us? I'm sure Dr. Wayne would love to have your help."

"Dr. Stiles has a job and a life in Nashville. We can't expect him to just give that up."

He turned but hadn't needed to in order to know Shelby stood there. He heard the voice in his dreams, remembering her cries of pleasure as she reached her peak.

She wore a dress tucked and darted in all the correct places to accent the curves of her slim figure. The pale peach color complemented her complexion perfectly. Her shapely legs were showcased to their best advantage by the knee-length hem and her small feet were adorned by a pair of silver sandals.

She'd pulled her hair away from her face on one side, giving her a sophisticated look. There was a hint of pink on her lips that made him want to kiss it away. Shelby took his breath. She was a shining jewel in a room of uncut stones.

"I guess we can't ask him to completely change his life," Mrs. Ferguson said in a voice that implied she wasn't convinced.

What? Taylor was so utterly captivated by Shelby that he'd forgotten what they'd been discussing. His gaze met Shelby's for a second before she looked at Mrs. Ferguson. Her eyes held a sad but resigned look.

"Happy birthday, Mrs. Ferguson." Shelby offered a present wrapped in bright red paper. "This is from Dr. Stiles and me."

Taylor had to work to keep his surprise from showing.

"Honey, you two shouldn't have, but I do love presents."

One of the little girls playing nearby got up and came over. The child started tugging the corners of the paper off the present. "This is my fifth grandbaby, Audrey," she said, glancing up at Taylor and Shelby. "Would you like to help me open it, sugar pie?" she asked the girl. She nodded and went at the present in earnest.

Minutes later Mrs. Ferguson lifted out a floral print scarf that she promptly wrapped about her neck. "I love it. Thank you both." She smiled her pleasure.

"You're very welcome," Taylor said. "It looks wonderful on you." The woman beamed. "Dr. Wayne has good taste."

"It's does look perfect on you," Shelby said.

When another guest drew near he said, "I think I'll take Dr. Wayne over for a bite to eat. Again, happy birthday."

He cupped Shelby's elbow, counting on her not making a scene.

"Happy birthday," Shelby said, before Taylor ushered her away.

"Thank you for including me in on the present. I'd not thought to get one and was going to send her some flowers tomorrow."

"You're welcome," Shelby said, without looking at him.

He let his hand drop when she moved far enough away that he could no longer cradle her elbow.

Shelby balanced her plate on her lap as she took a sip of tea. Taylor sank onto a chair next to hers. They ate silently, as if they were strangers. She missed that simple camaraderie they'd shared so many times, longed for it again. Grief filled her for what they'd so briefly shared and lost. She cared too much for Taylor for them not to at least part as friends.

"Taylor, I'm sorry about…uh…things."

"I am too. Will you walk me out to the car?"

She wasn't sure it would make a difference in the long run

but she couldn't say no. "I guess so. We just need to stay long enough not to be rude."

A few minutes later Taylor took her plate and cup. "It's time I headed out," he said. He stood, walked over to where the dirty dishes were being gathered and placed theirs with the rest.

Her gaze followed him as he moved away in his self-assured, loose-hipped stride. He was too handsome for words. Dressed in a light blue shirt and striped tie that was no doubt silk, he sported the air of a suave and confident male. His navy slacks fit his trim hips and molded to his behind perfectly. They were supported by a thin brown belt. She smiled as she remembered the day he'd arrived. Taylor had been wearing those same shoes.

Shelby committed everything about him to memory so she could bring them out in the blackest part of the night.

As Taylor walked back to her, he smiled. This one reached his eyes. Her heartbeat did a clip-clop. She couldn't help but return it.

"Ready?" he asked, offering his hand.

"Shouldn't we say goodbye to Mrs. Ferguson?"

He glanced over at her. A group of people surrounded her. "I don't think she'll miss us."

Shelby placed her hand in his. It felt right to touch him. She let Taylor help her stand. As soon as she did, she pulled her fingers from his. Letting herself hope would only make it hurt more. They'd reached the door when "Oh"s and "Help"s rang out. She turned. Mrs. Ferguson was slumped in her chair.

"Taylor…" She grabbed his forearm for a second before they hurried to Mrs. Ferguson.

"Someone call nine-one-one," Shelby called.

"Move back," Taylor snapped in an authoritative voice that made those surrounding the limp woman react. Even the children quit playing. There was no clink of utensils on plates or sounds of laughter. Everyone was focused on Mrs. Ferguson.

Reaching the woman, Taylor went down on a knee and brushed her hair away from her face. "Mrs. Ferguson, can you hear me?" Getting no response, he said, "Help me get her on the floor."

With the help of three other men Taylor maneuvered the large woman out of the chair, cradling her head so that it wouldn't hit the floor. Her eyes remained closed. She was deathly pale and her lips were a dusky blue.

Shelby went down on her knees and placed two fingers on Mrs. Ferguson's neck to check for a pulse in her carotid artery. Taylor came down beside her.

"No pulse. We'll have to start CPR."

She checked the airway for obstructions. "I'll handle the airway. You do compressions."

Taylor removed his tie with two quick jerks and threw it to the floor. He then located the correct spot on Mrs. Ferguson's breastbone to push. Stacking his hands one on top of the other, straightening his arms and locking his elbows, he began to push down on Mrs. Ferguson's chest.

The only sound in the room was Taylor's calm but firm voice counting, "Twenty-seven, twenty-eight, twenty-nine, breath." That was her cue to lean over and give Mrs. Ferguson two breaths. Taylor continued, "One, two, three..."

Sweat popped out on his brow but she couldn't take the time to wipe it away. For what felt like an age they worked in tandem to save Mrs. Ferguson's life.

The puff of breath from Mrs. Ferguson touched Shelby's face as she went down to breathe. She sat up. Mrs. Ferguson's eyelids fluttered. Taylor must have seen it too because he stopped compressions. The woman's eyes opened, closed and opened again.

"Mrs. Ferguson, nice to see you back." Taylor gave the

woman a weak smile but sounded much more composed than Shelby felt. "Don't move. An ambulance is on the way."

Standing, he dug into his pocket and brought out his keys. Tossing them to the man nearest him, he said, "Get my bag out of my car, front seat. Red sports car."

The man hustled away.

"Don't try to speak," Shelby instructed as she picked up Mrs. Ferguson's wrist and began checking her pulse.

The man returned with the medical bag. Taylor pulled out his stethoscope and listened to their patient's chest. Done, he stuffed the instrument back into the bag. "Heartbeat's strong but not as steady as I'd like," he told Shelby.

With great relief she saw the private ambulance personnel enter the building with a gurney in tow. Not for the first time she wished the area could afford EMTs to staff the transportation but that just wasn't possible.

Mrs. Ferguson opened her eyes and looked at Taylor. "Doctor?" Her voice quivered.

Taylor took her hand. "Don't talk. You're going to be just fine." His voice was low and sweet with concern, which told Shelby he'd come to care for the feisty woman. As the ambulance personnel worked to prepare her for transport, he continued to hold Mrs. Ferguson's hand.

Without releasing her, he'd managed to pull his phone out of his pants pocket. He punched one number and gave a succinct report and rapid-fire instructions that assured his directions would be followed. He'd arranged for a cardiologist to be standing by in Trauma when Mrs. Ferguson arrived at the hospital.

Shelby continued to monitor the woman's vital signs as the ambulance personnel worked with the help of Taylor and a number of men to lift Mrs. Ferguson onto the gurney and then into the ambulance.

"I'm riding with her," Taylor announced in a tone that

dared anyone to argue with him. He climbed into the vehicle without a backward look. The doors closed with a slam of finality before the ambulance roared off, siren blaring.

Shelby stood mountain still, staring at the back of the emergency vehicle as it pulled onto the highway. A lump of finality became thick in her middle. Her heart squeezed tight in anguish. Blinking twice, three times, she tried to prevent moisture from forming in her eyes. Everything in her wanted to scream *Come back* but that wouldn't happen. Taylor was gone.

As Taylor left Benton in the back of the ambulance headed for Nashville, he made the decision not to return. He'd convinced himself that it was best for Shelby if he sent someone for his car and belongings. The truth was that he was a coward. He couldn't look into her gray eyes that compelled him to stay and say goodbye.

Mrs. Ferguson made it to the hospital without further issues but had to have surgery for two blocked arteries. She came through the operation well and recovered nicely. The only glitch, as she put it, was the rigid diet and lifestyle changes she had to agree to. The feisty old girl would make it hard on her cardiologist but she'd do as she was instructed. This time she'd been lucky.

Taylor visited her daily and spoke to her cardiologist regularly. He'd been informed by the attending doctor that Shelby had called a number of times to check on the patient. Everything in Taylor wished he'd been the one to pick up the phone when she'd been on the line. He yearned to hear her voice. When the time came for Mrs. Ferguson to be released from the hospital, Taylor was there to wheel her out.

"You need to think about where you belong, young man," Mrs. Ferguson told him firmly as he helped her into her daughter's car.

On their ride to Nashville he would've argued that it was right here, being a trauma doctor. But now...

Taylor had been confident that he'd return to his position in the emergency department as if he'd never been gone. A couple of shifts later he'd recognized he was taking more time with his patients than he'd done before, listening more carefully to their needs. The nurses had looked at him oddly when he'd requested to speak to the family of one of his patients.

One of his colleagues had asked, "Taylor, what're you doing, talking to the family? You never did that before."

"The family deserves to hear how their loved one is doing straight from the doctor. Rules can sometimes be more in the interest of the hospital than the needs of the patient and their family."

A week after his return his superior pulled him aside. "I hear you're taking time to speak to the families. As commendable as that is, I understand that it's causing a backlog on your shift. Especially on the busy nights."

"Maybe so, but I think it's important."

"In this hospital that job falls to the social workers. You need to let them do their jobs."

Taylor nodded in understanding but not in agreement. If he had to pick a point where his disillusionment with working in a large hospital began, it was then. He was no longer satisfied with caring for patients and passing them off to another doctor. Taylor wanted to follow up his patients, see their progress, continue to care for them, build relationships with them. To his shock, he sought what he'd had in Benton.

His time outside away from the hospital didn't ease his discontent with his life choices either. He missed looking out the window and being able to see the stars at night. Living in the center of a large city, the glow of lights all night didn't allow for stargazing. Regularly enjoying the sun rising over the tops of trees was out of the question also.

He'd lived on the seventh floor of a high-rise apartment building for the last three years and he still didn't know his neighbors. In less than a week he'd met everyone on Shelby's street and could call them by name. He would've never imagined something like that would've mattered to him.

More than anything, he missed Shelby. Thoughts of her were as continuous as a movie replaying over and over. Her smile, her eyes, her laugh, her touch…

Often, when he cared for a patient, he'd wonder what Shelby would say about this. How would she handle this situation? Would she do this differently? At work, at home or at social gatherings thoughts of her intruded. More than that he missed their sparring, her intellect, her soft heart. With Shelby could he have a solid relationship? Did he love her enough to try?

He'd made an effort to continue where he'd left off with his social life but it seemed dull and uninteresting after being around Shelby. She and Benton had so infiltrated his life that nothing in his old existence satisfied him any more. He missed the belonging and acceptance that he'd searched for his entire life and found in Benton. Now he wanted it back. How had the small town and a petite firecracker of a woman managed to change him so quickly, so totally?

If he had any hope of Shelby accepting him as more than a partner in the clinic, as her partner for a lifetime, he had to face the demons in his past.

CHAPTER TEN

SHELBY opened the clinic at the same time she had every workday for years. The one exception was that she didn't have the same enthusiasm she ordinarily did at the thought of a new day. The sun had risen big and bright and all she could think about was how much she'd love to spend the day taking pictures. Maybe sit in the back-yard swing and sip lemonade.

She was going to start taking some time off.

Taylor had been gone for six weeks and the truth of what he'd said was ringing true. She should train the community to see her during the hours she was open. An emergency number would always be posted if she was needed. Wednesdays were usually slow. If she took those afternoons then she'd have most of the week covered.

She'd try it starting next week. That way the word could get out. With a plan in place she went about preparing for the day with a little more spring in her step.

Flipping the computer on, she quickly checked her emails. The name Dr. Mark Singer caught her attention. Tapping a key, she opened the email and scanned the text. Dr. Singer wrote that he was interested in interviewing for a position at the clinic. He'd like her to contact him as soon as possible. Shelby's fingers flew over the keyboard as she shot off a reply. She couldn't replace Taylor in her heart but maybe she could find someone to measure up in patient care. But even that was going to be difficult.

Taylor had been gone only a few weeks but she felt his loss at the clinic daily. She'd not realized how much her workload had consumed her life until he'd been there. Weeks later the patients were still asking about Taylor, wanting to know if she had heard from him.

There were reminders of him everywhere at the clinic, in the apartment, in her kitchen, and more painfully in her heart. Since he'd left with Mrs. Ferguson he'd not called. It hurt. Terribly.

She'd seen to it that his car had been driven to her house from the church. A couple of days later she had been both surprised and offended when a uniformed stranger had shown up at the clinic.

"I'm here to pick up…" the man had looked at a paper "…a Taylor Stiles's car. I was given this address." He'd looked around as if unsure he'd been in the correct place.

"May I see that?" Shelby's hand had shaken slightly as she'd taken the official-looking sheet. Taylor's bold signature had appeared on the line in the bottom right-hand corner. She knew it well. He hadn't even bothered to come and get his car. Was he done with anything that had to do with Benton, including her?

Shelby had instructed the man to follow her home. She'd stood in the drive and watched as he'd driven away in the car. It had been the final, indisputable statement that Taylor wasn't returning.

She phoned the hospital daily to get a report on Mrs. Ferguson's progress but never spoke to Taylor. She'd not really anticipated she would. The cardiology service was in charge of Mrs. Ferguson's care now. That knowledge still didn't stop her heart from beating faster as she waited for the doctor to answer the phone or prevent the disappointment she felt when the voice on the other end wasn't Taylor's deep, sexy one.

After Carly arrived at the clinic, they went to work seeing patients. By lunchtime Shelby was ready to get off her feet. She dropped into the chair behind her desk. Selecting the correct key on the computer keyboard, she brought up her emails. There was a reply from Dr. Singer. He and his wife were going to be in the Benton area that afternoon and wondered if they might stop in and see the clinic.

Overwhelmed at the possibility of finding someone to help her at long last, she quickly responded with her phone number and that she'd love to meet him and his wife. With the idea of impressing the doctor, Shelby hustled around and saw that everything was neat and tidy in the clinic before she left for lunch.

An hour later she sat at her kitchen table, having a sandwich with her phone nearby. She pulled towards her the pile of mail she'd gotten out of the mailbox when she'd arrived home. Releasing the rubber band, she found the photography periodical she subscribed to encircling the rest of her mail. She pushed the envelopes aside and straightened out the bent magazine. Six months' worth of the same reading material was stacked on the footstool in the living room. She'd not had time to open even one of them in a long time.

That was another change she was going to make. Taking a bite out of her sandwich, she explored the glossy pages of the magazine. A photo contest advertisement caught her attention. It called for pictures taken in the outdoors. All entries would receive a critique and the winner would have a showing of their work. The pictures that she'd taken at the old house certainly met the criteria. This would be a good opportunity to receive some easy feedback on her photography and a chance to move forward towards doing more with her hobby. The due date was soon. The pictures needed to be sent in right away. This would be her first step out into the world. She'd do it.

As she took her plate to the sink, the phone rang. Setting the plate down, she hurried back to answer the call. Dr. Singer was on the line and said that he was driving into town. Shelby gave him directions to the clinic, ended the conversation and snatched up her keys. Maybe the doctor would be the solution to at least one of her problems. Only time could heal how she felt about Taylor.

"So, Dr. Singer, do you think you might be interested in working with me?" Shelby asked an hour later.

"I think this just might be the right place for me," the silver-haired man said. "What do you think, Betty?" He looked at his smiling wife.

"For a supposedly retired doctor who won't give medicine up completely, I think it would be ideal. But no more than a couple of days a week. I'll need help with our dream home."

At Shelby's questioning look, Dr. Singer said, "We heard about the lake and thought it would be a nice place to build. We'll look for a place to rent until we can buy the right lot. Hopefully I can start work in about a week."

"That sounds absolutely wonderful," Shelby said, with her first true smile since Taylor had left.

Having Dr. Singer's help wouldn't entirely solve her staffing problem at the clinic but it was a step in the right direction. No matter how good a physician Dr. Singer was, he couldn't replace Taylor. Certainly not in her heart. No one could substitute for Taylor there. It was wonderful to have the requirements of the clinic being met but what about her needs? Only Taylor could give her that. The clinic's issues were resolving while hers had intensified to an unrelenting ache in her heart.

Taylor had been right. The clinic was more than a two-person operation but having another doctor would at least satisfy the state's concerns. She'd still need to look for additional help but there was a sense of relief and release knowing now she could occasionally get away from the clinic. She was already planning how to spend her extra time off.

Maybe she would go to Nashville. She recognized Taylor had been right when she'd gotten over being mad and thought about it. She had been using her job and Benton to protect her from further unhappiness. Staying in Benton was safe for her, familiar. It offered her a haven that meant she didn't have to risk herself, her heart. It was easy to stay there and not have any conflict. Keeping Taylor at arm's length had done the same thing but it wasn't living. She refused to let any time she could spend with Taylor disappear because she was too scared to grasp it.

Was it too late to contact Taylor? She'd wanted to call him hundreds of times. Pride had stopped her. But pride was a cold and lonely bed companion in the middle of the night. Would Taylor still want her? Had he moved on?

She'd never know unless she took the chance to find out. He'd asked her to meet him halfway and she'd refused. If she wanted Taylor, she was going to have to tell him. If they both desired a relationship badly enough, they could work something out. Snatching some time here and there was better than nothing. Better than thinking about him day and night, and carrying around heartache that seemed to never ease.

Decision made. Next Wednesday, she was going to Nashville to see if Taylor was still willing to find that compromise he'd pleaded with her to consider. She hoped with all her heart he still wanted her.

Taylor slowed his car as he entered the city limits of the town he'd grown up in. His stomach knotted but he kept going. He'd not crossed this particular line since he'd been eighteen years old and that had been on his way out of town. If he'd been a betting man, he wouldn't have put money on him ever returning. He huffed. He would've lost.

As with a number of things he'd done in the last couple of months, he would've sworn it would never happen. He'd amazed himself more than once.

He'd looked on the internet for his brothers' addresses. He wasn't even sure they were still living here. There were a number of Stileses living in the area. Both brothers had such common first names that the list of possibilities was great so he'd decided to drive there, then ask around. Before going to the police station for help, he wanted to see if anything had changed. If any of the bad memories had dimmed.

Circling the stately red-brick courthouse with the white dome that still commanded the square in the heart of town, Taylor found that much about it remained the same. The stores surrounding the county building were the same type that had been there years earlier with a few new ones here and there. People mingled on the sidewalks, talking or going in and out of businesses. Nothing seemed as horrifying or uncaring as he remembered. It could have been Benton's twin town.

Astonished that he felt no animosity but curiosity instead, he turned right out of town, driving past the high school. It appeared no different than he remembered from the outside. Was there a kid in there having to fight every day to survive?

Continuing on for another mile, he made a right beside the rustic general store where old man Carr had given him those words of encouragement. He smirked. Even now there were a couple of men sitting there, talking. Nothing had changed.

The road took him out of the populated area to where the houses were spaced farther apart. As he traveled, his stomach constricted. Hadn't he buried all those ugly feelings about his father long ago? All he had to do was ride down this road to have them resurface. He went round the bend in the road and slowed to a crawl. The house he was looking for stood on the right, or at least the one he thought he was looking for. This one was nothing like he remembered.

The tiny clapboard house was painted a pristine white. The porch had large ferns hanging along the front of the porch. There was now a white picket fence surrounding the yard and late-summer flowers were blooming in the beds on either side of the wide limestone stone steps leading to the door.

Taylor would've sworn that this wasn't the boyhood home where he'd spent eighteen miserable years. It was the same house, but then again it wasn't. Now it looked like a place where a happy family lived.

A man came out the door and walked towards a truck parked on the white rock drive. A jolt of disbelief rocked through Taylor.

Matt. He looked different than Taylor remembered him but still it was his older brother. Why was he here?

Taylor pulled off onto the shoulder of the road. Taking a deep breath, he climbed out of his car. The man looked at him questioningly. Then a surprised look came over his face.

"Taylor? Is that you?"

"Hello, Matt," Taylor said flatly.

Matt came toward him and Taylor moved to meet him. "I never expected to see you again."

"And I never expected to come here again."

Matt offered his hand. Accepting it, Taylor shook it then was pulled into Matt's hug. Taylor's body tensed for a second then he returned the hug. His animosity wasn't towards his brother. He'd endured living with his father just as he himself had.

"It's so good to see you," Matt said. "Please come in. My wife and children should be back soon. I'd love you to meet them."

Taylor looked at the house, and hesitated.

"Why don't we sit on the front porch for a while?" Matt suggested.

Taylor nodded his agreement.

As they walk toward the house his brother said, "I've kept up with you, you know."

The astonishment Taylor felt must have shown on his face.

His brother grinned. "The internet makes the world a small place. I tell everyone from the old days that you became a doctor. From what I read, a good one."

They each took one of the two rockers on the porch.

"So what brought you here?" Matt asked.

"Actually, I came to see if I could find you and Bud. But I didn't think it would be so easy."

"Bud isn't in town. He's in the state pen for armed robbery. He's not due out for another five years," Matt said matter-of-factly. "I tried to help him but he was too much like Dad to listen."

Taylor felt nothing one way or the other about his brother being incarcerated. Truthfully, he was surprised he wasn't dead. The life Bud had been living when Taylor had left town had led to nothing but destruction. He'd had to deal with men like his brother during almost every night shift he'd ever worked.

"How did you come to be living here?" Taylor asked, wonder filling his voice.

"I was on the same road as Dad and Bud." His brother spoke as if he was looking into the dark past and not liking what he saw. Taylor knew well how they had been. His older brothers had been coming in drunk and high by the time Taylor had been in middle school.

"I was in and out of trouble with the law and the same with jobs until my wife came into my life. If I wanted her, I had to make a change. A major change in my life. I did and I'm a better man for it. We now have two kids. A boy and a girl. Our family…" he pointed between himself and Taylor "…wasn't pretty, no place to see an example, and I still have to work daily to beat my addiction, but life is good. We all have a past and I just choose not to let mine control me."

That was what Taylor had let his do to him and still did. Shelby had pointed that out loud and clear. If it hadn't been for her, he wouldn't be here today.

Matt lived in the same town he'd grown up in and he had been able to put his past behind him. Taylor had run away and guilded it in fast cars, society women and an expensive lifestyle. Truthfully, his brother seemed to have done a better job of dealing with his past than he had.

They rocked in silence for a while. "Why live here?" Taylor blurted. "This house?"

"Because I thought I could replace so many of my ugly memories with happy ones if I raised my family here. I could try to make this house have what Mother wanted it to have. A family who loved each other. Do you have a wife? Any children?" Matt asked.

"No."

"A good woman can change your life."

That Taylor already knew. He should take a lesson from his brother. They'd taken different roads when they'd left home but each had needed to overcome their shared past. Matt seemed to have done so, now it was his own turn.

If he hadn't hurt Shelby so badly that she no longer wanted him.

Shelby agreed to take pictures at Mrs. Ferguson's postponed birthday tea turned welcome-home party. Word had gotten out about Shelby's skills at photography when the local weekly paper was contacted about her being a finalist in the photo contest she'd entered.

After Mrs. Ferguson returned home from the hospital, she

visited the clinic to let Shelby check her over. The woman begged Shelby to take pictures at the party despite her insisting she wasn't that type of photographer. Mrs. Ferguson wouldn't take no for an answer. Giving in, Shelby decided she might as well make the most of the opportunity to add to her portfolio.

The party was winding down now, and for that Shelby was grateful. On her feet most of the day, all she could think about was propping them up, watching a good movie on TV and having Buster sit on her lap. She loved the little dog dearly, though he was a bitter-sweet reminder of Taylor.

"Dr. Stiles," someone said.

Shelby went stock still. It couldn't be.

"Hello, Mrs. Ferguson, you look wonderful."

Shelby's heart went to her throat. *Taylor.* She'd recognize that voice anywhere, even in a crowd. With her back to the door, she'd not seen him enter.

She turned. Her eyes feasted on him. He was everything she remembered and more. Charming smile, dark hair, and too handsome for words. He wore a knit shirt, tan slacks and loafers. There was a relaxed appearance about him that hadn't been there the first time he'd come to town.

Her chest ached, reminding her to breath.

What was he doing here? Had he come to town just for this party? Was there some other reason he was here? Dared she hope?

Giving herself a mental shake, she brought her camera up to her face. She struggled to steady her hands as she clicked the shutter. After all, picture-taking was what she was here for, not to gape at the people who attended. Continuously snapping pictures, she rotated to get the last of the attendees.

"Hi, Shelby."

Act cool. Don't let him see that he rattles you. "Hello, Taylor. I'm surprised to see you here."

"I figured you might be."

"What brought you back? Were you caught speeding again?" She couldn't keep the bite out of the question.

He smiled. "I was. I threw myself on the mercy of the court and asked your Uncle Gene to sentence me to Benton again."

She lowered the camera. "You are kidding, aren't you?"

"Yeah, sort of."

"What does that mean?"

He looked around the almost empty room. "You done here? I'd rather not have my driving record discussed around town if I can help it."

Nothing was secret in this town.

"I'll have to let Mrs. Ferguson know I'm leaving."

She had no idea what was going on in Taylor's mind. What she did know was that until she knew what he was doing here she wasn't going to let him hurt her again. She'd only barely managed to stop thinking about him all day long. The nights were still out of her control. Taylor dropping in for a friendly visit would be enough to tip the balance.

He waited at the door and joined her as she stepped out into the evening breeze. When her lightweight flowing silk dress threatened to blow upwards she hurriedly pushed it down.

"You know, you're the most beautiful creature." The awe in his voice made her look at him. "I've missed you. The hardest thing I've ever done was to stay away."

"Please don't…" She couldn't listen to those kinds of words from him. She so desperately wanted them to be true. Another gust of wind caught her dress. Her camera case slipped off her shoulder as she reached down to hold her dress in place.

Taylor took the bag from her and looked around the parking lot. "Where's your truck?"

"Darn, I forgot. It's in the shop. Sam had to give me a ride."

"That Sam sure is a handy guy to have around." The sarcasm in his voice didn't escape her but she didn't take the time to analyze it. He placed a hand on her waist. "Come on, I'll give you a ride home. Kind of reminds me of old times." He grinned at her.

Shelby moved away from his hand. She saw a flicker of hurt in his beautiful eyes. "I guess I don't really have a choice. Where's your car?"

"I'm driving a truck now." He led her to a blue late-model mid-size vehicle. He helped her in and closed the door before going to the driver's side.

"What happened to your car?" she asked as Taylor pulled out into the road and headed towards her house.

"I decided to give it away."

"Away? Why?" She couldn't imagine someone willingly giving away a car that nice.

"I thought she might enjoy driving it more than I did."

Pain filled her. He'd given his car to a woman. If she'd harbored any hope that he'd come to see her or that there might be a chance for them, she didn't any more. He'd found someone else. She wouldn't let him see her cry. "That's one lucky woman," she said quietly.

"She's very special. There's no one else in the world like her." Shelby didn't have to look at him to tell that he cared a great deal about the woman.

"I'm glad for you."

"Are you really?" He glanced at her and Shelby turned away, preventing him from seeing the tears threatening to spill over. It sure hadn't taken him long to find someone else.

"Yes, I am. I want you to be happy."

"I hope she'll accept it and me along with it."

The fingers of Shelby's right hand clutched the doorhandle

as the one in her lap curled into a fist. Why didn't he drive faster? All she wanted to do was get home, close the door and crawl into bed. "Why wouldn't she? You're a great guy."

"I haven't always been. I hurt her and I'm not sure she'll have me now."

"Just tell her how you feel. I'm sure she'll forgive you." Her voice started to break. She didn't want to have this conversation. Giving advice to the lovelorn, especially where it concerned Taylor, wasn't something she was emotionally strong enough to handle.

"So all I have to do is say I love you?" he asked.

She turned to face him. "Why are you here, Taylor? Why're you telling me all this?" Thank goodness he'd turned into her street. She waited for his answer. "Why, Taylor?"

"Because I thought we were friends."

He had a twisted idea of what her friendship meant. She couldn't do this any more. "There's no need to turn into the drive. Just pull up in front of the house."

"I don't think so. A gentleman sees that a lady gets home safely."

She wanted to slap the grin off his face. Didn't he know this was killing her? How could he be so dense?

"Taylor for heaven's sake!"

"Okay, if that's what you want." He pulled to a stop at the end of her drive.

She gathered her camera bag and climbed out of the truck, not looking at him or even where she was going. She just needed to get away. To breathe again. All those hopes and dreams of going to him in Nashville had turned to ash.

Not looking back, Shelby hurried up the drive. She was halfway to the back door when she made out the color red through watery eyes. Rubbing the dampness away, she saw Taylor's car sitting there with a large silver bow on top. She slowly lowered her camera bag to the ground. Her body flushed. "What?"

"As large an apology as I owe you, I figured flowers might not cover it," Taylor said from right behind her. "I hoped the car might ease the way."

Shelby's heart had gone into warp drive and didn't seem to be slowing down. "I kind of like flowers," she mumbled, a grin forming on her face.

"That figures. My little she-cat never disappoints. I come to you with my heart in my hand and you're not satisfied." He chuckled dryly. "Shelby, aren't you going to look at me?" Taylor asked quietly.

"You said you loved the woman you gave the car to."

"I did, and I do. With all my being." He still hadn't touched her, as if he was afraid of her reaction. "I'll live in Benton if that's what it takes. I want you to be a part of my life, every day, always."

She still couldn't move. It was her dream coming true.

"Shelby, please turn around. You're scaring me."

She slowly rotated, looking at him. His dear face for the first time she could remember lacked confidence. Did he really believe she might turn him down?

"Taylor Stiles…" she punched him playfully in the shoulder "…why did you make me think you were talking about another woman?" She gave him a light swat on the shoulder this time before her arms slid up to circle his neck and pull his mouth down to hers. "I love you too," she said softly against his lips. Seconds later he crushed her to him and took control of the kiss.

Some time later Taylor pulled back but didn't let go of her. For that she was glad, she couldn't have stood on her own anyway.

"Nice to see you back, Taylor," Mr. Marshall called. "Planning to stay around, I hope."

"That I am," Taylor replied with such conviction she knew he meant it. "For ever," he whispered into her ear.

"Glad to hear it," the man responded.

Releasing her enough to pick up the camera bag, Taylor said, "Let's take this inside."

It could have been hours or days later for all Shelby knew she was so caught up in the fog of bliss that Taylor created by being in her bed. As she was lounging against him while they ate peanut butter and jelly sandwiches and drank iced tea, she couldn't remember being happier.

"You know, when the man from the service came to get your car, I was sure I'd never see you again."

"I thought it best at the time."

"Why?"

"Because I didn't want to hurt you any more than I already had. Now I know it was because I was afraid. I couldn't say no to you if you asked me to stay again."

"Was I that hard to resist?"

He kissed her shoulder. "Oh, yes, you were." Then he nipped at the same spot. "Still are. I've been running away. Now I'm running to what I want—you."

She smiled at him. "Uncle Gene said you needed to slow down some, take a look at yourself. I guess he knew what he was talking about."

"You should've seen the look on his face when I told him I planned to marry his niece." Taylor chuckled. A sound she loved.

"When he sent me here I'm not sure he meant for me to join the family."

"What made you change your mind about living here? You were so adamant."

"I found out when I got back to Nashville that I wasn't happy without you and by some measure without Benton. It was a physical hurt to be away from you. I wasn't satisfied with my work, my home or my life there any more. Here I felt good about myself." He paused a second. "I've never seen a healthy relationship up close. Heavens knows, my parents didn't have one. I'm not sure I know how one works. Please be patient with me."

She gave him a gentle reassuring kissed. "Not a problem."

Looking down at her softly he said, "I love you."

"And I love you."

Taylor shifted slightly. "I went back to my hometown. Saw one of my brothers."

She turned and placed a hand on his cheek. "I know that had to be hard for you. I'm sorry I wasn't there for you."

"That's okay. It was something I had to do on my own. I'd like to take you with me to meet my brother some time soon."

"I'd enjoy that."

Buster made a whimpering noise from the floor and Taylor reached down, picked him up and placed him on the bed. "Have you been taking good care of my lady for me, boy?" Taylor asked, scratching Buster behind his ears.

"Yeah, we took care of each other. He missed you almost as much as I did," Shelby said, petting the dog.

"I'm surprised you had time to miss me. I heard all about you being a finalist in the photo contest."

"Thanks to your encouragement and handsome face. How did you know?"

"Mrs. Ferguson," they said in unison.

"You were right about me hiding out here. The photo contest was my first step towards my new life. I was coming to see you on Wednesday."

"You were?"

"Yes. You just beat me to it by coming here today." She grinned up at him.

"Can I have my car back, then?"

She gave him a playful swat on the belly. "You cannot!"

His mirth was a low rumble in his throat. "What was that you said about my handsome face?"

"I sent in the pictures I took of you at the old house. The judges loved them."

He moaned.

"That's the price you pay for being so good looking."

"You're not hard on the eyes either." His hand slipped under the sheet to run along the ridge of her hip.

She grabbed his wrist, stopping it short of moving up the inside of her thigh. "Before you distract me, let me tell you my other news. I have a doctor who's going to help out at the clinic two days a week."

"So you liked Mark. I thought you would."

Shelby glared at him.

Looking unconcerned, Taylor's gaze focused on her bare breasts.

Pulling the sheet up to cover herself, she said, "You know Dr. Singer?"

He nodded and tugged on the sheet. It slipped to reveal the top curve of one breast.

"You sent him?"

"I did, but his agreeing to work at the clinic was all about your considerable charm. Do you think there's a place for me also?"

"You know there is."

He tugged on the sheet again but she held it securely. "I'd like to lease one of the larger spaces so that we could dedicate part of the clinic to trauma care. The people of Benton and the surrounding area need to have a place close to come in case of an emergency. What do you think?"

"That's a great idea. Thank you, Taylor. You do know that because of you Benton will get to keep its clinic."

His eyes darkened. "I think you should show your appreciation." He gave the sheet a harder tug but she didn't let go, giving him a teasing, come-hither smile. Her heart beat fast when his heated gaze met hers. With one swift movement of his hand the sheet was jerked away and he reached for her.

His lips met hers, replacing the past with the passion of the present and dreams of the future.

* * * * *

Lynne Graham has sold 35 million books!

To settle a debt, she'll have to become his mistress...

Nikolai Drakos is determined to have his revenge against the man who destroyed his sister. So stealing his enemy's intended fiancé seems like the perfect solution! Until Nikolai discovers that woman is Ella Davies...

*Read on for a tantalising excerpt from
Lynne Graham's 100th book,*

BOUGHT FOR THE GREEK'S REVENGE

'Mistress,' Nikolai slotted in cool as ice.

Shock had welded Ella's tongue to the roof of her mouth because he was sexually propositioning her and nothing could have prepared her for that. She wasn't drop-dead gorgeous... *he* was! Male heads didn't swivel when Ella walked down the street because she had neither the length of leg nor the curves usually deemed necessary to attract such attention. Why on earth could he be making *her* such an offer?

'But we don't even know each other,' she framed dazedly. 'You're a stranger...'

'If you live with me I won't be a stranger for long,' Nikolai pointed out with monumental calm. And the very sound of that inhuman calm and cool forced her to flip round and settle distraught eyes on his lean darkly handsome face.

'You can't be serious about this!'

'I assure you that I am deadly serious. Move in and I'll forget your family's debts.'

'But it's a *crazy* idea!' she gasped.

'It's not crazy to me,' Nikolai asserted. 'When I want anything, I go after it hard and fast.'

Her lashes dipped. Did he want her like that? Enough to track her down, buy up her father's debts, and try and buy rights to her and her body along with those debts? The very idea of that made her dizzy and plunged her brain into even greater turmoil. 'It's immoral… it's blackmail.'

'It's definitely *not* blackmail. I'm giving you the benefit of a choice you didn't have before I came through that door,' Nikolai Drakos fielded with a glittering cool. 'That choice is yours to make.'

'Like hell it is!' Ella fired back. 'It's a complete cheat of a supposed offer!'

Nikolai sent her a gleaming sideways glance. 'No the real cheat was you kissing me the way you did last year and then saying no and acting as if I had grossly insulted you,' he murmured with lethal quietness.

'You *did* insult me!' Ella flung back, her cheeks hot as fire while she wondered if her refusal that night had started off his whole chain reaction. What else could possibly be driving him?

Nikolai straightened lazily as he opened the door. 'If you take offence that easily, maybe it's just as well that the answer is no.'

Visit **www.millsandboon.co.uk/lynnegraham**
to order yours!

MILLS & BOON®

MILLS & BOON®

Why shop at millsandboon.co.uk?

Each year, thousands of romance readers find their perfect read at millsandboon.co.uk. That's because we're passionate about bringing you the very best romantic fiction. Here are some of the advantages of shopping at www.millsandboon.co.uk:

* **Get new books first**—you'll be able to buy your favourite books one month before they hit the shops

* **Get exclusive discounts**—you'll also be able to buy our specially created monthly collections, with up to 50% off the RRP

* **Find your favourite authors**—latest news, interviews and new releases for all your favourite authors and series on our website, plus ideas for what to try next

* **Join in**—once you've bought your favourite books, don't forget to register with us to rate, review and join in the discussions

Visit **www.millsandboon.co.uk**
for all this and more today!